Mistletoe & Magic

Lisa Cach, Stobie Piel, Lynsay Sands, and Amy Elizabeth Saunders

LEISURE BOOKS

NEW YORK CITY

A LEISURE BOOK®

October 2000

Published by

Dorchester Publishing Co., Inc.
276 Fifth Avenue
New York, NY 10001

ISBN 0-8439-4778-0

The Fairy
Godmother

Lynsay Sands

Chapter One

Roswald Keep, England—1324

The lid of the sarcophagus settled into place with a deep, low grinding of stone. There was silence for a moment, then everyone began to drift out, back to their daily chores and lives, leaving Odel alone. She was aware of their leave-taking and thought how funny it was that others still had chores to do. Unlike herself, life continued for them much as it had before the death of their lord and master, her father.

The priest patted her shoulder and Odel smiled at him stiffly, then watched him follow the others out of the building. He was leaving her alone to deal with her grief. Most considerate, she thought, almost ashamed that she was not feeling any. All she seemed filled with was an empty confusion, a sort of loss as to what to do next.

It seemed the whole of her life had been centered around the selfish wants and needs of the man who now lay entombed here. Without him to order her about, she really hadn't a clue what to do. At a loss, She stayed where she was, staring dry-eyed at the stone likeness laid out before her, waiting.

She was still standing there several moments later when the door opened again. An icy winter wind blew in, ruffling the black veil that shrouded Odel's still dry eyes. Positive it was the priest returned, she did not look about. But when a woman's voice rang out behind her, she nearly jumped out of her skin.

"Well, here I am. Late again as usual. But then, better late than not here at all, I always say," the high, clear voice chimed, sounding almost bell-like in the small stone building.

Lifting the black veil that covered her face, Odel tossed it back over her head and whirled toward the door. A round, little gray-haired lady dressed in the most horrid pink confection Odel had ever seen was trundling toward her. She was positive she had never met her before, but the woman's words seemed to suggest otherwise. The way she now charged up and enveloped Odel in a pink silk and perfumed hug also seemed to indicate they were not strangers. Eyes wide, Odel stood stiff in her embrace and wracked her brain for who she might be.

"Toot-a-loo, dear. I am sorry you have had to see to all of this on your own. I came as soon as I could. Howbeit, that never seems quite soon enough." Releasing her, the woman stepped back to glance down at the stern, stone effigy atop the tomb of Odel's father, then sniffed with distaste. "Rather grim, is it not? But then he was a perfectly grim man. I never met a more cantankerous lout."

When Odel gaped at such irreverent words, the woman arched her eyebrows slightly. "Surely you do not disagree?"

"I . . . He was my father . . . And he is *dead*," was all

she could come up with in answer. Lord Roswald certainly had been a cantankerous lout. But Odel would bite her own tongue off ere being disrespectful enough to say so about her own father.

"Hmm." The woman's mouth twisted at one corner. "I take it you believe that old adage about not speaking ill of the dead? Well, my dear, that is very good of you. I myself am of the firm belief that a man earns his praises or recriminations in life—and death—by his actions. And deserves every lick he earns. Your father, rest his soul, earned all the recrimination a body can spew. Why, what he did to your mother alone was enough to keep me recriminating for a century, never mind what he did to you!"

Odel's eyes widened and brightened suddenly. "You knew my mother?"

"Knew her?" The odd little woman's smile softened. "My dear, we were best friends. As close as can be. Until your grandfather forced her to marry your father. What a tragedy *that* was." She moved to the second sarcophagus in the room as she spoke and peered sadly down at the likeness of the beautiful woman it held.

"She was lovely. Even this cold stone cannot hide that," she murmured, then glanced at Odel. "They were not suited at all, of course. Your mother was young, beautiful, and lighthearted while your father was old and bitter. He had already had and lost one family—and he was determined to subdue and hold on to Lillith and whatever children she gave him in any way he could."

The woman's gaze moved back to the stone effigy and a sigh slid from her lips. She caressed the cold marble cheek sadly. "He choked all the joy and youth out of her ere the first year of their marriage was ended. Her death when you were five was a mere formality. All the life had left her long ere that."

Odel dropped her gaze to the likeness of her mother,

touched by the first real sense of grief she had felt that day. That sadness was quickly washed away by the woman's next words.

"You look much like her. Your mother, I mean. That should make things easier."

"Make what things easier?" Odel asked in confusion, but the woman didn't answer. A frown had suddenly drawn her lips down as she considered the pallor of Odel's skin and the thinness of the body obvious beneath the sack-like black gown she wore. Odel knew that while her features were the same as her lovely mother's, they were presently pinched with stress, and that there were dark smudges beneath her eyes that nearly matched the unrelenting black of the veil that shrouded her hair.

The woman moved so swiftly that Odel couldn't stop her start of surprise as the veil was suddenly snatched from her head. The action tugged loose several of the pins that had held her hair in place, sending them to the floor with a soft tinkle. Her hair slid eagerly down around her shoulders in waves of dull color.

Seeing the lifeless hair that should have shone fiery red-brown, the woman pursed her lips, concerned. "He did not choke the life from you as well, did he?"

Odel's eyes dilated at the rude question, then she blurted, "Who *are* you?"

The old lady blinked. "Who? Me? Oh, dear, did I not introduce myself? How silly of me. My goodness, no wonder you look at me as if I were mad, dear. You haven't a clue who I am. Why, I'm Tildy, child."

"Tildy?" Odel frowned over the name. Her memory nagged at her faintly.

"Your godmother."

Odel's eyes widened at that. "My godmother?"

"Aye. Aunt Matilda. But you may call me Tildy, dear. Matilda puts one in mind of large, horsy women with prominent teeth."

The Fairy Godmother

"Tildy," Odel murmured, obedience coming automatically to her, then she frowned as she stared incredulously at the little woman. Matilda had been her mother's cousin—a poor orphaned cousin who had been taken in and raised by Lillith's parents. The two girls had been as close as sisters. Closer. Best friends.

But Lord Roswald had not suffered his wife to have friends. It had been his opinion that all of Lillith's attention and affection should be shared only among himself and their children. He had forced her to end all contact with Matilda—or Tildy as she preferred—shortly after their marriage. Still, that hadn't stopped her mother from naming the woman Odel's godmother.

Unfortunately, it hadn't been long after that that Matilda had taken a fall from her horse that had ended in her breaking her neck.

Eyes widening incredulously, Odel whirled on the woman. "But you are dead!"

"Am I?" Tildy asked, seeming not the least perturbed. "Where did you ever hear a thing like that?"

"Well, from . . ." Turning, Odel gestured vaguely toward the stone image of her father, then glanced back sharply when the little woman clucked beside her.

"Aye. Well, we all have our faults, don't we?"

Odel stared at Tildy uncertainly as she tried to discern exactly to which fault the woman was referring. Was Tildy implying her father had lied? That seemed the obvious answer, since her aunt now stood before her, not looking the least bit dead.

"You're named after me. Did you know that?" Tildy asked cheerfully.

Odel blinked, distracted from her thoughts. "I am? But your name is—"

"Matilda Odel," Tildy told her promptly. Her expression softened affectionately as she reached out to brush

13

a stray strand of hair off Odel's cheek. "And I was so looking forward to being your aunt. But of course, then there was that riding accident, and—" She shrugged.

"The accident?" Odel asked with a frown.

"The one that ended my earthly life," Matilda said impatiently.

"You mean the accident *did* kill you?" Odel squeaked.

"Aye. In my prime, too," Matilda murmured tragically, then sighed and straightened her shoulders. "Alas, such is life. Anyway, I have been watching out for you all these years as a godmother should, but I couldn't interfere before. Vlaster said it wasn't—"

"Who is Vlaster?" Odel interrupted absently, her gaze shifting to the door. It wasn't that far away. If she could just distract this madwoman for a moment. . . .

"Oh, he's my supervisor." Odel glanced back to see the woman peer at the floor as if in search of something. "He is around here somewhere. He probably headed straight for the keep. He dislikes the cold, you see."

"I *do* see," Odel said carefully, easing a step to the side and a little closer to the door.

"Aye." Matilda made a face. "He was none too pleased to be coming down here at this time of year, but your case has reached a rather crisis point."

"Yes," Odel agreed, taking another sidling step.

"I was able to convince him, thank goodness."

"Of what?" Odel took another step.

"Why, that your father's treatment of you had made you afraid of love. That without some serious intervention, he will have succeeded in his efforts to make you as bitter and lonely as he himself was." The woman explained herself patiently, then beamed at her. "But 'twill be all right now. I am here, specially sent to see you happy."

Odel paused and stared at the woman in shock. "Are

14

you implying, my lady, that you are some sort of guardian angel?"

"Well." She made a face. "I am not quite an angel yet. Angels don't need canes and fairy dust."

"Canes and fairy dust?" Odel's eyes widened further.

"Aye. I am just a godmother, a fairy godmother. I need a little help performing my miracles," she admitted unhappily, then brightened. "Though if I succeed at helping fifty of my wards, I shall be graduated to angel."

"And what number am I?" Odel asked, curious despite thinking the woman quite mad.

Matilda winced, her answer coming reluctantly. "You are my first. I have been in training up until now, you see."

"Well, that figures," Odel muttered to herself.

"Never fear, though. I graduated at the top . . . Well, close to the top of my . . . I didn't fail," Tildy ended finally. She sighed and took Odel's arm, urging her toward the door Odel had been so eager to escape through just moments before. "Never mind that. All will be well. But there is much to do."

"Much to do with what?" Odel asked warily as her "guardian" dragged open the doors. Sunlight and a crisp winter breeze immediately washed over them.

"With *you*, dear. I am here to find you a husband."

"Find me a husband?" Odel paused and stiffened at the claim. That was the last thing she had expected—and the very last thing she wanted. "I have no need of a husband."

"Of course you do, dear. Oh, my goodness, yes. One cannot procreate alone, you know. A man is needed for that chore."

Odel flushed, then paled in turn. "But I do not wish to procreate."

"Of course you do. 'Tis your duty. As the bible says,

'go forth and multiply' and all that. Yes, yes it does and so you shall."

"But I am not even betrothed, I—"

"Aye, I know. Most remiss of your father. Terribly selfish, too, keeping you chained to him so. He wanted to keep you all to himself no doubt, but we shall fix that. We will have you betrothed and married off in no time."

"But—"

"Now, I'll have no arguing from you. I know your father insisted on your staying at his side until he died, but he's gone. And it is my job to look out for you now. I do so want to attain angel status—they have wings, you know—and after you I will only have forty-nine to go." Tildy's gaze settled on her determinedly. "But I do have something of a time limit. I have till Christmas to see you happy and married."

Odel stiffened. "Which is it?"

Tildy blinked. "Which is what?"

"Which are you supposed to make me? Happy or married?" she snarled, then turned to march across the bailey. Her heart was pounding something fierce, just as it had over the years when her father had raised his voice and his hand to her. Only this time was different. She wasn't feeling fear. Instead, she *was* furious.

She had spent the last twenty-five years under her father's power being ordered about. Every wish, every desire she had ever had had been belittled or thwarted by him. She had no intention of putting herself back under another man's thumb.

"But, my dear!" Matilda rushed after her, obviously alarmed. "Every girl wants to be married. Every girl wants a husband, children and a home."

"I am *not* every girl," Odel snapped, then suddenly remembered that this woman was quite mad. There was nothing to fear here; she didn't need to fear losing her freedom. Not truly. The thought made her pause.

She was free. A small laugh slipped from her lips, then she picked up her pace again and began to hurry up the steps to the keep. She was free! Why, she could go inside right now and . . . and sit by the fire if she wished. Her father would not be there yelling at her to fetch him this or do that. She could, well, she could do whatever she wanted. For the most part.

"Oh, my!"

At Matilda's exclamation, Odel paused just inside the door of the keep. She did not have to think hard to figure out what had brought that gasp from her lips, Roswald castle had done it. She felt all of her excitement of a moment ago slip away as she peered at the great hall. Her father's presence was everywhere. It pervaded the keep as if he were not truly dead at all. Odel peered about and sighed. "It is rather grim and gloomy, is it not?"

"Aye." Matilda nodded solemnly.

"Father never liked the sun much," Odel muttered unhappily as her eyes adjusted to the dim interior. "He always insisted the arrow slits be covered with leather, no matter the season, and—"

"There is only one chair in here," Matilda pointed out as if Odel had not noticed.

"Aye," Odel agreed unhappily. In the whole huge great hall, the only stick of furniture was her father's large chair by the fire. He had always insisted the tables and benches used at mealtimes be collapsed and leaned against the walls lest some "lazy loafer waste time sitting about."

"And there are not even any rushes on the floor," Matilda added with amazement.

"Father said that was just a lazy servant's invention to keep from having to scrub the floor daily."

"Scrub the floor? But these stone floors are so cold

17

without rushes that the air is seeping right through my slippers."

"I know," Odel almost moaned the two words. "I have always wished it were otherwise." She glanced at Matilda. "If you really wished to make me happy, you could send me a wagon load of rushes, not some useless bossy husband."

"That, my dear, is a very good idea," Matilda decided grimly. Immediately, she tugged open the small pink sack that hung from her wrist. She slipped her hand inside, pulled it out a moment later, then raised the closed hand in front of her face. After muttering a couple of sentences, she opened her fingers and began to turn in a circle, blowing, as she did, on the glittering dust that rested in her palm.

Odel was busy gaping at this, her mouth hanging open like a fish, when Matilda's little spin brought them face-to-face. Finding herself in the center of a small cloud of the glittering substance, Odel gasped in surprise, then quickly closed her eyes and mouth, and tried to step back out of the way. She was too late. She had already breathed in a good deal of the dust, and it sent her into a fit of coughing and sneezing.

"Oh, dear!" Matilda was at her side and thumping her back at once. "I am sorry, my dear. I had no intention of blowing it in your face. I am sorry."

"What are you doing?" Odel choked out, straightening slowly as her sneezes and coughs subsided.

"Aye. Well, I did mention that where angels could perform miracles without it, I need it to—"

"Oh, my God!"

"What is it?" Matilda asked, then turned to survey the room at which the girl was now gaping. "Oh." She grimaced uncertainly. "Too much, do you think? Perhaps I should have used a little less fairy dust, hmmm?"

"Fairy dust?" Odel repeated faintly, her eyes sliding

over the room in shock. The floor was now covered with a clean carpet of rushes, and the walls were so white that their brightness almost hurt the eyes. As well, several huge tapestries now adorned them. Odel had never before seen such beautiful, rich weaves and she marveled at them briefly before taking in the rest of the room.

The lone chair that had sat by the fire was no more, yet the room was full of furnishings. Several large carved chairs sat grouped around the fire, huge soft cushions on each, making them look remarkably comfortable. The trestle tables and benches that had been collapsed and leaning against the wall were now set up, long white cloths covering the tables' rough surfaces. Two dainty pillows on the center of the bench of the uppermost table denoted where she and Matilda should sit.

"My God," Odel breathed, then whirled on Tildy accusingly. "You *do* have magic!"

Matilda sighed. "Aye, dear. Did I not say so? I told you I have fairy dust to help—Oh! There you are, Vlaster." Bending, she picked up a cat that slid through the open door behind them.

"Vlaster?" Odel echoed, then her eyebrows rose as she recalled Tildy's earlier mention of the name. "Your superior is a cat?"

"At the moment, yes."

"At the moment?" Odel repeated. She started to turn away in dismissal, only to pause as her gaze took in the room again. Moaning, she closed her eyes and swayed slightly. "This cannot be happening."

"Are you feeling faint?" Tildy asked with alarm, letting the cat drop to the floor to put a supporting arm around her. "Just breathe deeply. Breathe."

Odel obediently took a couple of deep breaths, relieved when some of the tightness in her chest eased.

The buzzing that had been filling her ears began to fade.

"Better?" Matilda asked solicitously. Odel nodded.

"Aye, but—"

"But?"

"You have to put this back the way it was."

Matilda frowned. "Do you not like it? I could—"

She shook her head, her eyes opening and scanning the room. "I like it, but what will the servants think? They will know something is amiss."

"Oh, ta-ra," Matilda laughed and waved her cane in a vague circle. "There! They shall all now believe that my servants did it."

"You have servants?"

Matilda stilled and frowned at that, then peered down at the cat she had set down. "Vlaster?"

In the blink of an eye, the cat was gone. In its place stood a man. Tall and thin, dressed in a frock and brais of black, he wiggled a black mustache at her then ran one hand through his hair as black as the cat's fur had been.

"Oh, no no no." Odel began to back slowly away, her head shaking.

"Aye. It is perfect," Matilda said gaily. "My dear, meet my manservant, Vlaster. Vlaster, my niece, Odel."

"Manservant?" There was a touch of irritation in the man's voice, but Odel was too busy shaking her head to notice.

"Nay," Odel repeated faintly and Matilda hesitated, frowning.

"Aye, I suppose he alone could not have achieved all this, could he?" Turning, she marched to the door, peered out into the bailey, glanced around briefly, then stilled suddenly and smiled in satisfaction. Putting her hand to her mouth, she began making the most god-awful quacking sounds.

"What are you doing now?" Odel hissed, hurrying to

her side. "You sound like a—" Her eyes widened, and she stepped back from the door abruptly. Six of the brown female ducks that had been penned by the stables, came waddling through the keep door. "—duck," she finished in amazement, then frowned and closed her eyes, waving her hand impatiently in front of her face as Tildy unleashed another cloud of glittering dust.

Despite having seen some wholly inexplicable events in the past few moments, Odel was not at all prepared to find six women of varying ages and sizes suddenly standing where the ducks had been but a moment before. Each of them was wearing a gown the same dull gray-brown as the ducks' feathers. The ducks were no longer in sight.

"Oh," Odel groaned. Her hand went to her forehead in horror as her own thoughts rolled around in her head.

"Mayhap you should lay down, my dear. You appear to have gone quite white."

"Nay, nay. I . . ." Odel forced her hands down and her eyes open, but the moment her gaze took in the new room, the furniture, the six maids, and the tall, dark Vlaster, she closed her eyes again. "Aye, mayhap I should."

"Aye, I think so," Matilda said gently. The older woman took Odel's arm to urge her toward the stairs to the upper floor. "A nice little nap will do you the world of good. I will wake you when it is time to sup. No doubt you have been sitting up by your father's bedside since he fell ill, and are exceedingly weary. A little nap, then a nice meal, will set everything right."

"Aye," Odel grasped eagerly at that explanation of the odd things happening in her home; she was hallucinating. "I am just over-tired. A little nap, then something to eat and everything will be back to normal."

"Well, I hope not," Matilda muttered a little wryly. She opened the door to Odel's room for her.

"How did you know which room was mine?" Odel asked curiously, but as she entered, she had a sneaking suspicion. At what she saw, she quickly turned her back to the room.

"What is it?" Matilda asked with alarm, peering past her. Understanding crossed Tildy's face as the woman took in the large comfy-looking bed, the cushioned chairs by the fire, and the lush rose-colored curtains that hung above the bed. The chamber looked warm and cozy. It had *not* looked like that when she had left it this morning. Roswald had been too mean and cheap to see to his daughter's comfort.

"Hmmm," Tildy said with a shrug. "I did use quite a bit of dust . . . but this just saves me from having to tend to it now. Are you not happy with your new room?"

Eyes still squeezed firmly shut, Odel merely began to chant under her breath. "This is not happening, this cannot be happening."

"There, there," Matilda murmured, turning Odel back around and steering her toward the bed. "A nice nap is just what you need."

"This is *not* happening," Odel said under her breath, collapsing onto the bed when Matilda pushed her against it. "This cannot be happening."

Chapter Two

It was happening all right.

Odel stared around the redecorated great hall and shook her head for at least the hundredth time since Matilda had arrived. She had taken her nap, but things had not changed back to normal—and it had been a day and a night. The walls were still a smooth bright white, decorated with colorful tapestries; the floor rustled with rushes; and furniture filled every corner of the room. More than that, now the furniture was full of people. There were the usual servants at the nooning meal, the soldiers, and so on, but now the keep also had several guests. At least two dozen men lined either side of the head table. There had been half a dozen of them at sup last night—all young, wealthy, and single lords who had arrived while she slept. Another twenty had arrived since then, riding gaily into Roswald as if by invitation.

Matilda called them suitors; Odel called them pains in the arse. She had no intention of getting married. Worse, she felt extremely uncomfortable under their ob-

vious flattery. Even the lovely new gowns they praised—
she had woken up to find her chests overflowing—had
not eased her discomfort. Odel was not used to the presence of others. She had spent so long restricted to the
company of her father and his servants, she had no idea
what to say to these preening visitors—handsome
though they might be.

"Are you all right? You look flushed," Matilda leaned
close to murmur.

Shifting where she sat, Odel sighed unhappily. "I am
just a bit warm." It was true. Frowning slightly, she
glanced toward the doors leading outside and announced, "In fact, I think I shall go for a short walk
once the meal is over."

"What a lovely idea," Tildy said cheerfully, which
immediately made Odel suspicious. She didn't have long
to wait before her suspicions were borne out. Matilda
added, "I am sure that Lord Brownell or Lord Trenton
would love to join you."

"Do please stop trying to push those men on me,
Tildy. I have no interest in them," Odel said wearily.

Matilda's face fell like that of a child who has been
refused a treat. Odel felt guilt pinch at her and she
sighed, but she did not retract her words. She really had
no interest in marrying. The sooner Tildy accepted that,
the better.

"There is Roswald up ahead, my lord."

Michelle blinked the snowflakes out of his eyes and
glanced up at Eadsele's words. His gaze narrowed on
the castle rising out of the stand of trees ahead. Yes,
Roswald would suffice. The mounts were tiring and he
needed to find a place to rest them. It was an unexpected
occurrence, seeing as it was only past midday and they
had only set out for the last leg of their journey home
several hours before, but the horses were definitely

blowing and Michelle wasn't the sort who would run his animals into the ground. They would stop here until morning.

"Aye. So it is, Eadsele," Michelle agreed, vaguely amused by the boy's excitement. No doubt he was getting sick of traveling after these last two weeks trudging through the snowy landscape of England. Michelle really should have collected the lad in early autumn, but had been kept busy at Suthtun, the impoverished estate he had inherited this summer. He'd had little time to think much about his new squire, let alone chase down to southern England to collect him. If Eadsele's father hadn't been a friend and asked him to train the boy as a favor—

"Do you think they will have room for us?"

"I do not see why not. I have never met Lord Roswald, but I have heard that he does not entertain much." Michelle frowned to himself as he tried to recall what else he had heard.

His neighbor was wealthy, he had known that, but even if he hadn't, he would have realized it rather quickly as they rode through Roswald's main gates a moment later. Prosperity showed in the round rosy cheeks of the children, and their pets. Poorer castles and their attending villages often could not afford pets, or had ragged hungry-looking animals—not the shiny coated, muscular beasts at play in the courtyard.

A hollow sound drew his attention to the keep's main stairs as the cloaked figure of a woman exited the great hall. As she closed the door behind her, she turned. Her face was hidden by a fur-lined hood, but a scarlet gown peeked out from under her cloak with each step, she took. She briskly descended the snow-laden steps.

Was this Lord Roswald's wife, his daughter, or merely a guest? Michelle wondered as his horse came to a halt at the foot of the steps. Realizing he would have to ask to find out, he dismounted, moving inadvertently into her path.

"Excuse me, my lady," Michelle began politely. He found his words waved away impatiently as the woman did her best to move around him.

"Just leave your horse with the servants and go on in," she instructed without even a glance. "Vlaster will show you to your room."

"Ah," Michelle turned as she hurried past him, his confusion plain on his face if she had bothered to look. "Are you—"

"Aye, my lord. I am Lady Roswald. And I will surely be pleased to make your acquaintance later. In the meantime, Vlaster will see to your comfort."

"Thank you, but I think you may have mistaken me for someone else. I am—"

"I know, my lord," she interrupted again. At last, heaving a sigh, she stopped and whirled to face him. The impatient twist to her lips was all he could see beneath her cloak's hood as she spoke. "There are twenty more just like you inside. And no doubt, just like them, you are eager to inform me that you are the wealthiest, most handsome man for three counties. You find me beyond beautiful and exceedingly charming and want to vow you would willingly die a horrid and painful death if only I would smile in your general direction." Her words were a weary recitation.

Michelle blinked, then shook his head, a wry smile plucking at his lips. "Well, if you are comparing me to the village swineherd, I suppose I am all of those things. But I really had no plans to die today—not even for one of your undoubtedly beautiful smiles."

The woman stood still for a moment, then reached up to pull back her hood and peer at him. He suspected, by the way her eyes widened, that it was the first real look

26

she had taken at him. Just as this was his first real glimpse of her.

Her hair was a deep brown, shot through with strands of fiery red. Her skin was pale and smooth, her nose straight, her eyes a pretty blue, and her lips were not too full, nor thin. She *was* pleasant to look on, but not so lovely that a man would die for a mere smile—at least not this man.

Michelle had too much to do and too little time to be bothered with the needs and demands of a woman. He would leave off having to burden himself with one until he had Suthtun up to snuff. Then, he supposed, he would have to take a wife to make an heir, but he really wasn't looking forward to the chore. In his experience, wives were more trouble than they were worth. His own mother had practically sent her husband, his father, to the grave with her demands for rich fabrics and glorious jewels. The man had died in battle, one of many battles he had hired himself out for in an effort to appease her. Nay. There would be no spoiled, demanding wife for him.

Startled out of her annoyance by his nonchalance, Odel lifted her hood off to peer at the man. Now she stared at him with some amazement. When she had first come outside, she had thought him yet another of the suitors Matilda had invited. They had after all, been arriving one after the other all day.

Fair-haired men, dark-haired men, tall men, and not-so-tall men, they had paraded into Roswald like baby peacocks. Every single one of them was single, exceedingly handsome, and at least comfortably wealthy.

This man, though, he was different. He was tall and strong, like the others, but his dark, longish hair framed features too harsh to be considered handsome. Her gaze slid over the rest of him, noting that while his clothes were clean and of good quality, they had obviously seen better days. He obviously wasn't wealthy like the others. Still, the glint of amusement in his eyes made him somehow charming to look at. Forcing a polite smile, she said, "I am sorry, my lord. Obviously I have made an error. Who did you say you were?"

"The new Lord Suthtun."

"Oh." She recognized the name and a feeling of solemnity overtook her. "I was sorry to hear of your uncle's passing. He used to visit my father on occasion. He was a very nice man."

"Then you are Lord Roswald's daughter?"

"Aye."

He nodded briefly. "Aye, well, I am traveling home from collecting Eadsele here." He gestured to the young lad now dismounting behind him. "I realize 'tis only a couple more hours home to Suthtun and I dislike putting you out, but the horses are tired and I do not like to overtax them in such weather. Do you think your father would mind if we stopped for the night?"

"My father died several days ago," Odel told him distractedly, glancing over at the castle doors. Were there any rooms left? She suspected there were not. Truly the castle was full to its turrets with prancing dandies and—

"I am sorry." The man's words interrupted her thoughts, but when Odel glanced at him questioningly, he added. "For your loss."

"Oh, aye. Thank you." She looked away, still not comfortable with her own lack of grief at the loss of the man who for most of her life had treated her no better than a servant. Spying one of the stable boys waiting patiently a few steps away, she waved him forward. "Tend to his lordship's horses, please, Tommy." She gave the instructions, then gestured for Lord Suthtun to follow her up the stairs to the castle.

Odel didn't turn to see if he followed; she didn't have

to, she could hear his footfalls behind her on the steps. This was no tippy-toed dandy who moved as silent as a cat. Nay, his steps were solid and heavy behind her as she led him into the castle.

The noise and heat in the great hall rolled over them in a wave as they entered it, and that reminded Odel of her hope to escape, however briefly, from her suitors. Grimacing at the cacophony of laughing and jesting male voices she had been trying to flee only moments before, Odel sighed and peered about for Matilda or Vlaster. It only took her a moment to find them. In a room full of colorfully dressed men as tall and solid as trees, Matilda's short rounded figure, encased in another god-awful pink creation, stood out like a plump pink mouse in a room full of large and healthy gray rats. Of course, Vlaster wasn't far behind. His tall impossibly thin and dour black form was never far away.

Odel was about to raise her arm to catch her aunt's attention, when suddenly the woman was bustling toward them, Vlaster following her like a tall, dark shadow.

"There you are, my dear," Tildy cried brightly as she reached them. "I had begun to wonder where you had gotten to. I should have known that one of your handsome suitors had—" Her words died, her mouth opening soundlessly as she turned to peer at the man standing beside Odel. "Oh." Her gaze slid over his less-than-handsome face and worn clothes, her smile wilting like a rose cut from its stem. "Who are you?"

"This is Lord Suthtun, Aunt Matilda," Odel announced, glaring at the older woman for her rudeness.

"Suthtun?" Matilda's nose twitched, her forehead wrinkling with concentration. "Suthtun. I don't recall sending a missive to you, my lord," she announced unhappily, then turned to Vlaster. "Did I, Vlaster?"

"I do not recall one, madam," the man murmured, a dour look on his face.

"Nay, neither do I. Suthtun. Suth-tun."

"He is a neighbor to the north," Odel said through her teeth. "And quite welcome here."

"To the north?" Matilda questioned with a definite lack of enthusiasm, then she sighed and nodded. "Oh yes. Suthtun; that poor little holding of that friend of your father's." Her face puckered up again with open displeasure. Apparently Tildy had set her sights on wealthier game. Embarrassed by her godmother's openly rude behavior, Odel hurried to intervene.

"He is traveling home from court and sought shelter here," she explained quickly. "I assured him that would be fine."

"Oh. Aye, well of course, it behooves us to help a neighbor, does it not?" she said, but didn't look pleased at the prospect. In fact, she sounded decidedly annoyed. She turned to Vlaster to ask, "Do we have a room for his lordship? Or shall he have to sleep on the floor?"

"Aunt Tildy!" Odel gasped, giving Lord Suthtun an apologetic look.

"Do not be offended on my account, my lady," the nobleman murmured with the same good humor he had shown earlier. "I am an unexpected guest and would be pleased for even a spot on the great hall floor by the fire—if it is available."

Odel blinked at the man, amazed at his claim. Surely, had any of the other lords been asked to consider such a spot, they would have been wroth at the insult. They had all required a room from what she had seen, likely to house all their various clothing and finery. This man, however, appeared to travel light, a small sack dangling from his relaxed hand his only baggage. He also lacked the attendants the other noblemen seemed helpless without. Lord Suthtun had only a young lad with him—his squire, she supposed.

"I am sure that will not be necessary, my lord," Odel murmured, turning to her aunt. "Surely Lord Beasley and his cousin, Lord Cheshire, could room together for one night."

"Oh, nay," Matilda exclaimed at once with horror. "Lord Beasley has more gold than the king—and Lord Cheshire is quite the most handsome of your suitors. They are both most important men; I cannot think they will thank you for the insult."

Odel grimaced at that. Most handsome and wealthy they might be, but Lord Beasley was vain and Lord Cheshire was arrogant. Doubling them up could only help the two men's dispositions. "They shall survive the insult, I am sure," she said with a wry smile. "My neighbor is in need of a bed for the night."

"Aye," Matilda agreed reluctantly. "I suppose with the ague coming on his squire, his lordship could indeed use a bed. Very well, I shall see what I can do to smooth this over with the lords Beasley and Cheshire."

"Thank you," Odel muttered. She was grateful for her godmother's acquiescence, but confused by her words. Her gaze had moved to the boy in question. Much to her surprise, the lad did seem quite pale. He was also trembling as if with a chill. She had not noticed that outside. In fact, she thought she recalled him looking quite robust.

"Eadsele, are you not well?" Lord Suthtun asked the boy now, looking as startled as Odel by the boy's sickly state. Pressing the back of his hand to his squire's forehead, Lord Suthtun scowled. "You're on fire. How long have you not been feeling well?"

"I don't know, my lord. I was cold while we were traveling, but thought it was just the weather," he answered miserably, swaying where he stood. Lord Suthtun reached out and caught the lad's arm to steady him.

"Hmph." Matilda turned away with purpose. "You'd best put the boy to bed before he falls down. I shall send servants up to move Lord Cheshire's things."

"If you would follow me, my lord," Odel said. Suthtun lifted the boy into his arms and followed as she led him to Lord Cheshire's room, somehow managing to wave away any eager lords who might have slowed their progress.

"I shall have one of the servants arrange a pallet for the boy," she said as she let him into what had—until a few moments ago—been Lord Cheshire's chamber.

"Nay. Have them arrange one large enough for me." Crossing the room, he set the boy gently on the bed and pulled the furs up to cover him.

Odel was still for a moment as she watched him care for the squire. The man seemed extremely kind; his voice was soft and reassuring, his hands gentle. Her own father had never shown her such tenderness. Her thoughts were disturbed a moment later as the door opened behind her and servants began to file into the room. Within moments Lord Cheshire's things had been removed, and water and a clean cloth had been supplied. Lord Suthtun bathed the lad's head.

"Is he your son?" The tenderness the man showed was exquisite, and the question burst from Odel's lips before she had even realized it had come to mind. But Lord Suthtun didn't seem upset. He hardly seemed to notice, so busy was he with his caretaking.

"Nay, he is my squire, the son of an old friend placed in my care to train and raise."

His answer seemed to suggest that he would tend as kindly to anyone under his charge, and Odel pondered that. This man was an enigma. His clothes were old but well tended; he had claimed to stop for the night simply for the good of his horses; and now he showed dutiful care and even affection for a squire. He did indeed appear to tend well to what was his. What would her life have been like had her father been more like this man? she wondered.

"Might I prevail upon you for some mead, and perhaps some broth for the boy?" he asked suddenly.

Shifting, Odel nodded. Then, realizing that he could not see her nod, she murmured, "I shall have some brought up at once. And for the pallet to be arranged. Would you care for your supper to be brought here as well, or shall you join the table?"

His gaze slid to the window, then he glanced toward her. "I would not wish to trouble the servants anymore than I have to. I imagine I can manage joining the table."

"Then, I shall have one of the servants come and sit with Eadsele when 'tis time for the meal." Odel slid from the room to see to these things.

Downstairs, she had barely stepped off the landing before she found herself surrounded by suitors. It was as if they had been lying in wait for her return. Compliments, offers to escort her on walks, to play music for her, recite poetry to her, all smothered her like a cloying blanket as she tried to make her way to the kitchens. By the time she broke loose and escaped the great hall, she was thoroughly annoyed. She nearly trampled Matilda as she tried to enter the steaming kitchens.

"Oh, there you are, my dear," her godmother said, then paused to look at her more closely. "Oh, my, you do look vexed. Is Lord Suthtun's squire worse?"

"Nay, I just—" She gestured vaguely over her shoulder, then shook her head. "Never mind. I came to arrange for some broth and mead to be taken up for the boy."

"I already arranged that," Matilda assured her.

"Oh, good. Well, then, Lord Suthtun asked that a pal-

33

let be prepared for him. He wishes the boy to have his bed while he is ill."

Matilda's eyes narrowed, her eyebrows arching in displeasure. "Do you mean to say Lord Suthtun forced Lord Cheshire from his bed for a squire?"

Odel frowned at the woman's expression. "*He* did not force anyone. *I* suggested we put Lord Cheshire with Lord Beasley. Besides, I think it is terribly chivalrous of him to give up his bed for a sick child."

"If you say so," Matilda agreed irritably. "But I assure you Lord Beasley is smarter than to give up a warm, soft bed for a boy."

"Well, whether that is smarter is debatable," Odel snapped, then sighed as the kitchen door swung open to reveal one of her many suitors.

Smiling as he spotted her, the man let the door swing closed and hurried forward.

Chapter Three

"Would that be Lord Cheshire?"

Odel glanced up from her food to follow Lord Suthtun's gesture. He had taken a seat at the place she had saved him just as the meal was being carried out. Throughout the supper they had discussed the uncommonly cold weather they were having this winter, his squire's fever—which was still high—and various and sundry topics of less importance. Odel nodded and answered his question. "Aye, it is. How did you know?"

"Because he is glaring daggers at me," Michelle murmured with that ever-present amusement. "I think he is distressed at my pinching his bed."

"It wasn't really his bed to begin with," Odel pointed out dryly, her gaze moving over the man in question to his cousin, Lord Beasley. The two men sat side by side and neither of them looked pleased. Lord Cheshire looked especially resentful as he glared at Lord Suthtun. In truth, both men had already made their displeasure with the new arrangements known to Odel. When she had stood firm on the arrangements despite their complaints, they had settled into some unsubtle pouting. Odel didn't know whether to be amused or put out by their behavior, but it was obvious they both felt as her aunt had predicted; they were much too important to be forced to double up.

They had even been making noises about leaving. She guessed she was supposed to be overcome with dismay at the threat, but the only feeling she could work up was a vague relief. Really, having all these men fluttering around was quite wearing. Having a couple of them leave would hardly put her out.

"So?" The drawn-out word drew Odel's curious gaze and Lord Suthtun grinned. "Which one do you favor?"

Odel stared at him blankly for a moment, then felt herself flush. Apparently he had determined that the lords all gracing her table were suitors. Of course, she remembered, Matilda had said something about suitors when he and his squire had first arrived.

"Actually, I am not interested in any of them," she said at last, grimacing when his eyebrows arched in disbelief. "Having them here was my . . . Aunt's idea. I have no desire to marry."

"Ever?" he asked.

"Ever," Odel assured him firmly, then scowled at his expression. "You find that difficult to believe?"

"Well, aye, I guess I do. Most women wish to have a husband to supply all the riches and jewels they need to be happy."

Odel's mouth tightened at that. "I desire no man to supply riches and wealth. I have more than I need." More than she was even used to or comfortable with at the moment, she thought a bit unhappily. While it was nice that the keep was not as mean and cold as it had been, Matilda had rather overdone it.

Suddenly realizing that Lord Suthtun had been silent

quite a while, she turned to see him examining her as if trying to decide if he should believe her. She supposed he must have decided to take her word, because he next asked quietly, "Then what of a husband to provide children?"

Odel swallowed. She had never really even considered the possibility of children. She had given up on them a long time ago, when she had realized that her father had no intention of letting her marry and leave him. Now the possibility rose before her and she actually found herself tempted for a moment. Then she recalled that she would have to marry to have them—and that a man would likely make her children's lives as miserable as her own had been. "I would like to have children," she admitted quietly. "But, I fear, the price of a husband seems overly steep to me."

Lord Suthtun considered her briefly, then murmured, "Lord Roswald must have been even more of a tyrant than I had heard."

Odel peered down at her plate uncomfortably, then changed the subject. "Inheriting Suthtun must have come as something of a surprise."

He was silent for a minute, then followed her lead. "Aye. My uncle was still relatively young, and even had he not been, his son should have inherited. The fact that they both died within days of each other from a cold was a great surprise to all. How did your father die?"

"His heart gave out. In his sleep," she explained, then forced a smile for the servants who suddenly appeared before them. There were four in all, carting a suckling pig.

"Shall I?" Lord Suthtun murmured, withdrawing a small jeweled dagger from his waist and gesturing toward the platter.

"Thank you, yes." Odel watched as he sliced off some of the juicy white meat and moved it to her plate—a silver one no less, more of Matilda's magic. Many castles, she'd heard, had a silver plate and goblet for their lord on special occasions, but Roswald had never been one of them. Odel's father had been too cheap. Now everyone at the high table was eating off a silver plate and drinking from a silver goblet. Father would be rolling over in his sarcophagus, she thought with some enjoyment.

A small sound from her right made her realize that a small mountain of meat now sat on her plate. He was reaching to put more on, but looking quite perplexed. Obviously, he had been waiting for her to say "enough." Her father would have given her the thinnest, toughest serving he could manage, and that would have been that. She was not used to her wants being observed. Flushing with embarrassment, she murmured "Thank you," and was relieved when he nodded and turned his attention to filling his own plate.

It wasn't until he set the dagger on the table between them that Odel noticed its beautiful carved hilt. "Oh, my, how lovely," she commented, picking it up. "Wherever did you get this?"

"It was a gift from the king." He peered at his food as he answered, looking particularly embarrassed. Which only managed to make Odel more curious.

"What was the gift in honor of?"

Suthtun shrugged slightly. "I assisted him in an endeavor," he answered vaguely, then changed the subject. "Did your father never arrange a marriage?"

It was Odel's turn to look uncomfortable. "Nay."

"And your mother?"

"She died when I was quite young."

They were both silent for a moment, then her guest asked, "Is your Aunt Matilda the only family you have left?"

Odel nodded. "And you? Were your Uncle and cousin your only family?"

He shook his head. "The former Lord Suthtun was my mother's brother. My mother and my two sisters are both at Suthtun now, no doubt preparing for Christmas."

"Your father?"

"He died when I was young."

"Your sisters are younger than you, then."

He raised his eyebrows. "Aye. How did you know?"

"Well, you did not mention any husbands, so I just assumed."

He nodded. "Yes, my sisters are both quite a bit younger. There was another sister and a brother between us, but they didn't survive past childhood."

Odel murmured some suitable sounds at that, then asked, "And ere inheriting the title and estate of Suthtun, what—"

"I was a mercenary," he answered, apparently unperturbed by the question. And quite successful at it, Odel guessed, now understanding where his expensive clothes came from. As a mercenary without land or title to eat up his funds, he had been free to spend his earnings on such things. Now a lord of an impoverished estate, he spent his money more carefully.

Suddenly, all he had said began to ring bells in her mind. The knife was in honor of a favor he had done the king. He had been a mercenary prior to inheriting Suthtun. His name was Michelle—a French name, and not all that common in England. In truth, She knew of only two men with that name: the man seated beside her and a mercenary who had saved King Edward II from a suspected witch in Coventry.

She recalled her father having spoken of it with a laugh; he had been sympathetic to no one, not even his liege. The "witch", John of Wiltham, had been arrested for attempting to poison the king with a potion. Accusations of black magic had quickly followed. Wiltham had been arrested and held in Coventry to stand trial, but when the king had gone to question the man personally, Wittham had attacked him, trying to kill him with his bare hands.

It was said he would have succeeded, had a mercenary accompanying Edward not stepped in and killed him. The king had reputedly given this mercenary—named Michelle—his own jeweled knife in thanks. She recalled her father's jealous dismissal of the whole incident.

Odel's gaze dropped to the knife on the table, her stomach rolling over. "You are Michelle the witch-killer."

Michelle grimaced, then shook his head. "I have killed hundreds of men, yet I kill one accused of witchcraft and suddenly I am Michelle the witch-killer."

Odel relaxed somewhat at that, and even managed a smile. That was true; he had only killed one witch—and that had been one trying to kill the king. He was not exactly a witch hunter. "You have nothing against them then?" she said in a joking manner, but her gaze slid to where Matilda sat observing the guests.

"Well, I would as soon kill one as look at them," he admitted, drawing Odel's face back around in alarm. "But I am not interested in hunting them down. Witches are a nasty bunch. Sneaky, too. Killing with potions and elixirs rather than facing a man in fair battle. Aye. They are a nasty lot."

The knight turned his attention to his meal then, unaware that Odel was now trembling with fear. Her poor aunt! Tildy might call herself a fairy godmother, but anyone seeing her cast dust in the air and mutter over it would surely call her a witch. And Michelle would not need to hunt to find her. Dear Lord, if he saw her pull one of her stunts he would—

"Well, I had best go check on my squire," Michelle

announced suddenly, getting to his feet. Pausing, he turned to take Odel's hand and bow over it. "Thank you for the lovely meal, my lady."

Odel nodded, then watched him leave the table. He crossed the room and jogged lightly up the steps.

"Oh, my, that is a lovely dagger, isn't it?"

Turning, Odel glanced at Matilda, then down at the dagger she was gesturing to. Lord Suthtun had forgotten his blade. "It was a gift from the king . . . for killing a witch!"

Tildy's eyebrows rose, but rather than appear worried, she merely said, "Well that makes sense. The man obviously couldn't afford to purchase it himself."

"Wealth is not everything, Matilda," Odel said irritably, picking up the dagger and wiping it on a crust of bread.

"Well, it may not be everything, but it certainly helps to make a body happy," Matilda answered promptly.

Odel clucked in disgust. "Oh aye, it certainly did that for my father." She gave her aunt a pointed look, then rose.

"Where are you going?" Matilda shifted around in her seat to peer after her as Odel started away.

"I am going to return Lord Suthtun's blade and check on his squire."

She hurried away, and was at the top of the stairs before she realized anyone had followed. But just as she turned toward the room Lord Suthtun had been given, a hand on her arm made her stop and turn. The man behind her made Odel's stomach lurch.

"Lord Cheshire." She tried for a smile, but knew it was a bit stiff. She really wasn't in the mood to hear any more of his complaints about rooming with his cousin. "Is there something I can do for you?"

"Aye." He hesitated briefly, then lifted his chin. "I am a very handsome hu—man, am I not?"

41

Odel managed to restrain a grimace. Sighing, she nodded solemnly. "Aye, my lord." It was the truth. Lord Cheshire *was* quiet the most handsome man she had ever laid eyes on. His hair was a pale brown that flowed in waves down to his shoulder. His eyes were as black as Vlaster's jacket. His face and figure were perfection itself; she was being honest when she said, "You *are* very handsome." Then she continued with, "Now, if you would excuse me?"

Odel started to turn away to continue on to Lord Suthtun's room, but Cheshire grabbed her hand, drawing her to a halt. "Nay."

"Nay?" She peered at him narrowly as she tried to free her hand from his.

"First we must settle this. I am the most handsome man here. Would you not agree?"

Sighing, she nodded impatiently. "Aye, my lord. In fact, you are the most handsome man I have ever seen."

"Well, then, why do you avoid me? Do you not know how fortunate you would be to have me to husband? Why do you resist falling in love with me?"

Odel's mouth dropped open at the forward question. "I . . ."

"I would be a good husband to you. I would let you eat all the juiciest morsels. I would give you five or six babies. I *would* make you happy."

Eyes wide, Odel heard a high, almost squeaking sound slip past her lips. She quickly closed her mouth, then shook her head in the hopes of clearing it so that something useful might come to mind to say. She was still struggling when he suddenly swept her into his arms. Passionately, he breathed, "We would do well together. You *will* love me." Then his mouth descended on hers.

Odel wasn't very experienced when it came to kisses—well, all right, this was her first—but if this wet, mushy experience was what they were all like, she decided, she could do quite nicely without them. Her decision never to marry had not been a mistake. She began to struggle in Lord Cheshire's grasp.

"Unhand her!"

That voice was rather like the crack of doom, Odel thought faintly before Lord Cheshire finally released her. Steadying herself with a hand on the wall, she turned to peer up the hall. Aunt Matilda was barreling toward them. Who would have thought such a deep authoritative voice could have issued forth from her plump, usually cherubic countenance? Although she didn't look very cherubic at the moment. She looked furious. And, oddly enough, Tildy in a fury was quite an intimidating sight.

Odel almost felt sorry for Lord Cheshire. The man was suddenly looking terrified. Almost, but not quite, she decided, using the back of her hand to wipe away his slobbery kiss.

"How dare you overstep yourself so!" Matilda raged, coming to a halt before them, her eyes spitting fire.

"I . . ." The young nobleman looked away, anywhere but at the woman confronting him, then suddenly drew himself up and spoke. "She wanted me to. She loves me. She wants to be my wife."

"Poppycock!" Tildy snapped, not even bothering to look at Odel for confirmation. "You cannot fool me, I can see right through your lies. You thought if you forced yourself on Odel I would have to agree to a marriage. Then you would be set up here for the rest of your miserable days."

Lord Cheshire shrank slightly under her wilting glare, then whined. "Well, so what if I did?"

Matilda's eyes narrowed to angry slits. She flicked her cane at him once, set it down with a snap, then smiled with satisfaction. "That, is so what!"

Odel turned in bewilderment to peer at Lord Cheshire, but he was no longer there. A scuffling sound drew her gaze downward then. Her mouth dropping open, she gaped in horror at the rat now sitting where Lord Cheshire had been but a moment before. "Aunt Matilda!"

"What?" Tildy asked innocently, her gaze shifting curiously past Odel. The squeak of a door opening sounded behind her.

Odel whirled, her horrified gaze landing on Lord Suthtun as he stuck his head out into the hall. Peering down the dim hallway toward them, he arched an eyebrow in a silent question.

"Is anything amiss? I thought I heard—"

"Nay," Odel assured him quickly, rushing down the hall to urge him back into his room. It wasn't until she noticed the way his eyes had widened that she glanced down to see that she still held his dagger. No wonder he was backing away so quickly. "I—Here," She turned the weapon around and held it out to him, explaining, "I just wanted to return this . . . and Aunt Matilda followed to have a discussion with me. All is well."

"Are you sure?" he asked, accepting the weapon.

"I am positive. Everything is fine. Really. Fine." She nearly choked on the lie, vaguely aware her voice was unnaturally high and squeaky sounding. She grabbed the door and pulled it closed, adding a slightly frantic, "Sleep well."

After she shut the door in his face, Odel whirled and hurried back to Matilda. "You undo that right now!" she hissed fiercely, glaring at her godmother and pointing furiously downward.

"Undo what right now?" Tildy asked with bewilderment.

"Undo what?" Odel cried in amazement. "Do you not realize that Lord Suthtun would as soon kill a witch as look at her?"

The Fairy Godmother

Matilda looked unperturbed. "And so he should. But I am not a witch."

"Yes, but—" Odel began, then shook her head. This was no time to explain. Trying for patience, she ground out, "Turn Lord Cheshire back into . . ." Her voice died as she glanced down and realized she was pointing at nothing. The rat that had been Lord Cheshire was gone. A frown of dismay replaced her anger. "Where did he go?"

Matilda shrugged. "No doubt he just skittered off somewhere. Rats tend to do that." Never fear though, Vlaster shall find—Oh! There. You see! Vlaster has already found him."

Following the woman's gesture, Odel peered toward the stairs. She paled at once, her eyes dilating with horror. Her aunt's "servant" stood at the top of the stairs, holding the rat by the tail as if he were about to swallow it. "Vlaster!"

Pausing, the liveried servant closed his mouth, straightened his head, and turned to look at her in silence.

Odel was at his side at once. Snatching the squirming rat from him, she held it out in front of her and turned back toward Matilda with a determined expression. But she had only taken a couple of steps when the door to Lord Suthtun's room opened again and his head popped out once more. Obviously he had heard her shriek. Dropping her hand, she moved the rat behind her back and tried for an innocent expression.

"Aye, my lord?" she murmured, the calm image she was trying to project ruined somewhat by the way her voice rose at the end. She gave a sudden jerk as Lord Cheshire broke free of her hold, and was now scrabbling up the back of her gown. Biting her lip, she tried not to squirm as his little clawed feet scrambled over her rump and started up her spine. If he bit her, she was going to step on the little bugg—

"I thought I heard a shriek," Lord Suthtun explained quietly.

"Oh. Aye," Odel almost moaned the words as the rat crawled under her long hair and made its way to the nape of her neck. She felt its cold nose against her flesh, and she had to bite her lips to keep from shrieking again. *It is only Lord Cheshire,* she reminded herself. *It is only Lord Cheshire. Oh, God!*

"Oh, 'twas nothing, my lord," Matilda stepped in to reassure him. "Odel just thought she saw a rat."

"Ah." The man's gaze shifted from Matilda to Odel, then widened. "It would seem she did see one."

Odel closed her eyes with a groan. She had felt Lord Cheshire move to her right shoulder. No doubt the little beast was now peering from her hair. Putting her hands out before him as the rat started to climb down her front, Odel offered him a platform to stand on as she lied. "Nay. Not *this* rat. This rat is . . . er . . . a pet. I thought I spotted another *rat!!*" She shrieked, whirling away as, instead of moving on to the hand she had lifted, Lord Cheshire took a nose-dive down the front of her gown. He was now nestled between her breasts, and apparently quite happy from the way he'd quit squirming.

Pulling her gown away from her chest, Odel dug her other hand in to retrieve the wayward suitor. Matilda was there at once, her cane raised as if to zap her, or the rat, or both. Releasing her gown, Odel immediately snatched the cane with her now free hand, grabbed ahold of the rat with the other and ripped it out of her top.

"Are you quite all right?" Lord Suthtun was at her side now as well.

Taking a moment to glower in warning at Tildy, Odel handed the rat to her, then turned to Lord Suthtun. "I am fine, my lord," she assured him, her voice unnaturally brittle. "Just a little trouble. All taken care of now," she assured him, frowning as she realized that Matilda, Vlaster and Cheshire were now disappearing down the stairs. "I—umm—I really have to get back to my—er—guests, my lord." She began backing toward the stairs. "Is there anything you need, then . . ."

"Michelle. And no, thank you"

"Good night, then, Michelle." With a grimace, she whirled and set off after her aunt.

Matilda and Vlaster were nowhere to be seen when Odel reached the bottom of the steps. Muttering under her breath, she waved away the men who immediately began moving in her direction. Perhaps Matilda and Vlaster were in the kitchens. She had nearly reached the door to the steamy room when a cold rush of air swept through the great hall, rustling the rushes. Pausing, she turned to see Matilda entering with Vlaster on her heels. Odel promptly changed direction and rushed toward them.

"Where have you been? Where is Lord Cheshire? What have you done now?" Her words came out in a frenzy as she reached the pair.

Matilda patted her arm soothingly. "Nothing, dear. He went . . . er . . . home."

"Home?"

"Aye. He left."

"How?"

Matilda scowled. "What do you mean, 'how'? He—"

"Did you turn him back or not?" Odel hissed. "You did not leave him a rat, did you?"

"Oh." Her aunt gave a little laugh. "Well, no. You needn't worry about that, my dear. Lord Cheshire left here just as he came. Now, why don't you go for a nice little walk with Lord Beasley? He mentioned earlier that—"

"I do not *wish* to take a walk with Lord Beasley. I do not wish to walk with *anyone*," Odel interrupted wearily, her shoulders slumping as the tension left her body. "I do, however, wish you would give up on my marrying one of these men. I really have no desire for a husband, Tildy!"

Face softening with sympathy, Matilda reached out to briefly clasp Odel's hand. "I know, my dear. But then if you did, I would not be needed here, would I?"

Odel opened her mouth to try to convince the older woman to give up her quest and let her be, but instead closed it and shook her head in defeat. She did not have the energy to argue with the woman. She had been doing so for the last two days without result.

"You look tired. Why do you not go to bed? I shall see to your guests."

"They are not my guests. *You* invited them here, and . . ." Odel began impatiently, then shook her head and turned away. "Oh, what is the use? You do not listen to me, anyway. I am going to bed."

Chapter Four

"You should go below and eat."

Michelle let the fur drape fall back to cover the window and turned to find Eadsele sitting up in bed. The boy was still pale, but he looked a bit more alert than he had for the past week. "Are you feeling better?"

Grimacing, his squire shook his head apologetically. "I am sorry, my lord. I am never sick. Really."

Leaving the window, Michelle moved back to sit on the side of the bed. "Do not apologize. It is hardly your fault that you are ill."

"Aye. But 'tis only a week until Christmas, and I know you must be eager to return home."

"Do not worry about me, I am enjoying the rest." He meant to assure the boy, but didn't sound very convincing even to himself.

Not wishing to overburden Lady Roswald's maids when she already had so many guests, Michelle had insisted on nursing the boy himself. He had spent the last week stuck here in this room, trying to bathe down Ead-

49

sele's temperature when it was high, covering him with furs when he had the chills, and urging bowl after bowl of broth down the boy's sore throat. To a man used to days filled with activity, this was becoming unbearable. And yet, the nights had almost made the week pass quickly.

A smile curved Michelle's lips as he recalled the last several nights. While he had insisted on staying with Eadsele during the day, the Lady Odel had convinced him to let a maid take over his nighttime vigil so that he could spend his evenings below—and also get some rest. Since the first night, he had joined the table for supper, then fallen into the habit of chatting and playing chess with Odel.

Odel. He smiled slightly now as he thought of the way her eyes sparkled when she laughed. He'd found himself regaling her with all the funny little stories he could recall. He also liked the way she blushed when he complimented her, so that he found himself slipping them in, so that he could enjoy the pink flush that covered her cheeks.

Aye, Odel had helped to keep him from going mad this last week and he could hardly believe that the company of a woman affected him so. But he had come to know her quite well this last week, and what he had learned was that not all women were the greedy grasping creatures his mother had always seemed.

At least, Odel wasn't. She never seemed to take advantage of the servants around her as his mother did, ordering them to do this or that, and even, he suspected, making up things just to play the grand lady. Odel did most everything for herself.

Murmuring that the servants were busy with their own tasks, she would fetch the beverages while they played chess each night. She even often threw logs on the fire and built it up herself rather than asking a servant. Odel also hadn't worn a single jewel to adorn her gown this last week, though he was sure she must have many such items.

Aye, she was different than his mother, and Michelle liked her all the more for that. He could hardly believe his luck. With a keep full of wealthy, handsome men, he was surprised she gave him any time at all. But not only did she give him attention, she paid little if any attention to the rest of the guests.

"You would do better did you not spend all of your time in here with me, my lord," Eadsele suggested, interrupting his thoughts.

His gaze focusing on the pale boy in the bed, Michelle shrugged and smiled.

"Someone has to stay with you."

"The maid who sits with me while you eat offered to sit with me during the day—should you wish to enjoy the holiday diversions Lady Roswald is supplying."

Eadsele's voice seemed almost eager. Michelle was pleased to see in the boy's face the barest trace of color, too. His new squire had been an apple-cheeked lad when he had collected him, and had remained so through most of their journey. It had only been upon their arrival here that he had become so deathly pale, when he had been stricken by this illness. His pallid complexion since had been most worrisome. Now, the faintest flush of pink again touched his skin.

"Lady Roswald is beautiful, do you not think, my lord?" At the sly words, Michelle's eyes narrowed on the boy. Lady Roswald had visited Eadsele's sick room once or twice a day, sometimes staying to play a game with them to cheer the lad. She was very kind. And she was also beautiful, though he had not thought so at first. Hers was a loveliness that grew on you. Still, there was something about the boy's tone of voice that made Michelle suspect his motives.

"Why do I get the feeling you would be eager to see me go?" he asked abruptly.

The flush in the boy's cheeks stained his face a bright red, and Michelle's eyes widened slightly. He recalled the way the boy had brightened every night when the maid, Maggie, arrived, and suddenly he understood. The boy had a crush on the little serving wench.

Michelle didn't know why he had not picked up on the fact sooner, or why it so surprised him now. Eadsele was already fourteen.

"So tell me about this maid," Michelle murmured, his lips twitching when Eadsele flushed even darker.

"The maid? She tells me about the feasts and the celebrations," he said as if it were of no consequence. At the sound of activity in the bailey below, the boy gave a relieved look and glanced toward the covered window. "What is that? Do you think they are going on a hunt?"

Standing, Michelle moved back to the window and peered out at the snow-covered bailey. "Nay. 'Tis just a wagon load of flour."

"Hmm." Eadsele shifted restlessly. "From what Maggie says, there has been a grand feast every night."

"Aye," Michelle murmured, still looking down on the bailey.

"I would think they should need to go hunting soon then, should they not? The larders should be running low by now. It has been a week since we arrived and there has been no hunting done at all."

Michelle nodded at that, his mind suddenly fixing on the suggestion. He was tired of being caged indoors with Eadsele, but up until now he had felt it was his place to look after the boy. After all, the lad was his charge. But it seemed Eadsele had a more attractive nursemaid in mind. And now the squire had given him a good idea. He would enjoy a nice brisk ride right about now, and hunting game to make up for what he and Eadsele were eating was the perfect excuse. That would give him a chance to get outside without feeling he was neglecting his duties or overburdening the Roswald servants.

"You are right," he announced, letting the fur drape again fall into place to block out the bailey below. "A nice stag or boar should—" What he suspected was a trace of triumph in Eadsele's eyes made him pause. He got the distinct impression he had been manipulated. Still, he decided, it didn't matter. He wished to get out and about anyway. If Eadsele wished to gaze upon the little serving wench, let him.

"Good morning, my lady."

Odel felt a shot of alarm run through her on finding Lord Suthtun seating himself next to her at the table. During the week since his arrival at Roswald, Michelle had never once come below to break his fast.

Which was a relief to her of course, she assured herself. After all, it lowered the risk of his coming upon Matilda and her magical moments. She hadn't worried about that with the Roswald servants. Matilda had assigned the duck maids to serve in the great hall, which left the real maids to tend to the bedchambers and kitchens, safely away from the likelihood of seeing anything unusual. Odel also hadn't had to worry about the men-at-arms witnessing anything. It turned out that they were all quite disgusted with the preening ways of the lords lounging about Roswald hall, and did their best to avoid them. Her men still came into the hall for meals, but were quick about it and left as soon as they were finished.

It was only Lord Suthtun Odel had to worry about. His decision to nurse his sick squire had been quite convenient if he were to stay at Roswald. It left her with only the evenings to worry that her odd aunt might suddenly pull out some fairy dust, or wave her cane in front of, or even worse, at him.

Odel had done her best to keep him away from the woman. She sat between them at the dinner table always keeping up a lively chatter so that he would have no reason to address the strange godmother. Then, once the meal was finished, she had taken to playing chess with him each night by the fire.

The best thing about that was, Odel had found Michelle a worthy opponent. For every game she won, he won one as well. They were most evenly matched. Actually, she had enjoyed talking and playing with the man since his arrival, and she was suddenly aware that she would miss those companionable evenings when he left. Which was perhaps why the idea that the boy might be improving was presently upsetting her. Once Eadsele was better, there would be no excuse for Lord Suthtun to remain. And while she knew she should be relieved that his departure would vastly simplify her life, at the moment she was more concerned with the loss of a man who was quickly becoming a friend. Her first friend.

"Is Eadsele all better, my lord?" she asked, putting aside her own confused feelings for a moment.

"Nay, I fear not."

Odel felt relief rush through her and tried to stamp it down. She should be feeling disappointment. If she had any sense she would feel disappointed. Every minute he remained was risky. It appeared, however, that her good sense had abandoned her. "I am sure he will recover soon."

"Aye." Lord Suthtun agreed, then cleared his throat. "Actually, Eadsele mentioned something I had not thought of."

"Oh?"

Michelle nodded. "He mentioned that no one had gone on a hunt since we had arrived and I wondered—"

"Oh, what a marvelous idea!" Matilda crooned suddenly from behind them.

Odel whirled to peer over her shoulder. She hadn't heard the woman approach. Managing a smile, she then glanced back at Michelle. "Aye, my lord. You are very considerate, but that is not necessary. We have plenty of meat."

"No, we don't. In fact"—lifting her cane, Tildy swung it quickly toward the door to the kitchens, then set it down with a satisfied thump—"we are fresh out. I was going to suggest a hunt myself."

"Matilda," Odel growled, glaring at the woman in warning, but her godmother blithely ignored her. Instead, she beamed briefly at Lord Suthtun, then turned her gaze over the whole of the room.

"Everyone! Yoohoo!" She clapped her hands to gain the attention of the others in the room.

Her suitors, Odel sighed inwardly at the thought. She was going mad with their ridiculous compliments, their sessions of preening in efforts to gain her attention, and their long, drawn-out dissertations on how handsome, wealthy, or clever they were. She had never known that nobleman could be so vapid; but then, Father had never really let her socialize. Gazing at her guests, she was almost grateful. Added to that, she was starting to find her appetite affected by their presence at the table. Odel had come to notice that they all had the oddest way of eating. First of all, they ate constantly—all day long from what she could tell. But it was the way that they ate that disturbed her most. They each brought their food up to their mouths with both hands, keeping their backs straight, heads up, and eyes alert as if watching for some thief who might steal it. It was the oddest thing she had ever seen, made stranger by the fact that they *all* seemed to do it. Only Lord Suthtun did not. Odel had mentioned it to Tildy, but the woman had laughed and claimed that those manners were all the rage at court these days. To Odel, it was creepy. It reminded her of something she couldn't quite place.

All of this had managed to make Odel extremely grateful that Lord Suthtun came below for the evening meals. It gave her an excuse to escape the other men. And his habit of staying below for an hour or so afterward allowed her to stay away from them.

Nervous of what Matilda might do, Odel had urged him into a game of chess before the fire the second night after his arrival and every night since. She had used the claim that she was chilly as an excuse to rearrange the seats. Placing her own chair with its back to the fire had forced him to sit with his back to the great hall at large. His being unable to see what was going on in the rest of the room had allowed her to relax.

Odel had actually enjoyed their games. Michelle was a witty man and charming even, something she had not expected in a warrior. And he had not minded her beating him at chess; he even seemed mildly pleased by it. Which was very different than she was used to. Odel's father had always claimed she cheated and knocked the board to the floor when she won against him. But Lord Suthtun merely cast her an admiring glance and complimented her strategy, a reaction Odel shared when the knight himself won. She had woken up today looking forward to the evening ahead.

Now, she felt the beginnings of panic creeping up on her again. A whole day in the presence of Tildy and her magic. If Tildy should turn one of the men into a rat or perform some other magical act in front of Lord Suthtun . . . well, she doubted he would see a difference between a fairy godmother and a witch. Feeling helpless, she listened to Tildy outline her plan for a big hunting party. A feeling of doom was dropping around her shoulders even as she did.

The Fairy Godmother

*   *   *

"There!"

Odel glanced at Michelle at his excited whisper. She had been busy looking over her shoulder at Tildy and the others. Her godmother rode on a small plump mare that Odel was sure did not belong to the Roswald stables, following several hundred yards behind Lord Suthtun and Odel. The other lords rode in a group behind her.

Matilda was as stiff and tense on the animal as could be; she looked about as pleased to be on a horse again as Odel was to be on this hunt. Briefly, recalling that her godmother had died in a fall from her mount, Odel almost felt pity for her. Then her gaze fell on the pack of suitors bouncing around in their saddles behind her and Odel had felt all pity die. Good heavens! Not a one of them could ride. What sort of lords could not ride a horse?

"Do you see it?"

Turning away from the group trailing behind them, Odel followed Michelle's pointing finger. Their horses slowed. A huge wild boar was rooting in the bushes ahead. Drawing her mount to a complete stop, she reached instinctively for her bow, feeling excitement and fear begin to course through her. Wild swine had become rarer the last couple of years; to chance upon one now was quite lucky. The thought made her pause and glance back toward Tildy, her eyes narrowed. Any good fortune was suspect.

Expecting to see the others hanging back, Odel's eyes widened as she saw that Tildy and the men hadn't yet slowed. They were riding up at full speed, apparently unaware that she and Michelle had come upon game—and dangerous game at that. Her hand jerking on her reins, Odel instinctively shouted out a warning.

A curse from Lord Suthtun was followed quickly by an angry squeal. Odel whirled back to see what had hap-

pened. She realized at once that her shout must have
startled Michelle just as he had taken aim. An arrow now
quivered in the boar's hindquarters, and she was quite
sure that he wouldn't have aimed *there*. But there was
little time to think of much more than that. Michelle had
feathered the beast's posterior, and the boar wasn't at all
pleased.

"Oh, dear," she murmured, then tightened her fingers
on her reins in alarm. Michelle shouted a warning as the
boar charged.

The next few minutes became a swirl of chaos. Like
a pack of dogs on the scent of blood, the suitors who
had flanked Odel's aunt now charged onto the scene.
They swarmed around Odel and Michelle, crowding
them so much that there was no way to swerve or retreat
as the boar came at them, squealing madly. The horses,
smarter than their riders, began to whinny and snort,
rearing back in terror. Odel managed to keep her seat,
but the lords—lousy riders all—went tumbling to the
ground. Their shouts were added to the chaos as they
rolled and darted about, trying to avoid the feet of the
horses off of which they had fallen.

Given so many new targets, the boar suddenly
stopped, apparently unsure who to attack first. After a
brief hesitation, it headed after the nearest man. Shrieking, the lord in question charged for the nearest tree, the
boar hot on his heels.

Had she not been busy trying to stay in the saddle,
Odel would have marveled at the man's agility as he
scrambled up that tree. He was quickly followed by his
friends, one after the other, as the boar charged each.

It would have been the perfect opportunity for Odel
or Michelle to shoot another arrow into the boar, but
neither could get a clear shot from their bucking steeds.
Seated side-saddle as she was, and with her horse dancing on its hind legs, Odel began to fear she could even

stay mounted. Feeling herself begin to slide toward the ground, she desperately tightened her hold on the reins. Then, realizing that she was doomed to fall, she let go and concentrated on landing on her feet.

Now *she* was a target for the boar. But, unlike the others, Odel knew she couldn't scramble up a tree—especially not as she was dressed. Not wasting any time, the moment her feet hit the snowy ground, Odel grabbed up her skirts and began to run. Behind her she heard Michelle shout, the boar snort, and Tildy's high-pitched yell, but she didn't take the chance of looking back. She had no time. Boars with their vicious tusks were deadly—especially when injured and angry. She charged into the woods at full tilt, wishing that skirts weren't so hard to run in, wishing that the ground were not so slippery with winter snow, and wishing above all that she had stayed home.

Chapter Five

One minute Odel was running for her life and the next her legs were pumping uselessly in the air; she had been caught around the waist and lifted off the ground. Michelle now held her, and she hung down the side of his horse. Apparently he had regained control of his mount enough to rescue her. Odel had barely grasped that when something tugged at her skirts. Peering down, she cried out in horror. The boar was less than a heartbeat behind her, and one of the beast's tusks had caught in the hem of her skirts. She felt her stomach roil, but Michelle tugged his reins to the side, swerving away from the boar and ripping her skirts free.

Looking back, Odel saw the beast turn to charge after them, but Michelle put on more speed, urging his mount to a gallop. It quickly widened the distance between them leaving the snarling animal behind in the brush.

Several moments after the boar had dropped out of sight, Michelle let his mount slow then come to a halt. Using both hands, he lifted Odel and drew her around before him on the saddle. Seating her sideways, he frowned. "Are you all right?"

"Yes," she breathed, managing a weak smile. "But that was close."

"Aye." He didn't smile—in fact, he looked quite grim. He glanced back over his shoulder. There was no sign of the boar now. "You would think those idiots would know better than to charge in like that."

Odel heartily agreed, but merely murmured, "Thank you—for saving me."

Turning his attention back to her, Michelle's expression softened in a small smile. "It was my pleasure," he assured her. His voice was husky, and he raised one hand to brush a strand of hair off her cheek.

Odel covered his hand with her own, but glanced shyly downward. But not for long. Michelle immediately tilted her head back up, his lips coming down to cover hers.

At first, Odel froze under the gentle caress of his lips. Other than Lord Cheshire's slobbery attempt to drown her, she had never been kissed. And where Lord Cheshire's mushy ministrations had made her want to wretch, this man's kiss was heavenly. It was strong, warm, and demanding. Masterful.

It seemed so natural as he urged her lips apart for an open-mouth kiss, that Odel didn't think a thing of it. She merely slid her arms around his neck and held on as he invaded her. Her toes curled in her slippers and little moans sounded in her throat, shocking her, but she found herself terribly disappointed when at last he broke away.

Sighing, Odel opened her eyes slowly. She peered up at him, but he was sitting stiff in his saddle, his head up and alert as he peered over her shoulder. Still, it took a moment before the roaring his kisses had caused in her ears subsided enough for her to hear what had drawn his attention. Something was moving through the woods toward them. Odel leaned to the side to peer over his shoulder just as Tildy came crashing into the clearing on her ungainly little mare.

"*There* you are! Well, thank goodness you are all right." Matilda drew her mount to a halt and peered at the two of them. Displeasure tightened her lips as she noted the way Odel rested on the saddle before Suthtun, her arms around his neck; the way his own held her about the waist. Surely she was annoyed that one of the suitors she had supplied was not in Michelle's place.

"The boar was brought down, and a couple of the others even managed to fell a stag. They also bagged a couple of pheasants, so we shall have a fine feast tonight." Tildy pronounced this abruptly, then turned to head back.

"What? How is that possible?" Michelle asked. "We just left the clearing."

Odel closed her eyes. She knew how it was possible. Tildy's magic, that was how.

"Well, some of us were busy while you two were mucking about," Matilda snapped.

"We were not mucking about," Odel said at once, coloring. "I was running for my life and Lord Suthtun saved me."

"Hmmph." Matilda's lips tightened further. "And I suppose it was luck where he brought his horse to a halt?"

Michelle and Odel shared a perplexed look, then peered about in bewilderment. There was nothing but leafless trees and snow. Then Odel glanced upward, and a small gasp slid from her lips. *Mistletoe*. The upper branches of the trees sheltering them were laced liberally with the vine. She hadn't noticed it until now. And judging from Lord Suthtun's expression, neither had he.

"Your horse ran for home before anyone could stop

him, my dear," Matilda announced, drawing their attention back to her. "You shall have to ride back with me."

Odel turned her dubious gaze to the mare her aunt rode. It was extremely small, and really rather round—like the woman who rode it. Odel had her doubts as to whether the animal could manage both of them. Apparently Lord Suthtun did as well. His arm tightened around her waist. "There is no need for that, my lady. She can ride back with me."

Matilda gave a snort of displeasure, then without another word she turned her horse and trotted off, leaving them staring after her.

"Well," Odel said uncomfortably, avoiding his eyes. "It would seem the hunt is over."

"Aye." Michelle said. He peered down at her silently for a moment, then glanced up at the mistletoe overhead. "It would seem you owe me a kiss."

"Oh?" Odel glanced up as well. "I thought you already took one."

"That was for saving your life. This one would be for the mistletoe."

Odel blushed prettily, then leaned up to press a quick kiss to his lips. "How is that?" she asked a bit breathlessly. She settled back on the saddle.

"That was very nice," he said solemnly. "But there is an awful lot of mistletoe."

Feeling heat and excitement pool in her belly, Odel nodded just as solemnly. "Aye, there is, my lord."

With a smile he bent to kiss her. It was not the sweet, swift rubbing of lips she had just given him, but another of the long, hot, toe-curling variety. And this time, Odel's reaction was more violent. She was helpless; arching into him, her body responded of its own accord. Her tongue slid out to join his, her fingers curling almost painfully in his hair, and she shuddered. Surely, this was a Pandora's box, this reaction that burst to life within her, begging to be opened.

She wanted more, and that was frightening. It was a hunger she had never before experienced, that swelled within her.

The years under her tyrannical father had convinced Odel that marriage and children were not for her. She'd had no wish for a husband who might be as cold and dictatorial as her own father had been. But that had left her feeling lonely and empty. Until now. Now the emptiness was being filled, the loneliness abolished. And, she realized in some far-off part of her mind, it wasn't just the kiss that made her desire him so. It was the chats and chess by the fire, the soft laughter over dinner, his warm arms that had saved her from the boar. This passion that was licking at her insides had begun some time ago. She was beginning to care for this man, and couldn't lie to herself about it. She had wanted him from the first moment she'd seen him.

His presence at Roswald was a dangerous thing, she had known that from the start. If he saw Matilda up to her tricks, there would be trouble. But had Odel approached Tildy about using some of her fairy dust to cure the boy? Nay. Had she suggested he continue home and leave the boy to be nursed? She might have sent Eadsele home with one of her men-at-arms when he was recovered, but nay. Had she encouraged the man to stay above stairs for the evening meal to reduce the risk of danger? Nay. In fact, it was she who had suggested he might enjoy a break, it was she who had insisted he join them.

Why? Because Odel had enjoyed his presence at dinner, and their shared evenings. Too much to send him away. She had spent the last few days wandering about the keep waiting impatiently for supper to arrive. She had alternated between thinking up excuses to visit him and Eadsele in their room, and thinking up witty things she might say, stories she had heard that might amuse him.

Odel *liked* this man. She enjoyed his company. She found him handsome when he laughed. And now, she realized with a sense of foreboding as he slowly drew away to peer down at her, she hungered for his kisses and touch like a flower craves sunlight. Odel wanted to pull his head back for another meshing of mouths. She wanted to cleave to him. She wanted to strip off his clothing and feel his naked body against hers. To Odel, all of that was more dangerous than his discovery of Matilda's magic could ever be.

Dear God, she wondered with dread, how had she let this happen?

"You are so incredibly beautiful."

Odel blinked at his soft words and felt her fears momentarily dissipate. Did he truly believe that she was beautiful? For most of the last twenty-five years she had been a shadow, her face pale, her limp hair pulled tightly back off her face, her expression as unhappy as she had been. But in the week after her father's death, since Matilda's arrival, Odel had felt herself bloom. Her face had regained some color. Her hair now held a healthy shine and even a slight wave. And in the week since Lord Suthtun had arrived, she had even begun to smile.

"You are beautiful, too," she whispered shyly. Much to her amazement, he immediately threw back his head, and laughed.

"Nay, my lady. I am an old warhorse. Battle scarred and—"

"You are not old, my lord," Odel interrupted abruptly. "Why you cannot be more than thirty."

"Thirty-one," he corrected gently, brushing a tress off her face. "But I used to feel much older."

"Used to?" Unconsciously she tipped her face, encouraging him to stroke her face as if she were a kitten.

"I find that being around you makes me feel like a boy," he murmured huskily, then reached for the reins of his mount. Taking them in his hand, he blew a breath out. She found herself staring at those lips that had caressed hers a moment before, and he managed a crooked smile. "I suppose we had best return now."

"Aye." Odel agreed softly.

Nodding, Michelle started to urge his mount forward, then turned it toward the nearest tree. Drawing it to a halt, he reached out and plucked down a sprig of mistletoe. He set it in her hair just above her ear, kissed her quickly, then plucked a berry from the small sprig, and slipped it into his pocket. "A remembrance."

Swallowing, Odel smiled weakly, then turned to look ahead as he urged his mount forward again. *Remembrance?* For when he left and her life returned to the lonely place it had been.

That thought made her so sad that Odel found herself unable to think of a single witty or amusing thing to say during the ride back to the keep. Instead, they were both silent. It wasn't until they entered the keep that either of them spoke, and then they both gasped in surprise. The hall had been transformed. Mistletoe, pine bowers, and streams of cloth and ribbon hung everywhere, and the tables were covered with white linen and preparations were under way for a feast.

"There you are!" Tildy suddenly appeared and bustled toward them.

"What is all this?" Odel asked in amazement.

"Why 'tis for the feast," the woman exclaimed as if it should be self-explanatory. "And we are going to have wonderful entertainment. A traveling group arrived while we were out. We shall have jugglers and tumblers, and a dancing bear. It will be marvelous!"

"All of this just to celebrate today's hunt?" Odel muttered in disbelief.

"Well, not just that," her godmother exclaimed. "But Christmas is coming on rather quickly, and that is a time for joy and celebration."

"What? No Lord Suthtun this morning?"

Odel made a face at Matilda's slightly sarcastic comment and shifted to make room for her godmother on the trestle table bench beside her. It had been several days since the hunt, and there were only three more days until Christmas. Lord Suthtun was still at Roswald.

Michelle had been joining her to break his fast every morning since the day of the hunt. He had still spent a good part of the day above stairs with Eadsele, but he had started to take his meals below, claiming he did not wish to burden the servants with the extra work of carting a meal up to him. But today he had not come down. Eadsele was again very sick.

Though for the past several days the boy had appeared to improve—yesterday Lord Suthtun had even brought the boy below to sit by the fire and announced that tomorrow they might risk continuing on—during the night, Eadsele's fever had suddenly shot back up. This morning he was ill as he had been the first night. Returning home was now out of the question, of course, two-hour journey or not, and Michelle had decided to remain above stairs with the boy to see if there was aught to be done.

Odel missed him already. She had grown quite used to having the man around, a fact that was just as awful for her as his absence. Her feelings for the man had only continued to grow these past days, along with her desire. There had only been a few opportunities for stolen kisses since the hunt, and after every one, Matilda had shown up, eyeing them with disapproval. She was making it more than obvious that she was truly displeased with the time Odel spent with Michelle. But then, Matilda had been displeased with the man's arrival right from the first. Odel supposed that her godmother considered his presence a fly in her ointment. The goodhearted but damnably stubborn woman still wished to marry Odel off to one of the rich, handsome suitors she herself had provided.

Odel paused. Now that she realized that her feelings for Michelle had reached a point where his leaving would be painful, Odel found herself wishing that Matilda had found a way to remove him. In fact, it suddenly seemed odd that the old woman hadn't.

"I am sure Lord Suthtun is a very nice man," Tildy was saying, "but he isn't nearly as handsome or wealthy as the suitors I have provided. I wish you would waste less time on him and spend more with a lord like Beasley. Or perhaps Lord Trenton, he is—"

"Explain something to me," Odel interrupted. Matilda's eyebrows rose.

"What dear?"

"Why have you not simply cured young Eadsele and seen Lord Suthtun out of here? That would have left the way clear for the others." As she made the observation, Odel stiffened as her own words sank in.

"What is it?" Tildy asked warily.

"My God," Odel breathed, then shook her head. "Nay. It cannot be."

"What?" Matilda was suddenly looking wary.

"Nothing." She forced herself to ignore the brief thought that struck her. Had Matilda not cured the boy because she did not really wish Odel to fall in love with one of her supposed suitors? Had Michelle been the man Matilda was really trying to get her to fall in love with all along? After all, it was rather odd that Lord Suthtun had chosen to stop at Roswald to rest only two hours' journey from Suthtun. And it was rather odd that the boy's illness had come on so suddenly. But, no. This was all just coincidence, she assured herself. Wasn't it?

"Why did you not cure the boy?" Odel repeated.

"Oh. Well, my magic does not work on humans," Matilda assured her, but she was staring downwards as she said it, reluctant to meet her gaze. Odel felt her stomach clench slightly; her godmother was lying.

"This *was* your *plan,* wasn't it?" she said quietly.

Matilda's expression closed. "What?"

"You never intended that I should fall in love with one of the others," she accused. "You knew I could not fall in love with any of those vain, silly, shallow men. You gave me a castle full of them, then presented me with Lord Suthtun in the hopes that I would fall in love with him."

"Now that is just silly. Whyever would I do a thing like that?" Matilda gave a nervous laugh and Odel exhaled in angry disappointment.

"I should have realized that was what was going on sooner," she said sadly. "You were so rude to him." Odel shook her head. "But that was all just part of your plan. You were rude, so I was extra nice. Then, too, my fear that you might perform some magic trick around him meant I would spend an awful lot of time trying to keep him away from you and the others, which would constantly throw us together."

"Oh, really, my dear." Tildy gave a strained titter. "You give me far too much credit. I could never be so devious."

Tildy was a horrible liar. She wasn't very convincing at all. Odel almost wished she were. Then she could believe that Michelle's interest in her was real. But like all those handsome, wealthy lords that were sniffing about her like dogs around a bitch in heat, Lord Suthtun's interest was induced. She was not foolish or vain enough to imagine that any of their attraction was real. In fact, that was part of the reason she had found their presence at Roswald so annoying. Aside from the fact that she wasn't interested in a single one of her suitors, she had suspected that their interest in her had to be a result of Matilda's magic. And yet, she had thought Suthtun was different. Tildy had seemed to dislike him so much, Odel had thought—

"Excuse me." She stood up stiffly and walked away from the table, positive her heart was breaking.

Chapter Six

"Are you ready?"

Odel grimaced at Matilda's question, but nodded grimly. "Aye. Is it time yet?"

"In just a moment." Matilda sounded excited. Odel was not. This was the fourth time Matilda had said "in just a moment." Meanwhile, Odel stood waiting uncomfortably in the kitchens, trying to ignore the gaping of the cook and his staff. They had never seen her like this, she supposed. Well, they had best enjoy it, because it was doubtful they would ever see it again. She crossed her arms over her chest self-consciously. While the costume Matilda had created for her was lovely, she was positive her nipples showed through the diaphanous material.

Created. Odel rolled her eyes at that. The woman had made her strip naked in her room, then taken out a pinch of fairy dust and blown it on her. When the dust had cleared, Odel had found herself wearing this, the most amazing creation she had ever seen—a toga-like gown

71

made up of the gauziest material ever. It was like wearing nothing at all. Or wearing the stars. Even her skin seemed to glimmer, likely with remnants of fairy dust. It showed a lot of her flesh. It was indecent.

If she had realized she would be expected to wear a costume like this, Odel would have put a halt to the pageant Matilda had suddenly proposed. At the time her godmother had mentioned it, Odel had thought that arranging the skits might keep the woman out of trouble. Little had she realized that she was to be the feature attraction. When Matilda had begged her to be in it, the woman had sworn her part was a very minor role, that she would not even have to learn lines. And, the role called for a woman, Tildy had said, and Odel was the only suitable lady present. Her aunt had not bothered to mention the role she was to play. Although, even had she said as much, Odel may have still agreed, not realizing what it would entail her wearing. Now that she knew, Odel was wishing she had simply nixed the pageant to begin with.

"Now."

She glanced to Matilda questioningly, but the woman was stepping aside and pulling open the kitchen door. Six lords, also coerced into playing roles, immediately began to move forward, pushing her out into the great hall on another of Matilda's creations: a platform on wheels, covered with gauzy blue material somehow made to remain in the curved shape of waves. Odel was Aphrodite, the goddess of love, rising from the waves.

Sighing inwardly, Odel struck the pose Matilda had insisted on, clasping her hands beneath her chin and slightly arching her back. There was silence in the room as she rolled out, then Matilda's gay voice began to narrate the story of Aphrodite and Ares. Odel stayed where she was, her gaze searching the audience for Michelle, but he was nowhere to be seen. Perhaps he hadn't come below, she thought sadly and sighed. She had been avoiding him. She hadn't been rude to him or anything—this was not his fault after all—but for her own self-respect and sanity she had decided to keep her distance until he left. She had been hard-put to ignore the confused glances he'd been casting her way ever since.

Matilda had just introduced Ares. Odel glanced around to see the god of war step through the keep doors at the opposite end of the great hall where he had been waiting. Out in the cold, she thought with a grimace. She almost felt sorry for Lord Beasley, the man that Matilda had assigned the role of her illicit lover. But as the figure drew nearer, Odel's eyes widened. Her jaw dropped as she took in Michelle's wry smile. Dressed in a short—almost indecently so—toga and carrying a shield and sword, he mounted the steps to her foamy platform.

As Matilda narrated the tale of Aphrodite and Ares, lovers despite Aphrodite's marriage to Hephaestus, Michelle's expression turned apologetic. He took her in his cold arms.

"What are you doing?" Odel stealthily whispered in his ear as they embraced. "Lord Beasley was supposed to be Ares."

"Lord Beasley was not feeling well. Your aunt asked me to step in."

"Oh." Odel glanced distractedly at Vlaster. The man rode around the platform in a small chariot-like affair led by two more of her suitors wearing horse masks. Vlaster himself wore a long gold toga and was supposed to be Helios, the god of the sun, catching them in their infidelity. Honestly, the man looked more interested in the cock in a cage that he carried than in Odel and Michelle; he was looking at the bird as if it might make a tasty snack. When he rode out of the keep's front doors and out of sight, Odel shifted a little closer to Lord Suthtun. "You must have been freezing out there. You are still cold."

"While you are pleasantly warm," Michelle murmured, his arms tightening around her. Matilda droned on. The older woman was relating how Helios was quick to report Aphrodite's infidelity to her husband Hephaestus, and how the two plotted to catch the lovers in the act.

The keep doors opened again and Vlaster's chariot returned on a cold breeze. This time there was a second man with him, a rather large, muscular fellow carrying a hammer: the castle smithy. She recognized him after a startled moment and smiled wryly to herself. Who better to play Hephaestus?

"Your aunt said that when the chariot came back I was to kiss you," Lord Suthtun murmured next to her. Odel glanced up at him with surprise.

"She did?"

"Aye. She said it was to represent Ares and Aphrodite making . . . er—"

Flushing with embarrassment, Odel silenced him by quickly pressing her lips to his. After a startled moment, Michelle's kiss became real. Odel felt herself melt in his arms. Her hands crept up to clasp around his neck, her body shifting and arching into him. Without thinking, she gave in, breathing small sighs and moans of pleasure into his mouth. Then something unpleasantly cloying dropped over them and Odel and Michelle froze in surprise.

"Hephaestus's net," Michelle muttered. Odel suddenly remembered that she was in the midst of a pageant. Aye, of course, and Hephaestus, or the Roswald smithy, had just thrown a special net over his unfaithful wife and her lover to parade them before the Olympian gods. While Odel and Michelle embraced under the net, the platform was pushed around the room.

According to Matilda's narration, when presented with the unfaithful pair, the gods merely commented on Aphrodite's beauty. Many simply claimed that they would not mind switching places with Ares. Roswald's villagers and soldiers were more than happy to act the parts of the Olympians. Even a few of Odel's suitors made ribald comments.

Feeling herself blush from her forehead to her toes, Odel herself almost felt guilty. She was more than relieved when the circuit of the room was finished and Matilda continued her narration.

The net was pulled from them. Knowing she was expected to exit, Odel waited for the platform to begin moving again, but it appeared the wheels were stuck. The men who had pushed the platform out were straining painfully to move it, but it would not budge.

Frowning, Matilda recited the part where they left again, and again the men strained at the platform, but still it did not move. When Tildy frowned, then glanced toward Michelle expectantly, he hesitated, then swept Odel up in his arms. Striding from the platform, he carried her to and through the keep doors. Behind them came the sound of thunderous applause.

"Music!" Odel heard Matilda shout as the doors closed behind them.

No longer in character, Odel was terribly aware of her state of undress. It was a relief when Michelle set her down on the icy castle steps.

He frowned with concern, then around at the winter night. "It is rather brisk tonight. How long were we supposed to stay out here? Your aunt did not say."

Shivering, Odel made a face. "This is long enough, I think."

"Aye," Michelle agreed and turned to pull open the door, but it did not open. He pulled again. The door remained firmly shut.

"What is it?" Odel asked with a frown, reaching past him to give the handle a tug herself. The door didn't budge.

"Is it bolted?" Michelle asked with a frown.

"We hardly ever bolt the door. It should—" She shook her head with distress and tugged again, fully expecting it to open.

"Perhaps the bolt dropped into place when it closed behind us," Michelle suggested. Odel continued to tug impatiently at the door, not commenting. At last she began to pound on it in the hopes that someone would notice.

"I do not think they can hear us over the music," Michelle murmured after a moment. Odel paused to listen. Sure enough, the musicians were now playing a rather loud song. The audience members would never hear them.

"It is rather cold out here. Is there another door?"

Sighing, Odel began to rub her arms in an effort to warm them. She turned to peer absently around the bailey. "There is a door into the kitchens."

Nodding, Michelle scooped her into his arms again and promptly started down the stairs. "Which way?" he asked as they reached the bottom step.

Gritting her teeth to keep them from chattering, Odel pointed to the right and Lord Suthtun broke into a jog. He loped quickly along the outer wall of the inner keep, then around to the back and the door leading to the kitchens. Still holding her in his arms, he reached out and pushed at the door. It was as firmly shut as the front doors. Frowning, he let Odel slide to her feet on the snowy path, then grabbed the door firmly and pulled. Nothing happened. The door remained solidly closed. Michelle began pounding on it. He banged for several minutes straight, but no one came to open it. They were locked out.

Shifting from foot to foot, arms crossed over her chest, teeth chattering, Odel stood, miserably waiting.

"I do not think they can hear us here either. We should—" His voice died as he turned to peer at Odel in the moonlight. Frowning, he reached out and pulled her into his arms. "My God! You are freezing." He rubbed his hands up and down her arms, then suddenly swept her up in his arms again and began to carry her back across the snowy ground.

"W-where are we g-going?" she chattered, clasping her arms around his neck and holding on for all she was worth. She buried her face in his hair. She had hoped that his heat might warm her, but he was cold, too. He paused several moments later and she glanced around to see him pull a door open. Wincing at the loud creak it made, she squinted in an effort to see inside the room into which he now carried her. It was dark, but not pitch dark. The dying embers of a fire in the center of the small building gave off some light. Carrying her inside, Michelle set her down on a stool. Leaving her there, he hurried back to close the door, then moved to the fire to urge it back to life. Within moments he had a nice-size fire going again. He watched it for a moment, then moved to squat in front of her.

"The smithy's forge," she got out between shivers.

"Aye." Michelle took her bare feet in hand and began rubbing them, frowning at her icy flesh. "You are freezing."

"You, too," she muttered, and he laughed.

"These costumes were not meant for winter wear." His cold hands moved vigorously up and down her colder calves.

Odel was silent as she watched him minister to her, amazed that he would kneel on the ground to tend to her when he himself was likely freezing. His head was

77

bowed, his hair shining in the light from the fire, his hands moving over her flesh.

"Once I've warmed you up, I will go see if I can get them to let us in," he said, his voice sounding oddly husky. His hands moved over her knees and began to smooth up her thighs.

Without thinking, she reached out, gently touching his soft hair, then stilled when he raised his head. Flushing slightly at the way he looked at her, she let her hand drop away, but he caught it. He began to rub that now, his eyes beginning to smolder. They were both silent for a moment, then he raised her hand to his mouth.

Dragging in a ragged breath, Odel automatically began to close her hand, but Michelle held it open. He pressed a kiss to the tender flesh of her palm, then to the sensitive place between her first two fingers. Odel shifted slightly where she sat, her breath catching in her chest as his tongue swiped lightly at her skin. It tickled and sent little arrows of erotic excitement quivering up her arm. She bit her lip to keep from gasping aloud.

Raising his head, Michelle peered at her silently for a moment, then bent to bestow another kiss, this time to the inside of her wrist.

Odel raised her other hand to touch the side of his face, her heart swelling when he turned into the gentle caress. But then he turned back to what he had been doing, his lips nibbling her inner arm up to the crook of her elbow. Odel caught her breath and squirmed on the stool he had set her on, but the breath escaped on a low moan as he suddenly turned his face and pressed his open mouth to the side of her breast.

Shuddering slightly, she clenched her fingers in his hair, then watched, breathless, as his mouth traveled until it found and settled on her nipple. Through the soft material of the gown—the gossamer material may as well not have been there, it was so thin and translucent—he began to suckle at her nipple. The fabric rasped against her suddenly sensitive skin, and overwhelmed by the erotic feel and sight of his actions, Odel closed her eyes on a moan.

She opened them again at once, though, when he urged her legs open. Shifting to kneel between them, he lifted his head and pulled her face down for a hot and hungry kiss. It succeeded in raising Odel's temperature faster than any amount of chafing could have.

Sliding her hands around his shoulders, Odel kissed Michelle with all the passion and yearning of twenty-five loveless years. She felt his hand slide up her side, then around to one breast and she arched slightly, pressing herself into the caress with abandon. She wanted this. She wanted it *all*, and she moaned in disappointment when his lips left hers. They merely moved along her chin to her ear, though, then blazed another fiery trail down her neck.

Odel was absently aware of his hands at her back, but only vaguely until her gown pulled tight and Michelle muttered in frustration against her throat. Realizing that he was trying to undo her costume, she reached to help him, undoing it quickly. Yes, she wanted this.

He tugged the gown forward, drawing it off her shoulders, and pushing it down toward her waist until her breasts were bared. Forgetting the material then, he caught the two globes in his hand and bent his mouth to each. He feasted on them with an eagerness that made Odel's insides ripple with desire; she watched him pepper her pale flesh with kisses.

Even that, though, didn't prepare her for her body's reaction when his lips suddenly closed over one swollen nipple. It was as if her stomach had dropped right out of her and the blazing smithy's fire taken its place. Gasping for breath, Odel arched backward, her hands clutching his shoulders with excitement. Suddenly, the stool she was on began to overset, and her hands scrabbled against him.

Catching her against his chest, Michelle shifted her to the side, then lowered her to the straw floor. His body followed, half-covering hers, as his lips and tongue continued to tease and tug at her nipple. Feeling one of his legs slide between hers, Odel automatically spread hers slightly, then closed them around him. The brush of his leg against her bare inner thigh told her that her skirt had ridden up, but she didn't care. She wanted to feel more of him. With that intention, she grabbed at the shoulder of his toga, first tugging it loose, then using it to bring him higher.

Giving up his attention to her breasts, Michelle lifted his head and shifted upward, his mouth again covering hers. Odel kissed him back, but her attention was focused on his toga and removing it. Pushing it down between them, she let her fingers trail over his chest. She paused curiously at his nipples to see if they were as sensitive as her own, then she reached around to clasp his back and pull him tight against her. She arched forward to meet him. Her hands slid down to clasp his buttocks through the cloth of his toga, then slipped under it. Odel squeezed the flesh of his behind curiously, then hesitated when a breathless laugh slipped from Michelle. He broke their kiss to peer down at her.

Swallowing, Odel met his gaze uncertainly, her teeth coming out to chew her upper lip as she saw amusement mingling with the passion in his face.

"I thought I was ravishing you," he murmured in explanation. "And I was feeling guilty about it, but now I am feeling a little bit ravished myself." He gave her a wry look then, as she started to remove her hands, he added huskily, "I like it."

Odel hesitated, then smiled. She slid her hands back downward, this time bringing one forward to slide between them. He shifted slightly, watching her face closely as he gave her the access she wanted. Odel blushed, but didn't hesitate when her hand bumped against his manhood. Covering it through the cloth of his toga, she squeezed gently, watching the fire grow in his eyes. Encouraged by that, she slid her hand beneath the toga and grasped him again, her grip firm as it closed over his naked flesh. She had to pause then because she wasn't quite sure what to do next.

Michelle helped. He shifted his hips away slightly, drawing his manhood through her hand, then shifted forward again. Understanding, Odel began to caress him herself. She was rewarded with a quick hard kiss before Michelle caught her hand and drew it above her head. Holding it there with one hand, he slid his other hand down over her body until he was cupping the flesh between her thighs. Odel drew in a quick shaky breath, her free hand moving instinctively to push his away, but he caught that one and pinned it above her head as well.

Holding both of her hands fast with one of his own, he returned the other to again press it between her legs. He met her gaze and held it as he began to move his hand against her, pressing the silky cloth down between her legs. Then, drawing it out of the way until she lay open to him, his fingers slid over her honeyed center. Suddenly he was caressing her in a way that made her arch and squirm, and she could hear herself gasping raggedly through her open mouth as if she were drowning.

"Not fair," she groaned at last, arching into his touch. She shook her head, her hands tugging to be free.

"What's not fair?" he murmured huskily by her ear, then nipped at the sensitive flesh there.

"You will not let me touch you," she gasped, then groaned. His caress had changed in strength and speed.

"If I let you touch me, it will be over before it has begun."

"What . . . would?" she managed to get out, her body tight as a harp's string.

"This." One finger found and dipped into her and Odel cried out, her body straining as if he had branded her. Her eyes widened incredulously as spasms of pleasure shook her body. Bending his head, Michelle caught her cries in his mouth, kissing her passionately as she began to float back to earth.

Leaving that warm, fuzzy place to which he had taken her, Odel began to kiss him back. Her arms were free now, and they slid around his neck. She felt his hands on her back, then he shifted position, drawing his knees up beneath him even as he pulled her into a sitting position. Michelle urged her to kneel on either side of his legs and drew her forward until they were chest to chest.

Clasping him close, Odel returned his kiss, then let her head fall back as he again began to kiss his way down her neck. She gave a slight start when she felt his hand reappear between her legs, then sighed in pleasure by his ear. Though she would have thought it impossible, he began to rebuild the fire in her. His mouth slipped over one nipple and Odel leaned back further, holding on to his shoulders. Unconsciously, she rode his hand as he caressed her. This time when her body began to spasm with pleasure, he urged her upward with one hand on her bottom, then directed her downward.

Odel's eyes widened incredulously as she felt him enter her. He was frightfully large and she felt a bit of discomfort, but then they were joined. They stayed like that for a moment, before Michelle clasped her by both buttocks and urged her to move. Odel did her best, but she wasn't sure of what she was doing. After a moment, he shifted again, easing her gently onto her back.

"Tell me if the straw is uncomfortable," he whispered in her ear. For a moment, he withdrew, but it was brief before he was sliding back into her. Closing her eyes, Odel pressed against him, her hands sliding down to curl around his buttocks and urge him on. Together, they found completion.

Chapter Seven

"Are you warm enough?"

Smiling, Odel nodded sleepily against Michelle's chest, unwilling to move from where he had placed her. They had both found satisfaction this time, and afterward Michelle had rolled onto his back, taking her with him. She now lay upon his warm body, rather than the cold straw of the forge floor.

She felt his fingers in her hair and shifted, then raised her head to peer at him questioningly when he murmured, "Thank you."

"For what?" she asked in surprise.

He tugged her head up to his to kiss her before murmuring against her lips, "For my pleasure. Thank you."

Odel smiled gently when he broke the kiss. "You are very welcome, my lord. And thank you. And thank you. And thank you." She punctuated each thank-you with a kiss on his nose, chin, and chest.

Chuckling, he hugged her close, then began to run his hands through her hair. "Do you think the doors are still locked?"

"Who cares?" Grinning, Odel eased into a sitting position astride him, then added wickedly, "I could stay here forever."

"Aye." Michelle reached up to catch and caress her breasts, smiling when she moaned and moved atop him. Her lower body dragged over his manhood and stirred it slowly back to wakefulness. His voice had taken on a husky hungry, quality. "But we should return soon."

Odel opened her eyes and peered down at him, shifting her body. That told him better than words could that she knew what she was doing to him. "Are you *sure* you wish to go back?"

Michelle groaned at the sweet torture, then caught her by one hip. "Aye, I am sure, minx," he growled. Then his expression softened. "I would talk to your aunt. I must ask for your hand in marriage." He grinned. "Then we can do this all the time."

For a moment joy filled her face and Michelle felt all was right with the world. Then, just as suddenly as it had come, it was gone, she closed her eyes, her expression shuttered.

"Dear God, how could I have forgotten," she wondered aloud. Michelle felt alarm catch at him. There was something about her words and tone of voice that made him think that the happiness he had only just grasped was about to slip away. His hand tightened on her hip in reaction, as if he could physically hold on to his happiness.

"Forgotten what? What is it?"

Her eyes popped open and she peered at him sadly, then shook her head. "Nothing. It does not matter," she assured him. "You need not offer for me, my lord."

Michelle narrowed his eyes, feeling as if he had stepped into a roomful of cutthroats and couldn't be sure which would attack him first. How was he to react to her words? Was it best to proclaim his feelings and desire to be with her, or use a more pragmatic approach? As she began to turn away, he decided the pragmatic approach would carry more weight.

"Odel," he began carefully. "There is a good chance that what we just did may bear fruit."

Her eyes widened at that, then she suddenly struggled off of him and onto her feet. Bending, she picked up her gown and began to distractedly don it. Her voice was troubled when she finally spoke. "Aye. You are right, of course. But there is no need to panic. We should wait to see if—"

Michelle was on his feet beside her at once. Grabbing her arm, he spun her around to face him. "I *do not wish* to wait. I wish to marry you."

Turning her head away, she avoided his eyes and sighed. "No you don't. It is just a fleeting . . . fancy. It will pass," she assured him. "And then you shall be grateful we did not wed."

Michelle felt his insides grow cold at those soft words. "You have no desire to marry me?"

"I have no desire to marry anyone," she said carefully.

"You mean to say you made love to me with no intention of—"

Odel shifted impatiently at that, cutting him off. "You sound like this was your first time. You were hardly a virgin, my lord. Pray, do not now act the outraged innocent."

Michelle blinked at her accusation, drawing himself to his fullest height when he realized she was right. He had sounded just like . . . well, good lord! He had sounded like a bloody woman! Realizing he was becoming overwrought like a woman, too, he concentrated on calming himself. He watched her dress, then tried for a reasonable tone. "My lady—"

"Odel."

"Hmm?" he asked, knocked off track.

"I do think you might call me by my name after what we have just done, my lord," she pointed out.

"Oh, aye." He grimaced slightly, then politely answered, "And you must call me Michelle."

"Thank you."

She was still sounding a touch sarcastic, he noted with displeasure, but restrained his temper once more. "Odel, I do not offer marriage lightly. In fact, this is the first time I have ever proposed. I want to marry you."

"No, you don't," she repeated, sounding quite firm on the point, which only managed to annoy him more.

"Pray, do not tell me what I do and do not want."

"Fine, then I will tell you this," she snapped, stepping forward to poke him in the chest. "I have spent the last twenty-five years of my life under the thumb of a tyrant. I had to sleep when he said to sleep, eat when and what he ordered me to eat, and even wear, say and think what he insisted I must. But that is *over* now. My father is dead and I will never willingly put myself under another man's thumb again."

She started to whirl away then, but he caught her back, his eyes burning into her. "You look at me and tell me that you really think that I am in any way like your father. You tell me that this is not just fear speaking and I will walk out that door and leave you be. Otherwise, I will be speaking to your aunt—"

"Nay!" Odel interrupted, then looked away. "I do not believe that. You are kind and gentle and you treat even your horse better than my father ever treated me, but—" She shook her head. "But none of that really matters, my lord." Her eyes holding a sad finality that was more concerning to Michelle than her ridiculous outburst of a moment ago could have ever been, she said softly, "I know you think that you love me, but what you are feeling isn't real. You will wake up someday soon and find you do not want me. This is all magic. So, pray, just consider yourself lucky that I knew better than to accept you. Let it be, I will not marry you."

On that note, she turned and fled, leaving him staring after her.

"Here is where you have been hiding."

Odel turned from her window to peer at Matilda as she entered her bedchamber. "I am not hiding."

"Oh? It is nearly time for the nooning meal and you have not yet once shown your face below. What is that if not hiding?"

Odel shrugged and turned to peer out her window again.

Last night, she had hurried straight here after leaving the smithy's hut. The front doors had opened easily under her touch when she reached them, and Odel had suddenly known that the whole episode had most likely been more of Matilda's magic. Still, she had been beyond caring at that point. Weaving her way through the celebrating people, she had hurried above stairs to her room and cried herself to sleep. This morning she had woken up with the birds, changed out of her costume, and spent her time alternating between pacing and staring blindly out the window.

"I have just come from a discussion with Lord Suthtun," Tildy announced. "He is hiding it well, but he is quite distressed. He said that he asked you to marry him and you have refused. But he doesn't understand why."

"You should have explained it to him, then," Odel said bitterly.

"I would have, but I didn't know. It wasn't until he told me that you had said what he was feeling wasn't real that I understood why you had refused him. He left right afterward to check on Eadsele, however, so I came to talk to you."

"Lucky me." She sighed wearily.

"Odel," Matilda said firmly. "I told you this last night, my dear, but obviously you did not believe me. I have used no magic on Lord Suthtun. His proposal was sincere. His feelings are true. He loves you."

"Nay." Odel didn't even bother to face her. "You used your magic to make him love me. Do not deny it."

"Oh, child. If it were that easy, I could have simply made you love whomever I wanted you to. That would have saved me a good deal of trouble, wouldn't it?"

Odel stiffened, then turned slowly to find the older woman nodding.

"It is true. And I told you this yesterday. Why will you not believe me?"

Odel was silent for a minute, then asked, "Can you swear to me that you used no magic on Lord Suthtun? Will you vow it before God?"

Matilda hesitated, then crossed her heart. "I have used no magic on Lord Suthtun."

"You are lying," Odel said unhappily. "Your hesitation gave you away."

"Oh for Heaven's sake!" Matilda cried, then moved to sit on the bed. She sighed. "All right, I may have used a little magic to make his horses tired, and perhaps to put the suggestion in his mind that he should stop to rest here for the night. I may also have had a hand in Eadsele's falling ill to keep him here—"

"You made Eadsele sick?" Odel cried in horror.

" 'Tis just a fever. He will be no worse for the wear," she muttered, looking slightly ashamed.

Odel considered that briefly, then eyed her narrowly. "And that is it? You did not 'put a suggestion' in Lord Suthtun's mind that he should love me?"

"Nay. I vow before God himself that I have done nothing to determine Lord Suthtun's feelings for you." She shifted impatiently. "I cannot influence feelings, Odel. My magic will not do that."

"But the suitors," Odel murmured in confusion, not sure whether to believe the woman now or not. What she said made some sense. "They were . . ."

"The suitors," Matilda muttered irritably. "Of course."

"Aye, of course. Now you're caught." Some of Odel's uncertainty left her, replaced by bitterness. "I am not so foolish as to believe that they would all be so eager to marry me without some . . . *influence*."

"Yes, well, I can see how that would confuse you," Matilda peered down at the floor, then cleared her throat. "You were right that there is something amiss with them." She paused to clear her throat again. "They are not human."

Odel wasn't sure what she had been expecting, but it hadn't been that. "What?"

Matilda made a face. "Do you remember when you asked me if I had turned Lord Cheshire back into a man before he left? And I said, 'not to fear, he left as he arrived'?"

Odel nodded with bewilderment.

"Well, he left as a rat," Tildy admitted. Then, just in case Odel was misunderstanding what she was saying, she added, "He also arrived as a rat. All the lords who have filled Roswald these past two weeks—except for Lord Suthtun—were originally rats."

Odel stood gaping at the woman, picturing the men in question. She was recalling the way they had scrabbled so quickly up the trees. Then she remembered the odd way they had of eating and how she had thought it reminded her of something. Now she knew. *Rats.* She could actually picture them right now—eating. And as they ate they grew ears and whiskers. They were rats. All of them rats . . . And one of them, Cheshire, had—

"Oh, God," Odel breathed, her face paling and her eyes going round.

"What is it?" Matilda asked with concern.

"One of them kissed me!" she cried. She began scrubbing at her mouth a bit frantically. "Oh, yuck! Ick! Ptooey!"

Matilda rolled her eyes, but allowed her a moment of such behavior, then grabbed her hands impatiently to still them. "As I said," she repeated grimly, forcing Odel's attention back to her. "My dust cannot affect people—at least, not their choices. God gave man free will; he would hardly supply me with dust to take that away. I can change the inside of the castle, I can turn ducks into maids, and rats into love-struck men, but I cannot make you love someone, or make that someone love you."

Odel forgot about being kissed by a rat.

"Then, Michelle—"

Matilda nodded. "Lord Suthtun loves you."

For a moment, joy suffused her face, then it was immediately replaced with regret. "Oh no! What have I done?"

"Nothing that cannot be undone," Matilda assured her. Her godmother stood up, grabbed her hand, and dragged her toward the door. "Come with me."

"Where are we going?" Odel asked as she was led from the room and up the hall.

"You are going to straighten things out." Matilda announced firmly.

"But how?" Odel cried as they reached and started down the stairs. "What can I say? I thought my aunt had cast a spell on you? He will think me mad."

"You will come up with something," Tildy assured her, then paused at the bottom of the stairs. She glanced around before satisfaction crossed her face. "Look."

Odel followed her gesture to see Michelle standing in the doorway to the kitchens, talking to a servant. No doubt he was arranging for something to be taken to Eadsele.

"Go to him," Matilda urged quietly, digging a small pinch of fairy dust out of her sack. She blew it in the general direction of Lord Suthtun. All at once, the doorway he was standing in was suddenly alive with mistletoe. "Kiss him. Tell him you love him. Make things right."

Odel hesitated briefly, then swallowed, straightened and moved determinedly forward. She arrived at his side just as he finished with the servant. The girl retreated into the kitchen and Michelle turned toward the great hall, pausing when he found Odel in his path. She saw pain flash across his face, then it was gone, replaced by a smooth, emotionless facade.

"Lady Roswald," he murmured formally. "Is there something you wished?"

"Aye," Odel said huskily. "You."

At his startled expression, she pointed upward. He glanced up, spotted the mistletoe and his mouth tightened. She knew he was about to reject her, so she refused to give him the chance. Stepping forward determinedly, she reached up on tiptoe, catching his tunic and tugging him down to her. Their lips met.

It wasn't as easy as she had hoped. He did not melt into her embrace, did not take over the kiss and give his passion rein. Instead, he remained stiff and silent. Odel tried to coax some passion from him with her lips, but found it impossible.

Tears stinging her eyes, she drew back slightly. She whispered, "I was wrong, my lord. Last night . . . I was afraid. But now I am more afraid of losing you. Please, my lord. I love you."

Catching her upper arms, Michelle eyed her warily. "So you will be my wife?"

"If you are sure it is what you want," she said huskily. A smile blossomed on his lips.

"Aye, I am sure," he told her quietly. "I love you, too."

Joy filling her face, Odel started to reach up on tiptoe again to kiss him, but he lowered his head, meeting her halfway. This time the kiss was mutual.

A cat's hiss and a rustle of rushes distracted Odel and Michelle briefly from their kiss. They both glanced around in amazement as a pack of perhaps twenty rats fled through the open door of the keep and out into the cold winter day. Stranger, the long, thin cat that followed seemed less to be trying to catch them and more to be herding them away. *Vlaster.* It was a moment before Odel noticed that the great hall was decidedly empty of guests.

"Where did everyone go?" Michelle asked with surprise when he saw where she was looking. He glanced toward Matilda.

"Who, dear?" the woman asked innocently, not seeming to notice the panic growing on Odel's face.

"Lords Beasley and Trenton and—"

"Oh, my, well. They saw the lay of the land and retreated," Odel's aunt said sweetly. She arched an eyebrow at them. "Is there something you two wish to tell me?"

Michelle hesitated and glanced down at Odel, then smiled widely. "Aye. We shall be married tomorrow," he announced. He glanced down at Odel when she nudged him in the stomach. "What?"

"Tomorrow?" she asked pointedly.

"Aye," he said, then looked uncertain. "You will marry me tomorrow, will you not, Odel? I vow I shall work very hard to make you happy. I shall tell you you are beautiful every morning, brush your hair every night, and tend to you as kindly as I do my horse and my squire."

Odel burst out laughing at the proposal, then hugged

him tightly. "I could not have asked for a more romantic offer, my lord. Aye, I shall marry you."

They had barely sealed the bargain with a kiss when Matilda released a husky sigh, then began bustling toward the door. "Well, that's that then. I am off."

"What?" Odel pulled slightly away from Michelle. The woman had hounded her all this time to be wed, and now she wasn't even going to be present? "But tomorrow is Christmas. And I would like you to be there when we are married. Will you not stay for the wedding?"

"Oh." Her aunt's expression gentled. "I shall be there, you may count on that. But in the meantime, I have much to do, my dear. Forty-nine to go, you know. Besides, you should spend Christmas with Lord Suthtun's family. And marry at Castle Suthtun as well. If you leave now, you should get there in time for the feast."

"But we could not leave Michelle's squire. Aunt Matilda, you—"

"His squire is much better, I understand, and more than healthy enough to make the journey." The words had barely left her mouth when Michelle's squire came bounding down the stairs, the very image of a healthy young lad. One could almost imagine he had never been ill.

"Are you really all right, boy?" Michelle asked with a frown. The lad spotted him and hurried to his side.

"Aye, my lord," Eadsele said, then he shook his head in bewilderment. "Only moments ago I felt weak and feverish, then as suddenly as it came on, my illness was gone. I feel right as rain."

"There you are, you see?" Matilda called, gaily ignoring Odel's annoyed glance. She waved on the servants that came trundling down the stairs with Odel's baggage; apparently the woman had made them begin packing for her. "No reason at all for you to remain here alone through the holidays. Go on to Suthtun. His mother and sisters shall adore you, I promise. Why, by this time tomorrow you shall hardly recall me."

"Oh, but—" Odel began, but whatever protest she would have given faded from her mind in a fit of sneezing. There seemed to be dust everywhere. The door closed behind Matilda and the last of her servants. Turning with confusion, Odel peered at Suthtun.

Smiling, he pressed another quick kiss to her soft lips. "Come along. She is right. My mother and sisters shall adore you as much as I do."

Odel was silent for a moment, then she smiled slowly. "But no more than I adore you."

Laughing as Suthtun grabbed her hand, she ran with him toward the door and out into a whole new world.

A Midnight Clear

Lisa Cach

To Bill Yeaton

Chapter One

Woodbridge, Vermont
December 1, 1878

Her breath misted before her, a faint drifting ghost in
the cold night air. The train platform looked empty, illuminated by a yellow gaslight that was dim and soft
against the winter darkness. All was quiet but for the
hiss of the engine's steam and the rumbling of a freight
door. Catherine stepped down from the train onto the
wooden planks, her heeled shoes thudding on the hollow
surface. She was used to the frantic rush of New York,
and had forgotten the slower pace of home. Only a few
others were disembarking at this station, already walking
toward the exit, leaving her alone beside the blackened
steel wheels.

With each stop the train had made, each familiar
place-name called out, her excitement had built, and she
had peered blindly out the window at the depths of the
night, searching vainly for some known landmark, re-

99

straining herself from telling the others in the carriage that this was where she was from, this was where she was born and raised. And here she was at last, standing on the planks of the Woodbridge platform, unable to believe she had finally arrived.

"Catherine!" her father's voice called.

"Papa!" she cried, her nearsighted eyes searching him out, and finding him at last, a figure that became clear as he moved toward her. She hurried to close the distance, the long back hem of her velvet skirt, with all its folds and flounces, dragging fashionably across the wood, the opening of her silk-and-mink coat flapping. She was showing unseemly enthusiasm, she knew, and Aunt Frances would not have approved.

Her father caught her in a hug, enveloping her in the scents of wool and pipe tobacco, reminding her for a moment of her childhood. He patted her on the back, his broad hand over-strong in his enthusiasm, and then released her. He blinked rapidly, a suspicious sheen in his eyes.

"Did you get something to eat? Was the trip comfortable?" he asked. "Did you have any problems switching at White River Junction?"

"I'm fine, Papa, just tired. Two o'clock in the morning is a weary time for a train to arrive." Her original train had left New York at four in the afternoon, and she was stiff and sore from sitting on the poorly padded seats, her tight, elegant travel ensemble a constant reminder to sit straight and not lean back. She was exhausted, and the space between her shoulder blades ached with tension.

"Your mother is waiting up, and I shouldn't be surprised if Amy is still awake as well," he said, leading her into the station, where porters would bring in her trunks. "Your visit is all Amy's been able to speak of for weeks."

"I've missed her."

He glanced at her, the sheen still in his eyes. "We've missed you, too," he said, then looked away. "Porter!" he called, his voice loud in the quiet station, and went to fetch her luggage.

"Good gracious, where did you get *that*?" Amy asked, staring with wide green eyes, the plumed purple hat in her lap forgotten. The young girl was sitting cross-legged atop her bedcovers, clad in a white nightgown.

Catherine looked down at herself, at the red French corset and white silk chemise she'd just revealed by removing her bodice and camisole. "In Paris. There are dancers there who wear nothing but scarlet corsets and short petticoats, and they lift even those up to show their legs to the men."

"You saw them?" Amy asked, incredulous.

"Once. Aunt Frances thought it would be educational to go to such a dance hall show. She says that one can on occasion be daring if one is sure to behave like a lady whilst doing so. Of course, she also said it is even better if one can count on the silence of one's friends."

"What was it like at the dance hall? Were there *ladies of the night* there?" Amy half-whispered, eyes widening on the forbidden words.

Catherine laughed. "And what would you know of them?"

"I would know much more if anyone thought I was old enough to discuss them."

"You'd find them more sad than fascinating." She went to hang her bodice in the wardrobe. Talking with her younger sister was increasing the sense of unreality she felt, back in the room in which she had grown up. Amy in person was somehow different than Amy in letters, where Catherine had let her imagination fill in her sister's spoken intonation and expression. Was this Amy

101

the same girl she had thought she had stayed close to through the mail? Even Mama had been altered, more gray in her hair, her cheeks a little fuller than Catherine remembered, her figure a little heavier. It was a surprise to realize that her family had been living their own lives while she had been away, growing up and growing older.

"So there were such women there?"

"I don't know for certain. Aunt Frances forbid me to gawk, and it was too dark and smoky to see much, anyway."

Amy's eyes went once again to the corset. "Mama doesn't have anything like that."

"Do you like it?" Catherine asked, striking a pose with one hand on her hip, the other lifting her skirts to show a bit of stockinged leg.

"Do I! I got my first corset this year, you know, but it's a plain thing, all white cotton without any trim or lace or anything. I don't even need it yet," she complained.

Catherine smothered a smile. "You wouldn't remember, but I was the same shape as you at thirteen. In two years you won't recognize yourself." She remembered as well her own young fascination with pretty underthings, and how they had seemed both forbidden and unattainable, things that belonged to a very adult world. In her trunks was a pink, beribboned corset for Amy, and a chemise and drawers "combination" trimmed with Valenciennes lace. They were innocent enough for a girl, but pretty enough for any woman. She would give them to Amy in private, though, as she hardly thought her sister would enjoy opening such gifts in front of Papa.

"Truly, you looked like me?"

"Truly. But you'll be much prettier than I, with your eyes."

"I like your brown ones," Amy said. "They look like weak tea in white china cups."

"Do they?" Catherine laughed, and turned to look at herself in the mirror. Her eyes were slightly bloodshot, her pale skin showing the shadows under her eyes. Her irises did indeed look the same color as weak tea. "I suppose you're right." Her dark brown hair was still piled up at the back of her head, the large loose braids pinned over small cushions to give the arrangement the great mass that was fashionable. Her scalp and every muscle atop her skull ached with the weight.

She heard Amy moving behind her, the bed creaking as she climbed off.

"Cath, look! It's snowing!"

She went to the window, where Amy was already raising the pane, heedless of the additional chill to the room. Catherine stuck her head out beside her sister's, watching the fluffy flakes fall silently in the light from the window.

"It's the first snow of December," Amy said. "Do you remember what that means?"

"Of course I do. Wasn't I the one who told you in the first place?" Catherine said, remembering the myth her grandmother had told her. "With the first snow of December, the snow fairies come to celebrate the Christmas season. They grant the wishes of those with pure hearts, and then with the ringing in of the New Year, they return to their lands in the north."

"I'm too old to believe it anymore, but I like to pretend it's true."

"I do, too," Catherine admitted. She put her hand out, catching a cluster on her palm and watching it melt. The breeze picked up, and she shivered. "It's too cold to be hanging out a window in my underthings," she said, and withdrew into the room.

Amy lingered a moment longer, then followed, pulling shut the sash. "I'm glad you're back, Cath."

"I am, too."

The clock in the hall below was striking half past three when she finally blew out the lamp and pulled up the covers against the cold of the room. Amy slept in the bed next to hers, her final "good night" followed quickly by deepened breathing, her gray cat, Quimby, nestled at her feet.

Home, at last. It had been nearly two years. Catherine had been living and traveling with Aunt Frances, her mother's wealthy, artistically inclined sister, since shortly after Catherine's graduation from Mount Holyoke. Last Christmas had been spent in London, there had been months in Paris, long stays with friends in Italy, and weeks at a spa in Switzerland. For the past several months they had been in New York, in Aunt Frances's large town house, entertaining poets, painters, writers, and the more daring of the New York social elite, all while Uncle Clement had happily busied himself with his business affairs, remaining in the background of his wife's social world.

Aunt Frances had wanted to give her an education of a different sort than the scholastic one offered at Mount Holyoke, and Catherine had to admit that her aunt had succeeded. Perhaps she had succeeded too well, and home would now seem small-minded and provincial in comparison to such grand sights as the canals of Venice and the palace of Versailles, not to mention the dancers of Paris. Maybe she would no longer fit in here.

She stared into the darkness, listening to the faint creakings of the house and to Amy's breathing. There were no sounds from the street, Woodbridge asleep for the night. She was tense despite her exhaustion, the room feeling less familiar than the opulent bedchamber she had left behind in New York, with the mementos from her travels on the walls and strewn about on small tables. Would this house ever feel like home again?

She scolded herself for even thinking the thought. Surely she would feel more a part of things in the morning, after a good night's sleep, and after a few days she would find herself once more in step with the rhythms of her family's life. She would cease noticing the changes, and would forget that she had been away.

After all, if she didn't belong at home, then where *did* she belong?

Chapter Two

"No, Mrs. Harris, it is $9.32 that you owe. It says so right here," Will Goodman insisted, showing the older woman the accounts ledger where he kept track of how much credit had been extended to his customers. He brushed back the lock of brownish-blond hair that had fallen into his eyes.

"I was certain it was $14.32," Mrs. Harris protested, her brow drawn into ridges of confusion. "With the sausages from last week, plus the new shoes for Joshua and Ann, and then there were the five pounds of sugar . . . I thought I had kept track. I'm not forgetful; you know that, Mr. Goodman."

"Of course not. Much as I would like to take $14.32 from you, especially if you were to offer it in part as cookies and pies, I'll have to settle for the $9.32."

"I'm afraid all I have at this time is—"

"I was thinking," Will interrupted, as if he had not heard her, "that I might be needing some help around here through the month. I know this would be asking a great deal, but do you think that I could steal Joshua and Ann away from you for an hour or two after school every day?"

"I don't think they'd be much use to—"

"I know it would be an imposition, what with all the chores that I am sure wait for them at home, but I would pay them well."

Mrs. Harris blinked at him, her frown growing deeper. "What would you be wanting them for? What use could a ten- and an eight-year-old be to you?"

"Well, Mrs. Harris," Will said, leaning over the counter and taking on a confidential air. "You might not believe this, but other children are not so well-behaved as your Ann. At this time of year, what with all the shopping people are doing, they tend to let their little ones run round loose, knocking over displays, getting dirty fingers on clean goods, and making a god-awful amount of noise that distracts the other customers and affects my bottom line."

Mrs. Harris "mmmed" in sympathy, nodding her head.

"Now your Ann, she's a gentle, clever child. I was thinking that I would have her sit over by the woodstove there, with a stack of storybooks. When those rambunctious sorts of children come in, I can send them over to Ann, where she can read to them and keep them out of trouble while their mothers shop."

"She's very good with the young ones at home," Mrs. Harris agreed.

"And Joshua, well . . ." Will scanned the front room of his general store, his eyes lighting on the solution to this problem. "Besides for sweeping and dusting and keeping an eye out for thieves who pocket my goods—there are some who come in here, you know—"

"Ahhh?" Mrs. Harris breathed, eyes widening.

"Besides that, I have a rather daring advertising campaign in mind. I have some new sleds that have come in," he said, nodding toward the bright red sled on display in the front window. "Very high-priced, and they are not selling like they should. Now that it has begun to snow, I'd like to send Joshua out with one of those sleds. When the other kids see how fast it goes, they'll be begging their own parents to buy them one for Christmas. I need an athletic boy like Joshua to show it off to its best advantage."

"And how much would you be paying for the services of my children?" Mrs. Harris asked, her eyes taking on a speculative gleam.

"Let's see what we can work out, shall we?"

Will was putting his fake public account book away when Tyler Jones, his senior shop assistant, shuffled over to him, wrinkles set in disapproving lines.

"You go easy on her again?" the man asked, shaking his graying, balding head in disgust. "You're going to run yourself right out of business, doing things that way."

"Mr. Jones," Will warned flatly.

"Shhhhh," Jones said, eyes wide, hushing himself dramatically with a finger against his lips. "I didn't see a thing. I know nothing."

"Good man."

"As long as I'm not a jobless man. Yours is not the only general store in town, you know. You have to stay competitive, or they'll drive you out of business."

Will just looked at him until the old man threw his hands up, shrugging his shoulders up around his ears.

"But you're the boss! You know what you're doing!"

"It's good to hear that you remember that."

Mr. Jones rolled his eyes and began to shuffle away. "Ignorant pup," he muttered under his breath. "Practically *gives* things away. What type of way to run a store is—"

"And which of us owns this place, old man?" Will called after him, then cut off the rest of what he was about to say as the bell rang over the door, and business captured his attention.

Mr. Jones's complaints did not concern Will, knowing as he did that they had no basis in truth. He was a partner in the glass factory downriver, a shareholder in an iron-works, and had invested in an import/export company that had grown to pleasingly profitable dimensions. His ties to these businesses and others helped him to stock his store at minimal expense. Few in Woodbridge knew of the extent of either his investments or his philanthropy, which was how he liked it. It went against his nature to draw attention to himself, and there was a subtle pleasure to be had in keeping his true self secret, as if by doing so he maintained some element of freedom.

The day went quickly as he, Mr. Jones, and his other clerks helped customers, stocked shelves, carried parcels, measured out cloth, fitted shoes, weighed out butter, and balanced books. They sold gloves, candy, shaving gear, pots, dye, sheet music, irons, rolling pins, toys, stockings, winter coats, eggs, and pork. He sold anything and everything that would fit inside one of the large connecting rooms, and if he didn't stock something someone desired, he would order it for them. He loved his store, and the work of running it.

All considered, it seemed that he had everything he could desire. Work that he loved, money invested to guard against misfortune, a large house newly completed on Elm Street, and the goodwill and regard of his fellow businessmen and customers. Life, he reflected as he closed up shop that evening, was complete.

"So tell me, are there any young men who have caught your eye?" Catherine's mother asked, sitting down in her accustomed seat at the end of the dining table, a cup of tea before her. She was a tall woman, more stately than slender, her dark hair dusted with gray, and she had large, warm brown eyes of a deeper shade than Catherine's own. She wore a high-necked blouse and a cinnamon-brown skirt, bustled at the back in a style slightly out of date, but that nonetheless looked fitting on Mama.

"Perhaps one or two," Catherine replied obliquely, and looked at her mother from the corner of her eyes, checking for how well the bait was being taken. She knew that Mama liked nothing better than a tale of romance. She picked over the sausages and eggs in the warming dishes on the side table, slowly filling her plate.

"That viscount you wrote to us about, in London? Is he one of them?" Mama asked.

Catherine added a few slices of toast, then brought her plate to the table, setting it on the white lace cloth and taking her place to the immediate right of her mother. "I think he has become engaged to a Boston heiress."

"Oh. How very disappointing."

"Of course, the British are not the only ones with an aristocracy," she said, and paused to take a bite of food, remaining silent while she chewed.

Mama pursed her mouth impatiently, then made a noise of frustration. "Catherine Linwood! You're teasing me. You know very well I've been waiting all morning for you to get out of bed and come tell me all about your social life. A dozen times I almost went up those stairs and woke you myself."

Catherine laughed. "I'm sorry. I know how much you want to hear about my being courted, but there really isn't much to tell. There have been flirtations, but most have not amounted to much. The young men my own age all seem so . . . foolish. And the older ones are boring, with big bellies," she said, arching her back and arranging her face to match that of a self-satisfied businessman, thumb in watch pocket.

Mama's lips curled up in reluctant amusement. "You're a naughty girl."

"The best ones, of course, are already taken," Catherine said, dropping the pose.

"Did you say *most* flirtations have not amounted to much?"

She had known her mother would catch that small discrepancy. She chased a piece of egg around her plate with her fork. "There is one man who seems to have a certain interest in me."

"For heaven's sake, who?"

She gave up on the egg, and lay her fork down in the correct four o'clock position. "Stephen Rose. His family is filthy rich: They have money in railroads and shipping and ironworks and who knows what all else. Aunt Frances would scold me for speaking of their money, of course. She says it is not genteel to do so."

"It's not genteel only so long as you have enough money not to care. My sister cares about money and who has it, you can be sure, no matter her artistic airs. You'll notice she did not marry a poet," Mama added dryly.

Catherine had noticed that herself. It was amusing to think that Aunt Frances, with her elegance and sophistication, had once been a little girl having hissy fights with Mama. Although she knew they loved each other very much, Mama and Aunt Frances had always shared something of an abrasive relationship. "Mr. Rose must have enough money even for her standards, as she allows his visits and is always most eager to see him. I have the impression she arranges to throw us together."

"Is he handsome?"

"Terribly. He's all dark hair and black eyes, tall, and has the most graceful manners. He can charm anyone he has a mind to."

"And has he charmed you?"

She recalled the white flash of his smile, as he would lean down close to whisper something to her while listening to a concert; the skill with which he would sweep her around the dance floor in a waltz; the small thrill of pride when he led her in to dinner, and the other young women, more beautiful than her, watched in envy. "I suppose he may have," she admitted.

Her mother looked at her, eyes evaluating. "Are you in love with him?"

A nervous laugh escaped her lips. "Aunt Frances says I must be! There's no reason not to fall head over heels for Mr. Rose: He's handsome, rich, charming, and quite clever. He's considered an excellent catch."

"Mmm."

They were both silent for several moments. "Mama, how do you know if you are in love with a man?" Catherine asked, all trace of jollity gone. "It's true that my heart beats faster when Mr. Rose comes in the room, and his is the first face I look for in a gathering. I miss his company when he does not come to call for a number of days. Does that mean I love him?"

Mama reached out and squeezed her hand where it lay in her lap. "If you're not in love, then at least you are on the path toward it."

"I suppose I don't need to worry about the question now, though, do I?" she said brightly, trying to escape thoughts of her confused feelings for Mr. Rose. "I'm home, and he's far away in New York. I have all of you to think about now."

Her mother just raised her eyebrows.

The Linwood house was alive with the murmuring voices of guests, punctuated by bursts of laughter. The rooms, always chilly in winter, were growing cozy with the heat of bodies, the happy exchange of greetings adding an additional, intangible warmth to the evening air as friends and family gathered to welcome Catherine home.

"Will, this is my sister, Miss Catherine Linwood," Robert said. "Catherine, William Goodman."

"It's a pleasure to meet you, Mr. Goodman," she said.

Will took her gloved hand, her palm down, her fingers long and delicate as they rested lightly over the side of his hand. "It is a great honor to make your acquaintance," he said hoarsely, performing an abbreviated bow over her hand and earning a brief, puzzled look from her glorious eyes.

"Catherine will be with us through the holidays," Robert said. "She's been traveling the world, seeing sights that make Woodbridge look like a country backwater in comparison."

"And meeting men that make you look like a positive cave dweller," Catherine said to her brother, mischief in her eyes, and laughing at his falsely affronted expression. The sound was warm and melodious, sinking through Will's chest and wrapping around his heart.

A commotion at the door drew her attention. Will wanted to say something, but was tongue-tied, his lips parted and silent as Robert said something else to his sister. She laughed again, and then her eyes went back to the door with delighted recognition.

"Robert, Mr. Goodman, do forgive me," she apologized, and left them abruptly, hurrying toward the front hall, the scent of lily of the valley hovering faintly behind her.

Will stared after her retreating figure. She was wearing a burgundy silk gown, trimmed in black velvet and lace, the sleeves mere strips of material across her upper arms. She wore a velvet choker, the darkness of it emphasizing the creamy expanse of exposed bosom, and the gentle rounded curves of her shoulders. Her body was tightly corseted, the horizontal folds and gathers of her skirt around her hips making her waist look minuscule in comparison, the gathers at the back of her gown trailing yards of rich burgundy that dusted the floor in a short train.

Ludicrous, to be struck dumb by a pretty woman! He was thirty years old. He was no longer a giddy young boy. He was beyond adolescent embarrassments. He didn't believe in love at first sight.

And yet . . . In the space between one heartbeat and the next, when she had met his eyes and said, "It's a pleasure to meet you, Mr. Goodman," in a voice like mulled wine, Catherine Linwood had sparked to life a fire inside him.

The pleasure of meeting her was all his. But why? *Why?*

Earlier today he had congratulated himself on his life being complete. God had heard him and laughed, placing this woman down before him to prove his ignorance.

She was laughing, her gestures animated, her hand touching briefly on the coated arm of the visitor at the door. Will took his eyes from Catherine long enough to examine the newcomer, and felt a flush of jealousy run through his blood.

He'd never seen such a handsome man—the word *dashing* came ridiculously to mind—and dressed in a manner that bespoke such careless wealth. This man came from money. He'd been born to it, and had the air of one who had discovered that anything he wanted could be had for a price.

"Will? Will!" Robert said, stirring him from his staring.

"Huh?" he grunted, articulate as an ape.

"Good lord, man, you look like you've been kicked in the head."

Will blinked, frowned, and tried to focus on his friend.

Robert Linwood was a few years younger than he, but he and the Linwood family had become good friends over the past few years. Robert was a lawyer, who like many others in Woodbridge relied on the town's position as the county seat—and thus the home of the county courthouse—for his business.

"There is a saying amongst shopkeepers," Will said, still half-dazed, "that customers do not know what they want. A man may come into a store seeking only boot black, but then his eye lights upon a pocket watch and suddenly he must have it. He did not know he wanted a pocket watch. He got along fine without one for many years. But now he must have it, and if he cannot afford it he will leave the store with that watch haunting his thoughts until he finds the money to buy it."

"Are you feeling quite well?" Robert asked.

Will looked back to Catherine, who was introducing the stranger to her parents. Her excitement was palpable, even from across the room. "No, not quite."

Dinner was its own unique agony. The dining table was crowded, all its extra leaves put into use. Catherine was at the other end of the table, the newcomer, Mr. Rose, seated next to her and making himself the cynosure of the gathering.

" 'Well, I never!' " Mr. Rose was saying, imitating the voice of an affronted woman of the upper classes, to the great amusement of those guests seated near him. "And then she tripped on the train of her gown, falling into a servant and sending his tray of glasses crashing to the floor!" A drumming of laughter followed the denouement to the story.

Will did not laugh, watching instead how Catherine smiled, as if she had heard the tale before, and then glanced quickly at those near her, gauging their reactions as if seeking communal approval of this man. Her eyes flicked briefly down to his end of the table, squinting a bit, but then her attention went back to Mr. Rose, who had begun another anecdote about life among the upper crust in New York.

"*I* don't like him at all," Amy whispered at his side.

Surprised, Will turned to the girl with whom he had developed a small friendship during his visits to the house. She would not normally have been allowed to partake of a dinner party at her age, but an exception had been made tonight. "Do you speak of Mr. Rose?"

"I don't think he's a nice man."

"He appears to be entertaining everyone very well."

"All he does is mock people. I don't think that's a kind thing to do, do you?"

At the moment, Mr. Rose was doing a wicked impression of an Irish maid who did not understand the workings of water faucets. "No, not especially."

"I don't trust people like that."

"Did he say something cruel to you?" Will asked, catching the fiery look of resentment Amy cast at the man.

"No, it's just . . . There's just something about him. When we were introduced he said what a 'little doll' I was, and treated me like I was still in short skirts. I think he was even considering giving me a pat on the head. Then he ignored me completely."

"He and your sister make a handsome pair."

"Don't say that!" Amy grimaced, and gave a theatrical shiver of abhorrence. "I shouldn't like to have him as a brother-in-law." She was silent a moment, her dark brows frowning as she stared down the table at the object of her loathing. Then her gaze switched to Will, and her lips curled in a mischievous smile that was a younger version of her sister's. "I would much rather have *you* for a brother-in-law. Then Catherine wouldn't go off again to New York. She'd stay right here."

Will choked on the swallow of wine he'd just taken,

and after he finished coughing, tried to sound nonchalant. "Do you think I'd stand a chance against Mr. Rose?"

"You're a decent-looking fellow, and much nicer."

That didn't sound a ringing endorsement. "Nice" and "decent-looking" had not been known to win female hearts away from the "dashing" or "amusing." "I think your sister is barely aware that I exist. She never looks this way."

"That's because she's half-blind," Amy said.

"What?"

"She's nearsighted. Everything beyond about six feet gets blurry, and she refuses to wear eyeglasses. Even if she did look away from that man, she wouldn't be able to tell who was who down here. I do think that if she got to know you, she'd see that you were a much better choice than Mr. Rose. You think she's pretty, don't you?"

He swallowed, and suddenly found the plaster moulding on the ceiling to be of absorbing interest. "Uh . . ." he said noncommittally.

"You must. I think she's beautiful. And you need a wife. There's no one else you've got your heart set on, is there? Wouldn't Catherine do?"

He brought his eyes back to her intense green ones. "I suppose she might," he admitted.

Amy beamed at him. "I would be aunt to your children. Isn't that wonderful?"

Will blinked at her, thinking of the necessary steps to producing children with Catherine Linwood. "That would be . . . remarkable."

Voices from below were audible through the floorboards, the party continuing even as Amy got into her nightgown, shivering in the chilly bedroom. More guests had arrived after dinner, friends stopping by to welcome

Catherine back. If she hadn't had school in the morning, Amy knew she would have been allowed to stay up, but she couldn't say she particularly cared to as long as *he* was here.

She couldn't put her finger on why, exactly, she did not approve of Mr. Stephen Rose. He seemed to have charmed most everyone, and she should have thought it romantic that he had followed Catherine home, taking up residence in the inn next to the courthouse so that he could be near her. Instead she found herself wondering why the man couldn't go and impose his foul presence on his own family.

Worst of all had been the glow in Catherine's cheeks as Mr. Rose paid court to her. She deserved better than someone like that. She deserved someone kind and thoughtful, like Mr. Goodman. Even though Catherine was ten years older than Amy, she had never made Amy feel the age difference. She sent gifts from her travels, and wrote letters assiduously. Amy knew she couldn't have asked for a better sister—unless, that is, she had a sister who lived in Woodbridge, instead of in New York and over half of Europe.

If Catherine married Mr. Rose, she would never settle here, that much was plain. Mr. Rose would be quickly bored and dissatisfied with life in Woodbridge.

Her only hope was Mr. Goodman. She'd marry him herself if she were old enough, but she loved Catherine enough to sacrifice him to her. He wasn't as tall or handsome as Mr. Rose, and probably nowhere as rich, but he had kind, soft blue eyes that crinkled at the corners with humor. He didn't say much, but one always felt he thought you were important when you spoke to him, and deserving of his attention.

Not like Mr. Rose.

But Catherine, she couldn't see the truth of the two men, just as she couldn't see more than six feet in front of her. Mr. Rose had blinded her heart, with his funny stories that made you feel a bit ashamed of yourself for laughing, and with his romantic good looks. How could she ever get her sister to see the pure, hidden light of Mr. Goodman, when Mr. Rose was busy burning like a bonfire?

A wave of laughter rose up from the parlor below. Amy wanted to stomp her feet in frustration, get all their attention and tell them to throw Mr. Rose back on the train to New York.

She went to the window, looking out at the snow that had begun to fall once again. The lantern at the end of the front walk was lit, creating a pool of yellow light in which to watch the flakes, blowing in the wind. The neighboring houses, large and white like their own, were dimly visible, one or two windows glowing with lamp-light.

If only the snow fairies were real, she'd ask them for help. She had a pure heart, after all, didn't she? She might know about ladies of the night, but she'd never been kissed, and wasn't that supposed to be part of the contract? Wishes were always meant for virginal young girls, and what use was being a virginal young girl if the legends were not true?

A figure appeared beneath her, coated and hatted, walking down the path away from the house. She knew somehow that it was Mr. Goodman.

What did it matter that the fairies weren't real? She could still wish, couldn't she?

She left her room and went to the nursery, long since turned into a work and sewing room for her and her mother. She found a piece of white paper and scissors, and took them back to the slightly warmer confines of her bedroom.

She folded and snipped the paper, tiny triangles and diamonds of white falling onto her writing desk. Minutes later she unfolded a paper snowflake, airy and delicate. She dipped her pen into ink, and very carefully, in tiny script, wrote her wish upon the spines and crystals of the flake:

"I wish that Catherine could see Mr. Rose's and Mr. Goodman's characters as they truly are."

There. That was an honest wish, one that had Catherine's fortune at heart, and not Amy's own selfish desire to have her sister live in the same town. Amy loved her birth place, and intended to marry and raise her children here, when the time came. Life would be perfect if Catherine were living here, too.

She went to the window and raised the sash. The wind blew and blustered, sending flakes dusting into the room, then quickly changed direction, pulling at her hair and dragging tendrils across her cheek.

She kissed her paper flake, and threw it into the swirling snow. For a moment it dropped, and then it was caught in a gust and danced out away from the window, rising, rising, and she stuck her head out to see it go. Up it went, beyond the reach of the lantern's light, and then she could see it no more. She stayed hanging out the window for a moment more, silently asking the snow fairies to answer her wish.

Somewhere, in the distance, she could hear the faint jingling of sleighbells.

"Are you asleep?" Catherine whispered, sitting on the side of her own bed, feeling weary now that the party was over. The lamp on the dresser across the room was turned low.

Amy's eyes opened, and she smiled, her young features barely visible in the dim light. "What time is it?"

"Nearly one A.M. Everyone has gone."

"Mr. Rose, too?"

"To the Woodbridge Inn. He says he'll stay there

through New Year's, although he'll have to go see relatives in Boston for a bit."

"Why did he come, Cath?"

"What a silly question!" Catherine said. "To see me, of course."

"Doesn't it seem a bit strange to you, his following you here? It makes him seem like a dog without a home of his own."

"Of course he has a home of his own, and family, too. Don't you like him?"

"Are all the men in New York the same as him?"

"The same, how?"

Amy shrugged.

"Come, you needn't worry about hurting my feelings," Catherine said. "You don't have to like him just because I do. What's wrong with him?"

"He's not right for you. I don't think he's a good man."

Amy's words touched a deep, hidden doubt about Mr. Rose that Catherine had harbored for weeks, and she reacted against them. "You don't even know him. He's very attentive to me, and there is no scandal attached to his name. Why should you not think him good?"

Amy gave another shrug, barely discernible beneath the blankets humped over her shoulder.

"I think he's quite delightful, really," Catherine said crossly, and went to the dresser and began to remove her jewelry. "It was terribly romantic of him to come all this way to be near me. He charmed everyone who met him tonight. Even Papa seemed to like him."

"Papa seems to like everyone, but if you ask him, it's not always the case."

"I *shall* ask him," Catherine snapped. She tried to reach the buttons running up her back, and after a few futile tries gave a little huff of frustration and went back to Amy. "Give me a hand with these, will you?" she asked, presenting her back.

"Don't be angry with me," Amy said softly, as she sat up and went to work on the fabric-covered buttons.

Catherine's head bowed under the weight of that gentle plea. "I'm not, darling," she said quietly, and when the last of the buttons came free she turned and sat on the edge of Amy's bed, meeting her sister's eyes. "I'm tired of waiting, is all. I don't know if you can understand that. I like Mr. Rose better than I've liked any other suitable gentleman I've met, and I want to believe that he is the one for me, so I can finally stop looking. I want all of you to like him, so that I will know I made the right choice if I marry him."

"I only want you to be happy," Amy said.

Catherine smiled, and couldn't explain why Amy's words put the sting of tears in her eyes.

Chapter Three

"Catherine, you have a package!" Amy exclaimed, bounding into the kitchen, still wearing her coat and hat. The cold, clear air of the outdoors came with her, caught in the folds of her coat, streamers of it invading the warmth of the kitchen.

"Who's it from?" Catherine asked, setting her rolling pin aside and wiping her floury hands on her apron. She was wearing a blouse and skirt, but the skirt's train had become such a trial in the kitchen that at last she had pinned it up, the peacock-blue material twisted into an awkward pouch behind her knees. The heat from the ovens had brought out a fine sheen of perspiration on her skin, and tendrils of hair stuck to the sides of her face and neck. She was enjoying herself thoroughly, her mind having been lost for hours in the immediacy of dough and spices, fruit and sugars as she worked alongside the family's taciturn cook, Mrs. Ames. There was a French apple tart cooling on the racks, as well as a variety of cookies.

"It doesn't say. Here," Amy said, extending the small package toward her. "Ginger cookies!" she then cried, spotting her favorites, and quickly nabbed one off the cooling racks as Mrs. Ames raised a wooden spoon in mock warning.

Catherine took the package, examining the neat copperplate writing addressing it to herself. There was no other mark on the brown paper wrapping, nothing to say from whence it had come. "Where did you find it? The mail has already come today."

"Perhaps he forgot this, and came back. It was on the front step."

Catherine turned it over in her hands, then with a facial shrug took a knife and cut through the string. She unwrapped the paper, and into her hand fell a flat box about six inches long, and less than half as wide. It was padded on its outside, and covered with a pale blue silk that shifted to silver when she tilted it. There were silver hinges at the back. "Curiouser and curiouser," Catherine said, then opened the lid.

On a bed of white satin sat a pair of spectacles. She pursed her lips, then slid her gaze sideways to Amy, who was standing beside her, eagerly peering in, cookie held to her lips.

Amy looked up at her, catching her suspicious stare. "I didn't send them! Honest!"

Catherine looked back at the spectacles. No, Amy would not have had the money to buy them. The frames were gold, and so finely wrought that Catherine doubted their practicality. It would take barely a nudge, surely, to bend the ear pieces out of shape. The lenses themselves looked too thin to withstand a puff of air.

There was something written on the inside of the lid. She tilted it, and brought it closer to her face. Spelled out in gold embroidery she read:

A Midnight Clear

See far
And see near
But let your heart's
Sight be clear

She repeated it aloud for the benefit of Amy and Mrs. Ames. "What do you suppose that means?" she asked, genuinely puzzled now.

"Put them on," Amy said, her voice tight.

Catherine glanced at her, noting the intensity of her expression. "My eyesight is not half as bad as you think it is. I assure you, I can see well enough to make my way around the kitchen without falling into the fire."

"Please, let me see them on you," Amy asked, pleading.

"My hands are dirty. I'll try them later," Catherine said, and shut the box with a snap. Why was her family forever after her to wear eyeglasses? She could see what was in front of her, and wasn't that all anyone needed? It wasn't like she was a hunter who needed to spot a deer two hundred yards away. "Perhaps Aunt Frances sent them," she mused aloud.

An hour later, with the last batch of cookies in the oven, Catherine went up to the room she shared with Amy. She opened the pale blue box and looked down at the spectacles, frowning, wondering if they truly were from Aunt Frances. The more she thought about it, the less likely it seemed. Her aunt was as eager as she to let vanity overrule practicality in the matter.

She set the box down and took out the spectacles, carefully unfolding the ear pieces. She had her own pair of eyeglasses, but they were graceless, heavy things compared to these. With a glance at the door to check that Amy was not waiting and watching, she put them on.

And took in a startled breath.

The room around her was crisp and perfect. She blinked, and stared, and turned her head left and right.

Her own spectacles improved her vision, but only slightly. They were nothing like this.

Good heavens, she thought, *is this how everyone else sees the world?* It was no wonder her family implored her to wear eyeglasses, if so.

She went to the window, and looked out across the narrow front yard and the street, to the large white houses opposite, with their black shutters and doors, and the brass knockers surrounded by green wreaths. The bare trees were frosted with snow where the wind had not blown it off, and above it all the clouds were delicate streamers of candy floss across a blue-white sky. She felt tears start in her eyes. She had never in her life seen the details of real clouds, only how artists had chosen to depict them in paintings.

These spectacles were magic, pure and simple.

She would never take them off. She would sit here until the stars came out, and the moon, and she would see its shadowed craters for herself. She would walk in the woods, and see birds fly from tree to tree. She would go into town, and read shop signs from a block away. She would see everything as it was for the first time in her life!

She had been staring awestruck at the drifting forms of the clouds for she didn't know how long when a movement from the corner of her eye caught her attention. She turned, and coming down the sidewalk was Mr. Rose, in his elegant topcoat and hat, swinging an ebony cane.

She pulled away from the window, her hand going to her hair. She went to the cheval mirror, and when she looked into her own face saw something she wasn't expecting. Her eyes were sad and uneasy, not at all the way she thought she felt at this moment. She leaned closer to the mirror, looking into her amber-brown eyes, and as a knock came at the door below something of panic flared deep within them.

It was the eyeglasses, it had to be. She took them off, and immediately she looked like her usual self again, cheery and at ease. There must be something in the shape of the frames that gave her that illusion of looking like an unhappy mouse. She could not have Mr. Rose seeing her that way.

She snapped the lid shut on the spectacles, tucked up the straying wisps of her hair, and went down to greet him.

"You must find Woodbridge very quiet after New York," she heard Mama saying as she came down the stairs.

"There is a certain rustic charm to the village, almost as if it were caught in a past century," Mr. Rose said. "It's quite restful. One needn't worry that one is going to miss anything of interest."

"Indeed," Mama said.

"Mama is a director of the Woodbridge Drama Club," Catherine said, coming into the sitting room. "Everyone looks forward to the plays they put on. Many would be sorry indeed to miss one of their productions."

Mr. Rose made a half bow of apology toward Mama. "I can only imagine that the plays must be a great delight to the audience, with such a mistress at the helm. You bring elegance to all that you touch."

Mama's cheeks pinkened, and Catherine wondered if it was in pleasure or because Mama found the flattery a trifle fulsome. "Thank you, Mr. Rose. Now if you'll both excuse me, I must talk with Mrs. Ames about dinner," she said, and left them alone.

"Now why are you frowning at me, my precious lily?" Mr. Rose asked, coming to her and taking both of her hands in his own. "Are you not happy to see me?"

Catherine smoothed away the frown she had not

127

known she was wearing, and gave him a smile. "Of course I am. I just hope you are not finding Woodbridge to be terribly boring."

"I look upon it as an adventure into the wilds, worth enduring for the pleasure of one native's company," he said, looking deeply into her eyes.

She laughed nervously, and broke the gaze. "Did you notice the portrait on the wall, there?" she asked, seeking to divert his attention.

"The watercolor? Yes, I could not help but recognize your inimitable style. Was she truly cross-eyed, or was that your own special touch?"

Catherine tried to smile at the jest, going over to get a closer look at the portrait she had done of her grandmother when she herself was twelve. At the time she had not yet mastered the three-quarter profile of a face, and her grandmother did indeed look as if her eyes were not in concert with each other. One shoulder was higher than it should have been, and the hands were in an unnatural posture. Her grandmother had died a few months after the portrait was painted, though, and she knew her mother treasured it for reasons other than its artistry.

"It doesn't show much promise for my future as a portrait painter, does it?"

"Don't tell me you still intend to dabble?"

She shrugged. Mr. Rose, she sensed, would not be one to put one of her artworks on the wall for sentimental reasons. He'd likely be embarrassed for his friends or family to see such a thing, for they might doubt his aesthetic sensibilities. She wondered if he was thinking a little less of her, now that he saw she came from a town that was uncultured and provincial in comparison to the great cities of Boston and New York, from whence his own ancestors had sprung.

Mr. Rose's superior sense of what was fashionable and in good taste had been part of what had drawn her to him. He was so much more cultured and finely bred than she, she had gladly relied upon his aesthetic opinions to guide her, and had trusted his judgment as being more discerning than her own. She was afraid of appearing lacking in his eyes, an object worthy of his mocking ridicule, and in New York had constantly, subtly, sought his approval. She was surprised by the stab of resentment she now felt toward him, at his dismissal—however warranted—of her watercolor painting.

"I was thinking we might take a stroll. You can explain to me this fine metropolis where you were raised," he said, and waggled his eyebrows comically at her, lightening the mood, and sweeping away the shadowed thoughts that lurked in her mind. "Only, I do hope it is not the fashion here to go about in public with one's skirts pinned up behind."

She felt a burn in her cheeks, and excused herself to go let down the train of her skirt.

Chapter Four

The air was bright and chill, her breath freezing in her nose. A light dusting of snow last night had renewed the sparkling beauty of winter, concealing the dirty slush that had been accumulating along sidewalks and roadsides. Catherine pulled the door of the house shut behind her, and felt her heart lift at being outside and alone. Mr. Rose, who had danced attendance on her almost every day, had gone to Boston to pay a visit to cousins, and would not be back for a week. Amy was in school, Papa at the lumberyard. Mama was planning meals with Mrs. Ames, and training the new maid. She was on her own.

Once out of sight of the house, Catherine reached into her reticule for the box that held her spectacles. Mama and Papa had denied buying them, as had her brother, Robert. Mr. Rose she had not even asked, knowing instinctively what the answer would be. She had put them on once for Amy, and it had almost broken her heart how clear the hope and youth were upon her sister's face.

She had not yet come to terms with wearing them regularly. It was something she had resisted for so many years, she could not bring herself to give in so quickly to the seduction of that crystal vision. At least, she could not give in before her family, who had been pestering her for so long to wear eyeglasses. In private was different, and so was alone in public. Half the faces in Woodbridge might be familiar to her, but with the exception of her lifelong friends, no one else knew of her battle against ocular assistance.

The street her family lived on was only a five-minute walk from the center of town. She put on the spectacles, and felt a thrill race across her skin as the world leaped into focus. The picket fences, the bare maple and oak trees, the brook that was visible at the backs of several houses, running down to join the Ottauquechee River, it was all perfectly etched in sunlight and snow.

Her skirt swished along the sidewalk, the train and underskirt gathering matted clumps of snow. She knew she was smiling like a fool as she turned onto Elm Street and headed toward town. Houses gave way to shops, and then she was at the intersection with Central Street, where the tall iron fountain for watering horses stood like an island in the middle of a stream. The water was frozen now, she could see that even from the edge of the road.

She was about to turn right, to make a circuit of the village green, but her eye was caught by bright colors in the nearest shop window. She stepped closer, putting up her hand to the glass to cut out the glare, and peered in at the Christmas cards on display. They were a reminder that she had yet to buy any, and that her Christmas shopping was only half done. She went in.

Cinnamon-scented warmth greeted her, and for an instant she wondered if she had stepped into someone's kitchen. A woodstove sat at the center of the room, and

131

on the braided red rug in front of it sat four or five children, all listening raptly as a girl only a few years older read to them from a picture book. The girl sat in a rocker, her black-booted feet several inches above the floor.

Catherine moved closer to the stove, and saw that a vat of spiced cider sat simmering there, cups and cookies on a tray to the side, apparently for the customers to take as they pleased. She realized then that she had been in this store once before, a summer a few years ago, but only for a few minutes. It had been lemonade on offer at that time, and meringue cookies.

She moved away from the stove, listening with half an ear as the girl read her story, and gazed at the goods stacked upon the shelves and arranged under the glass counters. She had seen goods in stores before, but never all at once, the sheet music twenty feet away as plain to her vision as the roll of ribbon in front of her. There was a young clerk helping a woman across the room, and up on a ladder a boy was arranging cans. A few other shoppers milled about.

Catherine wandered through a doorway into a room displaying housewares, then into another with dry goods. She heard an odd, irregular rapping sound coming from behind a curtained doorway, and idly wandered toward it, her curiosity prompting her to pull the edge of the curtain aside and see what was making the noise.

A man stood in a storeroom, facing half away from her. In his hand was a can of peaches, and as she watched he turned it slightly, then with a hammer whacked a dent into the side of it. He set it in a box along with several others, then searched the shelves. It was potted beef this time that fell to the hammer.

She stared, transfixed by the odd behavior. He was slightly taller than average, his frame strong, his hair a dark brownish blond. When he turned the right way she

132

could see part of his face, and could not help but think that it was a good countenance, something level and steady in his features that spoke of a well-grounded man. The impression made it all the more difficult to understand what he was doing.

"Pardon me, sir," Catherine found herself saying, and the man tensed. "Is the owner of the shop aware that you are damaging his goods?"

He turned around, and she met the loveliest pair of soft blue eyes she had ever seen. It was as if the first warmth of spring resided within them, and she was struck speechless.

"Miss Linwood," he said, his cheeks taking on a faint tinge of pink. "You've surprised me."

"I beg your pardon—" she began, then stopped herself. "Mr. Goodman?" she asked, astonished, and not at all certain the name she had dredged out of her memory was the right one. Surely if she had been introduced to this man once before, she would be more certain of it. She could not have forgotten him!

"Did Robert not tell you that this was my store?" he asked.

"Oh! I see!" But she did not see. Her eyes went again to the box of canned goods.

He grimaced. "I don't suppose you could pretend not to have seen me doing that?" he asked.

"It is no business of mine what you do with your goods," she replied. "I should not have disturbed you in the first place. My apologies, Mr. Goodman. Good day." She started to let the curtain fall back into place.

"Wait!"

She opened the curtain again. "Yes, Mr. Goodman?"

He put his hammer down atop a box. "Was there something you were looking for?"

"Excuse me?"

"In the store," he said, gesturing vaguely toward the room behind her.

"Oh. Well, yes. Christmas cards. I have suddenly recalled that I have yet to write a single one. Those in your window are quite lovely."

He came toward her, and she stepped out of the way, feeling suddenly a trifle embarrassed that this man she had met in her own home was now going to wait on her in his shop. It felt a peculiar and awkward situation.

"I ordered them from Louis Prang, the lithographer in Boston. I wasn't certain they would sell well. Not so many here have caught on yet to the fashion of sending them."

She let him lead her back to the front room, and to the small collection of cards. One was of a girl lighting candles on a tree, one of a striped stocking stuffed with toys, there was a trio of trumpeting angels, and last a row of tiny toddlers alternating with songbirds on a branch, with the title "A Christmas Carol." Mr. Rose would have chosen the trumpeting angels, she was certain, but the silly, sentimental toddlers made her smile. "These will do, I think," she said. "Could I have sixty?"

His eyebrows went up. "You'll have cramped fingers when you're done with that lot."

"I suppose I shall."

He began to count out the cards, but was interrupted by a raw female voice.

"Mr. Goodman! There you are. Where is my order? I've been waiting these past twenty minutes, wondering where you'd gone off to."

He paused in his counting, casting a wide-eyed look at Catherine.

"Go ahead," Catherine said. "I'll count them out myself."

"I'll be back in a moment. Do forgive me."

She nodded, and took his place at the drawer of cards,

her mind only partially on what she was doing. From the corner of her eye she watched him hurry to the discontented woman, confer with her for a moment, and then disappear into one of the back rooms.

She had her cards counted out by the time he came back, carrying the small crate with the dented cans and placing it on the wooden counter next to several other goods, most of which were already wrapped in brown paper and string. Catherine moved slowly closer, keeping her eyes averted, her ears straining to catch their exchange.

"It's a good thing there are people like me who are willing to take damaged goods off your hands," the woman was saying.

"Indeed I am fortunate in that regard," Mr. Goodman said. "Every shopkeeper knows that it would not do to have such as these sitting on the shelves, giving an impression of poor quality. You, however, are a Vermont woman through and through, and know the value of your money."

She sniffed, her chin going up. "A pretty can makes no difference to me, so long as the contents are as they should be. Half off, you say?"

"One third."

The woman grumbled, then nodded her consent. Catherine surreptitiously looked the woman over, noting the faded fabric of her skirt and her aged coat, the seam at the corner of the pocket having clearly been mended. Her eyes went back to the woman's face, and the tough-jawed pride evident there, and finally comprehended Mr. Goodman's peculiar behavior with the hammer.

Mr. Goodman called over one of the younger clerks to finish wrapping the woman's parcels, and then he came back to her.

"I've taken half your cards," Catherine said as he came up to her.

135

"No matter," he said, pulling out a sheet of paper and stacking the cards neatly in the center. He would not meet her eye, his attention all upon the engrossing task of wrapping her Christmas cards. She thought she could detect a tinge of red color in his neck and cheeks, contrasting with his white collar. A lock of his hair fell forward over his brow.

He doesn't like anyone knowing what he does, she intuitively understood. *He'd rather people thought him a poor businessman, than that they be aware of his charitable nature. How very peculiar.*

"I'll put these on your family's account, then," he said, tying the string and finally looking at her.

"Yes, thank you." It would save the awkwardness of handing him money, turning him into a clerk who waited upon her. "I must congratulate you on your store, Mr. Goodman. The stores in New York may be larger, but they have not half the atmosphere of congeniality as yours."

"Thank you, Miss Linwood," he said, and favored her with a smile that transformed his face, taking his regular features for a moment into the realm of masculine beauty. Coupled with that warm gaze, it was a powerful combination.

Something stirred deep within her, a gentle shifting of she knew not what. She gave an uncertain smile, and picked up her package, suddenly feeling ill at ease and eager to be gone. "Good day, Mr. Goodman."

"Good day, Miss Linwood. I do hope we meet again soon."

Will watched her as she left his store, the sleighbells he had put above the door for Christmas jingling at her departure. He saw her pause outside the door for a moment, then turn to the right, toward the village green.

When the last glimpse of her figure, gowned in dark chocolate brown and a coat edged in mink, disappeared from sight, his shoulders sagged. He gave a quiet moan and grimaced, hitting himself upon the forehead with the heel of his hand.

What a dolt she must think him. Hammering at his own cans, babbling on about Boston lithographers and Christmas cards—what did she care if his cards sold well, or where they came from?—then grinning like a simpleton when she had complimented his store. "I do hope we meet again soon," he'd said, eager as a puppy. "You'll have cramped fingers." "Did Robert not tell you this was my store?" Lord save him from himself. He must seem crude as clay in comparison to the urbane Mr. Rose.

"Joshua!" he called, and a moment later the ten-year-old appeared from a back room. "I think we're in need of Christmas greenery. Round up a couple of your friends, and we'll take the wagon into the woods to fetch some."

"Yes, sir!" Joshua whooped, and ran for his coat.

"Ann, do you want to stay or come with us?" he asked the girl who was sitting in the rocker.

"I'll stay if I may, Mr. Goodman."

He nodded, having expected the answer. He'd never known a child more in love with books. "Give Mr. Jones a shout if you need anything," he told her.

He barked orders to his clerks, desperate now to escape the shop. Heat burned his cheeks at the thought of his encounter with Miss Linwood, and it seemed the only way to extinguish it was to throw himself into the cold of outdoors. He couldn't stand to remain here at the scene of his humiliation, replaying it over and over in his mind.

"Did you want to make those deliveries, since you'll be out?" Greg, one of his clerks, asked.

"Yes, fine." It was an excuse to stay outdoors even longer, so he might as well.

It was half an an hour before the team was hitched, the orders loaded, and the boys all installed with blankets amidst the groceries, gunnysacks, pruning shears, and handsaws. Will pulled on his monstrous bearskin coat and matching hat, and climbed up onto the buckboard. Behind him, the boys were already bragging about what they'd buy with their wages from the outing, their daydreaming far outmatching their imagined income. Their enthusiasm brought a half-smile to his face. He remembered what it was like to be ten and fundless, and how exciting the prospect of earning pocket money could be.

As his mood lightened, his bumbling with Miss Linwood began to seem less of an irretrievable tragedy. She *had* said she liked his store. She had been quite complimentary on that score, and that was after all the rest, including leaving her to count out sixty cards herself. He clicked to the horses and gave them a light slap of the reins, and the wagon lumbered out from behind the store and onto Elm Street.

She had not recognized him immediately, but he imagined he must look different to her now that she was wearing spectacles. Perhaps Amy was correct, and Miss Linwood had never properly seen him at all. He thought she looked quite fetching in those fine gold frames, her liquid brown eyes gazing intently and, he assumed, clearly. He felt, somehow, that the spectacles made her a fraction more accessible to him, and a bit less an untouchable angel from another realm.

A bobbing set of feathers and a swishing brown skirt, dragging in the snow like the tail of an exotic bird, caught his eye. His heartbeat thundered, and perspiration broke out under the heavy bearskin. Ridiculous! He had but barely made her acquaintance, and he was mooning over her as if he were in love.

He slapped the reins again, the horses picking up to a trot. He eased them over to her side of the street, and slowed their pace.

"Miss Linwood!" he called, not giving himself a chance to think better of what he was about to do. "Miss Linwood!"

She turned, stopping, her expression one of utter surprise. "Mr. Goodman!"

He was calling to her on the street from a wagon buckboard. He knew it was not the behavior of a gentleman to a lady. He drew the horses to a complete halt. "Miss Linwood! We're going up to the woods to gather greenery. Would you care to join us?"

She gaped at him, eyes going to the wagon load of boys, then back to his bearskinned self.

He welcomed the gaping. Let her see that he was not Mr. Rose! Let her reject him outright, and avoid his company forever after, thus freeing him of any hope that she might someday greet his arrival with the same pleasure she had shown for her wealthy suitor.

"I—"

He waited. Let the ax fall swiftly, the stroke clean!

"I suppose I might," she said.

Oh, good lord. He sat frozen for long seconds, immobilized by those simple words of acceptance. What new hell had he bought himself, full of false hopes?

Dazed, he jumped down from the buckboard and took her parcels, handing them up to one of the boys. "Miss Linwood, may I introduce to you Joshua, Tommy, Eli, and George."

"My pleasure," she said, nodding her head to the lot.

The boys had fallen silent, shy where moments before they'd been swaggering young cocks. He remembered that feeling as well, and wished it were further in his past. Miss Linwood was neither sister nor classmate, mother nor teacher. She was a woman full-grown and lovely to look upon, and the boys were scared to death.

There was a mumbled, barely discernible chorus of "Nice to meet you." Will helped her up onto the buckboard, then climbed up beside her. He snagged a blanket from the wagon bed, and unfolded it over her lap.

She smiled at him, arranged her skirts, then settled her gloved hands atop the blanket, her back straight as if held by an iron yardstick. "I had been intending to see the woods," she said. "Thank you for inviting me to join your excursion."

"The pleasure is mine," he said, and put the wagon in motion.

Catherine swayed with the motion of the wagon, and held her chin up. As Aunt Frances had said, one could do the slightly scandalous as long as one behaved as a lady whilst one did it. She was chaperoned by four young boys, and Mr. Goodman was a friend of the family. There was no reason she should not be sitting here.

She felt her lips twitch. Aunt Frances would not have approved, however much she tried to persuade herself otherwise. One did not ride wagons into the countryside with men of brief acquaintance.

So why had she said yes? To see the woods through her new spectacles without her family to observe her, perhaps. Perhaps because she hadn't felt like returning home yet, despite the cold that had seeped through her thin boots and was numbing her toes. Perhaps, just perhaps, because Mr. Goodman had piqued her curiosity, and now that that instant of startled attraction had faded, she wanted to know a little more about him.

She turned her head slightly, trying to watch him without appearing to. He looked like a flustered bear, his blue eyes peering out with consternation from beneath his bushy black hat. He appeared, now that he had her in his wagon, to be not entirely certain of what to do with her. Mr. Rose would never have been at such a loss. It gave her a sense of power, to think that for once she was the one with the greater social ease. She was the one who was one step ahead, whereas she never was with Mr. Rose.

"Tell me, Mr. Goodman, how long have you been in Woodbridge?" she asked.

"Six years."

"Ah, indeed. And your family? Where are they?"

"I have cousins in New Hampshire." He looked like he wanted to say more, but was restraining himself. Perhaps he did not think she would find anything he said of interest.

"And do you come from a family of merchants?"

"My parents were farmers, not well off," he said, and when she nodded, making eye contact to show her interest, he continued. "It was never a life that appealed to me. One of my earliest memories is of going to the general store, and the wonder I felt looking at all those *things*, and all that candy. I thought Mr. Johnson, the owner, must be one step down from God to be owning all that. Even getting a peppermint stick into my hand was like a holiday to me. Plowing and sowing and mucking out barns seemed to me a foolish way to spend my time, when working in a store might be an option."

"What did your parents think of that?"

He shrugged his shoulders, the bear fur rising up to meet his hat. "Mother died when I was eight, and my father seemed to . . . fade after that. When I told him I'd gotten an after-school job at the store, he just muttered, and jerked his jaw forward in what I took to be acceptance."

He glanced at her. She nodded for him to go on.

"When I finished school, I went to Boston, working

141

at a large store there for a few years. I thought I needed the experience of working in a large city. Then Father died, I sold what was left of the farm, and came here and bought a small dry-goods store that was for sale."

"I remember it. 'Cooper's Dry Goods,' wasn't it?"

"The very one."

"It seems you've made a success of your enterprise. Cooper's was not much of a store."

"I've been fortunate."

Catherine thought it was likely more than that. The man might have a soft heart, but he plainly had business sense. His merchandise was of good quality and sold at fair prices, and the welcoming atmosphere of the store made it the type of place one wanted to linger and browse, even if there was nothing one needed to buy. She well knew that was a circumstance that had caused many of her own coins to flow through her fingers.

They turned down a narrow lane, and followed it to a farmhouse. He drew the horses to a halt, and called over his shoulder to the boys, "Garfields'!"

Joshua stayed in the wagon while the three other boys jumped down, then Joshua started passing goods to them, which were carried up to the door in the passage-way that connected kitchen to barn. An old woman came out a moment later, and waved to Mr. Goodman. He leaped down and went to talk with her, and after a few words the woman—Mrs. Garfield, she presumed—looked over at Catherine, met her eyes, and nodded in silent greeting. Catherine nodded back.

Catherine sat and watched the rest of the exchange, and watched the boys running to and fro with their packages and burdens. She began to find herself feeling at a social disadvantage, sitting on the buckboard of a wagon in her fashionable, frivolous clothes, the jaunty, plumed hat atop her coiled hair ridiculously inappropriate to the occasion. Mrs. Garfield was wearing a dark woolen dress, apron, and half-mittens, her hair pulled simply back and covered in an outdated cotton cap. She doubted Mrs. Garfield would walk in the snow in thin leather boots with high heels.

When they were all back in the wagon and on their way again, Mr. Goodman said, "I should have asked before: Do you mind my making a few deliveries while we're out?"

"Certainly not, I'm enjoying the ride," she said. He seemed to sense her slight lack of conviction, his eyes on her for long seconds, and she felt a flutter of panic that he might actually turn the wagon around, drive back to town, and drop her at her house if she showed the least sign of wanting to return. She didn't want that, however out of place she might feel in her finery. She might look silly and useless sitting there, but her curiosity about Mr. Goodman was yet to be satisfied, and she would not leave until it was.

They rode in silence into the woods, the boys behind them having become accustomed enough to her immobile back that they had resumed their talk. She eavesdropped, smiling when one cursed and was abruptly hushed by the others in belated consideration of her presence.

"I must have come to Woodbridge at about the same time you left for college," Mr. Goodman said. "Robert tells me you went to Mount Holyoke, down in Massachusetts."

"I thought it was a huge adventure at the time," she said, and at his prompting told him of what it had been like, and talked as well of her travels with Aunt Frances. She paused when he halted the wagon and gave the boys instructions on what greenery to fetch, but then he prompted her to continue, staying with her in the wagon, as the snowy ground was too uneven and wet for her to walk upon dressed as she was.

It wasn't until the boys were coming back with their loaded gunnysacks and, surprisingly, a tree, that she realized she had been talking for at least three quarters of an hour. Mr. Goodman exclaimed over the unexpected spruce and climbed down, and she listened with half an ear to the boys' improvised explanations of how badly he needed a tree in his store. Her mind, however, was busy berating herself for talking on and on about herself and her travels.

He must think her a pretentious, self-absorbed braggart. He had coaxed her to talk, nodding and murmuring in the right places, making eye contact and giving her the sense that he *listened*, in a way that few men ever did, but any woman should know better than to take that at face value. Hadn't she herself gone through those very motions countless times with men these past few years, feigning interest in some stultifying tale, all the while wondering when the windbag would run out of air?

She half-turned and watched with a distracted smile on her lips as they maneuvered the spruce into the wagon, the top of it hanging well over the back end. Why was she so concerned about what he might think of her, anyway?

Because you admire him, a voice inside answered. Maybe she did. He was self-made, and yet maintained a kind and generous heart. He was free of pretension, and there was something honest and solid to him that she had found in very few men besides her father. He also looked, she thought, to be a happy man.

He caught her watching him, and smiled while cocking his head at the boys, as if to say, *See how they manipulate me?* She wondered how much extra the boys were demanding to be paid, for bagging such a large piece of greenery as a spruce.

Had Mr. Goodman ever married, ever been in love? It was not the type of question she could ask him on short acquaintance. She tried to imagine what it would be like to have him courting her, and failed. He was too far from the likes of Mr. Rose and the other men who had peopled her circle of late. Would he bring a small bouquet of flowers, that unruly lock of hair on his forehead ridiculously slicked back and subdued by pomade? Would he sit in the parlor with a cup of tea trembling on his knee, and try to make conversation?

He climbed back up beside her, the boys scrambling in behind. "Are you warm enough?" he asked. "There are more blankets in back."

"I'm quite comfortable," she half-lied, and felt a twinge of guilt for her thoughts on how he might court a woman. Whomever he chose to marry, she would be smart to count herself a fortunate girl.

Chapter Five

Catherine shoved the needle through a cranberry, then carefully pulled the dark red berry along the string until it nestled up against its twin. She reached into the bowl for another, shoving aside those that had black soft spots or were half white. Papa was hunched on a stool next to the fire, shaking the long handle of the popcorn popper, the seeds rattling across the bottom of the black mesh container. Amy sat with her on the floor, sewing small lace pouches that would hold candies for the tree.

"How late will Mama be?" Catherine asked her father.

"I'm to fetch her at nine, and none too soon, I'm sure. That drama club causes her more grief than joy."

"I think she enjoys complaining about them," Catherine said.

"It's worse this year. You know she and Maggie Walsch have written their own adaptation of Dickens's *A Christmas Carol* for the stage, don't you?"

"Dear me, no. Mama did not mention that part of it."

"Well. You can imagine the state she gets in when our local thespians question their lines."

Catherine pursed her lips and raised her brows, imagining the scene very well indeed. Mama was a lamb in the general course of things, but on the occasions that a creative project was put into her direct control, she became a field marshal who brooked no opposition. Those who questioned orders or threatened desertion were put to the firing squad. "Is Mr. Goodman in the play?"

"Mr. Goodman?" her father asked, eyes on the kernels that had just begun to pop. "Of course. He's Scrooge."

"*Scrooge?*" Catherine cried. "You cannot be serious."

Papa looked over his shoulder at her. "Who better than a shopkeeper? They're notorious for being tight-fisted."

"But Mr. Goodman! Or does Mama see it as a joke?"

Papa frowned at her. "I don't quite see what you're getting at, Catherine. He's an astute businessman, and living alone like he does in that new house of his, I think he fits the part rather well. It's easier to imagine him in the role than, say, Mr. Tobias, who has a wife and six children and is on the library board."

"Do people think him a miser, then?"

"I doubt that they think of him much at all. He's a bit of a cipher, our Mr. Goodman, and keeps himself to himself," her father said approvingly.

"Papa!" Amy cried, pointing at the fire.

"What? Oh, damn me," Papa said, turning back to his task and finding the popper full of flaming popcorn. He used the long handle to open the lid, and dumped the lot into the fire. "That's the third batch."

Catherine and Amy both giggled. Papa gave them a glare.

"Why are you asking so many questions about Mr. Goodman?" Amy asked her, as Papa refilled the popper.

"Who says I am asking 'so many'? I was curious, is all," she said primly.

Oh yes, she was curious, curious because at the second farmhouse where Mr. Goodman made a delivery he came back to the wagon with a pierced tin footwarmer full of hot coals, knowing despite her denials that she was chilled. Curious, because when he had again prompted her to talk about herself, she had looked into his eyes and known that he truly was interested, and not merely feigning it out of politeness.

"Is he courting you?"

"Amy! What a ridiculous question. Of course not."

"I don't see what's so ridiculous about it. I like him, and think he would make an excellent brother-in-law."

"Oh, really," Catherine said, rolling her eyes, feeling a touch of embarrassment on her cheeks. Married to Mr. Goodman? She, the wife of the man in that enormous bearskin coat? How Mr. Rose would laugh!

"Did you ever ask Papa about Mr. Rose?" Amy asked.

"Eh, what?" Papa said, settling back onto his stool, casting another look over his shoulder at them.

"I wanted to know if Catherine had asked you your opinion of Mr. Rose," Amy said.

"No. Why? Did you want it?" he asked Catherine.

She busied herself with a cranberry, then glanced at him from under her brows. "If you were willing to give it."

"Things that serious, are they?"

"I wouldn't say that, Papa, but I trust your judgment and Mama's."

He gave the popper a shake. "He'd be able to provide for you, there looks to be no question of that. He's personable, and cuts a fine figure. He seems to have taken quite a fancy to you." He chewed the inside of his lower lip, eyes focused on the distance.

Catherine waited. "And?" she prompted.

"Hmm?" he said, pulled from his reverie.

"And what else?" she asked.

"And nothing else. He appears an eligible enough young man."

"But—What of his character? What type of husband would he make?" Catherine complained, unsatisfied. "Is he a good man? Would he be a good father?"

"I don't have a crystal ball, Catherine, and I barely know the man. You are the one who has spent time with him. You know the answers better than I would."

She gave a little grunt of frustration. Why was it a parent never had an opinion when you most wanted one, but was free enough with advice when you were in no mood to hear it?

"Damn me!" Papa cried again, and Amy shrieked in laughter as another batch of popcorn went up in flames.

"You have no idea how jealous I am of you right now," Melinda whispered into Catherine's ear. "I think he's the most handsome man I've ever seen." They were standing in the doorway to Melinda's house, Mr. Rose a few steps away on the short bricked path through the yard.

Catherine smiled at her friend, and at the baby she held bundled in her arms. "Nor have you any idea how jealous I am of you." Her childhood friend was married and a mother twice over. Her house was small and untidy, and she could only afford one maid-of-all-work, but she looked content.

"Hurry up and go now, or some Woodbridge spinster will lose her senses and kidnap him right before our eyes," Melinda said.

"I'll call on you again soon."

"Do. I can never seem to get out of the house when I have a baby underfoot."

Catherine pressed a kiss onto the downy forehead of the child, said her final farewells, and joined Mr. Rose where he waited, leaning his right hand atop his ebony-and-gold cane.

"Your friend is quite charming," he said as she took his arm and they began to walk.

"I am glad you think so. She was taken with you, as well."

"Such a sweet, simple girl. I can see how you would like her."

"I've known her since we were two, and she is not entirely as simple as she may seem," Catherine said, a faint touch of annoyance spoiling her mood. Was that a patronizing tone she had heard in his voice?

Mr. Rose laughed. "I've offended you! My dear," he said and, tucking his cane under his arm, he reached over to pat her hand where it rested in the crook of his arm. "I meant 'simple' in the best of all possible ways. She is unspoiled, and possessed of those 'simple' virtues that any man would wish for in a wife."

"Then I apologize," she said, and wondered what was wrong with her. If Melinda was to be believed, she was the envy of every unwed young woman in Wood-bridge—and not a few of the married ones as well—and yet she was not entirely pleased to be walking beside Mr. Rose at this moment. He had returned from Boston the night before, and today when he came to the house had expressed his profound happiness to be once more in her company. He had made her mother laugh with stories about his Boston relatives, and then had readily agreed to accompany Catherine on her visit to Melinda. So why was it that she found herself ever so slightly irritated by his presence? Why, when he was so perfect a choice for a husband, did she find herself wishing he would go away?

"Your apology is most graciously accepted," he said playfully, and they turned a corner and began walking along the side of the village green. They had gone some distance in silence when he spoke again, somewhat puzzled. "Catherine, I do believe that man is waving to you," he said.

Catherine squinted into the distance, trying to make out of whom he spoke. She was not wearing her spectacles, and everything except the sidewalk a few feet in front of her was a blur. Her irritation rose a notch, for if Mr. Rose were not with her she *would* be wearing them, and seeing for herself who waved, thank you very much.

She knew it was her own vanity at fault, and not Mr. Rose, but that realization did nothing to improve her humor. "I cannot make him out," she admitted.

"He's stopped now. He's going into a store."

"Is he?" she asked, her grip tightening on Mr. Rose's arm. "Which one?"

"I cannot tell, the tree branches block the sign. Does it matter?"

"I thought it might have been a friend of the family, Mr. Goodman. He owns a general store at the corner of Elm Street," she explained.

"Did I meet him at your welcome-home party? Perhaps it was he. Shall we go say hello? I wouldn't like him to think you had cut him."

"No, that wouldn't do . . ." she said, her voice trailing off. Mr. Rose seemed not to notice, leading her briskly toward the store. She did not like the idea of seeing him in Mr. Goodman's store, the men speaking to each other and shaking hands. There was something to it that made the nerves in the back of her neck shrink in discomfort.

Mr. Rose opened the store door to the jingling of sleighbells, and stopped short when they had taken but a few steps inside. "Here now, this *is* quaint." The spruce from the woods was standing near one of the front windows, partially decorated with popcorn strings and paper figures. On a low table in front of it sat pots of paste, scissors, colored paper, popcorn, thread, and other materials for making decorations. Two small children, too young for school, were diligently snipping and pasting together a haphazard paper chain, as well as snacking surreptitiously from the popcorn bowl. "No one would believe this at home," Mr. Rose said. "Cookies and cider! And a rocking chair!" Someone's grandfather was sitting in the rocker, head on his chest as he snoozed near the warmth of the woodstove.

Catherine wondered what mocking stories Mr. Rose would tell his friends in New York about "quaint" Woodbridge when he returned. Would she have to sit and listen while he imitated Mr. Goodman and his quiet ways to the guests at the dinner table?

A figure approached, and even before he was clear to her eyes, she knew it was Mr. Goodman. "Miss Linwood, Mr. Rose. It's a pleasure to see you," he said, and as he came within her field of vision she saw that he was wearing a grocer's apron over his vest and shirt. His hair flopped down over his forehead as he shook hands with Mr. Rose, and Catherine could not help but think—and feel traitorous and small for the thinking—that Mr. Goodman suffered for standing next to Mr. Rose, tall and elegant in his well-tailored clothes, his wavy hair as black as midnight.

Mr. Goodman looked what he was, a shopkeeper in a town of middling size, shorter and broader than Mr. Rose, his coloring unremarkable. On the surface, there was nothing to set him apart from the dentist three doors down, or one of the innumerable law clerks at the courthouse.

Then his eyes met hers, and in an instant she found what she had seen before: kindness and understanding, humor that crinkled the corners of his eyes, and a quiet happiness in the soft blue depths that drew her with its promise.

"We saw you wave from across the green," Mr. Rose

explained, then took a considering look around the front room. "I've never seen a store like this. I almost want to steal the rocker from that old man, and settle down for a nap myself. You should take your business to New York. Such a style of store would make shopping a great deal more pleasant for gentlemen forced to accompany their ladies. You would make a fortune!" Catherine felt certain Mr. Rose was offering false flattery. He preferred his shops to have marble floors, and clerks who fawned.

"Neither I nor my store are made for a large city. The pace here pleases me quite well," Mr. Goodman said, and then added with a straight face, "My only regret is that there is no front porch on which old men can whittle and play checkers in the summer."

Mr. Rose stared at Mr. Goodman for long seconds, and then burst out laughing, slapping him on the shoulder. "There's more going on than meets the eye with you, isn't there?"

Catherine found herself embarrassed for Mr. Rose and Mr. Goodman both, for what they must think of each other. She sensed a wire-thin tension between them, growing stronger by the minute. She shifted in discomfort.

"I am no more than you see," Mr. Goodman said. "I should very much like to continue our conversation, but I'm afraid I must man the counter. Miss Linwood," he said, bowing his head toward her. "Mr. Rose."

"Mr. Goodman," she said in parting, hoping he could see in her eyes that she regretted the subtle incivility of this encounter. The corner of his left eye twitched, in the bare hint of a wink, and she tightened her lips to keep from smiling.

"I'm in need of new gloves," Mr. Rose said to her as Mr. Goodman went back to his counter. "Do you suppose I might find some here that suit me?" he asked,

153

and began to drift toward the glass-topped counters with their drawers of goods beneath.

"I told Mama I would not be gone long," Catherine said. "Would you mind terribly if we returned to the house?" She felt that Mr. Rose was but looking for the chance to find fault with the store, for no preordered gloves would pass the judgment of a man who had his sewn for his hands alone, at a cost ten times that of those to be found here. She could not bear the thought of standing by while he had Mr. Goodman bring out pair after pair, each found wanting, except for maybe one that he would deign to buy, if only to put Mr. Goodman more firmly in the ungentlemanly role of merchant by placing money in his hand.

"As you wish," he agreed amiably, and held out his hand for her to see the small place where the stitching in his glove had come undone. "I'll return later on my own."

She closed her eyes, shamed by her own thoughts about Mr. Rose and his motivations. She could no longer tell what was real, and what was imagined from her own doubts.

They walked back to her house, the sidewalks shoveled clear of snow but slick spots still making her glad to have Mr. Rose's arm for support. She wished she could wear her spectacles, and enjoy the light of the early afternoon sun on the snow.

At her door Mr. Rose stopped her when she would have reached for the latch, gently turning her to face him as they stood on the step. "You know that I care for you, don't you, Catherine?" he said, his gloved fingers touching lightly at the side of her cheek. It was the first time he had used her given name, and she was too struck by the look in his dark eyes to protest the familiarity.

Was this what love looked like? He gazed at her with

pleading, as if she were the sun, and all his world would be winter without her. It seemed to her in that moment that despite his wealth and good looks, despite his social standing and charm, he needed her to save him from some dark emptiness hidden deep within.

She took hold of the hand touching her cheek, and squeezed it. "You have become a dear friend," she told him. Propriety limited her to such a gentle declaration, but she did not know if she could in truth have said more. She was thankful she did not have the option, and thus was not forced to reject it with him gazing at her in such a way.

"I brought you a gift," he said, and reached into a pocket inside his coat.

"I could not—"

"Please, Catherine," he said, taking out a small package wrapped in red paper. "Do not decline me this pleasure. Take it."

Reluctantly, she took it from his hand and held it against her chest, feeling that her acceptance was creating a tie by which she did not wish to be bound. "Thank you. Shall I open it now?"

He touched her cheek again, briefly. "Open it later."

She nodded. He smiled, and leaned closer. Her eyes widened and she tensed, sensing that he wanted to kiss her. A moment later he had leaned away again, and then was leaving, touching the brim of his hat to her as he sauntered down the path. She stared after him, and then, not wanting him to turn and catch her doing so, she quickly let herself into the house, shutting the door firmly behind her.

"Catherine, is that you?" Mama called from the small sitting room that served as her office.

"Yes, Mama." She followed her mother's voice, finding her sitting at her desk with various lists and Christmas cards spread over it.

"No matter how much one accomplishes in preparation for Christmas, there is always something more to do," Mama complained as she came into the room. Catherine dropped the gift and her coat on the small settee, then went to the fire and lifted the front of her skirts to let the heat reach her legs. "It seems I spend the entire month of December preparing, and then when it is all over I spend another month cleaning up. It gets worse every year. We didn't have Christmas trees when I was a little girl, you know. Things were much simpler. And now there are cards I must send as well! 'Twas an evil fellow who dreamed that up."

"You must let me help you more."

Mama waved her hand, shooing away her concern. "I have it all organized up here," she said, and tapped her temple. "I have your duties mapped out, do not worry yourself on that score. What's that?" she asked then, spotting the red box.

Catherine let her skirts drop and sat on the settee, lifting the box onto her lap. "A gift from Mr. Rose. He insisted I take it."

"Did he?" Mama said, brows raised suggestively.

Catherine undid the ribbon, pulled off the paper, then opened the flat box inside. "Oh," she said softly. Mama was craning her head trying to see, so she lifted the hair comb out of the box.

"Good gracious," Mama said.

"Indeed." The long comb was carved of tortoiseshell, and set with cabochons of a clear yellow stone. She did not know enough to tell what the stones were, but given Mr. Rose's wealth, she doubted he had bought her polished glass.

"It's lovely, and Mr. Rose has exquisite taste, but Catherine . . ."

"I know, Mama." Although neither Mama nor Aunt Frances had ever expressed any rules of etiquette specifically concerning hair combs, the item was perilously close to jewelry, and as such was far too personal a gift. Wearing it in her hair would, in some way, be like inviting Mr. Rose to touch her hair himself. "Should I return it to him?"

Mama was silent, a frown on her forehead as she considered. "He might take that as a rejection of more than just his gift."

"I know." She put the comb back in its box, and set it aside, then slouched down against the settee, her corset holding her torso straight even as her chin doubled, settling atop her chest. She let her hands flop to her sides.

"Catherine?" Mama said, coming over to sit beside her. "Has something changed since last we spoke of Mr. Rose?"

She flexed her hands in a minimal-effort shrug. "I don't know. Perhaps." She frowned, and rolled her head to the side to look at Mama. "I fear he is much more attached to me than I to him. He has put his heart on his sleeve, and I find myself wishing he would put it back inside his vest, out of sight. *Why*, Mama? Why should I feel that way? He is handsome and charming and rich, and I should be delighted that he has lost his heart to me. Is there something amiss with my own heart, that I do not respond as I should?"

"Perhaps he is not the man for you, and your heart knows it."

"I must be a very spoiled sort of girl if I am not satisfied with the likes of Mr. Rose. Perhaps the next man who catches my interest, I will grow tired of just as quickly. Mr. Rose has everything: Why have I lost my regard for him?"

"Catherine, you cannot force yourself to love someone simply because he seems to everyone else to be a perfect choice. If you do not love the man, then all the good

157

looks and money in the world are not going to make you happy."

"I am not completely certain I could not love him," she said doubtfully. "And I do like him very much. Or I did. I do not understand why I have lately found myself so annoyed by his presence."

Mama patted her on the knee. "I think you will come to the right decision in time concerning Mr. Rose."

"What do you think I should do, Mama?"

Her mother smiled cryptically. "It would be of no use for me to say. Rest assured, when you come to your own conclusion, it will likely be the same I would have advised."

"Sometimes it is comforting being told what to do."

"And when have you ever wanted to do what you were told? No, I shall save myself the trouble and let you figure this out for yourself. If you want the comfort of being told what to do, you may smile prettily while I give you your chores tomorrow."

Chapter Six

"Mr. Rose isn't coming with us, is he?" Amy asked, fastening the side buttons on her skating skirt. They were in their bedroom, dressing for the outdoors.

"I did not invite him, although I think perhaps I should have."

"Why would you have wanted to do *that*?"

"Amy! Because it would have been a small enough gesture, especially as the poor man has been alone here all this week, thanks to me." After giving her the hair comb, Mr. Rose had come daily to the house inviting her to walk or go for a sleigh ride, but each time she had put him off with protestations that there was too much to do in preparation for the holiday. She had not even let him in the house, or offered refreshments, her discomfort with the gift and all it implied making her uncomfortable in his presence, and yet she was too cowardly to be frank about her feelings. After several days of such treatment, he had ceased calling.

For the past few days Catherine had been free of either the sight or sound of Mr. Rose, but with his absence had come a sense of guilt and obligation toward the man, for he had only made the journey to Woodbridge because of her, and had held her in high enough regard to pour out the secrets of his heart. It had been callous of her to brush him off as she had, and with no explanation. She had formerly believed herself a friend to the man, and knew she owed him a face-to-face conversation on what could and could not be between them.

The guilt she felt over her unspoken rejection of Mr. Rose was only compounded by her growing attraction to Mr. Goodman. For the past week her only break from making wreaths, ornaments, centerpieces, and decorated cookies had been walks to Mr. Goodman's store to purchase items that she convinced herself were utterly necessary to the completion of the projects Mama had set for her. She had taken to dawdling there, chatting with him when he was free, or watching him help a customer from the corner of her eye if he was busy, as she pretended to page through the most recent *Harper's Weekly*. Yesterday she had made certain to mention, as if in passing, that she and Amy would be skating today.

She wondered if Mr. Goodman thought her a pest, or at least a trifle strange, to be spending so much time in his store. She was likely making a spectacle of herself to those who noticed her repeated, lingering presence, but Mr. Goodman himself showed no sign of thinking her visits remarkable. He treated her, she supposed, with the same kindness with which he treated everyone. When he looked at her, there was no hint of the needy-dog look that had haunted Mr. Rose's eyes as he declared his love to her. Mr. Goodman was self-contained, and for all that his character was clear to see on his face, his innermost passions were still private.

She pushed her spectacles up her nose. She had started wearing them earlier in the week, and after a few surprised comments, her family had largely forgotten them, acting after a day or two as if she had always worn them. Except for Amy, that is. Catherine thought her sister possessed of an obsessive fascination with the spectacles, and Amy had given a wide-eyed shiver of excitement when Catherine had let her try them on.

"Are you two ready, then?" Papa called up the stairs. "The horse will freeze to death if it has to wait much longer."

Catherine rolled her eyes, and caught Amy doing the same. Papa liked to blame an animal for his impatience or bad temper, whenever the situation allowed.

Papa dropped them from the buggy at the edge of the road, the pond no more than a hundred yards off. A dozen or more townsfolk, children and adults, were already there, skating round the oblong that had been cleared of snow.

They trudged down the path to the side of the pond, and sat upon the logs that had been arranged there for putting on skates. A fire had been built behind one of the other logs, to warm those who either tired or had come only to watch. Catherine searched the skaters for an upright bear, disappointed when there was none to be seen. The disappointment lessened when she took a moment to remind herself what a wonder it was to be able to see the faces of skaters thirty feet away. She was in danger already of taking her new clarity of vision for granted.

"Have I caught you coming or going?" a familiar voice asked, as a bulk of bearskin sat down next to Amy.

"Mr. Goodman!" Amy exclaimed. "We've just arrived. It's been ages since Catherine skated here, you know."

"Has it now?"

" 'Twould be best if you showed her which places to avoid." And then, all innocence, "Is that Becky over there?" she asked, peering across the pond. She finished fastening her skates onto her boots, and stood up. "You don't mind if I go join her, do you, Cath?"

Catherine raised her brows at her. "No, not at all," she said, and Amy skated off.

"Did that wire work as you wished, for the wreaths?" Mr. Goodman asked companionably as he bent down to put on his own skates. It was as if they were simply carrying on where their conversation had left off the day before in the store.

"It was just what I needed, thank you. Papa is using what was left for fastening the candles to the tree." Had Mr. Goodman come to the pond because she had told him she would be here, or would he have come anyway? she wondered.

"I don't suppose you have much opportunity to skate in New York."

"On the contrary, the ponds in Central Park are quite crowded with skaters throughout the winter. They are an especially popular place for courting couples," she said, and to her embarrassment found herself giving him a coy, sideways look.

"Are they?" he said mildly. "I would have to say the same use is made of the pond here." He nodded his head toward the skaters, and following his gaze she saw a young couple, the man taking great care as he guided his companion's efforts upon skates, reaching out to catch her when she seemed in danger of falling. The young woman shrieked and laughed as she stumbled awkwardly about, clinging to her beau's arm.

"I'd wager my best hat that she skates better than she lets on," Catherine said.

Mr. Goodman laughed. "But that's not the point, is it? Shall we?" he asked, standing and holding out his hand to her.

"I warn you now I am not going to slip and fall like

that young woman, and neither do I shriek."

"I did not expect that you would, although laughing is not forbidden, so long as it is not at me," he said, giving that smile that turned his average face glowingly handsome, and made her heart contract.

She took his hand, gazing up at him and wishing he showed some sign of wanting to court her. From the way he behaved, she had no reason to think he thought any more of her than that she was the sister of a friend, the daughter of a family he respected, and perhaps a pleasant person with whom to converse. Had he even once looked at her as a potential sweetheart? she wondered.

Looking into his eyes, there was such understanding and interest, even admiration, it hurt to admit that he probably shared the same look with everyone. She knew somehow that he was a man whose kindness would not be limited to those he liked, and it ate at her that she could not tell if there was anything in that look meant especially for her.

"I shall have no limits placed upon my laughter, Mr. Goodman," she said, reaching the edge of the pond and releasing his hand as she glided out onto the ice. "If you fall, I shall laugh myself silly."

"Not if I pull you down with me," he said, and glided toward her.

She shrieked, then dashed away, and felt a flaming heat bloom on her cheeks. Had she truly just shrieked, after saying she would not? Oh, God . . . She glanced over her shoulder, and saw the bear was almost upon her. Another shriek pealed forth, and she dug her skates into the ice, racing to evade him. Her heart was beating wildly, perspiration breaking out, her muscles electrified by the thrill of being chased around the pond.

Will skated after Miss Linwood, the playful fun of pursuing her knocking up against the thought that she might be flirting with him. Might she be? It hardly seemed possible, but . . .

He caught up to her and grabbed her hand, swinging her around. She made another of those laughing shrieks, and he took her other hand as well, swinging her around him in a circle. "Stop! Stop!" she cried, laughing. "I'm going to fall."

He slowed, then brought her to a halt. She swayed, dizzy, and he pulled her closer, her feet motionless as she glided to him. She released his hands and grabbed higher up his arms for support, blinking her warm brown eyes at him as her vertigo passed.

"That was most unfair of you, Mr. Goodman," she said. "If I had fallen, it would not have counted, as it would have been entirely your fault."

"All's fair in love and war," he said, the words out before he could stop them.

She grinned mischievously at him. "And we both know which this is," she said, and skated away before he could respond, leaving him watching dumbly after her.

No, he didn't know which it was, not for her! And did she have any notion of what he felt for her, that it was deeply, desperately love, and not war?

She cast him one backward glance, as if daring him to follow and capture her again.

The shyness that had overcome him upon first meeting her was still with him, making it nearly impossible for him to show her that his interest was more than platonic. His natural reserve, which such a short time ago he had enjoyed, was in this case a torturous barrier that he did not know how to surmount.

The only way to prevent himself from gibbering like an ape in her presence was to pretend to himself that she was already a close friend. When she came to the store, he struggled to shut away his shyness into a dark, locked box, and refused to second-guess his actions and words. He coaxed her into talking about herself and her family's Christmas preparations, and as she talked he gradually forgot about his locked-away shyness. He teased her gently, making her laugh in those rich tones that grabbed at his heart. He helped her to find the goods on her list, discussions of each item wandering off into uncharted realms. The circuitous route of conversation led from ribbons to favorite desserts, from oranges to the time she had climbed Mt. Tom, from cloves to their mutual love of the novels of Wilkie Collins.

There was always one more topic to discuss, one more direction in which to take the conversation, and then she would take a glance at the watch pinned to her breast and give a start, apologizing for keeping him so long from his work. Each extra minute she stayed afterward was a victory, the visible reluctance with which she left him a boost to the morale of his advancing army.

He watched her figure gracefully moving through the other skaters at the opposite end of the pond, pausing briefly to skate a circle around Amy and her friend.

Miss Linwood's visits had given his attachment to her a deeper basis than a pretty face and infectious laugh. Her conversation was informed and perceptive, her mood usually one of quiet merriment. She was vivacious without being vulgar, mischievous without being cruel, intelligent without condescension. His heart had somehow known, at first sight, what it would find in her.

Even with her hints of flirtatious encouragement, though, the thought of openly courting her, exposing his heart for all to see, left him feeling ill. There was something within him that would not permit such a display.

He would not, could not try to persuade her to love him with sweet words and gifts of candy and flowers. He could not call on her, sitting like a lovesick fool in her parlor, while her mother hovered nearby as chaperone. By embarrassing himself, he knew that he would embarrass her, and put in jeopardy any fondness that she held for him. No, it was better to continue his attack of stealth.

"You shall become a snowman if you stand there much longer," Miss Linwood said, skating up beside him and scraping expertly to a stop. She had made the circuit of the pond while he stood frozen, contemplating his adoration of her. It had begun to snow, and glancing down he saw that a fine layer of it covered his coat.

"Of what were you thinking, to transfix you so?" she asked.

"Of how best to catch you, of course," he said, and raised his arms as if to do so. She gasped, and in her haste to back away lost her balance. He moved quickly, doing exactly as he'd said before she could fall. She was a welcome weight in his arms, her cheek pressed to his chest, her hands clinging to the fur of his coat, but he released her as soon as she had regained her feet. He skated away at a gentle pace, and after a moment she followed, gliding easily into place at his side as they circled the pond.

"You tricked me," she accused.

"I did nothing."

"Yes, and it was quite clever of you."

He smiled, but did not answer.

Chapter Seven

Catherine settled into her seat between Amy and Mr. Rose. They were in the McMahon family's old barn, converted two years ago into the drama club's theater. Doves and chickens were known to roost overhead, and the place would never completely escape the faint scents of its former use, but the fowl had been chased out for this night, and likely no one but Mr. Rose minded the smells of chickens and dust.

"My friends will never believe this," Mr. Rose said, shifting on his hard wooden chair and peering into the raftered gloom.

Catherine felt a spark of irritation invade her good mood. "Are you going to mock my mother's production to them?" she whispered fiercely, casting him a narrow-eyed glare.

"I would never do such a thing!" he exclaimed in a whisper, and grasped her gloved hand in both of his. "Catherine, you know I would not," he said, and gave her the wounded look that turned her stomach more each time she saw it.

167

"This play means a great deal to her," she said, and gently pulled her hand away.

"I know it does. And to you, too, so you may rest assured that I will applaud mightily at the final curtain."

Even those words annoyed her, sounding to her as if he doubted the play could possibly merit such grand regard. She wished she had not invited him along, but guilt had made her do so. After returning from skating, she had found a note waiting from him, explaining that he had fallen ill with some manner of ague and was only now near recovery, and that he was more sorry than he could say that he had been unable to call on her those past several days.

She felt it was too sad for anyone to be ill and alone during the Christmas season, as he had been. And so, the invitation to the play. He had accompanied her, her father, and Amy to the barn theater.

She hoped for some point later in the evening to have a chance to speak privately with him. It was easy enough to see that he had not been well, although he claimed now to be fully back to health. His skin was colorless, his eyes bloodshot, and when he moved she sometimes caught a strange scent wafting from him. A devil in the back of her mind wondered if he had spent those days of "illness" drinking himself prone. She quashed the thought as unworthy.

The last of the audience straggled in, finding places in the seats that remained. The hard wooden chairs sat on risers that thumped hollowly under their feet, and the rustling and whispering began to settle as the lantern lights were lowered. When all had quieted to an expectant silence, and all eyes and ears waited for the curtain to rise, there came a deep, gutteral cry from off-stage: "Bah, humbug!"

Catherine put her hand to her lips, smothering the laugh that wanted to slip forth as she recognized Mr.

Goodman's voice under the grouching exclamation of Scrooge. The curtain lifted upon the stark scene of Ebenezer Scrooge's counting house, the bare furniture and the meager coal scuttle, and she joined the others in applauding a welcome to the two actors sitting at their worktables.

Catherine rummaged in her reticule for her spectacles, slipping them on in the safety of the dark. She'd leave them on, too, and nevermind what Mr. Rose might think. She ought to have more backbone than to let his likely opinion of a pair of spectacles alter her behavior. If he saw fit to mock them, well, then, let him, she thought, lifting her chin and giving a little sniff. Perhaps he would find them so unattractive he would go back to New York and leave her to enjoy Christmas with her family in peace, with her having to say nary a word.

Mr. Goodman was all but unrecognizable in his costume, his hair colored gray and lines of miserliness drawn into his cheeks and under his eyes. He played the role of Scrooge with enthusiasm, being as sour and bad-natured as Dickens could have wished, if not more so.

Scrooge's nephew had come into the counting house, and for some minutes had been arguing cheerily with Scrooge about the worth of Christmas. "So 'a Merry Christmas,' Uncle!"

"Good afternoon!" Mr. Goodman barked, for the third time trying to dismiss the happy man.

"And 'a Happy New Year'!" the nephew gaily chirped, to the laughter of the audience. Catherine thought she even heard a reluctant snort of amusement from Mr. Rose.

"Good afternoon!" again, from Scrooge.

Catherine caught Amy's eye, sharing a smile with her. "He's good," Amy whispered. Catherine nodded. Seeing Mr. Goodman onstage, even playing the part of a despicable miser, had the curious effect of magnifying his attraction. She felt a queer sense of possessive pride over him.

The play progressed, flour-faced ghosts arrived and went, and then Mama was on stage, as Mrs. Cratchit serving the Christmas goose and pudding to her family as Scrooge and the ghost of Christmas Present watched from the side. Catherine and Amy both giggled to see Mama in costume, and then Bob Cratchit made his toast.

"A Merry Christmas to us all, my dears. God bless us!"

The Cratchit family repeated the toast, and into the following silence came Tiny Tim's voice, "Dog bless us everyone!"

Mama stared wide-eyed at the little boy, as did the rest of the Cratchit family. Scrooge winced in sympathy. The little boy's face turned scarlet, as he realized what he'd said.

"Mr. Goodman!" Mr. Cratchit said, trying to gloss over the boy's error by hurriedly raising his glass in the next toast.

Mr. Goodman, startled at hearing his own name on-stage, uttered an audible, "Eh?"

Suspicious coughing sounds rippled through the audience.

"Mr. Scrooge! Mr. Scrooge, I mean to say," Cratchit corrected, waving his glass and spilling his drink over both his hand and Tiny Tim, who looked on the verge of tears at this further insult to his pride. "I'll give you Mr. Scrooge, the Bounder of the Beast!"

"The *founder* of the *feast*, indeed!" Mama cried, to more muffled coughing. "I wish I had him here," Mama continued. "I'd give him a beast of my mind—*piece* of my mind, damn it!-" Mama swore, as the Cratchit family bowed their heads, their shoulders shaking, "—to feast upon, and I hope he'd have a good appetite for it!"

"My dear, the children!" Bob Cratchit reproached

softly, covering Tiny Tim's ears, his face as tenderly disappointed as a saint's. "Christmas day."

Hoots and snorts of laughter burst out, both onstage and in the house. Catherine, Amy, and Papa joined in, safe under the cover of the crowd from the wrathful glare Mama sent out into the darkened theater.

"It should be Christmas day, I am sure," Mama said with vehemence and a withering look cast over the audience as she carried on with her speech. By force of will she seemed to settle them all, although Catherine heard a whispered, "*Piece* of my mind, damn it!" behind her, amidst shushing and giggling. She bit her own lips to keep from joining in.

The play made it safely to its conclusion with only minor mishaps, the cast all assembling onstage as a narrator read out the ending of the story, explaining how Scrooge became a good man, who kept Christmas well and avoided spirits ever after. Tiny Tim stepped forward and with extreme care enunciated the final line. "God bless us, everyone!"

Tiny Tim's real parents, in the audience, leaped up and shouted "Hurrah!" and applauded wildly as the curtain came down. Catherine joined them, and then the whole audience was on its feet, clapping and cheering as the curtain came up again upon an empty stage. The actors re-emerged, one by one, accepting their applause with great grins upon their faces.

When Mr. Goodman came out, the applause turned into as much of a roar as could be gotten from a crowd of such small size, and Catherine found herself stomping on the echoing risers in her approbation, and then she yanked off a glove and stuck two fingers in her mouth to give a piercing whistle.

"Good Lord, Catherine, control your enthusiasm!" Mr. Rose hissed beside her.

"Control your*self*, Mr. Rose!" she snapped back, and

gave another whistle, twice as long as the first.

Mr. Goodman put his hand to his mouth, then threw a kiss to the audience, his eyes meeting Catherine's as he did so. She laughed, delighted, and was aware of Mr. Rose stiffening beside her.

The applause finally quieted, and the curtain fell for the final time. The lights were raised, and people began to leave, slowly, mingling near the exit and in front of the stage, talking about the performance as they inched their way outside. Some, like Catherine and her group, lingered inside, waiting for a cast member. Someone raised the curtain again, and a crew member appeared with a broom, quickly sweeping the stage and then disappearing behind the panels that formed the rear of the stage.

"She told me earlier she would need about fifteen minutes to change and put away her things," Papa said.

Mr. Rose touched Catherine's arm, lightly, and bent near her. "I'm going out for a breath of air. Would you care to join me?"

She shook her head, not looking at him, and pulled away just enough that his hand dropped from her sleeve. It would be a good chance to speak with him, but she was in no temper to do so civilly, after his attempt to shush her applause.

Mr. Rose hesitated, the answer plainly not what he had expected, then turned and pushed through the remaining crowd to the exit. Catherine saw that Papa was watching her, and she gave him a forced smile, trying to hide what she was feeling. He was usually obtuse to what the females of his family felt, but he had that look that said this was one of those rare occasions where his intuition and observations had come together to form a correct conclusion.

"Shall we take a look at the props?" Catherine asked Amy, for distraction. It was bad of her to snub Mr. Rose, after she had invited him here tonight, and yet she could not seem to help behaving coldly toward him.

She and Amy climbed the two steps up onto the stage, and inspected the furnishings of Mr. Scrooge's counting house. They could hear the excited chatter of the cast and crew behind the panels, as they changed clothes in the converted stalls and put all in order for tomorrow's matinee performance.

A few minutes later the cast began to depart, their earlier air of excitement subdued now as tiredness took hold. When Mr. Goodman came out, Catherine slid off Bob Cratchit's tall stool where she had been sitting, playing out the clerk's role to Amy's amusement. "You were wonderful, Mr. Goodman, wonderful!" she said. "I should never have thought you would make such a perfect Scrooge if I had not seen it for myself."

"That is high praise, coming from one who has likely seen the best actors that London has to offer."

"High praise, but deserved." She smiled up at him, her twinges of guilt about Mr. Rose vanquished for the moment by the warmth of Mr. Goodman's presence. "You seemed to be enjoying yourself onstage."

He ducked his head slightly, the lock of hair falling over his forehead. "I am surprised myself by my enjoyment. Except for in the theater, I do not like to be the center of attention. It is as if there is a side to me that only comes out upon a stage."

"Does that mean you aren't quite the reserved, noble man you seem?" Catherine asked in a purr.

He shot her a quick look, one that asked if that question was meant to be as flirtatious as it sounded. "We are none of us exactly as we might seem, nor are we as we might wish," he said.

She was about to ask him what he would change about himself—she could imagine nothing in him that was in need of alteration—when she felt a hand on her

173

arm. It was Mr. Rose. She had not heard him come back in, so absorbed was she in Mr. Goodman.

"Come, Catherine," Mr. Rose ordered, and started to pull her away. "It is time you went home."

She jerked her arm out from under his hand. "Mr. Rose, I am not yet ready to depart," she said, and looked up at him from behind her spectacles. She did not like what she saw. Every suspicion she had had of his character was written more plainly on his features tonight than ever before. There was something wild and unstable in his eyes, something desperate and needy that repelled her. She sniffed the air, catching again that strange scent coming off him. "Mr. Rose," she asked as quietly as she could. "Have you been drinking?"

He took her arm again, pulling her away from Mr. Goodman and leaning down to whisper at her. "If I have, whose fault is that?" Mr. Rose said, his breath making her step back. "You have been playing games with me, Catherine, first enticing me to follow you to this backwater town, then snubbing my attentions and trying to make me jealous by making eyes at that sorry shopkeeper. And what manner of affectation are *these*?" he asked, and pulled the spectacles from her face. "I don't know what joke you're making, except on yourself by wearing them."

She couldn't speak for astonishment at his temerity, and then her chest filled with air as that astonishment gave way to hot, poisonous fury. "How *dare* you, Mr. Rose!" she accused, her voice louder than she had intended. She could not recall ever being so incensed, and in a distant way was astounded by the rising, angry pitch of her own voice. "You have no right, *no right,* to lay your hands upon my person so! You have *no right* to blame me for your drunkenness, and you *certainly* have no right to address me by my Christian name. *Mr.*

Rose." Her next words were exactly enunciated. "Have I made myself clear?"

"You've made yourself clear enough, and shown your true colors, too," Mr. Rose said as angrily back. "Be careful, Mr. Goodman," he called past Catherine's shoulder, "if you allow such a one as this to lead you a merry chase. She has the heart of a whore, and won't be happy until she sees you grovelling in the dust for her favors."

Catherine heard her father give an angry shout, but it was Mr. Goodman who was first to respond, coming immediately to her defense. "No one may speak of Miss Linwood in such terms, sir," Mr. Goodman said in a steady, hard voice. "No one. You will apologize to her and to her family."

"Or what?" Mr. Rose sneered. "You'll make a play at chivalry and hit me? That will do nothing to change the truth."

"If you do not apologize," Mr. Goodman said lowly, "then we will all know that you are no gentleman, and a disgrace to your family's good name."

"No *gentleman*? Ha! And who are you to be judging who is and is not a gentleman? A shopkeeper! A peddler!"

"Do not make this more difficult than it has to be," Mr. Goodman warned.

"You want a fight, do you? You think you can best me?" Mr. Rose tossed Catherine's spectacles to the side, where they landed under a worktable and skidded along the floorboards. "I'll show you what gentlemen are made of." He lowered his head and charged.

Mr. Goodman stepped easily aside, and Mr. Rose, deprived of his target, stumbled past, unable to stop before running crown-first into a supporting post of the loft. He crashed down upon Scrooge's coal scuttle with a clamoring of metal and lay still.

175

Mr. Goodman bent and picked up the spectacles in the following silence, and wiped them carefully with his kerchief before handing them back to Catherine. "I'm terribly sorry about all this," he said. "I'll take him back to the inn."

"Oh no, Mr. Goodman, I couldn't ask that of you," Catherine said, and found to her surprise that she was shaking. She did not know if it was her own anger, Mr. Rose's unkind words, or the narrowly averted violence that had her trembling so.

"You do not need to ask. The man had too much to drink, and was not in his right senses. Please, try to forget what he said." He met her eyes, and the calm strength there helped to steady her, making her feel as if he held her safe in his arms. Her breathing evened out.

"You are being too kind," Papa said, coming up onto the stage and staring down at the sprawled form of Mr. Rose. "He deserves to be dragged to a snowbank and left there 'till spring."

"He's not worth the worry."

"Eh?" Papa asked.

"Of being hung for murder," Mr. Goodman clarified. "It would spoil my appetite for Christmas dinner. I do not think he is worth that."

Papa laughed. Amy went to Mr. Rose and glared down at him, with a look in her eye that said she'd very much like to kick him. Catherine felt her mother's hand on her shoulder. "It's time to go home," Mama said.

Amy came over and took Catherine's hand, squeezing it in silent support. The gesture put her on the verge of tears. The three of them left, leaving Papa and Mr. Goodman to deal with the unconscious Mr. Rose.

Chapter Eight

"Good gracious, Robert, what did you put in this?" Catherine asked her brother, after taking a sip of his eggnog. It was proudly displayed in an enormous crystal bowl surrounded by cuttings of holly, in the center of a lace-covered table. She would not have been surprised to see blue flames rising from the heavy yellow drink, for certainly there was more of the *nog* to it than the *egg*.

"I made it according to George Washington's own recipe. My friend from Virginia sent it to me. He says his family has made it this way for nigh on a century."

Catherine took another sip, her head filling with the fumes of brandy, whiskey, and God knew what else. "Then I am surprised they survived this long, and surprised as well that we were not left under British rule!"

Her brother laughed and filled a cup for another of his guests. He and his wife, Mary, had opened their house to friends and family for Christmas Eve, and the spacious rooms were crowded with New Englanders who had suspicions there was something irreligious in having a spirited Christmas party, but were reluctantly enjoying themselves nonetheless.

Catherine wandered over to where a fiddler was playing lively music, to which a few couples self-consciously danced. Children raced about from room to room, playing their own games, and in another room the more sedate sat and conversed near the tree, its candles lit and carefully watched by more than one eye, lest fire should break out.

Even as she watched guests and conversed with friends, part of her was constantly searching for Mr. Goodman. There was a small commotion at the door, and Catherine's eyes went to the figure entering there. Disappointment pulled at the muscles of her face when she saw the formal, well-tailored coat, but then the man turned and it was the face she sought above the wool muffler, bearskin nowhere in evidence.

After that embarrassing spectacle at the barn, she had become leery of any move that might be considered forward or flirtatious on her part. She did not want anyone thinking she had the heart of a whore, and so although every muscle urged her to go and greet him she checked the impulse, holding back with a shyness that was new and painful.

She stood half-hidden beside a potted palm, watching as the maid took Mr. Goodman's outerwear, and Robert went to welcome his friend. She willed him to look at her, to see her, and smile and come join her. She willed him to take her hand and lead her out to dance; to stand close and smile down into her eyes; to hold her hand against his chest and ask her not to return to New York, but to stay here with him, forever, as his wife and the woman with whom he would share his bed.

He looked her way, and their eyes locked. She knew that all she felt was writ plainly in her eyes. *"Heart of a whore,"* she heard Mr. Rose say in her head. She glanced away and to the side, her lids lowered, and then long seconds later she looked toward him again. The entryway was empty.

The heat of embarrassment touched her cheeks. For all that Mr. Goodman had defended her in the theater, perhaps he felt that she had deserved Mr. Rose's insults. Part of her believed he would be right to do so.

Miss Linwood was even lovelier than the first time he had seen her, Will thought as she met his eyes from across the room. Her gaze was intense upon him, hungry and yet still. The dark green fronds of a palm formed tiger stripes across her breast, bringing to mind a great cat lurking in the jungle. She was wearing that same burgundy dress he had so admired before, its dark folds inviting touch like an animal's pelt.

She broke the stare, suddenly glancing away in a bashful gesture that was not in character with the woman he knew. It took only a moment to understand that it was the altercation with Mr. Rose that had done this to her, that had made her doubt her natural instincts.

For causing that moment of Miss Linwood's self-doubt, Will would gladly stuff Mr. Rose through a hole in the ice of the skating pond. He had wanted to do much worse to the man at the theater, but the stricken look on Miss Linwood's face had stopped him. Further violence would have served only to distress her more. No, far better to let Mr. Rose lie before her in his drunken stupor, knocked senseless of his own doing, and then gallantly volunteer to remove the offal from her sight.

"Will, you must say hello to Mr. Abernathy," Robert was saying, and pulled him away before he could protest.

Mr. Abernathy, the elderly president of a local bank, began yammering at him in words he could not understand. He saw the man's mouth moving, bits of spittle on his lips, but it was just noise to him, his thoughts obsessed with Miss Linwood and her hungry gaze. Countless impatient minutes went by as he sought holes in the conversation through which to bolt, and then at last he was free. He went in search of her.

She was no longer near the palm, nor was she in the crowd around the table with its great vat of eggnog. He went from room to room, searching, replying to the greetings of others with only a fraction of his attention. Where had she gone?

"Miss Linwood," a hoarse, low voice said behind her.

She turned, happily expectant, then stepped back when she came face-to-face with Mr. Rose. "What are you doing here?" she exclaimed, and felt a sudden queasiness in her stomach, her heart beating rapidly in what was almost fear. She was in a hallway, having just come from the washroom, and at the moment there was no one else about.

"Please, let me apologize," he said, grasping her hand. "There is so much I need to say to you."

"We have nothing left to say," she said, trying to control her voice.

"Please. Hear me out." He squeezed her hand, his eyes pleading. "You can give me that much."

She didn't want to talk to him, didn't want to be in his presence at all, nor did she want Mr. Goodman to come upon them together and think worse of her, but Mr. Rose did not look like he would be easily sent away.

"Please," he said again.

"Not here," she said brusquely. It was not physical harm she feared from him, but another raw, emotional confrontation. If it could not be avoided, at least this time it could happen in private. After a quick moment of thought she led him down a different, unlit hall to the sunroom that had been shut up for the winter, its wicker furniture covered in sheets. She could see her breath on the cold air, the room dark and forlorn out of season, illuminated only by the blue reflections of moonlight off the snow outside.

"Miss Linwood—"

"Mr. Rose," she interrupted fiercely, gathering her courage and going on the offensive. "I thought I made myself quite plain in the letter I sent to you with the hair comb. Our acquaintance is at an end."

"My behavior was unforgiveable, I know that, but I am asking you to please hear me out. Please. Miss Linwood, you cannot fail to know how I feel about you. I love you. There! I confess it! I love you, and I cannot live without you. If you were to deprive me of all hope of making you my wife, I think I should have to kill myself."

Catherine looked at him in horror. "You don't mean that. You can't!"

"But I do." He dropped down to one knee, and taking her hand began to smother it in kisses.

"Stop it, Mr. Rose! At once!" she ordered, jerking her hand from his grasp.

"Marry me, Catherine!"

"No." There seemed no other way to say it, no way in which to soften her answer. She was completely repulsed by him. Even his drunkenness had been better than this. "I will not marry you, and I shall never change my mind."

"I cannot live without you," he pleaded, tears in his eyes, his hands grasping at her skirts. "I'll kill myself."

She was furious that he would try to lay that guilt upon her. "I will not accept responsibility for your actions, Mr. Rose," she said harshly, trying to hide the quavering of her voice, hoping that her words were true. "You will leave this house, and never speak to me again. Good-bye." She yanked her skirts out of his hold and left the room, slamming the door behind her against the sound of his sobs.

In the empty hall she suddenly had to lean against the wall, her knees shaking and her breath short, nausea roiling her stomach. The muted sobbing quieted, and then she heard the outside door to the sunroom open and then swing shut, and she knew Mr. Rose had at last gone. She closed her eyes and listened gratefully to the silence.

Minutes passed, and then she heard a concerned male voice, its timbre familiar and welcome. "Miss Linwood, are you unwell?"

Catherine opened her eyes, and saw Mr. Goodman silhouetted against the faint light from the end of the hall. She released a shaky breath. "No, just a bit shaken. Mr. Rose was here. He asked me to marry him, then threatened to kill himself if I refused." She felt more than saw the sudden tension her words created in him, and quickly added, "I turned him down, and he left. He offered me neither insults nor harm." And then, the guilt she had said she would not accept crept in. "Do you think he will do himself an injury?"

Whatever feelings he was experiencing, Mr. Goodman held them under tight rein, asking only, "Was he drunk?"

"I don't think so."

"Then he should be out of danger's way for the moment. I'll send word to the inn to have someone keep an eye on him." She heard him take a breath, his hold on his temper apparently not quite as solid as she had assumed. "That was an unkind, manipulative thing of him to say to you, and I hope you do not allow it to trouble your thoughts. Mr. Rose is responsible for his own actions, and you are in no way to blame for whatever he does or does not do."

She touched her temple, brushing back a wisp of hair, feeling the dampness of perspiration on her brow. She tried to meet Mr. Goodman's eyes in the dim light, still not as certain of her innocence as she wished to be. "Have I behaved badly toward him?"

He came closer, to where she could make out his features. His expression showed no hint of judgment, his eyes telling her that he understood what she was feeling. "You did not behave badly. There is no way to save a heart from being crushed, when you cannot return its regard."

Did he mean the he would have to do the same to her? She gazed intently into his eyes, and suddenly knew it was not so, however much her fears may have tried to persuade her otherwise. This warmth in his eyes was meant for her alone, speaking of a desire that matched that in her own heart. A tingling awareness of his nearness ran across her skin. She wanted to touch him, and wanted him to touch her. She wanted to feel his lips pressed against hers, and his arms coming around her, enveloping her in the quiet strength that hid beneath his humble exterior.

She swayed toward him, one hand rising to lie against the broad warmth of his chest. He inclined his head to where their lips were a bare inch apart, her breath mingling with his. She caught a faint scent of spices and soap from his skin, and felt his heart beating beneath her palm.

They held the pose for an eternal moment, their breathing the only sound in the dark corridor, and then he reached up and clasped her hand on his chest, bringing it down. "Your family will be wondering where you've gone off to," he said, drawing back.

She ducked her head, disappointment cold upon her skin. At his prompting she slid her hand up to the crook of his arm, and let him lead her back to the party.

* * *

183

It was almost 2:00 A.M. and still Catherine could not sleep. Amy breathed heavily in her bed, only her face visible under the mound of covers, and the house was quiet. Despite the late hour, despite the eggnog from earlier in the evening, and despite the questionable relief of having made a final, irrevocable, face-to-face rejection of Mr. Rose, she could not rest.

It was not the anticipation of Christmas morning that had her tossing and turning. It was that long moment in the hall, when she had been on the verge of kissing Mr. Goodman. He had known what she wanted, and had wisely, honorably, chosen against stealing a kiss from her in the dark hallway of her brother's house, while she was yet vulnerable from the trouble with Mr. Rose.

Damn Mr. Goodman, and his noble heart. She had wanted that kiss.

And what if she had gotten it? What if she had squeezed a declaration of love from Mr. Goodman, what would she have done then? Would she truly be willing to stay in Woodbridge, to be Mr. Goodman's wife, if he would have her?

In a heartbeat.

The opera, the symphony, the theater, the artists and the writers, the bustle and sense of something new around the next corner that was New York; all that she would gladly give up, perhaps even without Mr. Goodman to go to. She was weary of New York, and the lifestyle in which she did not fit except with constant effort. She preferred unsophisticated Woodbridge, where her awkward watercolor could hang upon a wall without comment. She could be herself here, and most especially she could be herself with Mr. Goodman.

She heard a faint jingling of sleigh bells, *jing a jing a jing,* coming from outside, breaking into her thoughts. A reluctant smile sneaked its way onto her lips. Santa?

Jing a jing a jing.

Who would be out at this hour? She slipped from under the covers, and wrapping her robe around her against the chill, went to the window, picking up her spectacles on the way. She put them on, and moved aside the curtain to look at the moonlit night.

A sleigh was coming down the middle of the icy lane, drawn by two bay horses. As she watched, it came to a halt and a figure in a bulky bearskin coat hopped out, rummaged in the bags of goods piled in back, and then came toward her house.

She dropped the curtain, heart thumping, standing frozen for a moment, and then she threw off her robe and dashed for her clothes, cursing under her breath at all the fastenings it took to get them on.

Corsetless, her skirt half unbuttoned and her coat covering the equally undone state of her bodice, she dashed down the stairs in her socks and sat on the seat by the door, shoving her feet into her boots, wrapping the laces several times around her ankles in lieu of lacing them. She was out the door a second later, taking only a moment to notice the two small packages on the front step, running carefully on the icy ground to where the sleigh now waited, several houses down.

She reached it just as Mr. Goodman returned from another house. He stopped in his tracks when he saw her. Her breath was coming in gasps after her slippery sprint, and she hung onto the side of his sleigh.

"Miss Linwood!" he whispered loudly, "What in God's name are you doing out here?"

"As if you should be the one asking me such a question, Mr. Goodman! What are *you* doing out here, is more to the point," she whispered back, as conscious as he of how easily their voices would carry in the night.

"It's a secret. No one was supposed to see me."

"You might have thought to take the bells off your horses, if you were so anxious to go undetected."

"I did," he said with exaggerated patience.

"For heaven's sake, I heard them from my room," she said, moving toward the horses to point out his obvious error. She squinted, then moved her hands over the leather harnesses. There were no bells.

He raised his brows at her from over the backs of the horses.

"But . . . I *heard* them," she said. "Did someone else go by?"

"You're the only moving creature I've seen. You know, Miss Linwood, you have an uncanny knack for catching me at tasks where I would prefer to remain undiscovered."

"Poor you," she said, and gave him a mock pout. She climbed into the sleigh.

"Miss Linwood! Come down from there !"

"I am going with you. I couldn't sleep, and this promises to be much more entertaining than staring at the ceiling all night."

He hesitated a moment longer, then climbed up next to her and took the reins, setting the horses in motion with a light slap. "I'm going to be out all night, you know. You're going to get very cold."

She found the buffalo skin that was shoved to one side in a crumpled heap, and shook it out. "I shall be quite comfortable." As the horses trotted down the center of the street, it began to snow, light feathery flakes that fell gently around them. "Look, it's snowing," she said, then cocked her head to the side, frowning. "It's odd to see that, with the moon so bright."

He looked up at the night sky with her, to where the sky was nearly free of clouds. "Perhaps it is being blown off the trees and rooftops."

"Mmm," she said doubtfully. There was no wind.

The snow, as if possessed of a mind of its own, followed them in gently gusting flurries as they made their

rounds of the town, and traveled out to the neighbor-
hoods where the mill workers lived with their large families, Mr. Goodman stopping at houses where there were
children and leaving gifts upon the doorstep. The snow
swirled behind them as they drove out to farms, and it
covered their tracks when they left, removing all traces
of their passing. At the far edge of her hearing, Catherine
thought she could detect the faint jingling of sleigh bells.

Catherine soon took the reins, leaving Mr. Goodman
free to dig in his sacks for the right gift for the next
house, and she did not feel the cold. They worked in
silent concert, anticipating the needs and movements of
each other. The hours of the night seemed to stretch into
infinity, even as they flew by. It should not have been
possible to make as many stops as they did, Catherine
knew, yet somehow there was always time for one more,
until the sacks were empty and the first faint light of
dawn reached into the sky.

With dawn turning quickly to morning, she handed
the reins to Mr. Goodman and he drove her back to her
house. He helped her down from the sleigh, and led her
up the walk to her front steps. During the night they had
said nothing of what was in their hearts, and yet Catherine felt that an understanding had been silently
reached, that during their early morning ride a bond had
been formed between them that was meant to last a lifetime.

"Mr. Goodman," she said softly, looking up at him,
as he paused with her atop the steps.

Silence held them, and Catherine felt a magnetic pull
as he looked at her, the corners of his eyes crinkling,
the soft blue loving and accepting her exactly as she
was. He bent his head down and his lips gently took
hers. She closed her eyes, feeling the warmth of his kiss
move through her. His mouth moved over hers, nipping
and caressing, and she happily answered with caresses

of her own, her arms going around his neck as he in turn held her close, exploring her mouth, her cheeks, her brow.

She did not know how many ages had passed when she came to her senses, her face tucked into his neck as he held her, his cheek resting atop her head. She blinked and pulled back, still slightly dazed. He had the hint of a smile playing on his lips.

"Mistletoe," he said.

She blinked at him, and he nodded upward. She followed his gaze, to the ball of mistletoe she had forgotten, hanging above the steps.

"I should have brought you here sooner," she said.

Will smiled, watching the snow settle on Catherine's hair, still not quite believing that he had won her heart.

"Just what did you leave for us?" she asked, bending down to pick up the packages he had left in front of her door. "One for Amy, I see, and look here," she said, grinning mischievously, "one for me."

"You can open it now, if you like." It was a small, portable set of watercolors meant for use outdoors. Amy had once told him that Catherine liked to paint, and he knew she'd done the touching portrait of her grandmother, in the parlor.

She tore the paper off, revealing a flat box covered in pale, silvery-blue silk. She froze for a moment, then touched the silk and glanced up at him with a knowing look.

He was too stunned to speak. That was not the box he had wrapped yesterday afternoon. He had never seen it before, and yet that had been his wrapping paper, and his handwriting addressing the box to Miss Linwood.

She lifted off the lid, and there in the center of a bed of white satin sat a platinum ring. "Oh, Mr. Goodman," she sighed, and lifted the ring from its bed. It was studded randomly with tiny diamonds. "Snowflakes," she said, and there were tears shimmering in her eyes.

He bent closer, and saw that indeed there were small snowflakes etched into the surface of the platinum, between the glittering diamonds. It was a ring he would have chosen for her if he had had the chance, after their magical sleigh ride tonight.

She pulled the glove off her left hand, and then held out her hand, fingers parted. He stared at that white hand, and at the ring she held in the other. There seemed only one thing to say, only one thing to do.

"Will you marry me, Miss Linwood?" he asked, his voice gone suddenly hoarse.

"Do you love me?"

"Beyond words."

"Then yes, Mr. Goodman, I will marry you," she said, and a tear like crystal ran down her cheek. "For I love you, too."

He took the ring and placed it upon her finger as the snow continued to fall, soft and pure as the feathers from an angel's wings. She threw her arms around him, and he closed his eyes in thanksgiving to whatever heavenly force had put that blue box and ring inside his wrapping paper.

He held her, and in the distance he heard the faint, magical jingling of sleigh bells.

Angels We
Have Heard

Amy Elizabeth
Saunders

*To my grandmother, Dorothy Hood, who
tried to expose Santa Claus, and paid the price.
Thank you for letting me tell your story in chapter six.
I was blessed to be born into a family of fine storytellers.
Merry Christmas to all.*

Chapter One

Black Diamond, Washington 1889

Rose Shanahan stood on the front steps, watching her children as they ran toward her from the schoolhouse, as if they were trying to outrun the early December wind rushing down from the mountain. It seemed to blow her children toward her, down the narrow road where the mud was turning solid with ice, past the row of little miners' company houses, all identical to her own, past the general store and false fronted hotel, the saloon and the bakery, and down to the little train depot.

Mount Rainier loomed above the tiny town, magnificent in the cold sun of the afternoon. It rose, a huge dome of snow and ice beyond the smoky gray line of hills, beyond the ancient green forests, and it felt to Rose that the wind was the very breath of the mountain, blowing December to them in a snow-and pine-scented gust. Behind the shining snow of the mountain, dark clouds gathered, moving toward them.

She pulled the worn fabric of Jamie's old coat tighter around her swollen stomach, smiling as the children grew closer. She felt a quick ache in her heart at the sight of Danny's threadbare sweater, and the way Katie's too-short dress blew above her knees, with no more hem to be let out. But no help for that, now. At least they were strong and healthy, and that was something you couldn't buy in the company store, or in all the world beyond, for that matter.

"It smells like snow," Katie cried out, as soon as she was within earshot. "Do you smell it?"

"I do," Rose said, allowing herself to share in the happy anticipation of the six-year-old. Katie leaped the two front steps in one motion, her little arms wrapping tightly around her mother's great belly.

The baby inside her moved energetically, almost as if he could hear the sound of his sister's voice.

"It doesn't smell like snow," Danny contradicted, with the surly superiority of his eleven years. "It smells like air. Cold air. That's all."

Rose watched him as he pushed past, banging the shanty door behind him. He had Jamie's face, handsome and dimpled and fair beneath shiny dark curls, but none of the dreaminess and laughter in the dark eyes, more like her own. Well, perhaps that was a good thing.

"It smells like snow," Katie repeated softly, snuggling closer to her mother.

Rose pulled her tightly against her, stroking the wind-reddened cheeks with the back of her work-roughened fingers, blistered by neverending gallons of hot water and lye soap and scrubbing against washboards. She had the hands of a laundress, red and rough.

"Are you done working today?" Katie asked, and Rose marveled at how the child seemed to follow her thoughts.

"All done. Forever. Mr. Svenson and Mr. Batinovich

will pick up their clothes tomorrow, and then all that's left is to pack the trunk and go to the train."

Katie's dark eyes brightened with excitement at the idea of the train ride down the mountains to the Green River Valley, and then to a new life in the city beyond.

"In Seattle," she said. "Perhaps you can find a fine job, in a beautiful house. Things will be lovely there."

"Perhaps," Rose agreed, trying not to show the fear that pinched her heart. Who would hire her, eight months huge with child and tired and clumsy? After the train fare was paid, and the money she owed to the store for food, she would have about seven dollars left in the shabby little purse hidden beneath her mattress.

That was all. Seven dollars standing between her beautiful children and the harsh world, until she was able to work again.

"Mama."

Kate had her little face turned up to her, the dark eyes glowing warm and brown, the face still with a touch of babyish softness around the chin.

"What is it, wee Kate?"

"Today at recess, I went to my secret place in the forest, and I prayed to the angels to make everything better. And do you know what?"

"Tell me." Angels, this week. Last week, it had been stories of fairies and elves.

"I heard one. Her name is Emily, and she had violets in her hair, and silver wings with frost on them."

"Silver wings, was it?" Rose repeated lightly. *Oh, Jamie, Jamie, couldn't you have left your child something a little more substantial than your gift for story-telling, the wild imagination that carried us from one place to another on nothing more than dreams?*

"And she said she has a fine house for us, all ready. For a Christmas gift. A carpet on the floor, and flowers

195

on my walls, and a big kitchen for you with a rocking chair, and—"

"No mention of new boots for your brother, I suppose," Rose interrupted, throwing the cold water of practicality onto the story.

Katie laughed, and Rose tugged the child's dark braids playfully.

"Whoever heard of angels speaking of boots?" Katie demanded.

"Whoever heard an angel speaking of rocking chairs?" Rose returned. "Get into the house, now, before this wind freezes the last of your good sense out of you."

The child smiled up at her with an odd resignation, as if she knew that her stories were disturbing to her mother, but also knew better than to stop sharing them. "Yes, Mama. Are you coming in?"

"No, not yet. I'm going to say good night to my mountain."

She wished that the dark clouds weren't shawling around the beautiful white and blue heights. She would have liked to have seen one last sunset with the mountain glowing pink and gold in the twilight.

But that was life. Sometimes you asked for pink and gold sunsets and got heavy gray clouds with snow blowing in.

Sometimes you married laughing men with brilliant dreams, and ended up with consumptive drunkards, coughing away part of their lives and drinking away the rest, until you were left alone in the cold wind, with nothing to help you but your own two hands, aching and tired.

And a little hope, Rose reminded herself. And a little hard-earned wisdom. And two beautiful children . . . no, three, soon.

Far up the road, the whistle of the Black Diamond Coal Company pierced the twilight, through the ancient pine forests. It was caught and carried on the mountain wind, through the little row of houses, past the tiny town and store and train depot, past the little graveyard where tomorrow she would leave James Shanahan forever.

But hadn't she really left him years before, in her heart? The laughing, bright-eyed young man who had charmed her so long ago had changed into a pathetic reflection of himself, dragging her and her baby, then two babies, from job to job, town after town. Silver mines under hot desert winds, copper mines in the Utah mountains, a gold mine in California where there was no gold at all except what the saloon owners lined their pockets with.

And finally, the last stop, here in Washington, the coal mines. They had arrived in the spring, the mountains intoxicating with their perfume of grass and pine and wildflowers, and the mountain sparkling and breathtaking above them, looking so close.

"There you are," Jamie had cried, his breath, even then, coming in gasps. "Look at that, Danny. Look at that, wee Kate. Here we are, up so high you can almost hear the angels singing."

Rose took a final look at the mountain as the sooty sky obscured it.

"I hope you hear those angels singing now, James Shanahan," she whispered, with the mixture of sorrow and resentment his memory always brought her. "Lucky for you that the Lord is more forgiving than I."

It was a queer, angry farewell to the man who had been her husband, she knew. But that was that. She could no more help the way she felt than she could help having dark hair or a sharp tongue. People were just what they were, and she had greater worries on her mind than that.

*   *   *

197

They ate their meager dinner of bacon and beans at the small, rough table that had been in the one-room shanty the day they had arrived. Drying laundry hung from lines criss-crossing the ceiling, making little curtained corridors that they ducked through and around.

Rose had already packed their few belongings. Her sad little iron was heating on the tiny stove, and as soon as the table was cleared she could press Mr. Svenson's giant Sunday-best shirt, and Mr. Batinovich's little tiny one, and that would be the end of her employment to the miners of Black Diamond.

And good riddance. No more tubs of coal-blackened work clothes, no more struggling with the great copper-bottomed boiler, no more stinging handfuls of lye soap.

"Your face might freeze like that, Danny," she commented, as she reached past him to take Kate's plate to the wash pan. "All long and sour. And that bottom lip stuck out so far that someone might take it for a table, and try to put their plate on it."

Kate giggled, but Danny rolled his eyes.

"Stop sulking, and put some coal in the stove for me. What did you learn in school today?"

"Nothin' much," was the surly reply.

"Nothin'?" Rose echoed. "Not even where the missing *G* went? I'm certain that there was a *G* on the end of 'nothing,' last time I looked."

Danny didn't answer, just bent over the stove with the coal hod. He was thin, too thin for a growing boy. She could count his ribs through the worn cotton of his school shirt.

"Perhaps," Rose went on, trying to tease a smile from him. "You used it up on growling. Or grumbling. Or . . ."

"Grouchy," suggested Kate, her smile bright.

"Is this all the coal?" Danny demanded, turning without a smile.

Rose nodded.

"It's not enough. Not enough for tonight *and* tomorrow."

"It'll have to do. Wash up now, and if you get cold, put a quilt on." She didn't mean to snap, but she was tired. Tired and frightened, and the baby was making her back ache.

"It's not fair!" he exclaimed, dropping the bucket with a heavy bang. "We shouldn't have to leave. It's our house—"

"It's not our house," Rose corrected. "It's the company's house. It belongs to Mr. Asher, and he needs it for a working miner. They let us stay a good year, Danny, even when your father was too sick to work, and a good eight months beyond that, out of charity . . ."

"And so they should have," the boy shot back, angry color staining his cheeks. "They owe us that much. What does old Asher need our house for? He's got a big, fancy one that he hardly ever uses."

"But he owns it, all the same." Rose threw a clean sheet over the table, and spread the shirts out to be ironed.

"It was his mine that killed Dad! And now he's throwing us out. And why should we be cold even one more night, when that old snake has a mine full of coal? I hate him!"

The fear and grief in the boy's voice took the anger out of Rose's answer.

"Danny, Danny. It wasn't the mine that killed your father, it was consumption. He had it long before we got here." And drink, she added to herself, but the children didn't need to hear that.

"Nobody forced your father to work in a coal mine; he chose to. And we've been lucky to be allowed to stay here as long as we have, and that's enough."

"No, it's not," Danny muttered.

199

Rose straightened up, one hand on her back, and glared. "I said that's enough. I'm tired to the bone, and we need a little less grief in this house. You're old enough to show your mother respect and understanding. Now fetch me that iron while it's hot, and let's have no more talk of hating anyone."

"I hate old Joshua Asher," Danny repeated, defiant. "I saw him going into his fancy house with his fancy rig and fancy horses, and I hate him."

"Then you're a fool," Rose snapped, her patience at an end. "Hating someone is like letting the person you hate live in your house, free room and board. You keep them with you all the time. Now, I said that's enough, and I mean what I say."

Danny slammed the door of the stove, and said nothing.

Rose sighed, and took up the weight of the sad iron in her hand.

The silence in the room was dark and angry. A cold wind shook the little house, stirring the drying laundry.

"It's snow," Kate said softly.

Rose went to the window and pushed back the calico curtain made from her old blue dress. Across the dark road the Gilhooleys' window shone yellow into the night. True enough, white flakes were sparkling past it, thick and fast.

Both children stood behind her, the anger in the room disappearing into the magic of the first snowfall of the year.

"Can we go out into it?" Kate asked softly, her tiny hand creeping into her mother's.

"What, in the dark of night? Into the cold?"

"Just to see the white? It's pretty."

"Why not?" Rose replied after a moment. "Why not? The cold won't kill us."

And the house might seem warmer, she reasoned to

herself, when they came back in. But already, the little shanty house was growing colder. She stopped Danny as he moved toward the stove.

"Save that last bit of coal," she said. "We'll certainly need it in the morning."

She finished ironing the shirts, and bundled Kate against the cold as best she could, hating the sight of the thin, darned stockings, the fraying sweater pulled over the child's dress, sighing at the sight of the missing buttons on the worn boots.

Everything looked tired and worn out, not strong enough to hold out much longer.

"Like me," she thought, then banished the thought. She would hold out. She had lived through longer, hungrier, more hopeless days. At least she would be directing their lives now, not following Jamie from dream to drink. She would survive, and the children with her.

But the fear of not knowing what tomorrow would bring was cold and deep within her, and she wished with all her heart that she, like little Kate, had faith in angels.

"Mama?"

Danny lifted himself cautiously on one elbow, peering through the dark room.

His mother didn't answer. She was sleeping more deeply these days than she used to. He wasn't supposed to know that she was growing a baby, but he was eleven now, and the whispers and veiled remarks of the neighbor women weren't lost on him as they were on Kate.

And he could see it in her face, the way it grew whiter and whiter as the day went on, the dark circles beneath her eyes, the way she had to stop and rest more often. When she lay down next to Kate on the other bed, she slept immediately, where they had used to giggle and whisper together.

He quietly slid back the worn quilt that covered his

cot, shivering when his bare feet touched the cold boards of the floor.

He kept his eyes on his mother as he reached under the bed for his clothing. In the darkness, her profile was very pale. She and Kate slept deeply, their arms wrapped around each other.

It was cold in the room, and the little stove gave off scant heat. The second to last piece of coal was in there, and he knew that it would be burned away before morning. They would wake up with their breath coming in great clouds, ice frozen in the wash bowl, feather patterns of frost on the windows.

It didn't seem fair, when there was mine full of coal just a mile away. More coal than in all creation. And that old skinflint, Joshua Asher, expected his own workers to pay for it at the company store.

Danny burned with the injustice. His father was dead, they were being turned out of their home, and waking up cold was just one thing more than he could tolerate.

Creeping quietly, he dressed himself, grabbed one of the empty coal sack from the peg on the wall, and slipped out the front door, into the brilliant white cold of the night.

It was harder going than he had reckoned. The walk up the road to the mine tunnel was a pleasure on a sunny afternoon, a mere annoyance in the rain, but in the frigid, biting cold, with snow soaking through the holes in his boots, soaking through his pants and numbing his shins, it was plain misery.

And still the snow fell, each flake stinging his already numb cheeks as he made his way up the hill, his breath coming in thick clouds. He tried pulling his arms inside his worn sweater, and wrapping them around his chest, but that threw his balance off, and slowed him down.

The snow-frosted forest around him seemed alive in

the dark and wild winds. The towering pines made hollow noises as the wind moaned through them. Every now and then a branch gave way and broke beneath the weight of the snow, making a sound like a gunshot, causing his heart to leap.

At last he saw the mine entrance, looming black and empty before him.

For a moment, his courage faltered.

Men had died in there, and there were always rumors of haunts. Danny usually didn't believe such things, but on a night like this, with the wind moaning, and the dark cave yawning black before him, and the familiar landscape shrouded and glowing eerie white, it gave him pause.

And then, too, he was stealing. A sin, most definitely, and beyond that, a practice firmly forbidden by the Black Diamond Coal Company. Each miner was given a monthly allotment of coal, and anything beyond that was to be purchased fairly at the store.

But, he reasoned, his mother didn't receive an allotment, and they had more than paid their dues to Mr. Joshua Asher. What was one bag of coal, against his father's life?

The anger that rose in his thin chest was enough to overcome his fear. He pulled an empty coal sack from beneath his shirt, and forced his numb legs forward.

Coal.

Why, there was no need to go much further than the very entrance. There was coal everywhere, glistening black rocks of it, hard and freezing, scattered around the mine entrance, great jagged piles.

It froze his already freezing hands as he gathered it, filling the bag as full as he could get it.

He smiled as he imagined his mother's surprise in the morning. He would stoke the little stove full before he went to sleep, and in the morning the shanty would be glowing with heat. They could have hot tea, and she wouldn't be angry at all when she saw his clothes black with coal dust. After all, there would be plenty of hot water to wash with.

She would understand why he stole, and they'd have a good laugh at how he'd fixed old Asher's flint, and they'd have one last day in the little shanty where they'd be warm and cozy until the noontime train went down the mountain, carrying them away forever.

He started back down the long road, dragging the heavy sack behind him with fingers that felt like frozen sticks, and still the white flakes fell, like broken pieces of light in the black sky.

Chapter Two

"There you are." George Critcher, the mine manager, pointed his gloved finger at the trail through the snow. "There's your thief, sir."

"Not a very bright thief," Joshua Asher observed. He reached into the inside pocket of his coat for a cigar, found none, and frowned. Of course. His cigars wouldn't be in the pocket of his black serge topcoat, designed for citywear and far too thin for this ice-cold morning.

They were in the pocket of his favorite coat, a heavy buffalo lined with soft wool. And now, presumably, in the possession of the not-very-bright thief.

He had taken off the buffalo yesterday evening, feeling overheated from readying the stables for the cold night ahead, and forgetting, had left it hanging by the stalls. This morning, he had made his way through the snow to retrieve it, and found it gone.

His favorite coat, three splendid Havana cigars, a small bag of hard candy, and—worst of all—his father's gold pocket watch.

The thief had, to his credit, left a clear trail, both in and out of the stables. In addition to his bootprints, he had been dragging a heavy bag, containing, presumably, coal. The trail through the pristine snow had been laughably easy to follow, dusted with black and the occasional fallen piece of coal.

"I can't tolerate thievery," Joshua Asher said, the thought of his missing cigars rankling him almost as deeply as the gold pocket watch. "And I can't tolerate stupidity. Whoever this son of a bitch is, I intend to ruin his morning."

George Critcher nodded, his hand reaching for his pistol. Both men stopped their horses and eyed the shanty for any sign of movement. Except for the telltale trail leading to the door, it appeared no different than the others—all were of unpainted lumber, had two steps rising to the doors, two small front windows, most still dark in the cold light of sunrise, and identical stovepipes smoking faintly into the air.

The stove chimney of the miner's shanty that interested them showed no smoke at all; the curtained windows were dark, with no movement behind them.

"What's the plan, Ash?" Critcher asked, trying to twirl his pistol. It stuck on the finger of his heavy glove, and he banged his hand and swore as he tried to loosen it.

"Firstly, you should avoid trying any more fancy doings with that gun, before you shoot yourself, or me. I'm in a right foul mood already, and getting shot won't improve it."

Embarrassed, the portly mine manager disengaged his finger.

"Secondly, I'm going to go in and wake that untutored son of a bitch and educate him in my opinion of thieves. You, Mr. Critcher, may then take what's left of him down the valley into town, and let the law take its due course. Third, I intend to smoke a cigar."

Having shared the details of his plan, Joshua Asher swung himself easily from the saddle, into the snow, and strode easily toward the quiet shanty.

Critcher was unsure whether he was meant to follow or not. One thing he knew for sure. Josh Asher was well above six feet tall, as hard-muscled as any five men, and not known for his good temper. Critcher would sure hate to be the man sleeping in the shanty.

Ash opened the door with one swift kick, letting the cold and pale light flood the dark room.

"I'd say good morning, if I was in a sociable mood, but I'm not. Get up, and keep your hands where I can see them. Time to pay the fiddler, gents."

He would have been ready for a fight, but none was offered. For a moment, there was no sound but the cold wind blowing through the door.

His eyes were adjusting to the darkness of the room, and he could make out two beds, their occupants well buried in quilts.

"Come on. You've wasted enough of my morning as is, and I'm not particularly pretty in the early hours. Move your useless asses, before I start kicking them."

There was a soft cry of alarm as his message began to register, and a figure sat straight up in bed, moving with the swiftness of fear.

"Great merciful heavens!"

The voice was female, and frightened.

He peered closer, and saw, through the half-darkness a tumble of dark hair, a very white face, and enormous dark eyes.

"Begging your pardon, ma'am. I believe I'm here to speak to the man of the house."

He spied an oil lamp on the table, and without taking his eyes from either bed, reached in his pocket for a match. It sputtered and flared. He carefully lit the lamp, pulled up a chair, and placed his revolver deliberately on the table.

In the small bed against the other wall, a child stared fearfully from beneath the frayed edges of a quilt.

"Ma'am? Is your husband here?"

She was staring at him with huge eyes, a pretty woman, a little sharp featured, but fetching enough. There was a movement next to her, and he caught a glimpse of a little girl, white as a ghost with long dark braids, before her mother pushed her back down to the bed.

"Don't move, Kate. Who are you, and what do you want?"

Her eyes were on the gun on the table, and then darting wildly about.

"Just the return of my property, ma'am. If you could see fit to tell me where your husband is—"

"In the graveyard." Her voice was sharp with fear, but she stared him down. "Dead these past eight months and more. Now get out, or I'll scream the town awake."

"Mr. Asher? Ash?" Critcher's call came from beyond the open door. "Everything all right?"

Ash gave a longer look around the room. There was nowhere for anyone to hide. An open trunk sat on the floor next to the bed, as if in readiness for a journey. The shelves were empty, stripped of everything but three cups and a tea tin. His buffalo coat and gold watch were nowhere in sight.

"Come on in, Critcher," he called.

The woman pulled the quilts closer, staring in shock as Mr. Critcher bumbled into the room wielding his gun in what he likely hoped to be a threatening manner.

The sight of Critcher, looking like a gun-toting bear bundled in layers of scarves, seemed to shock the woman out of her fear.

"Mr. Critcher! Explain yourself! What do you mean

208

by this intrusion? Have you completely lost your mind?"

Critcher hesitated, then lowered his gun. "Beg your pardon Mrs. Shanahan. . . ."

"And well you should. What can you be thinking?"

While George was stammering, Ash took another glance at the boy in the bed. Fear in those wide-set eyes, yes. But something else as well. Guilt.

He took another look toward the stove. It was cold and dark. Two empty coal sacks lay next to it in a puddle of dark water.

Frowning, he looked closer.

"Mrs. . . ."

"Shanahan," she supplied icily. "Rose Shanahan."

"Yes, I recall, now. Well, it seems that we had a thief abroad in the night. We were able to follow his trail quite easily. Not a very skilled thief, you see. Or maybe"—he tossed a quick look to the silent boy in the bed—"not a very experienced one. Left a dirty trail of coal behind him. Looked like he dragged a sack all the way down from the mine, then into my barn. He then helped himself to a loan of my favorite buffalo coat—"

"And one gold pocket watch," George interjected. "Solid gold."

"And then made his way here. Right up these stairs."

"You're wrong." The woman's face was tight with anger, and a crimson flush spotted her pale cheeks.

"I wish I was, ma'am. But the trail is there, if you wish to see it."

"I would, thank you."

Still holding a quilt tight to her chin, she reached for a shabby jacket that hung from the iron bedstead, and wriggled into it beneath the cover of her bedclothes. She murmured to the little girl, still silent, and pulled a protective blanket around herself as she stood.

"Now—" she began, and then her words broke off abruptly as she stared down at her feet.

Asher followed her gaze. There was water on the floor there, too, as well as by the stove. Black, sooty water.

"What in the world," she muttered, staring at the wet trail. She glanced quickly out the door, and then back into the room. Her eyes went from the empty, wet coal sacks by the stove, and then slowly to her son, silent and pale in his iron bed.

"Close the door, Mr. Critcher," she said. "We are quite cold enough this morning, thank you."

Critcher hurried to obey, and Ash watched with interest as the woman turned toward the boy in the bed.

"Get up, Danny," she said softly. She stood very straight, and even though she was bundled in the heavy quilt, with her dark hair hanging in disarray, she had a quiet dignity.

The boy obeyed, shivering. He had slept in his clothes, and they were stained black with coal dust. He avoided his mother's eyes as he pushed his feet into worn, wet boots.

"Did you steal coal, Danny?"

"Yes." It was only a whisper.

"Well, where is it? Return it to Mr. Asher . . . it is Mr. Asher, is it not?" She glanced at him swiftly for confirmation, and then back to her son. "Return it to Mr. Asher and Mr. Critcher at once, please."

The boy, his face pinched with guilt, and resentment, nodded to the stove. "Right there."

"Where?"

The boy looked at the empty coal sacks, laying in the sooty puddle, and looked back with utter bewilderment. "It was there. In them sacks—"

"*Those* sacks."

"—those sacks, last night."

Asher rose, and went to the cold stove. He lifted one coarse sack, and then another. Black water dripped from them.

210

"Where did you take the coal *from*, Danny," he asked, trying not to laugh.

"The entrance to the mine tunnel," the boy mumbled, still staring in confusion at the empty bags.

Asher fought back the chuckle that rose in his throat. "Well, I opined that you were not a very skillful thief, and that proves it. What you stole, my boy, was ice. Dirty ice, covered with coal slag and dust."

The boy's face flushed red.

"That's a mighty long piece to walk, in the cold, in the dark of night, for a bag of ice," Asher observed. "And you've made quite a mess of your mother's floor, to boot."

He almost felt pity for the boy, watching the shame and anger and humiliation fighting in the thin face.

"Mister?"

He turned to the small voice. The little girl was sitting up in bed, her small face peeking out from a cocoon of blankets. "Are you putting our Danny in jail?"

"For stealing a bag of ice?" her brother snapped.

"Stealing is stealing," Critcher announced, sounding once again like the authoritative company manager. "And a thief is a thief. And there's a matter of one buffalo coat and one gold pocket watch."

"Danny?" Rose Shanahan's voice sounded like a plea.

"I don't got 'em."

"Don't be a fool, boy," Asher said, a little impatiently.

"Of course they've got 'em," Critcher said. "Leaving town today, weren't you?" He nodded at the open trunk. "Probably in there."

"Danny?"

The shame in the woman's voice pained Josh Asher, but he couldn't let pity overcome his good sense. No point in letting a thief get away with it even once. Especially a thief this young. Let him learn his lesson, and hopefully he'd remember it.

"Well, boy?" he asked.

The child hung his head.

"Go ahead, and search, Critcher."

Critcher, with his usual lack of finesse, simply over-turned the packed trunk onto the floor. Ash winced, but didn't stop him. He carefully kept his face impassive as Critcher sorted through the meager belongings.

A few pots and pans, a few pieces of clothing, a worn-out man's wallet, a sewing basket, a carefully wrapped china cup . . .

"Here she is," Critcher announced, and held the watch aloft, gold and shining in the circle of lamplight.

Rose Shanahan made a quiet, soft sound, and for a moment dropped her face into her hand, her red, work-worn fingers pressing tightly against her eyes.

Asher waited for the inevitable tears, but when she lifted her face, it was cold and quiet.

"Well, Danny Shanahan, I hope you're proud. You've humiliated me, and brought shame on your father's name. What in the name of God possessed you?"

The boy was struggling not to cry. "I didn't mean to. At least, not at first. I just went in the barn to get warm. But there was that coat, and . . ." he swallowed.

"Where is my coat?" Asher interrupted.

"Under the step," the boy muttered, and the resent-ment in his face flared briefly as he glanced up, and then back to his mother.

"I didn't mean to take the coat," he repeated. "But I was freezing. I meant to put it back this morning. And then when I found the watch . . ." He pressed his lips firmly together, and then went on, hurriedly. "I thought he was so rich he wouldn't notice. And it could carry us through until you could work again. I'm tired of being hungry, and the other kids laughing at our clothes—"

"And you'd thought they'd show more respect to a

thief?" Rose demanded. "And where is Mr. Asher's coat?"

"Outside, under the step."

"Go get it."

"Begging your pardon, ma'am," Critcher interjected, "But that boy's under arrest. He ain't going anywhere."

Asher debated stepping in, but decided to wait. Let the boy have a good fright, and see if that didn't scare some sense into him.

"Arrest?" Rose Shanahan echoed, and the hot red color came back into her cheeks. "Are you mad, Mr. Critcher? He's done wrong, I'll agree, but he's not even twelve yet. He's never stolen before—"

"I doubt that," Critcher said, with all the pompous authority he could muster. "Takes after his father, I'd allow. Don't like to hire the Irish. It's always trouble. I wrote you, Ash, about James Shanahan, if you recollect. He was always showing up half-pickled, either goin' on a toot or comin' back off of one, and I asked you—"

"Mr. Critcher!" The woman's voice cracked like a bullwhip. "I shall have to demand that you desist. Daniel, Kate, go outside while I talk to these men."

The little girl scurried to obey, pulling her clothes beneath the quilt and dressing with all the energy of a squirrel stuffing its cheeks.

Danny stood his ground, his eyes dark and filled with hate as he glowered first at Critcher, than at Asher.

"Now," Rose Shanahan repeated, her voice shaking a little. "Put on your coats, and go outside."

"I don't have a coat," the boy muttered sullenly.

"Well, then, put on . . . a thing." She waved a vague, impatient hand. "Something. Put something on. Go find that buffalo coat, and don't come in till I call you. And you, Mr. Critcher, will hold your tongue until my children leave the room."

She had a kind of authority, Asher decided. Even

looking the way she did, wearing an old shabby coat over her nightgown, with her hair like a wild woman's, wrapped like a squaw in a tattered blanket, she had dignity. He liked the way her dark eyes snapped. If she hadn't been a laundry woman, he'd be tempted to fire Critcher and offer her the job of company manager. There weren't many men who would argue with that ring of command in her voice.

The little girl paused before she followed her brother out the door, and looked back. "Did you see?" she asked softly. "The snow is all pink in the sunrise. It looks . . . it looks . . . magicked."

"Enchanted," corrected her mother, her eyes softening for a moment. "*Magicked* isn't a word, Kate."

"It should be," the little girl said happily. "That's what it looks like. But enchanted is nice, too." She pulled the door closed softly behind her.

"Now, Mrs. Shanahan," Asher began, hoping to soothe her ruffled feathers, "I'm sure that you can understand that George here meant no offense. But thieving is a serious crime."

"That I know. Thank you for enlightening me. But that gives Mr. Critcher no excuse for speaking of my late husband in that way. Even if it is true. If he'd been half the worker he was a drinker, I'd own this mining company, and probably three others as well. But the children don't remember that, or if they do, they choose to remember what few redeeming worthwhile qualities their father had; and I'll not tarnish those."

"But surely, Mrs. Shanahan, you can appreciate—"

"Appreciate what? That you're sending an eleven-year-old boy to jail? No, Mr. Asher, I cannot."

"But, Mrs. Shanahan—" He was about to protest that he had no intention of doing so, but she gave him no chance.

"It is indecent, inhumane. My husband died working

214

in your mines, and Danny holds it against you. I'm sorry for what my son did, but you have to understand, he was just trying to help us. You can't expect a child to behave like an adult, nor can you punish him like one. Jail, indeed, Mr. Asher!"

He figured he'd better get a word in while she drew breath. "Now, really, Mrs.—"

Too late.

"And as if I didn't have enough grief, two fatherless children, and working my hands to the bone trying to keep body and soul together, scrubbing the coal dust out of at least thirty pairs of overalls a week—and a dirty lot your miners are, I could tell you—"

He genuinely hoped she wouldn't.

"And then getting put out of our home with a scarce two weeks' notice, and in the middle of winter, yet. It shouldn't surprise me if we end up starving in the street for Christmas. And the only worse thing than that would be starving in the street for Christmas with my only son in jail. But merciful lot you'll care—"

"Mrs. Shanahan—"

"—sitting up there in your grand house counting your money like Ebenezer Scrooge himself among the cobwebs, while we wander the streets begging—"

At what point, he wondered, had he become the villain in a melodrama? Even George was looking at him as if he expected him to twirl his mustache and give a demonic chuckle.

"Who told you my house had cobwebs?" was all that he could think of to say.

"Whereas, if you were a reasonable man, you would surely see that justice could be served without destroying what little family I have left. A mother's heart could break, Mr. Asher, just to think of it!"

She was something, all right. He wondered, as small and pale as she looked, where she found all that breath.

He was almost feeling bullied. And yet, no woman could look so pitiful, with that heart-shaped face, and the tears standing in those great, dark eyes.

"For pity's sake, Mr. Asher. For the sake of the Christmas season. Will you allow us to make compensation to you, for the wrong Danny did you?"

He waited for a moment, but she remained quiet. "I couldn't take your money, ma'am."

"Oh no. I didn't think, as a gentleman, that you would for a moment."

"What were you thinking, then?" he asked warily. Behind the glossy tears, he could almost see the crackle of energy in her eyes, and he waited uneasily for her answer.

"We could work it off."

"Now, I don't allow women or children in the mine. It's dirty and dangerous—"

"I agree entirely. But you will need a housekeeper, and, since Mrs. Louis left, and Danny can shovel coal and haul hay and keep those stables as neat as a pin. And little Kate can make herself useful at . . . something. I'm not sure what. Something. And that house is a disgrace."

"Says who?"

"Oh . . . people." Again that vague little wave of her hand, as if she couldn't be bothered to elaborate. "And I'm sure that the idea is more equitable than putting a widow and her helpless children out into the snow with Christmas coming. Don't you agree?"

"Well, of course—"

"Then it's settled!" She extended her hand, the color in her cheeks high, her eyes sparkling with happiness. "Thank you, Mr. Asher. You are a rare and noble gentleman, to allow us to make honest compensation for our family's shameful debt. It is truly gracious of you."

He didn't feel gracious. He felt as if he'd been run

216

over by a steam train. A very small steam train, but powerful all the same.

But there was her hand, small and thin and pitifully blistered, held out to him, and he'd be a real cad to refuse it. She looked so proud and poor and brave, standing in the cold puddles of melted coal and ice. . . .

He shook her hand.

For a moment, a brief flicker of triumph showed in her eyes, so quickly he was sure he'd imagined it.

"I thank you, Mr. Asher. And if you would, send the children in on your way out. And don't forget this, please." She picked his gun up from the table, holding it disdainfully between two fingers as if it were contaminated.

He pocketed it quickly, feeling as if he'd committed some breach of etiquette.

"Well," he managed. "Well. I suppose if you're going to be working in my house, we should discuss your duties. . . ."

"I know what to do."

He was certain of that.

"Mrs. Shanahan?" He stopped, one hand on the doorknob, and looked at her.

"Yes, Mr. Asher?"

"Do you gamble?"

"Certainly not."

"Thank God for that. You're a wily adversary."

Critcher behind him, Asher stepped out into the snow.

"I still think that—" George began.

"Don't, George. Don't say one damned word. Go get my coat from that boy. I need a cigar badly, right now."

Critcher started to speak, changed his mind, and waddled off to where the boy stood, silent and watchful, leaning against the wall of a neighboring shanty.

The little girl stood in the middle of the road, her face turned up to the pale sky. Under the rough gray wool of her knit cap, her face was luminous with pale skin and bright dark eyes, her cheeks glowing a delicate pink.

He looked up to see what entranced her, but saw only heavy wet flakes, falling from the pearl and gray sky.

"Do you know what I think?" she said softly, without bothering to glance at him.

"What do you think?" he asked, with another look upward. There was just cold sky, and snow.

"I think that when angels write us letters, they throw them into the wind. And then, they fall into little pieces and come down as snow." She peered over at him, and then at the snowflakes that had fallen on the deep blue of her sleeve, smiling.

"But then, how do we read them?" he asked, a little startled by the fancy.

"Oh, they don't need words. We can just see how beautiful they are. See?" She pointed a small, cold-reddened finger at his glove, where a large flake landed. "There's one for you. Who do you think it's from?"

"I think it's snow," he replied, shaking himself. "Your mother wants you to come in."

The child smiled at him, her dark brows lifting slightly, with a trace of disbelief. "I think it's a letter," she said, and turned to go. "From an angel who loves you."

He said nothing, just watched the odd little girl cross the white street.

He looked up again, trying to remember if he had had such fancies as a child. Letters from an angel who loved him—what odd whimsy.

Unbidden and vivid, the image of his wife came to him, gone and buried eight years ago. Funny, how the pain of it, while it struck less frequently, was still just as powerful. She had loved the snow. He'd almost forgotten that.

He stared at the falling flakes, graceful and pure, and for a moment he could almost believe that they were letters from Emily.

Chapter Three

"He must be at the mines," Rose said. "But I'm sure he expects us, so we'll let ourselves in. Let's leave the trunk on the porch, Danny, till I catch my breath."

It had been a long walk from the shanty, the two of them carrying them trunk, trying not to slip in the snow, while Kate tripped along behind, singing happy little songs that came out in white puffs of breath.

Joshua Asher's house stood on the rise of a hill, a good two acres of land cleared around it, right up to the edges of the great pine forests. Beneath the hill, and down the curve of the road, the little town lay quiet and white, smoke from the shanty stovepipes pluming into the sky. The white ribbon of road curved up the hill, past the house and east, over the hill to the mines.

And, Rose noted with satisfaction, from the broad front veranda she would be able to look directly at her mountain, on a clear day. Today though, she could barely discern the shape through the clouds.

The porch wrapped around three sides of the house,

with four broad steps leading up to the dark front door. Rose knocked again, staring admiringly up at the fan-shaped, leaded glass window above, badly in need of washing.

"From now on," Rose said, "we use the back door, up the kitchen steps. But just for today, we'll use this one. Just to celebrate."

"Celebrate what?" Danny asked, sullen faced.

"The fact that you're not in jail, for one; so wipe that look off of your face before I'm tempted to." Her cheerful tone never faltered. "For another, we have a fine, warm house to live in, and probably food to eat like we haven't seen for a few years. We're not walking the streets of the city wondering where we'll sleep tonight. And I haven't killed you yet. Be grateful, Dan."

She knocked a final time with cold fingers, then put her hand on the colder brass of the handle, and they went in.

She allowed her plaid shawl to slip to her shoulders, and let out a soft breath of happiness.

Behind her, Kate gasped audibly.

Poor little thing, Rose thought. *It's the grandest place she's ever seen.* One day, she would take her daughter to San Francisco, and St. Louis, and show her the towered, turreted, and gingerbread mansions there, and they would laugh at how Kate had thought this a palace.

But it was a fine house, to be sure, two stories, an attic, and a full cellar floor. A finer house than Rose had been in for years, except as a laundress, coming to the back door.

The floors were patterned with simple but elegant designs of dark and light wood, repeating up the wide staircase before her, and left and right, to the dining room and parlor. The rooms were identical in size and space, and thick layers of dust.

Rose wandered slowly into the parlor, immediately

pulling back the dusty wine-colored curtains. Cold winter light illuminated the rug on the floor, the high-backed parlor set of dark red, the dark carved tables, all frosted with dust.

"Cobwebs," Rose said. "Just as I thought." She shook a lace curtain, and watched the dust motes dance in the gloom. She touched the crystal prisms hanging from the globe of a table lamp. They would be so pretty, sparkling in the glow from the rose-painted globe.

The children stood in the wide hallway, as if they were afraid to enter.

"Well," she said briskly. "We certainly have our work cut out for us. Come on, this way. Through the dining room."

They followed her silently, as if they were in church. A brass-and-glass chandelier hung over the long, dark wood table and twelve matching chairs. As in the parlor, the fireplace looked as if it had not been used for some time.

The stillness in the room was overwhelming.

"Look," Rose said, her voice sounding almost forced in the silence. "How lovely. I could sit right there in the morning, next to the fire, and drink my tea and look right out the window at my mountain. Wouldn't it be lovely to be rich?"

She stopped to look at the built-in china hutch, the patterns of the dishes hidden under a layer of dust, and slid open a drawer. Silver, all tarnished. Beautiful forks and spoons of all shapes and sizes, and tiny salt cellars with wee little spoons. Wonderful linens, the lace yellowing from disuse.

She picked up a napkin ring of darkened silver filigree, and rubbed her thumb over the initials engraved there, a swirling "EA." It must have belonged to his wife. She had heard that years ago he had been married.

"More work," she said, replacing the napkin ring care-

221

fully and closing the drawer with a deliberate bang. Somehow, she felt the need to violate the dusty hush of the house, to make it light and clean and fill it with noise.

"Come along, you two," she ordered, pushing her way into the serving pantry. There she surveyed the shelves of dishes, towels, bowls, and cups.

"What is this little door for?" Kate asked, pushing open a little cupboard-like door that looked into the dining room.

"Ah. That? So that the kitchen servant can hand the food out to the servers, without the grand folk having to see her while they eat."

"Which kind of servants are we?" Danny asked, peering out at the silent dining room.

"Neither. Our own kind. And I don't imagine Mr. Asher bothers with those sorts of doings. They're mostly for rich women, in great cities."

"Well, I'm not handing him his cup through a little door," Danny said.

"You will if he asks, though I doubt he will. Look, here's our part of the house. It doesn't appear that he spends much time out there." She pushed the heavy, white-painted door open and walked into the kitchen.

"How did you know where the kitchen was?" Kate demanded.

"I should. I've worked in enough houses like this. Bigger, too. Until I met your father. Ladies don't like married women working for them."

It felt good to be in a nice kitchen again. Even with the windows all around, looking out at the white pastures and frosted forests, it was warm. The stove was a marvelous thing, huge and black and shining with nickel trim, two ovens, six stove lids. The coal hod next to it was full to the brim.

This was obviously the room Joshua Asher spent most

222

of his time in. A pair of boots stood by the back door, a coffee cup stood half full on the kitchen table.

"Look at the pump. While we're here, we'll never have to go outside for water," Rose said, pointing to the granite sinks, and even Danny was impressed.

"Why does one man need so many dishes?" he asked, looking at the glass-fronted cupboards and the stacks of blue-and-white china.

"In case an army comes by to visit," Rose answered, smiling. She sank into an oak rocking chair by the stove, and permitted herself a blissful moment of just sitting, enjoying the warmth and the space and the feeling of security. It was ironic. Where would they be now, if Danny hadn't gone out to steal coal?

"The Lord works in mysterious ways, His wonders to perform," she said softly.

She opened her eyes, and saw the children standing awkwardly by the table, looking around with awed eyes.

The child in her stomach rolled heavily, and booted her beneath the ribs. She wondered why babies always woke when you wanted to rest, and slept quietly beneath your heart while you worked. Another mysterious wonder, she supposed.

"Look. Danny, you bring the trunk to the kitchen, till we find our room. Don't drag it, you'll mark the floors. Take a few minutes to look around, but don't touch anything and don't go into Mr. Asher's room. After, we can work for an hour, and then we'll have something to eat."

"What will we eat?" Danny asked, looking happy at the prospect. It was good to see him smile.

"I'll find something. That little staircase there will go upstairs, just like the big one in front. And likely down, as well. That's our staircase. The big one in the hall is for Mr. Asher. Go on, learn your way around."

Delighted, they clattered off the way they had come,

and she shut her eyes again until she heard Kate's voice from the kitchen staircase. "Mama?"

"You found me. Did you see upstairs?"

The little girl came down the stairs, her worn, high-buttoned shoes appearing, then her slight legs and deep-blue skirt, and finally, her little face, glowing with excitement, her dark braids swaying as she skipped down the last few steps.

"Mama, it's the house."

"What about the house, little lamb?"

"This is the house the angel told me about."

"Oh, Kate. It's just a house."

"No, Mama. It's *the* house. See? There's your fine kitchen, and your rocking chair. And upstairs, my very room with flowers on the walls. And the bed is so lovely."

"I thought I told you not to touch things," Rose said. Really, how silly to feel that little chill of nervousness.

"It's all right. She said I might. It's our Christmas, Mama."

Troubled, Rose looked at Kate's shining eyes.

"Wee Kate, you know that it's just pretend, don't you? There are no angels here. This is just a dusty house that wants cleaning. There are no angels."

Kate regarded her mother patiently. "There are angels in the Bible, Mama."

"Yes, darling."

"And that's true, isn't it?"

"Well, yes, sweetheart, but that's different."

"Then there are angels," Kate concluded logically. "There is one that comes here, and she said I might sleep in the room with the flowers. And I said, 'Thank you very much, Emily.' "

"Kate," Rose said, and then stopped. "Never mind. It's a great imagination you have, but angels aren't like that. They sing to shepherds and visit the Holy Mother

224

A Special Offer For Leisure Historical Romance Readers Only!

Get Four FREE* Romance Novels

A $21.96 Value!

Thrill to the most sensual, adventure-filled Historical Romances on the market today…

FROM  LEISURE BOOKS

As a home subscriber to the Leisure Historical Romance Book Club, you'll enjoy the best in today's BRAND-NEW Historical Romance fiction. For over twenty-five years, Leisure Books has brought you the award-winning, high-quality authors you know and love to read. Each Leisure Historical Romance will sweep you away to a world of high adventure…and intimate romance. Discover for yourself all the passion and excitement millions of readers thrill to each and every month.

SAVE AT LEAST *$5.00* EACH TIME YOU BUY!

Each month, the Leisure Historical Romance Book Club brings you four brand-new titles from Leisure Books, America's foremost publisher of Historical Romances. EACH PACKAGE WILL SAVE YOU AT LEAST $5.00 FROM THE BOOKSTORE PRICE! And you'll never miss a new title with our convenient home delivery service.

Here's how we do it. Each package will carry a 10-DAY EXAMINATION privilege. At the end of that time, if you decide to keep your books, simply pay the low invoice price of $16.96 ($17.75 US in Canada), no shipping or handling charges added*. HOME DELIVERY IS ALWAYS FREE*. With today's top Historical Romance novels selling for $5.99 and higher, our price SAVES YOU AT LEAST $5.00 with each shipment.

AND YOUR FIRST FOUR-BOOK SHIPMENT IS TOTALLY FREE!*

IT'S A BARGAIN YOU CAN'T BEAT! A Super $21.96 Value!

LEISURE BOOKS A Division of Dorchester Publishing Co., Inc.

GET YOUR 4 FREE* BOOKS NOW— A $21.96 VALUE!

Mail the Free* Book Certificate Today!

(Tear Here and Mail Your FREE* Book Card Today!)

Get Four Books Totally
F R E E* —
A $21.96 Value!

(Tear Here and Mail Your FREE* Book Card Today!)

PLEASE RUSH
MY FOUR FREE*
BOOKS TO ME
RIGHT AWAY!

Leisure Historical Romance Book Club
P.O. Box 6613
Edison, NJ 08818-6613

AFFIX
STAMP
HERE

and things like that, but they don't go about dispensing rocking chairs and wallpaper. And that's that."

"But you said, the Lord works in mysterious ways. . . ."

"So I did, but that's not what I meant. Now let's get busy, and no more talk of angels, thank you."

"Yes, Mama."

Rose stood, rubbing her back, as Danny lumbered in from the pantry with the trunk. It looked very shabby in the clean, new-looking kitchen.

"Leave it there, for now. Run downstairs and see if there's a little bedroom. That will be our part of the house. Then bring some coal for the fire in the parlor and dining room, and we can begin there."

She started by throwing open the deep-red draperies, beating the dust out of them. Beneath, the fine lace curtains were so yellowed and dusty that the edges looked brown and burned, and she pulled them down from the rods. The snow was heaped almost a foot deep on the wide balustrade of the porch.

"I'll heat water and put these in to soak. Kate, I'll give you an old towel and you dust everything that's made of wood. Mind the lamps. Danny?"

"Right here," he said, turning the corner.

"Get the fires going, and don't burn yourself. Then come into the kitchen, and I'll get you ready to wash windows."

He rolled his eyes, but didn't answer back, thank goodness.

She stopped on her way through the dining room, and her eyes went almost involuntarily to the beautiful built-in sideboard with the heavy mirror over it.

She thought of the heavy napkin ring in the drawer, the engraving on it. "EA."

E for Emily, perhaps?

"Great merciful heavens, you're as flighty as Kate,"

she muttered to herself, and hurried to the kitchen. She found a large boiler, filled it at the pump, and began heating water while she inspected the pantry and the cold cellar.

No beans for lunch today; they would have a feast. Fresh-baked biscuits, and strawberry preserves. She found a smoked ham, and cradled it gratefully in her arms. She would bake it for supper, the outside basted with brown sugar. There was a full can of fresh milk. She would make potato soup, with bits of clear onion floating in a cream base. On her way out, she helped herself to a tin of peaches.

This would be a feast fit for Christmas, with a summery dessert of peaches. It was wonderful.

She hoped Joshua Asher would like it. She wanted him to be happy, so that he wouldn't object to them staying. Maybe he would even want it to continue on after they had worked off their debt. At least until the spring thaw. She knew she had bullied him into the agreement, and that he was more than likely to think better of it. They weren't out of the woods, yet.

But if she could just impress him . . .

It startled him, to ride up the drive and see the windows of the house spilling yellow lamplight onto the snow. For a moment he paused, startled, before he remembered Rose Shanahan.

He rarely used the front rooms. For that matter, he rarely used the house. He tended to stay in his city house, managing his sawmills and the financial end of the coal mines. He only stopped here every few months to make sure the mine was being managed properly. He'd stay for a week or two, then leave.

He didn't like staying too long in this house, so silent and lonely since Emily had died in childbirth. For years, it had been too painful. Now, it had simply become empty.

As soon as his horse was safely stabled for the night, he went up the kitchen steps and in the back door.

The snow had been swept from the steps, and he took care to knock the rest off his boots before he entered the kitchen, gratefully inhaling the rich scent of food.

And stopped short. Rose Shanahan was standing next to the stove, lifting a heavy steaming kettle in her slender arms, her dark hair coiled neatly at the base of her fragile neck, and she was looking very tidy in a deep-blue dress.

And very pregnant.

He wasn't sure why it stunned him so. Perhaps it was the memory of Emily, standing in the same place, in the same state. Perhaps he was just startled because he hadn't noticed Mrs. Shanahan's condition that morning. But then, she had been wearing that huge coat, and had quilts wrapped around her.

Kate was seated at the kitchen table, drawing on her school slate, and she smiled shyly at him. The boy was nowhere in sight.

"Mr. Asher," Rose greeted him quickly. "If you'd like to repair to the front of the house, I can serve dinner as soon as you're ready."

"I don't 'repair' to anywhere, as a habit. I usually have my dinner right here." He tried not to look at her stomach, but it was making him mighty nervous. He was no doctor, but he was relatively certain that women didn't get much larger.

Good God, a housekeeper was one thing, and he hadn't been altogether sure about that; but a housekeeper who could go into labor and drop dead at any moment was another thing altogether.

He resisted the urge to rush forward and seize the heavy kettle from her hands, but waited until she set it heavily on the stove.

227

"Mrs. Shanahan?" he said. "If you would be so kind as to 'repair' to the parlor, I believe we have some business to discuss."

"Certainly."

She followed him out of the kitchen, patting her daughter's head as she passed.

A fire blazed in the dining room, each place at the table was set with shining silver. On the sideboard, a copy of the *Seattle Ledger* waited. It was last week's paper, which he had already read, but the effort was nice.

He noted the small changes—the silver bowl on the table filled with pine boughs and apples, the shining windows, the dust gone from the heavy dark tables.

She had a fire in the parlor lit, too, coals glowing comfortably, warming the wine colors of the furniture and patterned carpets. It made a pretty contrast to the deep blue and white of the snowy night outside.

"I wasn't familiar with your habits," she explained hurriedly. "If you'd prefer your paper in the parlor before dinner, and what time I should serve. We shall have to arrange that. Also, what time you eat your breakfast, and what you like, and . . . all that sort of thing."

"I see." He sat in the armchair nearest the fire, and gestured for her to be seated. She sat awkwardly on the edge of the sofa, watching him warily.

"Mrs. Shanahan." He reached in his pocket for a cigar, and twisted it uncomfortably between his fingers. Best to be blunt. "This just won't work."

"What won't? Why?" Her face, which had been flushed from the heat of the kitchen, paled a little.

"To start with, Mrs. Shanahan, and forgive my being frank, but you are in an interesting condition, as they say."

She didn't blush, at least.

"Yes, sir, I am. But as you can see, that doesn't prevent my working."

"No, no, I can see that. But you must see . . . well, I just can't have it. You can't be cooking and lifting and getting up at dawn to make breakfast."

"I can do it," she said simply. "I'm used to hard work."

"I wouldn't feel right, having you wait on me, and working for me. And, if I may be frank again?"

She gave a quick nod.

"You just can't be here alone in that condition. What if you were to . . . to . . ." he struggled for a delicate way to put it.

"Begin labor," she supplied.

"Begin labor, and there was nobody here to help you? What would you do?"

She considered his words at length, tipping her head to one side.

"Mr. Asher? If *I* may be frank?"

He nodded.

"The fact is," she said bluntly, "I brought my first child into the world by myself, on the floor of a canvas tent on a ninety-degree day, outside a desert mining camp in Nevada. The only excuse for a doctor was an old medicine peddler with one leg, and he was so drunk I'm not sure he knew which end to look at. I threw him out of the tent before he had the chance to do any damage. It was dusty, dirty, utterly terrifying, and as hot as the fires of hell must burn. If that didn't kill me, nothing will."

"Well." He had never heard a woman speak so bluntly, and it surprised him that he had blushed before she did.

"Be that as it may, beyond that, I'm quite happy without a housekeeper. I'm set in my ways. I like dinner in the kitchen, alone, and I like to read the paper while I

229

eat, and put my dirty boots on a chair, and scratch myself, if I choose. And I don't want to be sitting there every night waiting for you to finish the dishes, worrying about you walking home in the dark."

"Oh. Well, as to that . . ." Her hands twisted the fabric of her blue skirts quickly.

"Hadn't thought of that, had you?"

"Yes, I had. And you see, Mr. Asher, as I understood it . . . That is . . . Mrs. Louis, when she was your housekeeper . . ."

"Mrs. Louis lived here," he pointed out. "She didn't have to fret about that."

"Exactly." She smiled that sweet, bright smile that he already distrusted. "How perfectly suitable. We shall be very comfortable here, and how kind you are to worry about us. I shall make sure that the children stay out of your way, and . . ."

"Woman, what are you thinking? I don't want a housekeeper at all, much less a housekeeper with two kids and a third ready to make an appearance God knows when. No sane man would hire you, in your condition. Are you crazy?"

Her dark eyebrows arched up at his outburst, stark against the pale white of her forehead. She appeared to consider her reply carefully, then spoke. "No, not crazy, Mr. Asher. Desperate. That's all. I'm alone, and I'm poor, and I'm desperate. What you say is true. No one would hire me in this condition. That's why I made such an effort to . . ."

"Bamboozle me."

"Secure the situation," she corrected, her voice prim.

"I'm sorry for your situation, but it can't be helped."

She lowered her head, and nodded. He watched her quietly, the way her dark head shone in the firelight, and the way her dark lashes made half moons over her pale

230

cheeks. He sincerely hoped she wouldn't cry.

She didn't. She simply drew two or three deep breaths, then smoothed her skirts over her knees. He noticed for the first time that the blue cuffs around her slender wrists were fraying.

"Well," she said, finally lifting her head. "Some things can't be helped. May we stay for tonight, or would you like us to leave for the hotel?"

"Oh, no need for that." He couldn't help but be impressed by her quiet dignity. A ridiculous guilt gnawed at him. "You can't leave town tonight, anyhow. I can take you to the depot myself, tomorrow."

"Thank you. If you'll excuse me, I'll see to supper."

He avoided watching her struggle to her feet. He had no reason to feel guilty. She was none of his business.

Still.

"Where will you be going?" he asked.

"Oh." She stopped, and put her head to one side while she thought. "Someplace. Seattle, maybe. Perhaps even Olympia. I haven't decided quite yet." She gave a quick little shrug and smiled, for all the world as if she was discussing making holiday plans abroad and it didn't really matter. "If you'll excuse me now."

Somehow, her brave nonchalance made him feel even more guilty than if she had cried.

He ate his dinner alone in the dining room, feeling slightly ridiculous in the formal setting. From the kitchen, where the Shanahans were eating, he could hear the sound of Rose's clear, firm voice, and the softer answers from her children. Occasionally, they laughed together, and he wondered what on earth they could find to laugh about.

She was no whiner, he'd allow that. She had spirit enough for ten women.

She also had a fine touch with a ham. It was a pity, really, that she couldn't stay.

But she couldn't. Tomorrow, when that coal train chugged down into the valley, she would be on it.

Chapter Four

It snowed again that night; not the gentle, wafting flakes of the night before, but a fierce, driving snowstorm that toppled ancient pines, buried roads, and collapsed roofs beneath its frigid weight.

In the morning, the little town of Black Diamond was snowbound, isolated from the rest of the world. One look outside told Rose that the coal train wouldn't be coming up through the foothills today.

She was delighted. Dressing herself quickly in the room that had lately belonged to Mrs. Louis, she hurried to the kitchen. Outside, pink and gold light touched the snow. She quickly added more coal to the fire, put the kettle on to boil, and started coffee in the speckled pot.

Lugging the coal, she hurried into the front of the house, stirred up the embers in the cold rooms, and started fresh blazes in the grates.

Shivering, she pulled open the curtains, and sighed with delight at the sight of the mountain. It was breathtaking, vivid, and sharp against the early morning sky of pink and lavender and gold. Soft, light clouds blew past its shadowed peak, like fairy boats in the sky.

Down the hill, Black Diamond was half-buried in the drifts of white, surrounded by the tall, frosted pines. The road was invisible, hidden somewhere beneath shimmering blankets of ghost white.

From one of the rooms above, she heard stirring, and after a few minutes, she heard Joshua Asher descending the kitchen staircase. She wondered if he ever used the front one.

He came out from the kitchen, and stared in amazement at the arctic landscape spread beneath the mountain.

"Son of a bitch," he whispered.

Rose laughed. "Not exactly my reaction, but yes, it's a powerful lot of snow."

"It's an all-fired lot," he agreed, crossing the room to join her at the front window. He raked his dark hair off his forehead, his blue eyes blinking in the light.

"Should have worn two sets of long johns," he murmured, and then glanced at Rose. "Begging your pardon, ma'am."

She smiled quickly, forgiving the impropriety, then went to fetch the coal bucket back to the kitchen.

He joined her there, sniffing happily at the scent of the coffee.

"Sit and have a cup," he urged her. "Get off your feet." He apparently thought that very pregnant women should be told to get off their feet, though he probably wasn't sure why.

"I've just gotten on them, thank you," she replied. "You're an early riser."

"You, too. What in tarnation are you doing now?"

"Hotcakes," she said, eyeing a scoopful of flour, and dumping it in a heavy bowl. After some thought, she added two more.

"Rose—I mean, Mrs. Shanahan—"

"Rose will do."

"I told you I don't like to see a woman in your condition waiting on me. Please don't go to any fuss."

She turned around and took a good look at him.

He was a handsome man, no doubt about it. Younger than she had imagined. Probably in his early thirties. And kind, too. Not the aging widower that she had imagined, citified with a topcoat and bristling side whiskers. She allowed herself the brief, vain wish that she had her figure back.

"I'm not fussing for your sake, Mr. Asher. I spied a tin of maple syrup in the pantry, and I've been awake for an hour waiting to get at it. And also, I have other selfish reasons for wanting to feed you well."

"I'm not surprised. Dare I ask?"

She laughed. "I want you to be so stunned by my cooking that you won't mind when you realize the train can't possibly run today. You'll ask me to stay until the tracks are clear, and I won't have to spend my money at the hotel. Then I can eat maple syrup every day for a week, if I'm lucky."

"Damnation." He hadn't thought of her being stuck in town. "You're probably right. I don't see any way around it, reasonably."

Suddenly, it seemed like the right thing to do. Hell, it was pleasant to have someone to talk to in the quiet morning hours, and to drink coffee without grounds floating on top, and to hear laughter in the huge emptiness of the house.

The tranquility of the moment was shattered by a clatter on the staircase, and her children came rushing up from downstairs, their faces eager at the sight of the snow outside the windows.

"Enough noise!" Rose exclaimed. "And you may as

235

well go to school today, so get your books. Mind your manners; say good morning to Mr. Asher, who has been kind enough to let us stay until the train can pass."

Danny offered him a perfunctory "good morning" that lacked enthusiasm of any sort, but the little girl smiled brilliantly, revealing a missing tooth.

"How long will that be?" she asked.

Her bright-eyed look of adoration made him uncomfortable. "Well, that depends."

"Till Christmas?" she persisted. Her face shone beneath her mussed hair, and the hope in her eyes was too keen to shoot down.

"Till the end of the month," he said, and then wondered what in the devil had possessed him.

The child clapped her hands with delight, and Rose's shoulders drooped with relief.

He stood, taking his cup of coffee, suddenly uncomfortable with his role of benefactor. "But I expect you two to keep the noise down, and behave. And you, young man"—he turned to Danny—"I expect you to get up and start the fires in the morning. That's no work for your mother. You're old enough to be helpful to her."

"Yes, sir."

Kate was whispering in her mother's ear, and Rose nodded. "Run down to our room, and take my shawl. Hurry."

The child disappeared down the hall, came back up wrapped in her mother's shawl, and rushed out the back door.

Ash watched her out the back window, plowing a trail to the outhouse, chattering away to nobody he could see. Odd creatures, little girls.

A thought occurred to him.

"Are you all down in Mrs. Louis's old room? All three of you?" he asked.

Rose nodded, smiling absently as she watched her daughter out the window.

"Well, that won't do. May as well make yourselves comfortable. There's a room upstairs that will do for you and the little one. End of the hall. Flowery paper on the walls."

Rose stopped abruptly, her hand still on the wooden spoon she was holding, and an odd expression passed over her face.

"Thank you," she said quickly, and turned her attention back to cooking.

"You don't mind staying in the room you're in, do you?" he asked Danny.

"All for my own? A room to myself?"

It was the first time the boy had looked at him with anything but distrust. He watched Danny struggling for his usual nonchalant expression. "Thanks," the boy said casually, as if it meant nothing.

He caught Rose's smile out of the corner of his eye, and suddenly Asher needed to be away from them, to find his solitude.

Without even an "excuse me," he left for the quiet of the parlor, the fire now blazing and warm, the room pleasant with the bright morning sun streaming through the clean windows.

He stopped, and sniffed curiously. A light, flowery scent wafted by his nostrils, and then was gone. Asher looked around, and sniffed again, trying to place it.

He couldn't. He sat by the fire, sipping his coffee, wondering why such a pleasant odor would make him uneasy.

He had eaten breakfast, saddled his horse, and was halfway to town before he realized; the aroma had been uncannily like Emily's favorite perfume.

Dismissing the thought, he guided his horse through the drifted snow, and rode on to town, hoping the telegraph lines were still up and that the storm hadn't done too much damage.

The morning passed pleasantly for Rose. She starched and rehung the lace curtains, now whiter than the snow they framed, acquainted herself with the contents of Asher's pantry and cold cellar, washed the breakfast dishes, and started several loaves of bread. It was a pleasure to have all the things she needed, and so readily at hand.

She took her spare dress and Kate's Sunday dress from the trunk, and sprinkled and ironed them.

Finally, she went upstairs, using the front staircase. It came out on a landing with high windows. A writing desk stood there, its surface covered with dust. She picked up one of the books that sat there, and opened the cover.

Emily Asher. 1878.

The sloping, pretty handwriting startled her, and she closed the book quickly, looking around guiltily.

"Don't be silly," she said aloud. It was coincidence that Kate had named her imaginary angel Emily. It was coincidence that they were in a beautiful house with a rocking chair in the kitchen.

She replaced the book firmly, and made her way down the hall in search of her new quarters. The first door she opened was simply an empty room, large and light, but with heavy round marks scarred into the wood floor where a bed had once stood.

The second door was obviously Asher's room, when he was in town.

"Saints preserve us," she said, staring at the chaos. Shirts, pants, long johns, boots, newspapers, and coffee cups were scattered over chairs, hanging from the mirrored dresser, and in heaps on the floor. His traveling trunk lay open in the middle of the floor. One sock hung from a lamp, and it took all her self-control to close the door without removing it.

She crossed the hall, and opened another door. A bathroom. White tiled and beautiful, with a huge curving bathtub, and a mirrored dressing table. She opened the linen closet, and saw stacks of Turkish towels, thick and costly.

The thought of bathing in such a tub was so tempting that she was ready to head down the stairs and start heating water, but the thought of Mr. Asher coming home and catching her was terrible.

With a longing look, she left the bath, and opened the fourth and last door.

This was her room. A huge bed, with a dainty coverlet of crocheted lace, a matching wardrobe of dark walnut, and a dresser as well. A dainty chair, upholstered in needlepoint flowers.

And, of course, there were flowers on the walls. A delicate ivory paper with a pattern of roses, pale pink and burgundy, running up the walls in vertical stripes.

Unable to resist, she lay full length on the bed, sighing at the softness of the feather mattress. No straw-filled ticking in this house.

For a rare half an hour, Rose Shanahan did nothing but lie there, hands wrapped around her huge belly, feeling the comforting rolling movement of the child inside her. She closed her eyes, and pretended that this was truly her house, her beautiful room, her full pantry downstairs. She imagined dresses she bought for Kate, and then the boots and wool coat she would buy for Danny. She would mail-order a beautiful cradle for the baby. She would buy them a sled for Christmas, shiny wood with painted red runners.

In the springtime she would plant a vegetable garden, and eat fresh green peas off the vines. She imagined her handsome husband coming home, and sitting beside her on the front porch in the summer, watching the mountain as it turned rose-colored, glowing in the warm twilight.

He'd turn to her, and she'd say, *"Do you know, Ash, what the baby did—"*

"You ridiculous creature," she said aloud, and sat straight up, feeling silly. She stood up slowly, wincing. Her boots were getting too tight; her feet were swelling, but she couldn't bear to leave the buttons undone and go flapping about the house like a slattern. She looked bad enough, waddling about like an overstuffed duck.

It had been a long time since she had worried about her looks.

She hung her and Kate's dresses in the wardrobe, closed the door with a bang, and used the kitchen staircase to go back down, as was proper.

"He thinks he's some pumpkins," Danny grumbled to Kate, as they made their way toward the house. "Mr. Fancy. I allow we'd have done just as well for ourselves in the city."

A week in Joshua Asher's house hadn't changed Danny's feelings about the man, not one bit. He was the enemy.

Kate struggled behind her brother through the snow, anxious to get back to the warm house. "I like him. I like our house. And the food . . ."

Danny couldn't argue about the food. He had never eaten so well. And every day, his lunch pail was a delight. His classmates couldn't mock him anymore for bringing nothing but a cold biscuit. Now he had soft, fresh bread, tangy pieces of cheese, and apples from the cellar. But food was one thing, and Joshua Asher another.

"It's easy for him to give away food, with all his money. But he doesn't really like us."

Kate was stung by the thought, and stopped right there

on the road. "He does!" she cried, her breath puffing out in great clouds. "He likes us! And he likes Mama. They sit and talk every morning."

For some reason, this seemed to infuriate Danny even more. "He does not!"

"He does. You're just mean because you don't like Sunday school, and Mama made us go."

"There was no reason to walk all that way. This was supposed to be a day of rest."

Kate quoted her mother. "You should have rested when you got there, while you listened to your teacher."

"I already heard it from Mama, I don't need to hear it from you."

Kate ignored him, and hummed happily as she walked along.

Danny rolled his eyes, and cursed his broken boots that let the snow in at the toes.

"I'll tell you a secret," Kate offered, trying to cheer him up.

"What?"

"Don't tell Mama."

"What?" He was interested now, but wouldn't let on.

"Mama's going to have a baby."

Danny turned and regarded his sister with a look of utter contempt. "I know that. Mama knows that."

"She does?"

"For corn sake, yes! You're such an idiot, Kate."

"You're mean. I bet you don't know the baby's name."

"No, and neither do you. Race you." He started up the long drive at a dead run, anxious to reach the warmth of the house.

Kate stood in the drive, watching her brother. The wind whispered past her cheek, and made a pretty sound. She took a deep breath, and smelled snow, clean and clear, and then, a breath of flowers.

"Emily?"

She closed her eyes, and felt a gentle sparkle of warmth near her. "I know you're there, Emily."

She looked around, but saw nothing but snow and trees, and up ahead, Mr. Asher's beautiful house.

"Danny doesn't mean to be like that, but he is. Do you think it's because he's sad? Like Mr. Asher? He never smiles, or laughs, but he's not mean. Maybe Santa Claus will bring Danny something nice. That would make him happy."

The little girl walked on toward the house, chatting away.

"Grown-ups don't get things from Santa," she said then. "They give each other things. I'd like to give Mr. Asher a present."

She tilted her head into the wind, and smiled, as if she heard an answer.

Ash stood by the front window, watching the children. There went that little girl, chattering to the air again. She spun in a circle in the snow, her arms spread wide, and laughed at nothing. Then she put her hand on her hip, and stood, nodding thoughtfully, as if she were listening to someone.

"Weird kid." He wandered into the kitchen where Rose was banging pots and pans around, doing whatever she did in there all day. He always felt at odds on Sunday, when the mine was closed.

Danny had just come in, and was wiping the snow from his boots, frowning. His cheeks were red with cold.

"What did you learn today?" his mother was asking.

He shrugged. "Something about God."

"Well, I should hope so. Never mind, I'll ask Kate. I hope one of you pays attention." She was elbow-deep in suds, washing something. She was always washing something. Ash wondered if there was anything left in the house that hadn't been cleaned.

"Rose?"

The boy shot him a resentful look at the use of his mother's first name. Too bad, he found himself thinking somewhat irritatedly.

"Yes, Mr. Asher?"

"May I ask you something personal?"

She stopped scrubbing, and turned, giving him her full attention. Her coffee-colored eyes were wide with curiosity as she dried her hands on her apron.

"I suppose."

"It's about your little girl. Is she . . . well, normal?"

"In what way?" Her spine stiffened a little, and her left brow lifted slightly.

He was a little sorry he had asked, but they'd always been frank with each other. "The way she talks to herself. You know. And . . . listens."

"Her hearing is fine."

"That wasn't what I meant. But . . . oh, come on. You know what I mean. Every time I round a corner, she's chatting away to nobody, and laughing, and I just wondered . . ."

Rose Shanahan nodded briskly. "Yes, I know. Kate is a very normal little girl, thank you very much. She just has a very vivid imagination, and talks about it. I believe many children have imaginary friends."

"Emily," Dan put in, rolling his eyes.

"What?" Ash asked with an involuntary start.

"—never mind," Rose said at the same time.

"Her friend," Dan explained, helping himself to an apple from a bowl on the kitchen table. "Kate says she's an angel named Emily. And she really believes it."

Ash said nothing.

"Yes, yes, with silver wings, and violets in her hair,"

243

Rose said briskly. "A little girl's fancy, Danny. That's all."

"Violets?" Ash asked, and his voice sounded a little uncertain to his own ears. They were Emily's favorite flower.

"A vivid imagination, Mr. Asher," Rose repeated. "That's all. Nothing to worry about." She gave a quick nod at the back door, and he saw the little girl coming up the steps.

"She believes it," Danny persisted, swallowing a bite of apple. "She's making me as crazy as a loon. Emily this, Emily that. And now Santa Claus."

"That's enough." Rose's voice was sharp as Kate came through the door, letting in a cold gust of fresh air.

The little girl ran straight to her mother, wrapping her arms as far around her middle as she could. Rose pulled off the girl's gray knit cap, smoothed the part of her dark hair, and bent to kiss her.

"What have you got there, darling?"

"A present. For Mr. Asher." The little girl turned to him with her gap-toothed smile, and held out her hands.

Red-berried holly branches, and vines of green ivy.

"How pretty," Rose said, smiling with the soft look of a loving mother.

"They go over the mantel, in the sitting room," Kate told him. "For Christmas. You know?"

He knew. He remembered. He didn't know what to say.

He remembered Emily, light brown hair shining. Their first year in the new house. She was wearing pale green, something loose and full over her pregnant stomach, her hands full of dark green ivy, and glossy, red-berried holly branches.

"We'll put them over the mantel, to bring Christmas

in, Joshua. Look, how pretty. Now it feels like Christmas is coming, doesn't it?"

The little girl was looking up at him with bright, innocent eyes.

He cleared his throat, awkwardly. "Well. Thank you, Kate. I . . . umm . . . I don't really keep Christmas, anymore."

Her brow wrinkled. "Keep it? No, you can't keep it. It's coming, and then it goes away. Here. It's a present."

Hesitantly, he took the branches. He glanced at Rose, and saw the troubled look in her eyes. She knew that something was wrong.

"Tell me, Kate," she said quickly, "for your brother can't remember. What lesson did you learn in Sunday school today?"

The child smiled proudly. "I remember. 'With belief, all things are possible,' " she quoted. "Can I have an apple, too?"

"May I," Rose corrected. "You may. But go wash your hands, first."

Rose turned away deliberately, and went back to her dishes.

Ash backed silently out of the room, the branches still in his hands. He looked down at them, shaking his head.

"Just a vivid imagination—"

"An angel named Emily—"

". . . and violets in her hair."

"—put them over the mantel, to bring Christmas in. . . ."

". . . all things are possible."

Almost unwillingly, he walked to the mantel, and laid the branches gently over dark wood.

They looked right. They *felt* right.

A sudden sunbreak pierced the cloudy sky, and shone through the windows, making little prisms of the leaded glass designs and warming the wine-colored patterns of the carpet.

He looked around. Something was different.

But nothing was. The room held the same furniture, the same carved what not in the corner, the same coals glowing in the grate, the same everything. Only the glossy green leaves on the mantel were different, yet it seemed as if the whole room had transformed.

Yes, it *was* different. The house felt warm and lived in, like a happy place, instead of an empty, waiting shell.

Laughter came from the kitchen, and the warm smell of baking. There was snow outside, and cinnamon within.

For the first time in years, Joshua Asher felt Christmas coming.

Either that, or he was losing his mind.

Chapter Five

The weather showed no signs of warming, and the citizens of Black Diamond were stranded together in the pine-scented, icebound hills.

The miners still worked the mines, freezing in the dark caverns, until Joshua Asher announced that until the thaw, men would work only half days, but still receive their regular pay.

A week before Christmas, another heavy snow fell, collapsing the roof of the schoolhouse. Since no one had been hurt, there was more rejoicing, this time among the children. Homemade sleds of varying sizes and shapes appeared, and Main Street took on an unusual holiday air as children slid, skidded, stalled, and shrieked through town.

The postmaster, once the telegraph system was up and running again, reported that Seattle had been blessed with rain, but it immediately turned the snow to mud. The streets were impassible, and there was a rumor—unconfirmed, but believed by all—that a horse had fallen into a mudhole and drowned.

247

Amy Elizabeth Saunders

The general store was filled with more visiting gossips than shoppers, but that was nothing new. The storekeeper paid tribute to the season by removing the picks, pans, and boots from the window, and laying out his annual Christmas display—a slightly dingy blanket of cotton wool, and a few cotton bolls hanging from threads (meant to resemble falling snow) and an assortment of enchanting, if mostly unaffordable gifts. Tin banks, paper dolls, pull toys, books, and a couple of china-headed dolls and bags of marbles provided much entertainment for the younger set, who, if they couldn't actually own such riches, could always stare at them and dream.

Reverend Quigley frantically rehearsed the little church choir every day, in preparation for the Christmas Eve service—considered a highlight of the year—and lamented that the only really true soprano in town belonged, most unfortunately, to the town's woman of ill-repute. And yet, bad or not, she showed up for every rehersal—and the fact that the other women sat at a distance from her only seemed to confirm her place as featured soloist.

All around, Christmas was coming, and there wasn't a man, woman, or child in Black Diamond who could ignore it.

Joshua Asher wanted to. He felt isolated, removed from the community. He longed for the peace of his Seattle house, where he had his lumberyards and warehouses to occupy him. Critcher managed his coal mines perfectly, his accounts were balanced and there was nothing else to interest him here.

He was at odds with himself, not used to having so much time on his hands. He couldn't very well sit by the stove in the general store playing checkers, and he was uncomfortable watching Rose lumber around the kitchen. Instead, he rode into town every day, telegraphed his Seattle offices, heard that everything was fine, and rode home again.

And every night, he sat in the dining room at a table meant for twelve, ate his dinner, and felt utterly alone. Funny, he thought, he had been alone for eight years now, and it had never bothered him.

Bored, he picked at his plate of chicken and dumplings, and entertained himself by trying to eavesdrop on Rose and her children.

They were laughing, but he couldn't tell at what. After a moment's thought, he reached over with his dinner knife, and opened the room's never-used service cupboard. The little open space, while affording him only a view of the shelves, let the Shanahan voices drift more clearly to him.

Danny was speaking. "—and then Sid knocked down Charlie, and Charlie knocked down Sid, and they both say they won. Then their ma came out, and knocked them both down for fighting."

"They're bad. Will Santa bring them anything?"

"If they're sorry, maybe." Rose's voice. "I'm not sure about Mrs. Gilhooley, though. It's bad form to be knocking your children down in the street."

"Danny washed Tessie Gilhooley's face in snow, and made her cry. Will Santa bring *him* a present?"

"Hmmm. Maybe not. Though maybe he should worry more about what Mrs. Gilhooley might do."

Apparently, Mrs. Gilhooley was a force to be reckoned with, for Danny gave a cry of mock horror, and Kate and Rose collapsed with giggles.

"Put your plate in the sink, Danny, if you're finished. Here, I'll get it."

"I'm not done yet. You're so clean, you're trying to wash our plates while we're still eating."

More merriment in the kitchen. Funny, he didn't ever remember hearing Danny laugh before.

Ash looked up, and caught a glimpse of himself in the reflection of the windows.

Suddenly, it seemed ridiculous. Here he was, alone in this huge room, eavesdropping on his housekeeper and her children for company. He reached out with his knife, and poked the service cupboard closed.

It was pathetic. He was so bored that he was sitting out here listening in on the latest strategies of snowball wars, and wondering which shanty the Gilhooleys were in so that he might catch a glimpse of the formidable missus. All this when what he really would like was—

The door swung open, and Rose was there.

"Mr. Asher?" She held a cup of coffee out to him. "If you're finished with your supper . . ."

She bent over to retrieve his plate, and he looked away, wincing at the awkward way she had to move around her belly.

"There's a brown-sugar apple cake, if you care for any."

"I would. But I'll sit in the kitchen with you, if you don't mind. I've been considering . . . I think it's as stupid as all creation for me to sit out here every night."

"I'm afraid our chatter would bother you." She looked slightly puzzled, as if unsure of how to respond. "Of course, we could leave you the kitchen, if you prefer. . . ."

"I'd prefer, with your permission of course, to spend some more time in your company." Damn! That had come out wrong. He had sounded for all the world as if he was asking permission to court her. But he had simply said exactly what he meant to, hadn't he?

"Mr. Asher." Her voice was always so solid. She never seemed to falter. "You had only to say so. We'd be delighted with your company. I'm afraid being snowbound must be very tiresome for you."

Of course, she understood. He looked up at her, and

250

saw that brilliant, dimpled smile in her heart-shaped face. It was a kittenish sort of face, too narrow at the chin and too wide at the forehead, and nose a bit too pointed, but somehow, all of it came together with a grace and symmetry that was uniquely Rose.

And suddenly, he didn't notice the swollen stomach or awkward gait, but saw only the pale glow of her skin, and the way her dark eyes shone.

For no reason that he could account for, he found her beautiful.

He followed her into the kitchen, and the children fell silent as he joined them at the table.

Maybe this hadn't been such a good idea.

Rose carried the cake to the table, and joined them.

"Any news in town?" he asked, after a moment of silence.

"There are toys in the store window," Kate volunteered. "And Charlie Gilhooley threw a snowball into the saloon, and hit Mr. Svenson, then had to run away."

"They sound like a boisterous bunch, the Gilhooleys. And how about you, Danny? Any good snowball fights?"

"No, sir."

The boy's face was set and sullen.

"All ready for Santa Claus?"

The boy raised his eyes, dark brown like his mother's, but with none of the warmth and humor. "That's bunkum," he replied rudely. "I'm not a baby."

"Danny." Rose spoke quietly, but with unmistakable warning in her voice.

"What's bunkum?" Kate demanded, looking anxiously up from her cake.

"It's slang," Rose replied with evident displeasure. "It means your brother's getting too smart for his own good, and had better watch his step."

251

"Done any sledding?" Damned if Asher knew why he was trying so hard to be sociable.

"No sled," was the quick answer.

The silence was flat. He tried to remember what he had liked best at that age. Horses.

"Well, I'm planning a ride out to Dussler's farm in the next couple of days, to see what he's got in the way of livestock. How does a goose sound, for Christmas? Or maybe some fresh pork?"

"It sounds wonderful," Rose said quickly, her eyes brightening. "It's been years since I cooked a goose. I wonder if I'd remember how."

"Oh, I'd bet you do. It's a far place to go, though. Could use a little company. Dan? Care to ride along?"

The boy's expression was blatantly hostile.

"No."

"Daniel. You may leave the table. And apologize to Mr. Asher for your rudeness."

"I apologize."

"And I'll take that apology as kindly as you gave it." Asher said, meeting the boy's eyes evenly.

Without a word, Danny left the table. A moment later, the door slammed behind him.

Rose started to rise, her eyes snapping, but Asher caught her hand.

"Let him go. It's a hard age to be."

"It's no excuse for rudeness. That child wears my patience thin."

"He isn't mean," Kate said softly. "Just sad, Mr. Asher. Sad and lonely."

Sometimes, the child's dark eyes seemed so adult, so at odds with her tiny face.

"You're a good girl, Kate," Rose said. "Go wash up, and get ready for bed, and I'll come hear your prayers."

"Yes, Mama. Good night, Mr. Asher."

Her footsteps were light as she ran up the stairs.

"Mr. Asher."

He turned to Rose, and saw that her dark eyes were wide and worried.

"Yes?"

"Are you aware that you are holding my hand?"

"I am?" He looked at her hand, laying beneath his own on the table. It was such a small hand, but a hand of considerable strength. Every blister and scar on her palm spoke of her ability to meet life's blows, and endure them.

It had been years since he had held a woman's hand.

"Does it offend you?" he asked softly.

Her eyes lifted hesitantly to his face, and he saw her uncertain for the first time since he had met her. She looked down at their hands together, and then back up with an expression of wonder.

"No," she answered slowly. "No, it doesn't offend me."

They sat in silence for a long time, neither moving or speaking, simply feeling the warmth and comfort offered by each other's touch.

He was deep in sleep, burrowed beneath the heavy blankets, dreaming something about violets. They were vivid, velvety purple splashed with yellow as brilliant as sunshine. Violets in the snow, sparkling like diamonds.

Rose was in the kitchen, singing softly as she made coffee. Footsteps came outside his door, quick and light, soft laughter like silver bells. The little girl, passing by the closed door, spoke softly so as not to wake him. Emily answered her, her voice soft with happiness, leaving the scent of violets in her wake.

He spoke to Emily in his dream. *"Do you like her, Em? Is it right?"*

And in his dream, Emily answered. *"Oh, yes, Joshua. She's brave and strong and good."*

A door slammed, below in the house. Danny and his mother, speaking in the kitchen.

Joshua opened his eyes, startled.

He didn't dream often, and it disturbed him, the way this dream seemed to hang over him in the cold morning air. For a moment, Emily's words seemed to hover in the room, and he could almost smell the scent of violets.

"Horse shit," he muttered uneasily. The room was exactly as it always was. He reached for his clothes, and found his pants thrown over a chair. He hurried to put them on over his red flannel long johns, then threw on a plaid flannel shirt.

He froze as he heard it again—the soft step in the hall, a whispering voice. He exhaled sharply. It was just Kate.

But still . . .

Silently, in his heavy socks, he crossed the floor, and stepped out into the hall. *Empty.*

A quick movement caught his eye, and he turned rapidly toward the back staircase. He followed quickly, and looked down. Nothing, just the murmur of Rose's voice, and Danny's answer rising from the kitchen.

Damn it, he had heard or seen something. He turned, and looked up, where the staircase narrowed and turned toward the attic. A cold breeze moved down to meet him.

Quietly, he turned the corner and peered up into the dark stairwell.

"Katie?"

The little girl turned swiftly, her dark braids flying.

Of course it was Kate. Of course, she was alone.

"Hey. What are you doing up there?" He squinted up at the dark stairwell, and saw her expression of alarm.

She bit her lip, and stared at him with doe eyes. "Looking for something," she whispered.

"Did you lose something?"

She shook her head.

"Then what are you looking for? There's nothing up there but an old dirty attic."

"Oh, no sir. It's in there."

"What, honey?" The poor little thing looked nervous. "You can tell me."

"No, sir. I mustn't. Mama said I mustn't upset you."

"Ah. Well, your mother makes the laws, as usual. But if I guess, that's not telling me, is it? And if I'm not upset, no harm done."

She considered that.

"Make you a deal. If I guess why you're here, and I'm not upset, I'll help you look."

She smiled. "That's not disobeying, is it?"

"Not a bit. Now I would guess . . . hmmm. You've been talking to angels again."

"You guessed!" She peered down at him. "Are you upset?"

"Not a bit. Now, what do you think is in the attic?"

"Let's go inside first."

Curious, he followed her up, and unlatched the hook on the door. "See? Good thing I happened along. You're too little to reach that."

He went first, his breath showing in the frosty air. The light was dim, slanting in two dusty windows set beneath the peak of the roof.

"How about that? I think we found the one place in the house your mother didn't clean."

"Two places. She won't clean your room. She says it looks like the wreck of the Hesperus. What's the Hesperus?"

He choked back a laugh. "A ship in a poem. Your mother's a smart woman."

The little girl nodded, smiling. "Now. Let me see. We're looking for a box."

He looked around the dusty room. "Take your pick. There's about twenty of them."

She moved quickly across the floor, her little boots leaving footprints in the dust, and walked slowly around the neat stacks of boxes, trunks, and crates. The headboard of the bed that had once been his and Emily's leaned against a wall, gathering cobwebs.

She stopped next to a broken chair, and pointed. "This one."

He walked over, and lifted it. It was an old vegetable crate, covered in faded newspaper. "What is it?"

"Christmas," she said simply.

He knew what he would find even before he lifted the corner of the paper.

"You said you didn't keep Christmas," Katie said softly. "But you do. You keep it in a box."

He tossed the newsprint to the floor, and lifted out a tiny swan of silver glass, and then a little house made of shining glass with a powder of sparkling snow painted on the roof. Next came golden walnut, delicate and fragile. A string of glass beads, still shimmering with jewel-bright colors.

These were Emily's precious Christmas ornaments, some from Germany, some from England. All were wrapped carefully and carried with her all the way from Boston, now gathering dust in the attic.

"Well," he said, and had to clear his throat. "Well. What do you make of that?"

"Do you know what Mama would say?" Kate asked solemnly.

"No, what?"

"God works in mysterious ways, His wonders to perform," the child quoted softly.

He didn't know what to say, or what to believe. There had to be a logical explanation. Maybe Kate had been poking around in the attic, and found the box days ago.

But even as the easy thought occurred to him, he thought of her little bootprints, making a trail through dust obviously undisturbed for several years. And the latch.

"Is that what your mother would say?" he asked finally. "Well, I guess if she says it, it's so. You know what else she'd say?"

"What?"

"She'd tell us to get out of this dust and cold before we catch our deaths, and wash up for breakfast, and that's that."

His imitation of Rose's no-nonsense manner delighted Kate; she stifled her giggles behind her small fingers.

"Come on. I'll carry the box I keep Christmas in, and you get the door. We'd better hurry. We have a lot to do today."

"What do we have to do?" She was almost skipping beside him, her eyes fastened longingly on the box of treasures in his arms.

"What do you think? These things are no good without a tree, are they? Have you ever had a Christmas tree, Kate?"

"No. But there was one in church last year, and we made paper chains for it. It was beautiful."

"This one will be better," he promised, as they went down the stairs. "I've got an idea. Let's hide these, and surprise your mother."

Together, they slipped the box inside his bedroom door and hurried downstairs to the kitchen.

Rose was standing at the stove, laying thick strips of bacon in a pan, and she gave them a sharp look as they entered.

"What on earth have you two been up to? You look like the cats who stole the cream."

"Exploring the attic," Asher answered innocently.

"Of all things. You're lucky you didn't catch pneumonia in that dust and cold. Saints preserve us. Go wash up for breakfast."

"Told you," he whispered to Kate, and the two of them choked back laughter.

Danny, coming in from the front of the house, looked suspiciously at them.

"Do you mind if I borrow your children this morning, Rose? I need their help."

"Not at all. What on earth for?"

"You'll see."

"I'm busy," Danny said, shoving his hands in his pockets.

Josh bent down, smiling a false, cheerful, smile. "Look here, you surly little hellion," he whispered, never breaking his smile. "We're doing this to make your mother happy, and you'll come along, and like it, or I'll kick your ass to all creation. Now, smile."

The boy's smile looked more like a grimace, but it would suffice.

"What are you doing in that sitting room?" Rose called through the dining room door, as if she didn't know.

"Don't come out!" Kate shrieked. "Not yet."

"Oh, all right." She retreated back into the kitchen, and eased herself into the rocker by the stove. She closed her eyes, and ran her hands over the firm mountain of her stomach.

The baby was quiet today, and she knew its time was drawing near. She offered up a silent prayer for his safety.

How long now? she wondered. As much as she dreaded the labor, she longed to have it done with. She wanted to be lithe and quick again. She had taken her old dresses out of the trunk this morning. The gray wool was in deplorable shape, but the sage green calico, sprigged with yellow and pink flowers, was still wearable, if faded. The corsets she had been so happy to discard were washed and waiting. It would be good to have a waistline again.

Out in the sitting room, she heard Kate give a cry of alarm, and, for the first time, heard Asher laughing without restraint. What were they doing to that poor little tree?

"Rose?" Asher came through the kitchen door. "Are you all right?"

"Fine," she said, opening her eyes.

He didn't look convinced. His eyes, blue as springtime skies, were worried beneath furrowed brows.

She suddenly felt huge and ungainly in front of him. She must have imagined it, that feeling she had in the kitchen last night. No man could find her attractive, swollen, and graceless, moving with the lumbering step of a bear.

"You don't look fine. Do you want me to fetch the doctor?"

"Great merciful heavens, no."

"You're sure?" he persisted.

She had never noticed before, that he had a scar on his forehead, one clear white line running above his eyebrow. It didn't make him any less handsome.

"I'm sure," she told him.

"You'll tell me in plenty of time, won't you, when I need to go? I wouldn't want . . . I don't want you to . . ."

"Mr. Asher." She met his eyes directly. "I'm not going to die. That's what you're thinking, isn't it?"

"I've considered the possibility," he admitted, flinching slightly at her harsh words.

"Put your mind at ease. If the Holy Mother could give birth in an old barn, I can certainly manage in a feather bed in a warm house. I'm actually looking forward to getting it over with. Now, stop fussing at me. Is it time for me to be surprised yet?"

259

A smile curved his lips. "Yes, ma'am."

"Good. And I hope you didn't track pitch and pine needles all over the house."

"Rose? Are you this formidable when you're not . . . in an interesting condition?"

"Oh no," she said, trying not to smile. "Not at all. I'm much, much worse."

"Lord help us all. Here, let me help you up."

"I don't need help." But she let him take her hands, and pull her to her feet.

"You're a tiny thing," he remarked.

"I'm as big as a house," she contradicted.

"A tiny house," he conceded.

That made her laugh, and it felt good to stand there, her hands clasped in his. There was something so stable and good about him. His very touch made her feel safe. What would it be like, she wondered, to be with a man you could depend on?

"We had best go out," he said. "Those kids are awfully anxious for you to see it."

She almost hated to ask. "Was Danny any better today?"

"A little. He's a hard nut to crack, Rose."

"He's grieving. It will pass."

He had to ask. "And you're not?"

"I'm not a child. I spent eleven years grieving and angry. Not to speak ill of the dead, Mr. Asher, but mine was not a happy marriage. I'm sorry for Jamie, but I quit loving him long ago. And this . . ." She nodded at her belly, and tried hard to find words to explain what there were no socially acceptable words to explain.

It had been months since she and her husband had been together that way, but there had been one night last March, cold and bitter and dark. James had been silent, finally, after hours of rough, rasping coughing, and they were huddled together for warmth. It had been a sad joining, a kind of farewell. She had never expected a child to result.

"I never expected this," was all she could think of to say. "It was a surprise. But for some reason, it was meant to be. I don't understand why, but there it is. God works in mysterious ways. And," she said, drawing a deep breath, "that's that."

He brought his hand to her cheek. "I'm sorry for asking."

She looked up at him. He was going to kiss her. She could see it in his eyes.

"Mama—"

They stepped apart abruptly as Danny burst in through the door. But not quickly enough.

His eyes darkened as they looked from Asher to his mother, and the eager happiness faded from his face. Silently, the boy retreated.

"Damn! Bad timing." Asher remarked.

"On all counts," Rose agreed, then she sighed. "But it can't be helped. Now, let me see this tree."

Even though it was still light out, the lamps had been lit in the sitting room, and the room glowed with warmth.

She didn't need to feign surprise.

A little tree was enthroned in a place of honor in front of the window, and the scent of pine, tart and rich and clean, filled the air, perfuming the room with the scent of the ancient mountains.

Beads of brilliant red and starry blue, gold and green and magenta draped through its branches, and amazing little glass ornaments sparkled and swayed beneath them. At least thirty candles were clipped to the branch tips, slender and white.

"I've never seen the like," Rose said, her voice soft with awe.

She held Kate's hand while the child pointed out the

261

little snow-sprinkled church, the pinecones of silver glass, and the golden walnut and acorn. There were birds of gold and red, with real feathers in their glass tails, and a silvery white swan and tiny golden trumpets. A bell of pure white glass, painted with red roses, dangled alongside a tiny Santa Claus, improbably short and fat, but Santa all the same.

"That is the most beautiful thing I've ever seen, in all my born days," Rose proclaimed. "I don't know what to say."

Asher beamed with pride, Kate danced in a circle, and even Danny managed an uncertain smile.

And then, to all their shock, Rose burst into tears.

She couldn't help it. Everything was so good, too good, and it had been years since she had hoped, or even dreamed that life might offer her anything other than the rest of her days bent over a steaming tub of laundry, scrubbing her fingers raw and hoping for nothing more than one good night's sleep.

And she was terrified that it was going to end.

At her sobbing, panic ensued. Kate cried, and pulled at her mother's skirt. Danny rushed to take her arm, begging her to tell him what was wrong. Nearby, Asher shouted at them to get her to the sofa, apparently sure that the baby was coming.

"Is it time, Rose? Should I go for the doctor?"

"Are you sick, Mama?"

"Please stop, Mama—"

She was being pulled and clung to and pleaded with from all directions, and as suddenly as she had started crying, she was laughing.

"No, no, I'm fine. It's all right, Katie, don't cry. *There*. Gracious, Danny, don't push me, I'm sitting. There, I'm sitting. Get back here, Joshua Asher, you're not sending for the doctor so that he can tell me I'm a goose."

They all watched her carefully, and their faces were so full of uncertainty that she laughed again, still wiping tears from her eyes.

"See? I'm fine."

"What happened?" Danny demanded, still clutching her arm.

"I got too happy. My cup ranneth over, I guess." She wiped her fingers beneath her eyes. "I just overflowed."

"Don't do it again, all right?" her son said, somewhat grumpily.

"I'll second that," Asher agreed, raking his hand through his hair. "Good Lord, woman. You scared us half to death."

He was pale, she noted. Amazing. Did he really care for her? She could hardly credit it, but he certainly appeared to.

"When do we light the candles?" she asked to get her mind off of the subject.

"Not now," Asher replied, with a wary glance at the tree. "I'm afraid of what you might do."

"Tomorrow, Mama," Kate said. "Tomorrow night, before Santa comes."

"*If* he comes. You two still have a whole day to be good."

"I can do it," Kate cried exuberantly. "I know it."

Danny rolled his eyes, returning to his usual removed demeanor now that the crisis had passed.

"Show me," Rose said. "Go wash up for dinner, the both of you. Your hands are black from that tree."

Rose waited until they were gone, and turned to Asher.

"Mr. Asher, I have a favor to ask you."

He lifted his brow. What did she want from him? "Go ahead."

"Tomorrow, when you go into town, will you stop in at the store for me?"

"What do you need?"

She dug in her pocket, and withdrew a carefully knotted handkerchief. "Just a little something extra, for the children. I thought maybe a harmonica for Danny. A little doll or a book for Kate." She held out a thin dime and nickel. "That should suffice."

"Oh, let me, Rose. I can't take that."

Her left brow shot up, something he was beginning to recognize as a sign of displeasure. "No indeed. That would be wrong, and I can afford this. Between this and whatever Santa Claus brings, that should be plenty."

"Hmm. Rose?"

"What?"

He looked around stealthily. "There is no Santa Claus, you know," he whispered. "I believe you're supposed to take care of that."

She laughed softly, and pushed at his shoulder. "You fool. I know that. I guess you didn't know . . ."

"Know what?"

"The church arranges it. Somebody—usually George Critcher—dresses as Santa, and goes from house to house, all through the town. All the children get something. It's really very exciting for them, and that way, no child in town is without a present."

"I didn't know that. Critcher?"

"He's very good. Reverend Quigley arranges it all. For a lot of the miners' children, it's all the Christmas they've ever had."

"I didn't know," he repeated. "I guess I should have contributed something."

"Hard to do, when you never go to church," she pointed out. "Now, give me a hand up, and let's see if I can't manage to get supper on without falling to pieces." She smiled up at him. "Thank you again for the tree. I could just sit and look at it all night."

"Hell, why don't we? Let's eat in the dining room.

I'll fire up the chandelier, and we'll make a party of it."

"Why not?" she agreed. "That'll be fun. I can take off my apron, and sit in that elegant chair, and look at that beautiful tree, and pretend I'm a great lady."

"Rose," he said softly, laying a strong hand on her shoulder. "You are."

Chapter Six

Rose stood on the kitchen porch, staring up at the sky. It was Christmas Eve. It always amazed her that no matter where she was, no matter how poor or unhappy she had been, she was always able to feel something extraordinary on this night.

There was always some point that she was able to steal away, and look at the sky, and believe in miracles.

It was easy this year. She was warm, and her children had enough to eat. Their Christmas Eve dinner had been served at a beautiful table, off of porcelain dishes with bouquets of spring flowers painted around the edges. There had been food to spare, beautiful pork roast and bowls of hot apple sauce, and green beans speckled with bacon and soft potatoes.

The house was full of the smell of gingerbread cookies and Christmas cake bursting with walnuts and raisins, and also the scent of the magical tree, shimmering in the soft yellow lamplight.

A miracle.

And Asher. Though they had not spoken one word about the future, she could feel a promise hovering in the cinnamon- and pine-scented air between them. All through dinner, whenever she looked up, his eyes were on her, pale and bright in the tan of his face, and he would smile. It was a bemused smile, a little puzzled, as though he was not sure exactly how this wonderful feeling was growing between them, or why.

She understood his expression perfectly, for she felt it on her own face, whenever she smiled back.

It seemed another miracle. But on such a night, she could believe in them. She tipped her head back, and stared into the ink-dark sky. The moon was almost full, its silver light glowing through mist. The pines around the cleared land were silhouetted perfectly black against the indigo night, and stars shimmered randomly, appearing and disappearing between the shifting, moonlit clouds.

Rose marveled that this was the same moon, the same stars that had shown on Bethlehem. And suddenly she knew that miracles existed.

"Mama? What are you doing out here?"

Danny stuck his head out of the back door, and she held her arm out to him.

He stood awkwardly, allowing her to hug him for a moment. He was growing. She felt a stab of longing for the little boy he had been, who had come to her for hugs and kisses as easily as he breathed.

"Looking at the stars. Thinking about Christmas."

"You always do," he said. "Remember Silver City?"

She laughed softly. How old had he been—maybe five or six? They had stood together in the night, outside of their canvas tent, and looked at the stars. And then the singing had started, Christmas carols rising into the frosty night.

He had asked if it was angels. She hadn't had the heart

to tell him it was the drunken women in the whorehouse down the hill. She had let him believe what he wanted.

"I remember."

"You're wearing Dad's coat," he said, fingering the fraying sleeve.

"I don't have another, do I?"

"Do you miss him?"

She was silent. "Not in the same way you do," she finally answered, honestly.

"Would you marry Mr. Asher?"

"If he asked me, which he hasn't. Yes. Yes, I would."

"I hope he doesn't," Danny said, his voice husky. "I don't want him to."

"I'm sorry for that. But life could deal us far worse. And I don't want to hear another word about it, and that's that."

Her son was silent for a moment. Finally, "Mr. Asher and Kate want you to come in. They want to light the candles on the tree." He shrugged off her arm, and yanked the door open, stomping back into the kitchen with the awkward, noisy gait unique to eleven-year-old boys, as if they hadn't yet learned to manage the size of their feet.

She sighed, and cast a last, longing look at the sky. *Oh, Danny. Don't spoil this for me.*

She wondered if she was hoping for one too many miracles.

"Are we ready?" Asher held the match up, and looked to Rose for approval.

A bucket of water stood ready with a mop in it, just in case. Kate bounced on the edge of the sofa, her braids bouncing off her shoulders in rhythm, almost trembling with excitement.

"Oh yes! Please!"

"Oh, maybe we should wait." Grinning, he went to put the match in his pocket.

"Don't tease," Rose ordered, laughing.

"Oh, all right. If you're sure."

"We're sure," Kate cried.

Slowly, ceremoniously, he struck the match. He lit one candle, then another, working from top to bottom. Slowly, the fir came to life, its beads and ornaments shimmering and twinkling like stars.

Kate and Rose let out simultaneous sighs of pleasure at the sight, and they looked so alike with their dimpled smiles and dark eyes glowing that it made Joshua smile.

Danny sat alone in the chair by the fire, his face pale and his eyes mingling sorrow and resentment. He looked very dark in the shadows, as if the Christmas light touched only those within its enchanted circle.

"Danny!" Kate danced up to him, and tried to take his hands. "Look! Look at our tree? Isn't it beautiful?"

He shook her off and shrugged.

Confused but undaunted, Kate persisted. "Come and look! Why aren't you happy? Santa's coming. Oh, what do you think he's bringing?"

"There isn't any Santa." The words burst out, from some dark, sorrowful and ugly place deep within him.

Rose whirled around. *"Danny."*

Usually, that would have been enough. But there was something in him, some lonely, bitter sorrow that none of them seemed to feel or understand—heck, none of them *tried* to understand. He was shut out, the orphan in their midst, and it was eating him alive. He wanted to strike out, to ruin their happiness.

"There *is*," Kate stated, softly, her voice quivering. "There is a Santa. He comes every year. He came last year, and he can come here. Can't he, Mama? Can't he, Mr. Asher?"

269

"He will," Rose said, in a voice that invited no argument.

"He won't!" Danny spat out, and now that the words were coming, they just kept spewing forth. "It isn't Santa, it's just dumb old Mr. Critcher, all dressed up in a red suit. He does it every year. And we know what he's going to bring; the same dumb things he brings every year. Just a few pieces of candy and a pair of old mittens that the church ladies knit. Isn't that what you got last year? And the year before?"

The boy's face was red, his voice harsh. "Isn't that what everybody gets? Didn't you ever notice that the kids with money get more, no matter how good you are? Ever wonder why? Now you know! Cause it's just old Critcher with our charity candy and our church mittens, and there ain't no Santa Claus!"

Asher stood frozen, shocked by the boy's anger. Kate stood perfectly still, her little face white, all the joy drained from it. But Rose stood straight and calm, her eyes clear and steady.

She moved quietly toward the children, and took Kate's hand. "It isn't true. It isn't true, Kate."

The child looked at her mother with tear-filled eyes, and Asher marveled at her expression of perfect trust.

"It isn't true," Rose repeated. "And Danny, you should be ashamed, trying to steal happiness out from under her. You know better. And Santa Claus can hear you, and you won't get a present."

Danny was white now, but still defiant. "He can't hear me. It's old Critcher, and he can't hear me. And he'll still bring my old mittens and candy, unless you take them away."

"Daniel James Shanahan." Rose's voice remained perfectly soft and calm, but there was a gleam in her eye that Joshua Asher hoped he never had to see again. "Christmas or no, one more word out of your mouth and

I will beat you like a dirty rug. Don't you ever, *ever,* try to steal another person's joy again. It's a cruel, ugly thing. It's wrong. And that's that."

They all stood, breathless, waiting.

Danny sank back into the depths of the chair, his eyes hot, but mercifully silent.

And then there came the sound of bells.

Soft and clear, down the drive in the cold night. Horse's hooves on the snow.

"He's here," Kate breathed, and her huge eyes, still filled with tears, turned toward the door with awe. She looked at her brother, and her expression said clearly that she was thankful not to be in his shoes.

The bells came to the front porch, and stopped.

Rose, still pale, managed a smile. "Open the door, Kate. Let him in."

The child stood rooted to the floor, trembling with excitement.

"Shall I?" Rose asked, and managed a shaky laugh. She gave Asher a quick, troubled look, and swung the door wide, letting in the cold night air.

"Santa Claus! We're so glad you could come."

It was Critcher, Asher noted with amusement, his short, robust figure perfectly suited to his red robes. His cheeks were red with cold behind his false beard, his sandy hair hidden beneath his fur-trimmed hat.

Santa Claus glanced at his boss, and turned a little pinker, but he nodded with as much dignity as he could muster, then, gave a deep belly laugh that really did sound like a proper Santa.

"Mrs. Shanahan! And Daniel and Kate! Merry Christmas! Have we been good this year?"

"Oh yes!" Kate came to life again, bouncing frantically on the toes of her boots, braids bouncing. "Mostly always! I tried!"

Danny, to his credit, said nothing. He lifted his chin

271

defiantly, and went to stand by his sister. He cast a quick, sharp look at his mother and Asher. *"See?"* the look seemed to say, *"I'll get my mittens and candy, and damned be the rest of you."*

Asher wanted to give him a good whack upside his head.

"Well, well. Let me see. It seems that I must have something in my bag, for two good children."

It was funny, the way Critcher was enjoying his role, acting so different from the glum, no-nonsense mine manager that Asher knew. It seemed that many things were different than he'd thought.

"Now, what have we here?" A package appeared from the burlap sack, tissue paper tied with red yarn. "What does it say on that?"

"It says, 'Katie Shanahan,' " Kate read, clapping her hands and bouncing again, proud to show off her reading skills. Her face was flushed with delight.

"It does indeed. You're a right smart little girl. You must be doing your schoolwork."

"I am," she said, her hands trembling. She wanted the package, plainly, but was afraid to reach out to such an exalted personage as Santa.

"Well, there you are, and Merry Christmas to you."

She accepted the package from his gloved hands, and clutched it to her heart. She held it, as if all the treasures of the world were contained within.

"And what have we got for you, young man?" Santa asked, and he looked into the burlap bag.

Asher glanced at Rose, who stood silently now, her mouth tight.

Santa frowned into the bag, and searched again.

Danny stood defiant.

"Don't worry, it's here," Santa Critcher assured them. "Just saw it, over at Svenson's. 'Danny Shanahan,' written right on it, plain as day."

272

He searched the bag, looking up at Rose, his face creasing with concern; then he searched again.

"It *was* in here," he repeated, confused, starting to sound more like Critcher and less like Santa. "I know it was. I just saw it."

Kate's eyes grew round with awe, and she looked at her errant brother with worried eyes.

"Now, don't that beat all?" Santa asked, straightening up and looking at Rose with troubled eyes. "I can't think what happened. Saw it there not ten minutes ago. And it's plumb gone. Just disappeared."

"I'll be damned," Asher whispered under his breath. He and Rose exchanged bewildered glances, Santa staring at them with baffled concern.

Danny stood, his defiance gone, his face utterly bewildered as he looked at the three adults.

Kate regarded her brother with solemn, pitying awe. The boy had sinned. He had doubted, he had shouted his disbelief of the great one, and Santa had found him out. His gift had mysteriously vanished.

Rose recovered first. "That's fine, Santa. I guess that's how it goes. We're always happy to see you, though." She took him firmly by the arm, and propelled him toward the door. "Thank you, and happy Christmas."

Critcher glanced worriedly over his shoulder, confusion plain on his face. Joshua couldn't restrain a wink.

"Merry Christmas, Santa Claus," he called, trying to keep the laughter from his voice.

"Uh . . . Merry Christmas," Santa answered, and Asher could hear him mumbling to Rose that he didn't understand, that he had seen the present—

"Good night, Santa," Rose said, sweet but firm, then she closed the door.

When she returned, they all stood quietly and looked at Danny. His anger and defiance were gone.

He stood there, confusion and suspicion playing

273

across his face, looking from his mother to Asher, and back again.

"How did you do that?" he finally asked, bewildered and forlorn sounding. "How?"

"I did nothing," Rose said, simply and truthfully. "Nothing at all. God moves in mysterious ways, Danny, His wonders to perform. And so, apparently, does Santa. Let that be a lesson to us all."

The boy stood stock-still, then ran from the room.

"Don't you dare laugh," Rose said to Asher.

"I wasn't even thinking of it," he answered truthfully. "I was thinking about what you said. I'll be . . ."

"And don't swear."

"Yes, ma'am."

Kate stared up at them with awed eyes. "He knew," she whispered. "Santa knew. Poor Danny."

"Yes, poor Danny," Rose agreed. "But he'll be all right. Now let me see what Santa brought you."

Kate tore open her package without hesitation, and her face lit up at the sight of her new mittens of red yarn, and a striped bag of ribbon candy. If Danny had tried to spoil her surprise, he had failed miserably.

She counted out each piece of candy, admiring them in turn—the red-and-white striped one, the solid green, the pink-and-white one rippled like a piece of ribbon caught in the wind, the lemon-yellow and orange ones.

She exclaimed over each as if it were a work of art, arranged them in a row, and then carefully tucked them back into their bag. She looked up at her mother.

"Should I share them with Danny?"

"Do you want to?"

She nodded, her face troubled. "He was bad, but I don't want him to be sad anymore."

"You're a good girl," Rose told her. "You may, in the morning. I think Danny wants to be alone now, and you need to go to bed. Christmas comes early."

Asher watched, smiling as Kate hugged her mother's neck, and bid him good night. She raced up the stairs wearing her red mittens.

"Will she sleep in them, do you suppose?" he asked.

"Probably. If they came from Santa, they're magic, you know."

"I should put those candles out." He stood, and started extinguishing them, one by one, carefully cupping his hands around the little flames. "Speaking of magic," he began.

"I don't have the faintest idea," she answered, before he could finish. "Wasn't that the oddest thing?"

"I almost felt sorry for the boy."

"Almost," she agreed with a grimace. "But not quite. He was horrible."

"Agreed." He snuffed out another candle, and started to laugh. "Critcher was a sight, wasn't he? He should forget the mines and go on the stage. Hell, *I* almost believed in Santa tonight."

He settled back on the sofa next to her, and they both laughed softly.

"Rose?"

She looked up at him, her eyes soft and dark in the lamplight.

He cleared his throat, uncertain of how to begin. "I'm not much good at speaking," He started confidently, but then stopped, suddenly tongue-tied.

She waited, wide-eyed and silent, and the look of hope in her eyes was somehow heart-wrenchingly sweet to him.

"I guess I'll just say it, plain out. This has been the best Christmas I've ever had. Ever."

"Even with Danny's sideshow?"

"Well, that was something, wasn't it? I still can't figure out . . . well, never mind that. What I want to ask is . . . I know it's too soon, but . . ."

275

He drew a deep breath, and spoke. "Will you be here next Christmas? That is . . . what I'm trying to say is . . ."

"I know what you're trying to say." Her voice was soft and trembled a little. "And my answer is yes. I would be happy to stay, Ash. I agree, it seems soon, but . . . I want to stay. As long as you want us to."

"Maybe forever?" He caught her hands, and squeezed them tightly between his own.

She closed her eyes, and her heart sang until she thought it would fly out of her chest and shoot away into the moonlight star-sprinkled sky. "Can you mean it?" she whispered.

"More than I've ever meant anything in my life."

A miracle. It was a miracle. This was the most beautiful night in all the world, in all time.

"I think I love you," she whispered, too honest to observe the proprieties, too honest to be ashamed of her own boldness.

"Oh, Rose." He gathered her tightly to his chest, and she let her face rest in the hollow of his neck, and breathed in the scent of his skin and dark hair. He smelled of soap and cigar smoke and clean hair.

"I love you, too," he whispered, and she felt his heart beating against her own. She wept with joy.

"Damn . . ." he said after a few minutes. "There you go again, running over. Stop that. Here—give me a kiss."

Blushing, laughing a little, she turned her face up, and they kissed, slowly and softly, until her face glowed pink, and she was breathless.

There was a soft sound from the ceiling above them, and they parted quickly, looking up.

"Kate," she said, unnecessarily.

He smiled at her, and wiped a tear from her cheek.

"I should go up," she said, her cheeks flaming again. "I forgot to listen to her prayers."

"Go ahead. You've already answered mine."

"Can you mean it?" She shook her head, joy and disbelief mingling in her heart.

"I can and I do. Now go to bed, Rose, and I'll see you in the morning."

She felt as if she were floating. The weight of her body seemed to have vanished, and she laughed with pure joy as she stood.

"Good night, Mr. Asher. And Merry Christmas."

"Good night, Mrs. Shanahan," he replied formally, his eyes twinkling. "And many more merry Christmases to come."

She couldn't help but look back at him as she climbed the staircase. He was standing in front of the tree, smiling as he bit off the end of a cigar.

She looked out the windows, up at the ancient, starlit sky, and her heart sang a prayer of thanks.

Kate was already asleep, still wearing her red mittens. Rose changed into her nightgown, shivering, and climbed into bed, hugging her daughter tightly.

She listened to the already familiar sounds of the house settling, and the sound of Kate's peaceful breathing. She listened as Asher climbed the stairs and went into his room across the hall, and smiled in the darkness.

She blessed the snow that had shut down the train, her son that had stolen Asher's coat, her daughter that listened to angels, and the man who had stolen her heart. As an afterthought, she even blessed Jamie Shanahan, for bringing her to these enchanted mountains.

At peace, she slept deeply and soundly, until the first pain shot through her back like fire, waking her in the dark and silent night.

Chapter Seven

"Ash. Oh, Ash, please wake up."

He rolled over immediately, blinking. "Rose?"

"Oh, Ash. Danny's gone!"

She was pale, paler than he had ever seen her. She stood in his doorway, a kerosene lamp in her hand. She was still in her nightgown, that shabby coat that hung to her knees thrown over it.

"What? Gone where? What time is it?"

"Three-fourteen," she responded immediately.

"What do you mean, gone? Gone where?"

"I don't know. I went downstairs and he's gone. His clothes as well."

"I'll kill him." He rolled to the edge of the bed, and grabbed for his pants.

"Oh, don't be angry. Just bring him home. He can't have been gone very long."

She turned away as he pulled on his pants. It was the first time he had ever seen her with her hair down. It hung to her waist, wavy from being constantly constrained in a braid.

"Any idea where he might be?"

"Not the vaguest. But he shouldn't be too hard to find."

"You reckon?" Damn, it was cold. He put on an extra pair of socks. "Why is that?"

"It's snowing again. He will have left a trail."

"Good for him. I won't be too tired from searching to kill him."

Knowing he was mostly joking, she managed a wan smile. "All right, kill him if you must. But, Ash, before you do, send him for Dr. Tunbridge."

"Great merciful hell, Rose!" His boot fell from his hand, and his heart fell into his stomach. His face must have been a sight, for she almost laughed.

"Don't look like that. Should I fetch you some smelling salts?"

"Damn it, Rose, this is not funny." He shoved his foot into his boot, realized it was the wrong foot, cursed, and switched it around. "I'll fetch the doctor first."

"Don't you dare. I have hours, yet."

"How do you know?" He felt sick. He *was* going to kill Danny. Where the hell was his buffalo coat?

"You cleaned your room," she said softly, looking around.

"Hellfire, Rose! How can you stand there chatting like that?" There was his coat, hanging neatly in the wardrobe.

"What would you like me to do? I told you, I have hours, yet."

"You're sure?"

"I have done this before, you know." Her voice grew sharp, and abruptly she closed her eyes, her lashes laying like dark fans over her pale cheeks. Her mouth pressed into a tight line, and she took a deep, shaking breath.

"Rose?"

"I'm fine." Her voice still sharp. Then, just as suddenly, her face relaxed. "I'm sorry. I didn't mean to sound huffy."

"You go ahead and sound however you want to. Do you need anything?"

"I need to sit down. I need you to find Danny, and bring him home out of the cold, so I can quit worrying."

"Sit. Sit. Where's a chair?"

She did laugh, then. "Right in front of you. Now, go on. And promise me—you find Danny before you even *think* about fetching Doc Tunbridge."

He sighed. "I promise."

"Thank you, Ash." She smiled, and turned toward the stairs.

"Where the hell are you going?"

"To the kitchen, where it's warm. I've got the kettle on. I thought I'd have some tea while I waited. And stop swearing."

"Tea," he repeated in disbelief. "Tea, she says."

He followed her down the stairs, jamming his hat over his ears. "Are you supposed to drink tea? Should you be walking all over the house?"

"Until I feel like doing otherwise. Are you sure you're all right? Should I get those smelling salts?"

How could she be so calm?

He followed her into the kitchen. "I don't like to leave you alone."

"Well, there's no help for it. Tell Doc Tunbridge the pains are eight minutes apart."

"Is that bad?" His heart raced with fear.

"No, it's one less than nine and one more than seven. That's all. I figure I've got three hours, at least."

"You're sure."

She calmly took a cup from the shelf, and reached for the tea tin. "As sure as I can be. Now, go find Danny, or I'll go myself."

"The hell you will," he said, and started for the back

door, reciting his list. "Find Danny. Wake the doc. Tell him eight minutes apart. Kill Danny—"

"No, no. Come home, so that I can see he's alive, then kill him."

"Right. Come home. Kill Danny."

"Good," she said. "Thank you."

"You sit down," he told her. "And don't . . . clean anything, or any such foolishness."

"Saints preserve us," she replied, stirring her tea. "Hurry up, before that snow gets worse."

He tried to smile as he left, but it felt sickly. He didn't want her to see his fear, but it was there, keen and cold as a freshly sharpened razor.

He knew she was strong; he knew she was healthy. He even knew she had been through this twice before. But in his mind, he kept seeing two things he had never wanted to remember again—Emily's face, still and white in the darkness of the bedroom, and her blood-soaked mattress. Afterward, he had hauled that thing into the yard and burned it, while cold tears trickled down his cheeks and the dark smoke rose into the winter sky.

He had never seen the child. Never even wanted to know if it had been a boy or girl. Reverend Quigley had buried the stillborn baby in its mother's arms, and said that they were together in a better place. It had been damned small comfort for Asher.

"Not this time, God," he said aloud as he saddled his horse. "You hear me? Not again."

That was as close to a prayer as he could manage. It would have to do. He swung his leg easily over the bay's back, and started out into the snow. He was following Dan Shanahan's trail for the second time in a month.

He lost the trail in town, where a thousand footprints trailed in all directions over the silent, frozen street. For a moment, he felt sick, but he kept his head. He circled around behind the buildings, and rode a few feet into the woods, and sure enough, there was a single trail through the fresh snow.

He followed it down the slope of the hill, out of town. White flakes fell from the sky, heavier and faster, already filling the path he followed. It felt like forever since he had seen Rose, but he knew, logically, it couldn't have been more than fifteen minutes. Twenty, at most.

Where the hell did that fool boy think he was going?

He stopped his horse at a gateway of pines, and saw him, a single, almost invisible figure sitting in the graveyard, so still that Josh almost missed him. He could have been one of the tombstones, or a statue dusted with falling snow.

Asher slid down from his horse, and walked through the snow-covered plots, heaving a sigh of exasperation and relief.

Danny glanced up briefly, and then looked away.

Ash's anger slipped away like dust between his fingertips. He had never seen such a woebegone look, such misery on such a young face. Well, he knew what that felt like.

Danny sat by a plain wooden headstone that was painted white, its lettering already faded.

James Shanahan.

Asher lit a cigar, the match sputtering loudly.

"Come to talk to your dad, huh?"

He crouched down in the snow beside the boy, and waited. After a minute, Dan nodded.

"Kinda bad time for it. Your mama's pretty worried." He paused. "You miss him?"

Danny turned and looked up at him with Rose's brown eyes, snowflakes resting on the lashes. "A lot," he said finally.

"That's hard. It hurts. Sometimes it feels like it's

never going to get better. And there isn't another person in the world that understands how you feel."

"There isn't." Danny swallowed hard. "He was . . . mine," he said simply. "He loved me best." He dashed a tear away with the back of his hand, angrily.

"Your mama loves you pretty fiercely, it seems to me."

"Maybe. But it ain't the same."

"Likely not. Nobody loves any two people exactly the same."

"He was mine," Danny said again. "You know how Mama and Kate are? Always understanding each other, always knowing what the other one's thinking about? He was like that with me. I know . . ." He stopped and swallowed hard. "I know what people say. I know he drank too much. But it didn't matter. He still loved me. Sang to me sometimes." He snuffled loudly. "Next time anyone says anything bad about him, I'll knock their head offa their shoulders."

"You do that," Asher said, watching the end of his cigar glowing. "A boy oughta take up for his dad."

Danny looked at him again, slightly curious. "That's not what Mama would say."

"Well, Dan, I'll have to kill you if you tell her I said this, but"—he looked over his shoulder, as if she could hear him—"your mother doesn't really know *every-thing*."

The boy gave a weak smile, the first one Asher had ever directly received.

"Now, get your stuff, and let's get home before you freeze. Your mother's worried sick about you."

Danny looked ill. "I bet she hates me. I ruined everyone's Christmas."

"Ah, the hell you did. Maybe your own, but tomorrow's a new day. And one day, you'll laugh about tonight."

"I don't think so."

"Trust me, you'll laugh. As to your mother hating you, that's just not possible. She couldn't if she wanted to."

He reached down into the snow, and picked up the small bundle of clothes lying there. "Come on. Let's get."

"Sir?"

Asher turned, and looked. Damn, that boy needed a decent coat. The ratty sweater he wore was truly sad-looking.

"I'm sorry. I'm sorry if I spoiled things. I just felt . . . like everybody in the world was happy except me."

"Ah." Ash nodded. "Kind of like, you're lonely and miserable, and your heart's aching, and it seems like everyone in the world has somebody to love them except you? You feel like the only person who ever could love you is gone? Like you're going to be shut out and alone forever?"

"Just like that," Dan said, in a tone of wonder.

"Come here. I want to show you something."

Together, they walked through the silent graveyard through the falling snow, until they stood by a tall tombstone with a kneeling angel holding a lamb.

"That's where Emily is. My wife. And my baby. And you know, I felt just like you, for a long time. And you know when I felt it most?"

"No, sir."

"When I'd sit alone at dinner, and listen to you and your mother and your sister talking. Everybody else had someone to love but me."

"Really?"

"You bet. But, Danny, love isn't like a bowl of sugar. It doesn't just run out. There's plenty for everyone. Enough to go around, and then some. Your mother can love Kate, and you, and me. And I can love all of you, and still love Emily. Hell, I don't love her any less just because she's gone. But I can still love your mother, just as much. The same way you'll love your dad. Forever. That's just how it works. It doesn't run out, it doesn't go away."

"Yeah, but sometimes it hurts."

"It sure as heck does," Asher agreed, then he grinned. "But not as much as your mother's going to hurt us if we don't get back." He reached into his pocket, and pulled out his gold watch.

It had been almost an hour since he had left.

"Come on, Dan. We've got to get moving."

Danny looked back across the graveyard at James Shanahan's grave, sad but dry-eyed. He nodded.

"We've got to stop by Doc Tunbridge's. There's a baby on the way for Christmas."

Chapter Eight

"Rose!" The kitchen was empty, and his voice echoed through the house. "Rose?"

Her cup of tea sat half empty on the table.

"You sit by the fire and warm up," he ordered Danny. "I'm going to talk to your mama."

He thundered up the stairs, his heart racing. "Rose?"

He threw open the door to her room. Kate slept peacefully, still wearing her red mittens.

He closed the door. "Rose?"

"In here. Your room."

"You gave me a turn—" he stopped, horrified.

She looked awful. Her face was stark-white, gleaming wet with sweat, her hair hung like dark seaweed to her shoulders. Her eyes were glazed.

"You found him?" Her voice was very small, and uncertain.

"Oh yes, you bet I did. He's downstairs."

She let out an audible sigh.

"Doc's on his way. Everything's going to be fine."

"I'm sorry . . . I took your bed. I didn't want to wake Katie."

"That's fine. That's fine." He took his coat off, and threw it at the chair. "Do you need anything?"

She nodded, and then suddenly an incredible spasm of pain contorted her face. She rose to her knees, and clutched frantically at the footboard of the bed.

"Oh, Rose. Oh, hell . . ."

Then, just as quickly, it was over. She stayed where she was, her hands still and white against the dark wood of the bedstead, and drew in a long, shaking breath.

"Tell Danny to stay downstairs," she said quickly. "And . . . oh, no."

He couldn't bear to look at her face. Instinctively, he reached beneath her arms, supporting her, his heart wrenching as he felt her body tighten and heave.

She went limp, gasping.

"Oh, holy hell, Rose."

"Don't swear. In the bottom drawer of my dresser, there are some blankets . . ."

"I'll get them." He tried to ease her back against the pillows, but she cried out, and he felt her body twisting again. Her fingers dug into his shoulders.

It seemed to go on forever.

"There. There. Lie back now."

She let him rest her against the pillows. She closed her eyes, her face still, her lashes dark against her white face, and he tried hard not to think of Emily.

"Hurry," she said softly. "Tell Danny, and then come back, fast."

He hurried. He thundered down the stairs and told Dan to stay there, thundered back up, and burst into his room just in time to see her weathering out another pain, her small face contorted in pain like he'd never imagined.

287

"Doc's on his way," he repeated. "He's on his way. I'll go check—"

"*Don't you dare leave this room*," she cried, her eyes flying open. "The baby's here. Right now. Do you hear me?"

He froze. Her eyes blazed at him like the fires of hell. He wouldn't have left that room if the house were burning.

"You said *hours*."

"I was wrong, you son of a bitch." She certainly still had spirit.

He took a deep breath. She wasn't going to die. He wasn't going to let her die. That was his Rose, no matter what she'd just sounded like, and she was going to live through this.

"All right, honey. I'm staying. Just tell me what to do."

He stroked her forehead, and she gave a long, terrible sigh. "Cold fingers." she whispered. "That's good."

Good. He'd done something right.

"Lift my back," she cried suddenly, in a harsh, pained gasp.

And then he was praying, hard and humbly and silently, lifting her shoulders forward and letting her fingers grip the skin of his hand so hard that he wondered if she would break it.

"Now!" she cried, her head arching back, and tears of pain coursing down her white cheeks. *"Now!"*

Somehow, through some ancient instinct he never really understood, Joshua Asher moved around to face her, and without hesitation, reached out and brought a baby into the world.

A headful of dark hair was cradled gently in the palm of his hand, and then a tiny shoulder.

"It has a face," he whispered—which he would later recall as one of the most idiotic things he could have said—and it seemed amazing to him. It was a perfect rosebud of a face, perfectly miniature, its expression so calm, eyes tightly shut and mouth held closed, as if disapproving of the rough entry into the world.

And then another shoulder appeared, Rose gave one more heart-stopping cry, like a wild creature, but it didn't bother him, and suddenly he was bent over a perfect human being, little arms quivering, tiny legs drawn up.

"She's a girl," he said, and his voice sounded a million miles away. "Rose? She's a girl."

For a moment he couldn't move, so stunned was he by the sight of this miniature human being in his own hands. Then he heard, for the first time in his life, the joyous cry of a baby girl announcing to the world that she was here, and alive.

He lifted his head and looked at Rose. Her eyes were huge in her face, but there was color there, too, a healthy pink flush spreading across her cheeks.

She held out her trembling arms, collapsing back against the pillows. "Oh. Oh, Ash . . . give her to me."

"There we are. There she is." He was suddenly afraid to move, afraid of dropping her, afraid of the snuffling kitten noises she made, afraid of the cord that still linked her to her mother. He laid her in Rose's arms as carefully as if she was made of glass.

"Oh, littlest baby," Rose whispered, and he found it amazing, the way her arms held the child so perfectly, so easily. She pulled the sheet up around the tiny, wet body, and touched the little face with one finger.

The child opened her eyes, and seemed to stare at her mother with a calm accepting expression, as though to say, "Oh. There you are."

"You did it," Joshua Asher said.

"I didn't have a choice," she answered softly. "Oh, she's beautiful. Oh, look at my angel."

"Is that her name?" he asked.

Rose looked up at him her great dark eyes shining. "What? Angel? It may as well be."

He heard the sound of a horse approaching. "Doc's coming."

"Fine." He had never heard her voice so soft, or seen a face with that particular tranquility. It was astounding. A few minutes before, she had been a wild creature, sweating and wild-eyed, and now she was Rose again, that quickly.

Starry eyed and pink cheeked, and beautiful. His Rose.

He bent and smoothed the hair off her face, kissed her forehead, and went downstairs. The sun was rising. Danny came racing from the kitchen, his face white.

"Is she . . ." he looked helplessly at Ash, and couldn't finish.

"Fine. She's fine, Dan. I'm no doctor, but they both look good to me."

The boy sagged with relief. "I heard the baby."

"Her name's Angel, I think."

"Hmm. Well, Kate oughta like that."

"And you better pretend to."

"Here comes the Doc," the boy announced, and opened the front door.

"Good morning, Daniel. Merry Christmas. Ash."

"Little late, Doc."

The white-mustached man raised his eyebrows as he removed his bowler hat. "Am I? Well, well. Babies have minds of their own. I take it everything went smoothly?"

"Smoothly?" Ash felt as if he'd been laid in the road and a herd of cattle let loose to run back and forth over the top of him. "Everybody lived."

"Can't ask for better than that. What do we have?"

"A little girl. Lots of hair."

290

"Show me to her. Take a look-see, count those fingers and toes."

Relieved to hand the responsibility over, Ash started up the stairs.

"Whoa there," Doc said. "Almost forgot. You lose something in the road, Daniel?"

"No, sir." The boy's face wrinkled. "Leastways, not that I know."

"Hmmm. Found this. Has your name on it." The doctor produced a small red package, tied with white yarn. "Must've fallen out of Santa's sleigh, eh?"

It was wet, the ink on the name tag was running, but there it was. Danny's Christmas present had miraculously returned.

Shocked, his small face full of wonder, Dan accepted the package. "Thank you, sir."

When Asher found him at the kitchen table, he was smoothing his fingers over his new mittens, smiling at the gray wool, a striped stick of candy hanging from his mouth like a cigar.

"You know what your mother would say now?" he asked.

Dan removed the candy, and they spoke in unison.

"God works in mysterious ways, His wonders to perform."

Chapter Nine

"You should let me buy you a cradle," Asher said.

"Nothing wrong with a dresser drawer," Rose said. She was back in her own bed in the pink-flowered room, her hair combed and braided, and looking healthier than she had a right to.

"She deserves a bed of her own." He looked down at the baby in his arms, wrapped so tightly in a blanket that all he could see was her tiny face. "I thought blue was for boys."

"I thought she was a boy."

He peered down at the child. "Do you see how your mother is? She bullies her way into my house, steals my heart, swears at me, and makes you wear blue and sleep in a drawer."

"I never swore at you!"

"She did," he said to the baby girl, jiggling her gently as he leaned back in the chair. "She called me a son of a—"

"Asher!"

"Something like that," he said, and grinned at Rose. She smiled back, reluctantly.

Outside, they could hear Kate's high cry of delight, and an answering whoop from Danny.

"Great merciful heavens, what are they doing out there?"

He stood up and looked out the window.

"Sledding."

"And where did they get a sled?" Rose raised her left brow.

"Oh, some dumb son of a bitch bought it for them."

"Ash! Stop it! Saints preserve us, will you ever let me live that down?"

"Nope. Not if you live to be a hundred. I'll say to my grandchildren. 'I remember the first Christmas I met your grandma, and do you know what she called me?' "

Rose laughed so hard that it hurt, just imagining it. "You'd better not. I intend to tell them that it was a Christmas miracle."

"It's a heck of a good Christmas, isn't it?"

"A miracle," repeated Rose firmly. "Look at that child in your arms. Is it any wonder that the greatest miracle of all started with the birth of a child? There's nothing more beautiful than a new baby."

"She's something, all right. She's beautiful."

"And Santa, dropping Danny's present in the snow? That's a miracle."

"If you say so."

"It is, Ash. There's nothing miraculous about miracles. I mean, they just don't happen to faraway people. There are miracles all around. It was a mircle that Danny stole your coat, and a miracle that the train wasn't running. It was a miracle when Santa lost the present. You see? There are miracles everywhere."

"I know it's a miracle that I met you," he finished, reaching out to touch her cheek. "And that you love me."

She snuggled back into her pillows, smiling. "Miracles exist, and that's that."

Out in the yard, Kate watched as Danny climbed the hill, pulling the sled behind him, its red runners tracing lightly over the snow.

This was the most beautiful Christmas ever. She spun in a circle, her arms out, until everything swirled around her. Sky, mountain, house, trees, sky, mountain.

She stopped abruptly, sniffing the air. Snow, and the smell of smoke from the chimneys, and very faintly, the scent of violets.

She looked up, high into the blue and rose and gold of the sunset, and for a moment, tears stung her eyes.

With a great whooping shout, Danny came whisking down the hill, snow flying up behind him, and skidded past her.

"Your turn," he shouted.

She gave a last look up into the Christmas sky. "Thank you," she whispered. "Good-bye, Emily. Good-bye."

Here Comes Santa Claus

Stobie Piel

To Isabelle Bonney and Kim Brown,
because you both have brought unlimited kindness,
compassion and wisdom to my life. Thank you.

Chapter One

Vale of Snow, 1890

"Either he goes, or I do. It's that simple." Ariana drew a quick breath, and realized it had been her first since she stormed into Saint Nicholas's private chamber. Her voice quavered with outrage, but the old man didn't look up from the papers on his desk. Instead, he just sighed and looked more weary than usual.

The door slammed behind her. She knew who it was without looking.

Taran stomped across the room and stood beside her, but she refused to look at him. She felt him like a dark shadow, one that towered over her because he was so much taller than she. Ariana kept her gaze pinned on Nicholas, but her chin trembled with restraint.

"Something must be done about *him* at once, or . . ."

"Or what? You've put my schedule off by weeks, Ariana, you and those small Welsh demons you call helpers." Taran sounded almost as angry as she was. His

usually low, mesmerizing voice came out stilted with
fury.

She closed her eyes to resist the temptation to look at
him. Looking at Taran always had the effect of confus-
ing her. "I had every reason to disable your current production."

"By the most demonic means you could think of.
Painting tiny gowns on my soldiers! And you did it because you're jealous, competitive, and a *fiend*."

This wasn't the first time he'd called her that. Ariana
whirled so fast that her long, dark hair spun over her
face. She jabbed it aside and glared up at him. Her lips
parted for speech, but no words came. By all the saints,
he was handsome. Never once could she look at him
and not be stirred. His hair was blacker than hers, and
his eyes, an impenetrable brown tinged with a far-off,
earthen warmth.

Her gaze drifted unwillingly down from his face to
his body. It was so strong, so perfect. *Curse you for
having this effect on me!* She forced her gaze from his
broad shoulders and powerful arms. The sight invoked
too much confusion, and too much memory. How could
one night hold such devastating power so long after it
was over?

His full, sensual lips quirked upward at one corner. If
he dared mention her attraction . . . "What? Surely you
can hurtle some retort back at me, Ariana. Or was sab-
otaging my studio enough?"

Nicholas still hadn't looked up. A twinge of nervousness stabbed at Ariana. Perhaps she had gone too far this
year. Much could be excused in these last days before
Christmas. Much had been excused in years past, after
all. But a quick glance told her the old man's chin beneath his white beard seemed set.

She forced a tight smile, which soon gave way to
anger. "*Sabotage* is a strong word, Taran. I had no

choice but to stop your current production . . ." As she spoke, her voice grew tremulous with rage. "I had to stop you, you black-hearted barbarian, because you had obliterated my lovely dollhouse with those marauding Huns you call toys!"

Yes, her voice was raised to excess and she was shaking her fist. Realizing the aggressive nature of her posture, she straightened her fingers and shoved her hands behind her back.

Taran appeared remorseless. "It is true that my testing period went somewhat awry, but since one of your small dollhouses made its way from your workshop into mine, I assumed it was a cast-off—and best made use of."

Her fist flew from behind her back and she shook it at his jaw. "It was no cast-off! It was flawless in every way! And it wasn't in your workshop, it was in the doorway of mine."

She trembled with anger. In all her lifetime before being invited to serve the legendary toymaker, Nicholas, she had never known this kind of passionate anger. Things had been different, simple. She had lived in Wales, had been the daughter of a renowned carpenter and had traveled with him from village to village in a time when the English monarchs were taking power over her people through bloody warfare. But watching her father, Ariana had learned to make small replicas of the homes he built, and found her greatest joy in presenting these as gifts to children of war ravaged families.

The devastation she had witnessed inspired her courage, and when she was twenty-three, Ariana defied her father, staying behind in a Welsh village to free children held by the English. She freed the children, but had been taken captive herself—and there, when faced with brutal execution, Nicholas had appeared and offered her a life in his service. It seemed he recruited helpers from those who had shown great courage and compassion.

Ariana treasured this life, and the chance Nicholas had given her, and she found it strange that any other emotion might dampen her gratitude. But she trembled with anger on a daily basis; she seethed with passion. Now, all the honor and courage of her lifetime in Wales had been cast to the wayside because she hadn't the strength to ignore a tall, strong-bodied barbarian.

They had been at odds since they met. She had arrived well after Taran had established himself in the Vale of Snow and had already ingratiated himself with Nicholas. She knew his story—in the first days of her arrival, it had thrilled her when she first heard the tale. When his village was overrun by an army of marauding Huns, Taran had sent all his soldiers and all the villagers into the hills to safe hiding. But to delay the pillaging army, Taran had ridden alone to forestall them, giving his people time to evade the attackers.

His people survived. Not a soldier was lost. But Taran had been surrounded, fighting until the last of his strength ebbed. Broken in body, his soul defiant, a storm rose up, clouding his attackers. And there, Nicholas had appeared to him, offering the same choice he would later offer to Ariana. Assured that his people were safe, and that his own life was ending, Taran had accepted.

But Nicholas hadn't chosen Taran for his courage alone. A warrior whose skill and bravery had elevated him to almost legendary proportions, Taran had been even more renowned for his kindness. He had defended his people from invaders, crafted the swords and the armor for his sovereign, and in those rare times of peace, he'd made tiny soldiers with perfect little weapons as toys for children. Something he continued to do in Nicholas's service.

As much as he annoyed her, Ariana had to admit Taran was skilled at making toy soldiers. No deadpan expressions had they, but instead, each one had a unique character. The villains looked fierce, the heroes proud and even perhaps a little weary. Even the toy horses had expressions. Because of this, Ariana knew the hard warrior hadn't gone through his life without caring. He had noticed everything, and remembered. He was sensitive—to everything.

Except her. To Taran, Ariana had been an amusement. He had played to her when she was new to the Vale. Then, when he tired of her, she had become an annoyance. But Ariana refused to be relegated to nothingness. She *would* matter to him, even if she had to be an eternal thorn in his side.

The situation was unfortunate, too, for Ariana had almost never been happier. Nothing Ariana had seen during her lifetime equaled the glory of the service she now performed, working for Nicholas.

The only dark spot in her life was Taran. As noble as she knew him to be, as handsome and as proud, he frightened her—so deeply that she had no idea how to combat it. He looked at her, and seemed to see inside her. And the fear that plagued her most was that if he asked, she would do whatever he wanted.

She knew, because she had done it once before. How that night haunted her! The chill in her heart made the mountains of snow outside seen like summer hills.

Ariana turned her attention back to Nicholas. His aged head was bowed, and he appeared pained by their conversation. She gulped, but she had to do something to remove Taran from her life. "Sir, I know it's our busiest time, and I hate to trouble you this way . . ." She felt sure she heard the old man sigh, faintly, but she had no choice but to go on. "I realize you can't send him back . . . probably . . ."

She paused, hoping Nicholas would do just that. Taran appeared confident beside her. "You'd like that, wouldn't you, Ariana? But my workshop produces toys that are much-valued with small boys, and a surprising number of girls, too. As much as you want me to leave, they *need* me to stay."

Her teeth ground together. He made it seem as if he cared more for children than she did. She had to restrain herself, but it wasn't easy. "Couldn't you move his workshop away from mine?"

Taran huffed. "You would make trouble with anyone."

"That's not so! Kiya the Egyptian has never once complained about my procedures or my assistants. You, on the other hand, would do well to be given an isolated studio far away from the others. It is well known that you and that Viking, Hakon, are always fighting, engaging in battles that disrupt *all* of us."

Her accusation did nothing to disturb Taran's composure. "My skirmishes with Hakon have been orderly, for the purpose of testing our creations. Every such event has been approved, and never employed with a spirit of hostility and rancor—unlike that which motivated your assault on my studio this morning."

"Those battles were disruptive all the same." Disruptive, because rather than attending to her own work, Ariana had hidden herself nearby to watch. She was never sure why she did so, except that Taran looked so happy with his Viking friend, laughing as they aligned their small toy armies. The scene always reminded her that he, too, had once been a child. They showed her his deep capacity for joy.

He didn't look happy now. "Disruptive, am I? And what do we say of your past misdeeds? Each year you wreak new havoc in my life, and each year it's worse than the one before."

"I've done nothing—"

"You set my hair on fire."

A tiny smile formed on her lips before she could stop it. "That was an accident."

He leaned toward her, dark eyes blazing. She remembered seeing that expression once before, but in a different mood, and a powerful tingling coursed through her veins. He was so close that she could imagine the heat of his body, the power of him as he reached out to hold her. . . . "I had almost no hair for a year."

Ariana puffed an impatient breath. "It grew back, didn't it?" If possible, it had grown back even shinier, even more glorious than it had been. From the moment she'd first seen him, she had longed to entangle her fingers in that dark black mane. One night, she had done so, and the sweet bliss of the touch still lingered in her memory.

She pried her attention from Taran to Nicholas. "Sir, that incident was thoroughly investigated, and I was found innocent of any attempt to intentionally harm a fellow craftsman."

Taran glared. "You were found innocent of trying to murder me. It is clear you had every intention of destroying my hair."

"I never considered any such thing." She had. It had been months since their one night of bliss, and he had shown no inclination toward trying to win her heart. It was clear that she had been only an amusement, a pastime. Perhaps he had toyed with her for the sake of his own ego. She had endured the shame as long as she could, then in a manner befitting her Celtic ancestors, she had taken action, setting his hair—accidentally—on fire.

Ariana met Taran's dark gaze and saw no yielding there, just anger. Most of the time, she felt that anger, too, but sometimes, late in the night when no one could hear, she found herself crying. Sometimes, the icy cold outside seemed nothing against the frost of her own heart. What was wrong with her?

Taran moved past her and placed his hands on Nicholas's desk. "This woman has long been a miscreant, trouble practically since she arrived here." He paused as Ariana wondered where this was heading. Taran glanced back at her. "It may be that Ariana herself would be better suited by a new chance at life."

He was trying to get rid of *her*! She felt her face blanch. Why it should hurt so, she didn't know. After all, she had come to Nicholas's chamber for just the same purpose—to get rid of Taran. But she'd never dreamed he loathed her; she simply needed to have him far away.

"But I . . . I don't want to go." Her voice sounded very small, not at all the impermeable shell she wanted to portray. He straightened and glared down at her.

"Nor, my lady, do I."

Tears of anger and hurt filled her eyes. "I am *not* leaving."

Taran stood as if carved from marble. "I'm not leaving, either."

"You're *both* leaving." Nicholas spoke for the first time, stood up from his desk, and gazed miserably at them. He wasn't a tall man, but he was fat, and his presence was always imposing. Ariana stared at him aghast.

"What?" She spoke in unison with Taran, who appeared equally shocked by the old man's announcement.

Nicholas fingered his beard. "You two have squabbled since you met. Perhaps you don't understand the reason, but I do. . . ."

Ariana's shock gave way to anger. "I understand perfectly! He is selfish, ill-mannered, and he cares nothing . . ." She stopped, horrified. She had been about to say, "for me." "For the work I do."

304

Taran frowned. "*I* am selfish? Your studio takes up more space than all the others combined. Perhaps Kiya doesn't object, but you don't torment her as you do me. It is impossible to work beside you, Ariana. You are a distraction—" He stopped and cleared his throat. If she hadn't known him better, she would have suspected he blushed. "Your work is a distraction . . . and one I would soon be rid of."

Nicholas glanced at them. "The battle between you two is disrupting everything."

Desperation seized Ariana. She loved her work. She loved living in the Vale of Snow, the quiet walks amidst ice-laden trees, the small animals, the beauty and peace. She didn't want to leave. "I have never missed my dead-line, sir. True, I'm a little behind now, but that's *his* fault." She paused to glare at Taran. She was hurt, and furious, and though she was sure Taran was solely to blame, a small part of her still felt guilty. "My studio has always produced the required toys, and their quality has always been the very highest."

The old man's expression softened. He wouldn't send her away. He loved her, as he loved all those he enlisted. "Both of you serve me well . . . when you're not busy battling each other. This year, though, the conflict be-tween you has escalated, and I cannot be sure either of you can perform your work as scheduled."

Taran's dark eyes formed slits of anger. "Had my toy soldiers not donned *dresses*, my quota would already be met."

Ariana made a fist. "Had you not destroyed one of my finest dollhouses, I would have more than enough time to finish its furnishings!"

Nicholas held up his hand, then cast his gaze heaven-enward as if fighting despair. "Neither of you can see beyond your personal difficulties." He glanced out his frosty window to the snow-covered forest beyond. A wistfulness crossed his face, and in response, Ariana's own heart suffered a dull ache. She had no name to give that pain, but she had felt it often of late. She had felt it while still a young girl and into womanhood.

Looking into the old man's face, she saw a shadow of herself. Only once could she remember that empty space inside her heart filled, only once had she felt complete—in Taran's arms. She reminded herself that fulfillment had caused her far more pain after it was over.

Nicholas looked back at her, then came around the desk to stand between her and Taran. "I rarely make mistakes, but perhaps I brought you here too soon."

That didn't sound promising. Ariana held her breath. "What do you mean? Have I not done all that you asked me to do?"

"You have served me well, and you are both skilled at what you do. But there is something you both have yet to find. I thought you would find it here. It is plain you have not."

Ariana hesitated, not daring to ask what he meant, or to look at Taran. "What do you intend to do with us?"

The old man considered this for a long while, long enough for Ariana to begin to squirm and fidget. She chewed her lip, and stole a quick peek at Taran. One glance told her he endured the same nervous anticipation.

Nicholas went to the large, round spyglass he used to investigate mortal deeds. He studied it, turning dials and muttering to himself. Ariana looked on with dread, not daring to look over his shoulder. At last, he nodded, then turned back to them.

"Britain, I think, might offer you a chance to redeem yourselves. . . ." Nicholas looked thoughtful, and a slow smile grew on his face. Ariana's nervousness soared. "In the land of your birth, you will find a test worthy of redemption."

"Do you mean there's some sort of good deed to be performed?"

"There is."

"What is it?"

"That is for you to discover, Ariana. Half the challenge of helping the world is recognizing a problem where none appears to exist."

Taran's dark brow slanted. "That's not much to go on."

The fat man glanced out his window again, his expression unreadable. "There are many dangers in the world, my friend. Many you both have faced yourselves. But there is another, less threatening, that causes more pain than all else."

Ariana chewed her lip. "That is cryptic, sir. Can't you tell us something helpful?"

"Where I will send you, there is a person who is suffering. You two must find this person, and then heal the wound no one else can see."

Ariana considered this. Since Nicholas was the patron saint of children, this task must naturally involve a child. She knew children well, felt comfortable with them, and understood them. She had the utmost confidence in her ability to identify anything troubling to a child, and fixing it.

Nicholas's quest didn't sound too bad, but something in his tone left her uneasy. "Much has changed in Britain since I lived there. It's no longer the same world I knew."

Nicholas appeared unaffected by her words. "The world you knew was medieval, far more savage than the Britain of today. Instead of your warrior kings, a gentle, fat queen rules."

"Queen Victoria. I know." Ariana hesitated. "I should fit in fairly well in her realm."

Her heart fell, but she wasn't sure why. She glanced

at Taran, fighting the ache that formed in her chest. "What about him? Are you sending him back to his birthplace, too?"

"I am sending him with you."

Ariana tried to affect disinterest and irritation, but she couldn't quite contain a spark of pleasure. "I suppose I can endure his presence until our task is complete."

Nicholas studied her awhile, then shook his head. "You don't have much time, Ariana. There are two days before Christmas."

She bit her lip. "Do you mean we have to solve this dilemma before Christmas?"

"I make my deliveries on Christmas Eve. Your task must be completed by Christmas morning."

Taran folded his arms over his broad chest. "What happens if we fail?"

"If the problem I spoke of is not resolved, then I will know beyond a doubt that I brought you to my domain in error." Nicholas's tone was ominous.

Ariana shifted her weight from foot to foot. "So then you'll leave us in Britain?" That didn't sound so bad. At least she would be with Taran in a world where she belonged—and one where he was a stranger.

"No, Ariana. That, I cannot do."

"What will you do, then?"

"I will have no choice but to return you both to the lands and time from whence you came."

Ariana stopped fidgeting and stood still as stone. "Back to medieval Wales?"

"Yes, and Taran will go back to the mountains of his birth."

Ariana gulped, fighting a fear she didn't fully comprehend. "But . . . we come from different times. If we go back, there would be no chance—" She stopped herself and felt her cheeks grow warm. *No chance of seeing each other again.* They would be separated by more than anger or resentment—or fear. They would be separated by distance and time, forever.

Nicholas's eyes glowed brighter. Sometimes, she forgot how ancient he was, and how wise. "You understand that much, at least."

Her chin quivered, but she couldn't let Taran know how much the thought of losing him terrified her. "I don't want to be sent back. I have learned so much in this time. I will be out of place."

Taran cleared his throat and seemed tense. "I, too, would find myself at a loss in the world I once knew. My life is here."

Nicholas looked between them. "We will see where your life is, Taran. I have appointed you a task, seemingly simple, yet which is filled with mysteries. Hopefully, it will lead you two to what you have not yet seemed to have found. You have two days to find it. If you fail, nothing I can do will change your fates."

Ariana's heart labored. *I can't lose you.* "Can't you advise us in some way, so that we might know how to avoid this dark fate?"

Nicholas placed his broad hand on her shoulder, kind like a grandfather. "Advise you? No. You must find it yourselves. I will tell you only this: There are many forces in you, Ariana. In everyone. Some are dark and pull you away from your heart's most true desire. They are the forces of fear and hate and anger. Sometimes, not fully understanding what we want can be enough to let the darkness seep in and rule us. When what we want is stronger than what we fear, no darkness will be strong enough to hide the light."

Taran sat outside his studio, ignoring the cold and new falling snow. He glared at the southeastern horizon, where the winter sun rose only a sliver, then set again. The icicles glittered on his roof. "I have no wish to go to England. What is he thinking, to send me there with *her*?"

Hakon stretched his long legs out before him and leaned back against the wall. "I don't envy you, my friend. England is at peace, and no excitement is to be found at all. Would that you were returned to some other land—north to mine, or farther south to where your land still twists in strife. There, you might make an impact that would regain your stead here."

Taran nodded, liking the idea. "Instead, he sends me with *the fiend*."

Hakon looked thoughtful. "If it were possible to seal shut her small mouth, perhaps she would be . . . Ariana *is* among the loveliest women I've ever seen." A smile formed on Hakon's lips and he sighed.

Taran glared at him. He had tasted that mouth, held that small, perfect body next to his own . . . and the memory of its perfection had still not abated. She was a goddess who offered the sweetest promise of his soul, then denied him its true satisfaction. *Herself.*

"Her loveliness is obliterated by the shadow of her scheming and pride." He said the words, knowing they were false. Nothing obliterated Ariana's beauty. Even when she had set his hair on fire, he had absurdly noticed only the beauty and charm of her devious expression, the way the flames reflected in the green irises of her eyes. *I am pathetic.*

She was a distraction, more so even than he could begin to tell their benefactor. Not the noise of her small, tapping hammers, or the constant singing of her tiny Welsh assistants, but because every time he saw her, he forgot what he was doing. He forgot where he was, and thought only of the one fleeting night she had been his. He had proven, too well, that he couldn't control himself when she was close.

There had to be another way to avoid a second humiliation. "I'll have to avoid her."

Hakon eyed him doubtfully. "You have had opportunity to avoid her here, yet find occasion daily to engage her in some squabble or other."

Taran felt a too-familiar heat rise to his cheeks. "Only because, daily, Ariana finds reason to torment me."

A half-smile twisted his friend's face. "It seems to me that the simple act of her walking past your studio is enough to torment you." The Viking paused while Taran fought for an excuse to deny the obvious. "Is it her deviltry, or the pretty sway of her slender hips that distracts you?"

Taran started to object, then found himself bowing his head into his hands. He groaned miserably. "What am I going to do?"

Hakon sat forward and crossed one leg over his knee. "Make the best of it. What choice do you have?"

"If only he hadn't ordered us to enter this struggle together! I would rather be most anywhere than locked on some secretive quest with her."

"That is a sentiment I concur with heartily." Ariana's small, lilting voice pierced through him like an arrow.

Taran looked up, shoved his loose hair back from his forehead, and saw her standing before him. Her hands were poised on her hips, her bright eyes glittered, and her small, lovely mouth twisted with its usual tight irritation, curled upward at one side. Despite all his anger, and all the humiliation he had endured at her hands, the only thing he could think of was kissing her.

She wasn't dressed in her usual medieval overgown, and her long hair had been wound into some kind of loose bun behind her head. Whoever had assisted her in the task had been artful enough to leave spiraling tendrils to frame her cheeks and cascade with tantalizing care along her slender neck.

She looked ravishing. Ariana always looked beautiful, and while he had somewhat gotten used to her appearance, he had not mastered the brief pang the sight of her always produced. He'd gotten used to her long, flowing hair, with its haphazard curl and gentle sway as she spun to march away from him. He'd gotten used to her long, green velvet gown that followed the lines of her body.

This new garment she wore, chosen undoubtedly to blend with those women were wearing in modern Britain, had the unfortunate alteration of a lower neckline and a tighter waist than her usual attire. Rather than peaceful green, this gown was dark red and trimmed with lace. Something about the shift in color suggested passion. Its snug bodice drew attention to her breasts, which though fairly small, were round and well-shaped. He remembered their pert fullness in his hands, and the familiar ache in his body resurfaced.

She noticed his attention upon her body, and her frown deepened. "I am clothed as befits a lady under the reign of Queen Victoria." She looked him up and down and shook her head. "You would do well to suit yourself in something fitting the times, also. We don't want to attract undue attention."

He rose to his feet so that he towered over her. He had always enjoyed the way her back straightened as if she wished somehow to force herself to be taller than he was. Her bright eyes slanted in suspicion, as if she knew he had stood up to make her feel tiny.

"I will go as I am dressed now."

She assessed his attire, slowly, with her usual intent and critical scrutiny. Her gaze fixed on his snug leggings, and intense displeasure covered her small, lovely features. "What you are wearing is completely inappropriate for male garb in this period of time."

Hakon rose and joined Ariana's scrutiny. "She has a

312

point, Taran. You look more like a barbarian warrior than a British gentleman."

Taran fought irritation. "That is because I *am* a barbarian warrior." He wasn't the sort of man Ariana wanted and he'd stopped fighting it. In her lifetime in Wales, he had no doubt she had been courted by many lovers, renowned and wealthy, men who could offer her anything she wanted. True, she had never married, but she had been still a very young woman when Nicholas had saved her from death.

Taran had been a strong man, noble and brave, but he had never cared much for his position in society. Ariana surely wanted something more. Well, she was welcome to it. One night with a barbarian hadn't changed her. He couldn't allow one night with a lady to change him.

"I will go clothed as I am."

She rolled her eyes. "You will be seized and thrown into a dungeon the moment we get there." She looked brighter at the idea. "But so much the better. I will handle whatever quest arises without you."

His jaw clenched. Fiend. From what he'd quickly learned about Queen Victoria's prim society, they might be crazy enough to do just that. Without a word, Taran turned, went to the costume workshop and found himself a suitable garment. He dressed silently, furiously, as Natasha the Russian seamstress looked on.

His leather leggings had been traded for black linen trousers, and his rough tunic was now a cumbersome black coat with tails, over a white shirt and the most abominable, useless article of clothing he'd ever encountered: the cravat.

"You are vision, Taran. Englishwomen will fall to feet before you." Her words were heavily accented.

Taran wondered what foolish period of history Natasha came from if she approved of such outlandish attire. She could be from any time. Nicholas had been taking people into his service for many years—long even before the notion of saints, though Taran had heard that the man had recently become canonized. However, his helpers had come from societies so far back in the past that Taran had never heard of them. She might be from one of those. Her sensibilities were certainly not like any he knew. Fortunately, Nicholas had bestowed all his minions with a magical gift of comprehension—at least of language. Otherwise, with all of Nick's helpers coming from different periods and countries, interaction would have been difficult. However, they could all converse easily enough—albeit in accented speech—even if their sensibilities remained different.

Even more than Natasha, Ariana's land and people in particular seemed strange to Taran. Even compared to Egyptians, Mayans, and Sumerian priestesses, Ariana seemed a world apart. Maybe it was because he paid more attention to her, but there was something about her Celtic nature that was fascinating.

"You will need this cap, Taran." Natasha passed him a tall, black hat and Taran repressed a snarl.

He crunched it into a ball. "I am not wearing this."

She took it from him uncertainly and looked nervous as if she knew her next suggestion was doomed to fail. "You will cut hair, to level of ear."

"I am not a boy. I am a man. My hair stays as it is."

"You look like Mayan priest. You will shock English."

That was possible, but still not enough reason to savage his appearance. His long hair was the symbol of his virility, his right after his passage into manhood. "I will enter England as a foreigner. Much that I don't know of the English ways will be explained by that."

Natasha eyes him, then sighed. "You will attract attention, no? Yes. That much is certain. But I suppose you are used to it."

Taran smiled at those words, pleased. Ariana should realize how much other women appreciated his masculine appeal. Though she had chosen to cast him aside, she might find it grating when others desired him.

Taran studied his reflection in the looking glass. He was tall, and the somber black suit had the effect of highlighting his uniqueness rather than making him look like a prim gentleman. He tried the top hat, hated it instantly, then tossed it aside. His hair looked favorable hanging over his shoulders, which were unquestionably broad, and his height served the garment far better than it might have on a smaller man.

He adjusted the unpleasant neck cloth, then decided to lose it at the first opportunity. He thanked Natasha, then went to the door to embark on his journey.

Ariana was waiting for him, impatient as always. She turned, her pink lips open to speak, but no words came. He watched with a deep thrill of satisfaction as her green eyes widened. For only a second, he saw a flash of admiration in her eyes and his pulse quickened.

She had looked at him that way once before, that festive Christmas night when he had first asked her to dance. They had danced and danced, forgetting their mutual animosity. Much that had simmered unspoken between them had come to the surface that night, and ended in the most perfect bliss Taran had ever known.

As much as he tried to forget it, he relived that night over and over with careful memory as to the exact details. He remembered every sigh from her lips, every touch, the look of her small hand, pale against his dark skin, as she pressed her palm over his heart. She haunted him like a ghost, even as her impatient self stood waiting.

The momentary admiration he had seen in her disappeared, and she replaced it with a familiar smug smile. "You will terrify British society dressed like that, Taran.

315

I see that it is easier for me to maneuver from the past into the future; for you, it is clearly a grievous strain."

"You dress well, Ariana, yet inside . . ." He paused while her smile faded to suspicion. "Yet inside, you are as much a barbarian as I. I wonder if you can conceal your wild, Celtic impulses. If the English have the slightest sense, it is you they will fear, not me."

She started her retort, but a trio of short Laplander— elves—arrived with the sleigh Nicholas used to disperse gifts on Christmas Eve and she fell silent. The sleigh would bear them across the endless winter, and back to the mortal world, driven by the elves. Taran didn't know how it worked, but the system had never failed. Rarely were the elves sent out for anything but collecting the chosen few from near-death, that and for the yearly Christmas excursions. Today obviously proved an exception.

Nicholas came out from the main house and stood silently as if assessing their potential for success. His expression indicated he was giving them relatively low odds.

Ariana, however, seemed enthused and ready for their journey. Her expression left Taran deeply uneasy, as if she might be plotting some deviltry at his expense. He came up beside her. Even in the cold, he detected the delicate, feminine fragrance of her soft skin. "You appear cheerful, Ariana, I take it our punishment has appeal for you."

She looked up at him, alert and bright as always. "It does, in fact. I am pleased with the thought of rejoining society, of the intrigues and excitement of life. People who have worked overmuch can benefit from a holiday, and I will view this journey as such."

Nicholas overheard her, and his heavy brow arched. "With that spirit, my dear, looking to the bright and hopeful side, you may be ready to face your challenges, after all."

Ariana glared with pride and self-assurance. "That is so, sir, and quite the way I have always dealt with adversity. In fact, I thank you for this opportunity to remind myself that such small disturbances as a barbarian can produce are truly nothing significant." She paused. "And I am looking forward to sitting in a pleasant room, partaking of sweets and wine—"

Taran coughed to repress laughter. "A holiday, indeed. It may please you to remember, my lady, that we have but two days to accomplish our task. I trust you can fit that in, somewhere amidst your parties, revelry, and sweets."

"I am well up to that task, Taran. You will be a stranger in my land, and *you* are likely to feel lost and out of sorts. But you can trust me to guide you in proper behavior—and if need be, cover for your unavoidable blunders."

She climbed into the sleigh and adjusted a soft gray cape around her shoulders. Taran got in beside her. In two days' time, they might be parted forever, he to his old land, she to hers. Apparently, that prospect didn't affect Ariana half as much as it tormented him. Well, if she felt that way, he wouldn't allow his own weakness for her to show.

"Let us go, Ariana. This might be a pleasant holiday, after all."

Chapter Two

"You can't drop us here at night, in the dark, in a storm! I have no idea where we are!" Ariana sputtered in fury, but the Laplander elves simply dumped her small bag at her feet, then hurled Taran's after it.

Her little sleigh-drivers appeared unmoved by the disaster into which they had pitched her. "Nicholas instructed us to deposit you a good distance from any dwellings, lest your arrival bring suspicion that might threaten your quest."

Ariana hopped from one foot to the other. "I didn't dress for the winter wilderness! Wait!"

The sleigh rose and disappeared before she had the chance to jump back in and try to wrest away the reins.

Taran stood beside her, glaring into the darkening gray sky. Then, he looked around at the shadowy landscape. "They have dropped us in hell," was all he said.

Ariana shivered and pulled her soft gray cape closer around her shoulders. She couldn't see much of her surroundings, but from what she could make out, they appeared to be amidst rolling hills and snow-covered farmland. "Not hell." She paused, then nodded. "Scotland."

Taran glanced at her. "You're Welsh, not Scottish. Why here?"

Ariana shrugged. "The object of our rescue must be here." She looked around. "Somewhere."

Taran's dark brow slanted. "Probably frozen in the snow." Fat flakes fell from the sky and lodged themselves in his hair. He looked disgruntled, but still devastatingly handsome. "If we could see a light from a village, or even a hut . . ."

They studied every horizon. Ariana squinted to see through the snow. "Nothing."

"You profess to know this land, Ariana. Which way do we go?"

Ariana shivered again. "South."

An exasperated smile formed on Taran's lips, but she appreciated it. She loved it when he smiled. It reminded her of how enjoyable his company could be, and how much pleasure he took in life. They started off together, plodding through the snow in the direction that seemed most southerly. The snow was deeper than it looked, and the journey therefore far more tiring than she'd anticipated. After a short time, her legs ached. Every step came as an effort.

Taran walked on ahead, his long legs providing him an advantage Ariana didn't share. For a while, she felt competitive and she forced herself onward. When he glanced back, she hopped forward so that he wouldn't notice how far she'd lagged behind.

He stopped and waited, though it hadn't been her intention for him to do so. "Are you all right, Ariana?" he asked.

She seized a quick breath and tried to hide her discomfort. "I'm perfectly fine. Why are you stopping?"

"You're bounding through the snow like a hare." He paused, assessing her. "You must be more rugged than you appear, if you have enough energy to leap about so."

"I am."

He shrugged, and headed off again. She drew a long, miserable breath and followed. An hour passed, and at last Ariana could no longer keep up. The evening cold had numbed her flesh; she couldn't feel her fingers or her toes, and her legs throbbed with pain. Night had darkened all around them, mercifully, so Taran didn't notice the tears frozen on her eyelashes.

Ahead, he stopped to survey the landscape, and Ariana pretended to have stopped for the same reason. He came back to her, a tall, dark shape in the night. "There's a light on the hillside to the east. I suggest we head in that direction."

She looked to where he indicated and her heart crashed. It was at least another hour's walk, in good weather. A sharp fear surfaced inside her. *I can't make it that far.* But neither could she simply collapse.

"Very good." Her teeth were chattering, so she said no more, but Taran moved closer to examine her.

"Is your cape providing enough warmth, Ariana? It appears somewhat thin."

Death first. She would never admit weakness to her handsome nemesis. "My cape is extremely well made, and very warm. It is so warm that I am almost hot. I may perhaps shed it after a while, as its warmth is so extreme." She straightened her back, with effort, and marched off to where he had pointed.

He hesitated, shrugged, then followed. He caught up within a few strides. She didn't want to let him pass, but neither could she increase her own speed. She stopped and stretched, casually. He stopped, too. How like him to investigate signs of her weakness!

"Are you tired?"

She frowned. "Certainly not! I could walk all night, if it happens to be necessary." She hoped fervently it would not. "But if you're tired, we can certainly rest."

She felt his penetrating gaze upon her, so she avoided meeting his eyes. He studied her awhile, no doubt seeking evidence of her deceit. "Since I'm not tired, and neither are you, I think it would be best to reach our destination as quickly as possible. If you're sure you're well enough, we will walk on."

Her heart fell, but she kept her expression even. "I am perfectly fine. Proceed."

Taran started off ahead. The moment his back faced her, Ariana's shoulders slumped and the frozen tears returned. She wished desperately for a mug of something hot and pleasant to sip, a warm fire for her toes, a blanket. . . . But she had only water in her pack, and it was frozen.

Snow swirled around them, increasing as the night deepened. Fate seemed against her surviving their walk. The light on the eastern slope grew brighter, veiled in the snow, but Ariana's hope dwindled. She fought panic, but the cold seemed to reach inside her and freeze even her fears. She walked on by rote, feeling less and less, her gaze fixed on Taran's back.

After what seemed an eternity of trudging through the gathering drifts, Taran stopped and pointed. "We're not far now, Ariana. I can see the glow of a well-lit hearth through a large window. Do you see it?"

He glanced back but Ariana felt too weak to care about their quest now, when each step forward was agony. "Yes. It's lovely." She saw nothing but Taran, but she couldn't let him see how weak she had become.

He started off, and Ariana followed, but her thoughts spun and wandered aimlessly, first to the days of her childhood, to the mystic hills and vales of her Welsh home, then to the festive dances of spring. She remem-

321

bered wanting love so much that it hurt, wanting to believe that the most magical of unions could happen to
her.

Young men had courted her, and several times, she
thought she had found "the one." But always, there was
something that proved her wrong. One man found another bride more profitable, revealing a shallow heart.
Another found himself torn between Ariana and a
woman his family had chosen. In the end, he obeyed his
family's wishes, grieving ever after that he had lost Ariana. But the moment he wavered, Ariana had known he
wasn't the one she had been seeking. True love would
never waver. It might hesitate and it might fear, but
when the moment of decision came it would never fail.

After a time, Ariana had considered entering the nun-
nery; that would spare her the pain and disappointment
of love. But the lingering, deathless hope of someone
unforgettable—someone so rare that in all the world,
there was only one such man—that had kept her from
taking the veil. Somehow, she had always known—
prayed—that she would find true love, and had been
unable to give up.

She had grown older, then, and lost hope. That was
when she had made her daring rescue of her village's
stolen children. Life had held no more meaning. And it
was then that she had been saved by Nicholas. There,
doing the noble work that was as close as she would
ever come to fulfillment, she had found Taran.

She had loved him on sight, and it was then that she
felt the first true terror of her life.

Ariana closed her eyes as she walked. She stumbled,
but didn't fall. He had been talking to someone else—
Kiya, the Egyptian, she thought—but when Nicholas introduced them, Taran had looked at Ariana as if he'd
never seen anything like her in his life.

His whole being had seemed focused on her as he

took her hand and held it. His skin had been warm, vibrant with the power of life. She recalled the embarrassment of suddenly feeling he saw into her heart as she peered up at him, spellbound. He had spoken, excited because he had found her—or so she had believed at the time. He asked her about her origins, had told her of his own. He had truly seemed to care.

And when he walked her to her new cottage, he'd kissed her cheek.

Ariana's boot lodged in the snow. She tried to pull free, but it held her captive, so she just stood for a moment, lost as Taran continued on oblivious into the night.

Somehow, they had become enemies. She was never sure why, except that she had become terrified after that first meeting. He had been so bold, and that had made her unnaturally shy around him—and that had increased the tension between them. He had told her she was special, and beautiful, and that he wanted to know her. He had held her hand and she had felt truly safe for the first time in her life.

They became enemies because she had been afraid.

Ariana pulled herself free of the boot and continued on, not caring about the pain of the ice burning at her foot. She limped forward. She had lost sight of the welcoming light, but it no longer mattered. She couldn't see Taran anymore, but perhaps that was for the best. . . .

She no longer felt cold, and that was some comfort as night deepened around her. Her limbs felt light and warm, and a strange contentment settled inside her. *I am free; this is all over.*

As she sank down to her knees, then into the warm, enveloping snowdrift, she had one last fearful thought. She had never truly lived at all.

"Ariana! Wake up, don't do this." She heard his voice in her dreams. Though he yanked her from a pleasant sleep, she couldn't help harking to it.

Annoyed that he was so insistent, still . . . that he cared at all gave her joy. She felt him pick her up, but she remained groggy. Maybe it was best she didn't answer, lest he put her down again and be angry that she had been sleeping when they had so much work to do, so many toys to make.

She felt his hand on her cheek. The palm felt hot. She opened one eye and saw him leaning over her. He appeared frightened. Well, she could understand that. She battled terror every time he walked by her studio.

"You feel hot, Taran. Are you fevered?"

He groaned, then tore off his heavy cape and wrapped it about her. He didn't seem capable of answering.

"You mustn't take that off. You'll catch a death of cold. We still have many toys to make, you know. And yours are so beautiful. I know they're violent, but still beautiful. Like you . . ."

Every word she spoke seemed to increase his fear. He pulled out a leather canteen and held it to her lips. A bitter liquid met her tongue and she grimaced.

"Drink it, Ariana."

She shook her head. "It's awful."

"It's grog, and yes, it's awful. Drink it anyway."

She squinted to better see his face. "Are you trying to poison me?"

He looked hurt, deeply, but it didn't seem such a far-fetched question. "I'm trying to help you. Please drink."

"I know I've been difficult at times, Taran, but I think you would feel a certain element of remorse if you killed me." She paused, her brow scrunching as she considered. "At least, I assume you would." She paused again. "I have been very difficult, I know."

She closed her eyes, wishing her fears had perhaps not been quite so strong, wishing she hadn't pushed him away with quite so much force. Maybe he would have pursued her, and not become her enemy.

A warm, soft touch pressed against her forehead. She peeked up. He had kissed her, gently. His breath became labored as if he were fighting emotion. He rested his cheek against her head and lifted the canteen to her lips again. "Please drink."

His kiss warmed her far more than anything else could, but she obeyed. The liquor burned her throat and stirred her senses. Suddenly, she felt the cold again; her toes hurt, and she noticed that her eyelashes hung low with ice.

Taran had found her missing boot and pulled it from the snow. He held her icy foot in his hands for a moment, then slipped the boot on. She shivered uncontrollably and her teeth chattered. He wrapped her tight in his cape and then lifted her into his arms. "You'll be all right now, Ariana. I won't let anything happen to you."

He had already "happened" to her, but her senses had returned enough to prevent her from saying so. To her surprise, she noticed icicles forming on his own black lashes. For an instant, she wondered if he had cried, then realized it was probably a result of the exertion required in hoisting her.

She gazed up at him dreamily. "You can't help it, can you?"

He looked down. "What?"

She smiled, though her frozen lips cracked in the effort. "Being a hero. It's in your blood. Even to save me . . ."

She drifted off toward sleep, but he jogged her and she frowned. "You can't sleep, Ariana. Not yet."

"Oh . . ." She sighed. "Very well. You will keep me safe, I know."

Even in the dark, she saw his eyes glitter, and this time, she felt sure that tears were the cause. "I'm sorry, Ariana." Yes, his voice sounded tight with emotion. Maybe he really did care, after all. "I should have known

325

you would hide your suffering from me." He bowed his head, then looked at her again. "I should have protected you, even from yourself."

He cradled her close against his chest so that she heard his strong heartbeat. She placed her hand over the spot and remembered lying naked beside him, touching his skin, feeling his power. She looked up into his eyes and knew she had been frozen for a very long time.

"Please warm me."

For an instant, she saw his heart in his eyes. He hesitated, then kissed her mouth, softly. All his warmth seemed to pour into her. She wrapped her arms around his neck and kissed him back. It had been so long, and she had relived his kiss so many times. . . . The music of their dance still echoed in her ears.

She slipped her tongue between his lips and she heard him moan deep in his throat. The sound inspired a sweet delirium that she hadn't known in a very long time. She tangled her fingers in his hair, then kissed his face. He felt so warm and so strong.

The passion between them drove away the cold, and Ariana felt as if their last kiss, so long ago, had never really ended. The time between, the battles and arguments, the tears at night, seemed like nothing.

Taran kissed her with equal fervor. She felt his desire, and something more. It was as if seeing her vulnerable and in pain had made him forget his hostility for her. For a moment, she thought he would lower her to the snow-covered ground and make love to her. She wanted nothing more.

Then he broke their kiss and tipped his head back. He looked away. She sensed he was trying to regain control of himself, so she pressed soft kisses against his jaw. He shuddered, but he didn't kiss her again.

"Ariana, you're weak. I'm sorry."

She caught her lip between her teeth, fear flooding through her. "But . . . I'm getting warm."

She caught his reluctant smile, but he closed his eyes. "I can't let this happen again. We've both seen where it leads."

Several tears felt hot against her cold cheeks, but she refused to let any more fall. "Put me down."

He seemed startled by her abrupt command, but he didn't release her. "We have to get through this, and do what we came here for. If you would in the future alert me to your suffering before it has gone this far, we might better avoid . . . circumstances dangerous to both of us."

He meant their kiss. He meant that she was dangerous to him. He had said so the night they met, just before he kissed her cheek. The cold of the winter night was no match for the sudden chill of her heart.

Why had she thought, even delirious from cold, that anything could ever change between them? Like the night they'd shared, it had been the briefest insanity, and she had obviously been bitterly confused. From now on, she would maintain her distance, and make it clear to him that she was not his for the taking—even if briefly she had dreamed of nothing else.

"You can't carry me the whole way. Put me down."

"You're not that heavy."

"The light has gone anyway. I noticed that it had disappeared just before I fell."

He smiled. "It hasn't disappeared. You had turned in the wrong direction." He paused. "You were going north."

He truly intended to carry her. How could she bear that, with her head on his shoulder, his arms around her, knowing that he didn't want her half as much she wanted him? "There has to be a better way."

"I'm sure there is a better way." He stopped and

327

sighed. "But neither of us has found it. I doubt we ever will."

Before she could answer or further object, Taran lifted her up and carried her toward the light.

Ariana's body felt tiny in his arms. Taran carried her with ease, but her intermittent shivers tortured him. He knew her so well. He should have known she wouldn't admit that she was weakening. She would have marched into hell without saying a word before admitting that to him.

He wanted nothing more than to have her close, and to protect her. From the first moment he saw her, he wanted to hold her and keep her safe, with him. Yet she still looked at him with suspicion, then and now, even to the point of thinking he would poison her.

Her doubt hurt him, but he had done nothing to ease her fears. Maybe he was so afraid himself that when she truly came close to him, she would find him lacking. Then she would reject him. He had opened himself to her once, then felt her withdraw afterward. He had waited for her to tell him she loved him, that he was inside her heart as well as her body, but she had said nothing. She'd just lain quietly beside him, looking pensive and alone.

He had always known he wanted more than sex from Ariana. There was too much passion and too much emotion between them to ignore the demands of his heart. He wanted to ask her what would please her, what would make her love him, but was afraid that would be a secret she would never reveal.

Her head rested against his shoulder, inspiring tenderness against his will. She shivered, but he saw she kept her eyes ahead as if suspicious he would take a wrong turn and lose them again. Despite her obvious doubts, they drew closer to their goal, and the light began to illuminate a large stone building, accessible through a well-tended winter garden of juniper and small pines, all decorated with Christmas ornaments and bells.

As they crossed the garden, he saw many windows lit, and heard sounds of music coming from within. Apparently, the hall's inhabitants were in the festive mood of Yuletide.

Taran glanced down and saw Ariana's eyes drift shut. Fear stabbed at him, and he lifted her body higher against his chest. "Ariana, we've made it. Don't sleep, not yet."

She opened one eye and her lips curled to the side, disgruntled. Still, on her small, lovely face, every expression had charm. "I was not sleeping."

Stubborn to the end. He resisted the impulse to kiss her forehead. "We will find shelter here, and food. Don't worry."

Her delicate brow arched. "I was never worried."

He shook his head and sighed, then banged the iron knocker against the heavy wooden door. A large pine wreath hung at the door's center, as carefully made as the decorations at Nicholas's abode. He heard footsteps from within, and Ariana squirmed in his arms. "Put me down!" He hesitated, but her squirming increased. "I cannot be seen in your . . . in this condition. Put me down."

He lowered her to her small feet and watched with a dull ache as she scrambled away. She straightened her robe and her hair, which had come loose from its bun. She adopted a formal, proud expression as the door opened.

An old man appeared in the entryway, dressed formally in black. He eyed them closely as if seeking recognition. Finding none, he stepped back. "Lady Emilia not be expecting ye." He eyed Ariana and apparently liked what he saw. But then, what man wouldn't? "Ye

329

look to be near frozen, dear maidy. What's befallen ye and yer poor husband?"

Taran liked the man's erroneous impression, but Ariana braced. "He is *not* my husband!" She was indignant, predictably, at even the thought they could be bonded so closely. He wondered how she would explain their connection.

The old man's eyes narrowed. "Then yer servant, miss?" Taran frowned, but at least the man had the grace to pose the question doubtfully.

Ariana looked tempted to accept this explanation, but Taran cast her a dark look of warning. Her small mouth twitched in irritation. He knew how much she would have liked to march about this mansion with him acting as her footman. "He's my . . . cousin." She paused. "Second cousin." She paused again, as if the connection was still too close. "Once removed."

The old man looked between them. "Yer not of the same breed."

Ariana puffed an impatient breath. "His side of the family was . . . removed to a kingdom across the sea, where I have only recently been visiting. My cousin here was . . . escorting me back to my home . . . in Wales, and we were waylaid by . . . ruffians . . . who stole our coach and our horses, and most of our bags . . . except these we have here.

"We are quite lost, and very cold. Could you offer us some form of shelter for the night?" She paused, not as breathless from her speech as Taran felt from listening to her. "By the way, would there be anyone suffering, generally unhappy, or otherwise in need in this residence?"

Taran rolled his eyes. Subtle, very subtle! He seized her, set her aside and addressed the old man. "My cousin is addled from the cold. If you could make arrangements to accommodate us for the night, we will offer payment for your kindness."

The old man appeared suspicious both of Taran's size and his accent, but then he cast a fond glance at Ariana, who looked pert and slightly confused. "Dear little thing, toes frosted, are they? I'll speak to the lady of the house, and see what can be done."

He motioned for them to enter, then led them to a square room to wait. Ariana glared up at Taran. "I am *not* addled."

She was obviously healthy enough to be angry. She looked so delicate and so fierce. He couldn't help a surge of affection. "It's a little early to start pressing them for information, isn't it . . . cousin?"

Her eyes shifted to her feet. "I couldn't let them think we were married."

Why did her rejections still have the power to hurt him, so long after he had accepted there could be nothing between them? "That would be inconvenient, wouldn't it?"

She looked up at him, but didn't answer. She suddenly looked sad and tired, as if the night's stress had finally taken its toll on her. "You are right about waiting until we've been introduced to the household. I wouldn't want them to be suspicious of our presence."

"Then, cousin, I suggest you let me explain our presence next time. Your story was implausible at best."

She sparkled with annoyance. "I am perfectly capable—"

The old man returned, cutting off Ariana's objection. A small, plump woman accompanied him, smiling, her hand already outstretched to Ariana. "Dear child! I am Lady Emilia of Gurthington Manor. My man has told me of your plight."

She seized Ariana's hands in hers, then rubbed them vigorously between her palms. "You're frozen to the

331

bone! Come inside, and sit by the fire with me and my guests. We'll see you're taken care of as well as by your own kin."

Lady Emilia made a clucking sound with her tongue. "My man has told me of your misfortune! Waylaid by ruffians! And you would be spending this fine, festive season among your own. I am so sorry, dear heart." She clucked again. It was possible this woman spoke faster and more breathlessly than Ariana herself. "Highwaymen. They are a problem, aren't they? But I do believe they act only from necessity and not from true evil. If we could, perhaps, lend them some measure of our good fortune, they might treat the world more kindly." She paused, presumably to take a breath. "Don't you agree, my dear?"

Ariana looked both confused and overwhelmed by Lady Emilia's energetic words. The Scotswoman reminded Taran of someone, but he wasn't sure who it was she resembled. "I am sure you are right, Lady Emilia."

Lady Emilia squeezed Ariana's hands. "Then you would forgive them for their deeds, my dear?"

Ariana glanced at Taran and looked guilty. "Of course."

Lady Emilia beamed and nodded sagely. "They did you no real harm, after all, seeing as you are here safe and sound. Likely they just needed some provisions. Probably for wee ones, who are at home with nothing. We do as we can here, to send out gifts and foodstuffs to our poorer neighbors, but there are always more in need of kindness during this cold time of year."

Ariana's brow furrowed and her lips twisted, which meant she was pondering something. Taran knew what likely occupied her thoughts. In a home as kindly run as Lady Emilia's, it seemed implausible they would find the suffering object of their quest. At least Ariana would be well cared for, and for one night, that was all Taran wanted.

He stepped forward and Lady Emilia squealed as if a delightful sugarplum had been offered. "My word, you are a tall one, aren't you?" She grabbed Taran's hands with the same vigor she had assaulted Ariana. "And handsome! I don't believe I've ever quite seen your like." She winked at Ariana. "Your cousin, is he? Oh, to have such relations dotted about the land!"

Taran's face felt warm, but he couldn't let Ariana detect his embarrassment. "I am Taran de Vaas, my lady. I was escorting Miss . . ." He stopped. He had no idea of his 'cousin's' surname, nor did he know the Welsh language enough to make one up.

Ariana cleared her throat. "*Glyndwr*. I am Ariana Glyndwr. My poor second cousin once removed has not mastered Welsh pronunciation."

Lady Emilia laughed, a tinkling, infectious sound. "And no wonder! Have any of us, save the Welsh alone, mastered that tongue? No, even the shortest Welsh words leave the rest of us, even we Celts, staggering over our tongues." She tucked Ariana's arm in hers. Beside the stout, round woman, Ariana looked tall. "Tell me, my dear, why do your people avoid *vowels* so?"

Ariana peeked nervously back at Taran as if fearing she might say something that would give them away. "Vowels are vastly overrated."

Emilia laughed again, then tugged Ariana down the hall. "They are indeed! And where are you from, dear girl? Northern Wales, or the south, or perhaps the rugged shores?"

"I am from Llangollen in the north, my lady."

"Beautiful country! Oh, how I love the Welsh hills and dales, with the mists and pleasant pastures and wild streams! Have you been away long, child?"

Ariana hesitated. "Quite long, yes."

Emilia glanced back at Taran and winked. "Visiting your relations abroad? I see that you picked the plum and brought him back with you. Your family will be pleased to meet this one, I think."

Despite Ariana's claim of family, Lady Emilia obviously believed they were betrothed. Taran sighed. Well, she would soon see through that mistaken impression.

Ariana opened her mouth to speak, but Emilia was still chattering. "He should tower over your wee family, I'm afraid. I've rarely seen a Welshman stand half so high as your handsome cousin."

Ariana hesitated, then nodded. "That is true. I was a hand taller than my late father."

Emilia beamed. "What a dear little pixie he must have been! But sad to say, he's no longer with us."

Ariana bit her lip. "He passed on some time ago."

Taran imagined himself standing amidst Ariana's tiny family. Would they all have been bright-eyed and quick like Ariana? Did she miss them now that they had been dead for nearly three centuries?

He thought of his own family of tall, strong-bodied warriors, and proud, silent women. He remembered the warmth that had bonded them despite their stoic nature. He saw Ariana among them, amusing them with her quick wit and imaginative mind, and a steel band tightened around his heart.

Lady Emilia led them into a large room warmed by a hearth. A giant pine tree stood at the far end of the hall, decorated with lavish attention to detail. It was similar to Nicholas's style, but more feminine. Several guests mulled around the tree, all laughing and comfortable. He heard the faint sigh of admiring women as he entered, followed closely by a young man's appreciative murmur when Emilia presented Ariana to her guests.

"Let us make these two lost angels welcome, my dear friends and family. Let us treat them as one of us, for while they are here at Gurthington Manor, it shall be their home."

Lady Emilia's guests crowded around, all friendly and happy, separating Taran from Ariana. His companion scrutinized them with unveiled interest, no doubt seeking out an unhappy face in their midst. It was not to be found. Everyone there looked pleased and well-fed, enjoying life to its fullest. Despite the festive atmosphere, Ariana didn't appear happy.

Taran made his way back to Ariana's side. She now sipped a pink-colored punch, frowning and pensive. "Doesn't it suit you, Ariana?"

She looked at him quizzically, and he nodded at her crystal goblet. "Ah, the punch. It's adequate." She took another sip. He loved the way her lips moved, always delicate but purposeful. "What do you think? No one appears in need of our service. What should we do?"

"I see no evidence of want or despair, that is certain." Except in himself, when he sat so close to her and couldn't touch her.

She drummed her fingers on her goblet. "Perhaps there's someone hidden in an attic, or cast out in the stables."

"Given Lady Emilia's temperament, that seems unlikely."

Ariana's shoulders slumped. "True. What do we do?"

"Nicholas told us that we must recognize a problem where none appears to exist." He looked around at Emilia's smiling guests and sighed. "It seems we've found a home worthy of that test."

Ariana nodded. He liked the way her chin set in determination. "Then we must commence interviewing her guests for weakness." She glanced at a pretty blond girl, then at Taran. "I will question that girl myself. You take the pear-shaped older woman in the corner."

Taran repressed a smile. Sometimes, Ariana's behav-

ior seemed jealous and possessive. How silly he was to
think so, though. A tall young man caught his eye, because the boy had fixed his admiring attention on Ariana.
"And I will interrogate that one. You, perhaps, might
see fit to question the gentleman seated by the fire."

Ariana looked doubtful. "The very old one sleeping
in his chair by the fireplace?"

Taran endured a flash of embarrassment. "Yes."

She shrugged. "I can't think I'll get much out of him.
Yet . . ." She paused, her eyes narrowing. "It's possible
that he is resting to avoid the overwhelming heartache
of lost love, or some such tragic affliction. I will discover its cause, bring it to rights, and we can return to
the Vale."

Chapter Three

The old man was interested in frogs. Apparently, he had even traveled to Africa in search of a renowned giant frog. He had brought one back to Scotland with him, but it hadn't survived the journey.

Ariana hesitated, trying to think of something helpful to say, in case this sorrow was the one she was to ease—although that seemed rather absurd. "Perhaps if you had made the journey during the summer months."

The old man sighed. "Nay, lass. The giant frog, he kenned for his home."

"Ah. Well, then. To have found such a specimen at all must be a source of pride for you, sir."

The old man's pale blue eyes sparkled. "Aye, it is, indeed! Had him stuffed, I did. Looks a bit puffier than he did in life, but maybe a smart lass like yourself would like to see—"

"No!" Ariana coughed and cleared her throat. "I don't think now is a good time for such a viewing." She glanced around nervously for Taran, but the pear-shaped woman had him cornered near a piano. The blond beauty she'd spotted earlier was dangerously close to him. Ariana decided her aged companion had no serious grief, other than an overstuffed frog. "Sir, it has been good to make your acquaintance, and I wish you many more such fascinating discoveries."

"Have to wait for spring, lass, but there's always something new to discover." The old man yawned and fell promptly back to sleep. Ariana adjusted his red tartan blanket to cover his bony hands, then left him snoring comfortably by the fire.

Ariana made her way to the piano. The pear-shaped woman had taken control of Taran's left arm and seemed to be squeezing it as if testing for ripeness. He looked uneasy and rather pained. Ariana considered rescuing him, but the woman appeared powerfully determined.

"We don't get lads half so brawny here in the lowlands. You look more like a mighty highlander." Clearly, Taran had no idea of the difference between highlanders and lowlanders, and even more evidently, didn't care. The rotund woman again fingered his arm. Ariana suspected the next inspection of Taran's firm flesh would involve the woman's teeth.

The blond girl maneuvered closer, too. Ariana frowned as Taran gave her a brief smile. Perhaps she resembled the tall, stoic women of his homeland. She didn't appear to be particularly full of personality, but Taran hadn't revealed any affection for Ariana's fanciful nature. Perhaps her very down-to-earth nature, too, might be considered a benefit.

Bad enough to be abandoned with him, but to watch him form an attachment for a pretty, sweet-tempered girl would be more than Ariana could endure. She knew all the women in the Vale of Snow—none had proven a temptation to Taran. She had grown accustomed to him without a woman. And in Nicholas's service, nothing had been likely to change. But now that they had been pitched out of their sweet complacency, anything was possible.

I want to go on as we were, separate but together, but Nicholas had made her wish impossible now. They had two days together. Two days in which to find someone suffering, here in a home just as happy as could be. It didn't seem possible, and they had so little time.

Ariana wedged herself casually between Taran and the blond girl, who was smiling patiently as the pear-shaped woman chattered on about Taran's strength and masculine charisma. Her "cousin" drew a long breath, then forced a polite expression in response. "Do I gather, madam, that your husband has passed away?"

The woman's brows arched dramatically. "Oh, why, no! He's over there." She gestured at the old man by the fire, then clucked her tongue. "Married him when I was just a wee lass, I did. Fine old man, but all he thinks about are toads."

Taran's eyes narrowed and Ariana wasn't sure what he was thinking. Was he judging these people? Was he beginning to think that all people of Celtic background were odd—just because one man loved to study toads? Ariana adopted a proud expression. "My people, too, have a undeniable affection for toads. They feature in many beloved children's stories, and in art, as in symbolism of the gravest nature." There, that would confuse him.

The blond girl eyed her in surprise. "Once, I considered it an odd hobby, but I must say that grandfather's enthusiasm for the creatures is infectious." Ariana decided to keep far from the old man, lest she become similarly afflicted.

The pear-shaped woman hugged the girl. "This is my granddaughter, Jane. Her father is an English parliamentarian, and most of her life has been spent in the far more exciting world of London society."

Jane was assessing Taran, too favorably, so Ariana took the girl's arm and eased her toward a small sofa. "Tell me, Jane, it must be quite difficult to be in Scotland, caught here in a storm, rather than in London for Christmas."

Jane's blue eyes widened. "Oh, not at all!" She lowered her voice conspiratorially. "You have no idea how tiresome the hustle of London can become." She stopped and sighed, looking happy. "When I am with Grandmother and Grandfather, I can forget all the pressures of making a good match, of fulfilling my parents' wishes for me."

Ariana endured disappointment. "And you don't find the toads terribly awful?"

Again, the girl smiled, and Ariana had to concede a growing fondness for her; she was sweet. Jane giggled. "Grandfather has a huge fat frog stuffed and kept over the mantlepiece. Some find it odd, but it is truly a source of fascination for me. I have a collection of stuffed frogs from every Christmas. He always presents me with a new set each year."

Ariana grimaced. "You have stuffed frogs, too?" Scotland was, by far, odder than Wales. Perhaps Taran should believe that these people were bizarre.

Jane laughed and patted Ariana's arm. "Not real ones. Toys, made of velveteen and cotton."

Ariana breathed a sigh of relief. "That is more pleasant, I imagine." She looked around the room. "So you are happy, then?"

Jane lowered her eyelashes, looking prettier than ever, and a shy smile formed on her lips. "I am tonight."

Ariana's heart suffered a sharp tug. "Why is that?"

Jane bit her lip, shy. "I hesitate to say, so soon."

Oh, no. The girl had developed a crush on Taran.

Ariana leaned back in her seat, defeated. "He is handsome, I know. But there is much to his character that wants inspection before fully committing yourself to a pursuit."

Jane's brow angled. "I didn't realize you knew him."

Ariana sat up. "You're not referring to my . . . cousin? My second cousin once removed?"

Jane laughed again. "Of course not! Though your cousin is handsome, I admit. Very well-built. But my heart is already given." She paused, assessing Ariana more closely. "As indeed I thought was his."

Ariana guessed where this was leading and she sighed. "If you mean to me, then you are mistaken. He can barely tolerate my presence."

"Indeed? For a man whose tolerance is so low, his attention seems often cast your way."

Ariana glanced at Taran. Jane was right. He had been looking her way, but as soon as she met his gaze, he turned his attention back to a tall young man. "He's probably afraid I'll say something wrong, or bungle . . ."

"Bungle what?"

Ariana resisted an urge to confess her entire story to Jane. The girl would only think her insane. "He has no faith in my social abilities."

Jane studied her a moment, then nodded. "I think you suffer from the same fear I myself felt with David—that you can't imagine any woman as good enough for him, let alone yourself."

Ariana swallowed hard. It was true, so she had to change the subject at once. "Who is David?"

"David is the gentleman speaking with your cousin. We arranged to meet here at Auntie Emilia's so that we might find a way to approach my parents on the subject of our marriage."

"And Emilia will be sufficient help with this?" Maybe

a forbidden wedding would require Ariana's intervention, but Jane didn't appear concerned.

"My parents always listen to Auntie Emilia. Everyone does."

"Then you are assured of a beautiful wedding, and a lifetime of love." For a reason Ariana didn't understand, her own heart sank even lower. She had assured herself there was no feminine threat to Taran present at the manor, which was some comfort, but her feelings of loneliness refused to abate. "Everyone seems so happy here." She couldn't restrain a wistful tone in her voice. "Are there tenants on this property? It seems so far removed from everything."

"There are crofters nearby."

That sounded promising. Crofters lived in small, draughty huts and often suffered during the winter months. "Perhaps I might go out to visit them."

Jane gestured toward the punch bowl. "There's no need to leave. My aunt's tenants are already here. Her home has always been welcome to all."

Ariana noticed a group of farmers and their wives chatting and laughing as they filled their plates with food. Their dress was less sophisticated than that of the noblemen, but they all seemed well-fed and healthy. "Are there any children?"

"Auntie has them all in the east wing, where she has the largest collection of toys in all of Scotland. We'll be hard-pressed to get them to their beds tonight."

That sounded good, but children were often seized with secret sorrow and pain. "Would it be permissible for me to see them at play? I have some interest in toy collections."

Jane indicated a staircase. "I'm sure Auntie would be pleased, and the children as well." She glanced toward David, who smiled. "It is the first suite on the left. If you don't mind, I won't accompany you. David and I have much to discuss."

Jane left and Taran came to sit beside Ariana. He appeared equally dumbfounded as to which guest might be in need of assistance. Ariana peered up at him. She liked that he wore a dark glower despite the festivities. He had never been a man who hid his emotions well; and that emotional honesty appealed to her.

"I take it you discovered the same thing I did. Nothing."

Taran nodded, then glanced back at David. The young man was now holding Jane's hands lovingly in his own. "At least he wasn't interested in . . ." He stopped, looking slightly abashed.

"Interested in what?"

Taran looked uncomfortable. "In anything besides his fiancée."

Ariana hesitated. "Did you think he was?"

"I thought it distinctly possible."

Ariana waited awhile, but Taran refused to look at her. "Me? You thought he was interested in me."

For an instant only, he looked vulnerable, and Ariana's heart felt swollen with pleasure. Taran shrugged, but still didn't meet her eyes. "I can think of no reason he wouldn't be."

"Other than his obvious love for another woman. A woman who appears to cause no mischief." Ariana hesitated. He had practically admitted that he was jealous. In turn, she felt safe almost admitting the same. "I had thought you might prefer a woman like Jane."

He met her eyes. "Why would you think that?"

"I have wondered what sort of woman you would choose."

He smiled, but he looked sad. "Don't you know?"

She felt uncomfortable with this subject. Too much

of her own secret heart might be revealed. "I suppose . . . someone like yourself."

"Is that what you want for yourself, Ariana? A man just like yourself? Small of stature, spirited of temperament, with bright eyes and a mind that can wander to the most fantastical realms?"

She knew what she wanted to say, if she dared. *I want a man exactly like you. Except he would love me back.* It seemed wiser to answer more carefully. "It would be nice, yes, to have some shared characteristics."

"Such as what?" He seemed genuinely interested, but Ariana felt cornered, as if he were only desirous of learning her weakness.

"I would like him to care for others, to be kind. I would like him to be of an imaginative temperament, so that he cares less for social standing than for the desires of his heart.

Taran nodded, seeming to like her answer. "I believe those are admirable qualities."

She brightened. "You do? But I imagine that you would find those characteristics to prove quite difficult at times."

He snorted, then muttered something in another language. "No question, they *would.*"

She sensed offense, though his words had started out as complimentary. "In what way would a vivid imagination cause *you* trouble?"

His dark brow slanted as if she should know the answer. "Perhaps a woman of such an 'imaginative' bent would see fit to set a man on fire rather than voicing any complaints directly to him."

Ariana's lips tightened, then twisted. "It occurs to me also that a man of like mind might also react strangely, and cause destruction to a woman's good work, all because he refuses to tell her what he really wants from her."

His eyes seemed darker than normal. "If the *woman* cared more for truth than for hiding her feelings, the man might be able to talk to her."

Ariana's face heated in anger. What was he implying? "If the man were truer of purpose, rather than leaving the woman to struggle to understand his true meaning, she might find her own truth easier to speak!"

Emilia's guests had fallen silent, and Ariana realized her voice had risen substantially. Taran paid no attention to the stares he was now receiving. As always, he focused solely on the matter at hand, which was her. "A woman who invites attention, receives it with obvious and memorable delight, then spurns it afterward might find truth difficult indeed." Taran's voice had lowered but it resonated with emotion.

Ariana leaned toward him, her fists clamped in tight balls on her lap. "When a man dallies with a woman for the sake of his own amusement, and toys with her affections, there can be only one reason, and that is for the sake of conceit—which wants more flattery than any woman can give."

Taran bent closer to her, his dark eyes glittering with passion. "The flattery was not demanded by the man, but by the woman, whose need for it is boundless."

She felt tears burning and blinked to prevent them from falling. Clearing her throat, Ariana took several shallow breaths to calm herself. "It is plain we have nothing useful to say to each other on this subject."

He nodded vigorously. "No, indeed." They moved away from each other, then stood up at the same time. "We have a task to perform, and clearly the object of our rescue is not in this room." He paused, his jaw tight with anger. "Have you learned anything at all to point us in the right direction?"

She refused to look at him. "There is a room of children playing upstairs. I heard nothing to indicate unhappiness among them, but I can think of nowhere else to search."

"Children have been known to be unhappy."

"I thought so myself."

Taran hesitated. "We will question them, then."

"Yes." She still couldn't look at him. She had come too close to admitting that she still harbored feelings for him, and incited nothing but anger. She couldn't allow that to happen again. Once, she had believed love was the greatest gift, that in its grip all things would be clear. With love, she had believed, all things false would be washed away. But as she headed upstairs after Taran, she realized the one thing that could make her happy was the one thing she trusted least. Love, itself.

Taran stormed up the staircase, Ariana close behind him. He heard her skittering to keep up as he hurried down the hall. What an infuriating woman! Every time he felt tempted to reveal his affection for her, her pride rose up and pushed him away. No, speaking his true heart to Ariana would be nothing but a mistake.

The sound of children playing stopped him outside a painted blue door. Small, round flowers had been stenciled on its panels. The door reminded him of the decoration of Nicholas's own studio, painted with love and attention to the most cheerful detail.

He looked down the hall at several closed doors, each painted with different scenes. Ariana stepped up beside him and touched the door. "It's very pretty work. I would like something such as this for my own workplace. When we get back, I shall set about painting something similar."

Taran sighed. "*If* we get back, you mean. Our success so far has not been promising."

She offered a rueful smile, then pushed open the door.

346

Several children of varying sizes sat playing in the room. A tiny girl with wild brown curls was tinkering with a makeshift dollhouse. The quality wasn't as good as those made in Ariana's studio, but the child seemed happy. As the girl worked, a red-haired boy lined up small soldiers and a chariot as if to lay siege to the dollhouse.

The little boy crept closer to the unsuspecting girl, but in his efforts at stealthy movement, he pressed his soldier too hard to the floor and snapped off its leg. Clearly, the toy lacked quality. Taran would have crafted much stronger figurines.

The little girl looked up and sighed. "You've broken his leg again, Robin." She stood up and placed her small hands on her hips.

The boy shook his broken soldier. "My man is still strong enough to conquer your measly dolls!"

The girl scoffed. "My dollhouse is a castle, and *all* my dolls are queens." She picked up a pretty one in a green dress and held it up in a threatening manner. "This is the biggest queen."

Taran and Ariana looked at each other. "A familiar scene."

A faint smile played on her lips. "It is."

Robin fiddled with the soldier's leg, and managed to break the other one, too. Taran seated himself cross-legged beside the boy. "It might be that I can mend that." The boy looked at him with large, brown eyes, suspicious, but willing to try. He passed him the soldier and waited without a word.

As the children watched, Taran withdrew a pocketknife, made a few cuts in the broken pieces, then fitted the legs back into place. He looked over his shoulder, and Ariana was smiling. He felt as if he were dreaming; this was a room filled with truly happy children. He felt as if this was where he and Ariana both belonged. For

347

a moment, they looked at each other, and he believed she was feeling the same thing.

The little girl took her hand and pulled her away, and Ariana set about reworking the dollhouse. She lay on her stomach, her small feet propped up and crossed at the ankle, chatting with the children that surrounded her. Taran found himself engaged in an elaborate military campaign taking place on the carpet. No matter how he tried to redirect several of the boys, they always seemed to be targeting the girls.

Ariana noticed the prospective siege, and her bright eyes glittered. "Ladies, line up your soldiers."

The little curly-haired girl positioned her queen at the top of the dollhouse, but the other girls hesitated. One held a doll close to her chest in protection. "Our dolls are ladies, not soldiers."

Ariana huffed. "Women can be warriors, too. They can be Celtic warriors whose dresses are just disguises to fool their male enemies."

Taran couldn't take his eyes from her bright face. "I suspected as much." She looked at him and her smile grew. She was enjoying the imminent encounter, and so was he.

They positioned their toy armies, with Ariana's dollhouse as the fortress to be assailed. They played for what seemed to be hours, until one by one, the children dropped off to sleep, scattered about the floor like dolls themselves. When the last child had dozed off, the game finally stilled.

Ariana lay on her stomach again, her feet crossed at the ankles. Taran liked the position because it gave him an unobstructed view of her small, firm backside. Her relaxed posture made him feel intimate, and he remembered that night long ago when she lay naked beside him, her long hair trailing over his chest.

She cupped her chin in one hand, propped up at the

elbow, and tapped her lip thoughtfully. "It may be that I will have to expand my production once we return home."

He crossed his arms over his knees, watching her. "To what?"

She sat up and faced him. "To castles. And it should be possible to create collapsible walls, for instance, so that children can pretend at a victorious siege without destroying the actual structure."

"I would appreciate that feature."

Her lips quirked to one side. "I'm sure you would." She leaned on one hand and her lovely head tipped to one side. "And what would you contribute?"

"I notice that small girls prefer more conversation and emotional involvement with their toys than boys do. I would make my soldiers with more distinct personalities, so that girls might form attachments to them."

"So you'll have some in pretty skirts?" Her eyes glittered as she spoke, and he fought an urge to kiss her.

"I will make a few fierce Celtic warrior women. Would that please you?"

"It would." Ariana yawned and her eyelids drooped sleepily. "It is good to see what happiness toys can bring." She paused. "Do you think that this is what Nicholas wanted us to discover?"

"It is a joy, but neither of us doubted the importance of our work. Nor can I believe that a toy soldier's broken leg was the sorrow of which he spoke."

She yawned again, then stretched. Every sinew of her body attracted him, and he longed to touch her. "No, I suppose not. Well, we've tried. Perhaps tomorrow will show us something we've yet to find."

Lady Emilia appeared at the door, smiling. Her presence seemed warm and comforting. Taran stood up to greet her, and Ariana scrambled to her feet beside him. "We were wondering where you'd gotten off to." Emilia smiled at the sleeping children. "You've worn them out, I see. There's no better evening spent than with happy children at play, is there?"

Taran looked back to where the curly-haired girl lay curled in a ball. "Shall we place them in their beds?"

Emilia held up her fingers to hush them, then tiptoed into the room to lift up the smallest child. She placed the child in one of the small bunks that lined the room. Taran hurried to help with the others. He saw Ariana do so, too, and she place a gentle kiss on a sleeping boy's forehead. He imagined her as a mother. No distance would arise between Ariana and her children, that much was certain. They would have much love, and enough spirited fun, to keep them happy for a lifetime.

They tucked the children into bed, then left them sleeping and went out into the hall. It was still brightly lit. Ariana closed the door quietly, then turned to Emilia. "It is a perfect room for children, even so many."

Emilia smiled. "When my parents died, I remodeled the east wing for them. It is a joy to me to have so many visiting and making use of these pleasant rooms." She touched Ariana's arm gently. "But you are tired, my dear. It may be that you should also retire for a lovely night's sleep."

Ariana bit her lip. "I should hate to put you to any trouble, setting up a bedroom for me."

Emilia laughed and squeezed Ariana like a daughter. "My dear, my guest rooms are always prepared for company. Because it is the Christmas holiday, and my guests are snowbound for the night, most of my rooms are filled, but as it happens, two remain unused."

It was impossible that they'd be left in the same room, "cousins" or not, but Taran couldn't help a tug of disappointment. He glanced at Ariana. There seemed to be no regret on her face. She kissed their hostess's cheek and yawned again. "Thank you, Lady Emilia. It has been a long day, indeed. Where is my room?"

The woman pointed at the last room on the right, painted lavender with cheerful suns decorating the panels. "You will be comfortable there. The bed is soft and warm. You will sleep well, I know."

Ariana looked at Taran, but he couldn't read her expression. "What about my cousin?"

"I have a fine room for your handsome cousin in the west wing. It was made for a tall man such as himself."

Ariana eyes her quizzically. "For your husband?"

Emilia's brow rose. "I have no husband. No, this room was designed for my brother, who is now abroad in Rome. Come, let me settle you in, and then please join us for breakfast. Not too early, of course . . ."

Emilia chattered happily as she led them to Ariana's small but pleasant room. Taran took one look around and envisioned himself on the bed, holding Ariana as she slept, or making love to her. He closed his eyes and went to the door to wait. *Why do I torture myself this way? She doesn't belong to me. One night without promises should have long ago been forgotten.*

Ariana seated herself on the edge of her bed and gazed sleepily up at him. Her long hair had come loose around her face and fell in soft curls, grazing her cheeks. Her expression changed as she looked at him, and for a moment, he thought he detected longing so exquisite that it almost equalled his own.

She wanted him, too. He felt it. It *had* to be true. But passion fueled his imagination, it had done so before. He could never be sure that what he saw in Ariana was not simply that. They looked at each other, and for a moment Lady Emilia's presence was forgotten. Their purpose in Scotland was forgotten. Everything but that one spark of passion faded into oblivion.

"How very lucky you are, the two of you!" Emilia's

351

voice startled Taran from his daze. He eyed her doubtfully.

"Why is that, lady?"

Emilia smiled and again he was struck by her deep
compassion. "Don't you know?"

Obviously, the woman thought she knew something
that they did not. "We are indeed fortunate to have found
your welcoming home, Lady Emilia."

Emilia glanced between them, and looked thoughtful.
"My dear young man, I believe your fortune began long
before this night. But sometimes the best thing in your
life can be right in front of you, and your own fears can
stop you from seizing it." She opened an upright wardrobe closet, revealing several long, white nightgowns.
Turning to Ariana, she said, "Use anything you like, my
dear. And for tomorrow, there are suitable gowns that
you are welcome to try. There's one of dark blue velvet
that would suit you especially well, I think."

Ariana took one of the nightgowns and played with
the hem. She seemed to be avoiding Taran's eyes, but
she nodded graciously to Emilia. "You are a very kind
hostess, Lady Emilia. I never dreamed when we . . . left
home . . . that we should find such a welcome refuge as
this."

"Nor did I expect such dear guests on a stormy night.
But fate brings together those most in need, don't you
agree? Even if I don't know where you've come from."

Emilia didn't wait for an answer. Ariana looked too
surprised to give one, anyway. The older woman kissed
her cheek like a long-lost relative, then went to the door
with Taran. "Come now. I will show you to your room.
It is larger than this, though perhaps a bit chillier. Your
coverlets are warm, and the hearth in the corner is well
filled."

Emilia picked up a lantern and went out into the hall,
but Taran couldn't resist one last look at Ariana.

She sat on her bed looking confused and delicate, and maybe a little lonely. Her gaze met his, then jerked away as if she feared to reveal too much of herself. Maybe she remembered that he had kissed her out in the storm, and realized his passion for her had never abated. Maybe she was afraid he would try again.

He knew that he should look away lest the desire in his eyes threaten her. But it coursed through him, as if the very essence of what he was reached out for her. He imagined his fingers caressing her soft cheek, easing her hair back over her shoulder so that he could kiss her neck. He remembered the feel of her swift pulse beneath her skin, he heard echoes of her quick breaths as he incited her further into desire.

She was looking up at him now as if she read his thoughts. He expected her to turn away, but her eyelids lowered and she dampened her lips with an innocent sensuality he had never been able to resist. He couldn't stop himself. His gaze shifted to her body and he saw the rise and fall of her nervous breathing. He remembered touching her softly, cupping her small, firm breast in his hand and feeling the peak grow taut beneath his fingers.

Emilia was already walking down the hall, but Taran remained at Ariana's door, making love to her with every part of himself but his body. She knew, and she didn't avert her gaze. Instead, he felt her receptiveness, her need that went beyond pride or anger or fear.

She was tired and confused, no longer at the home she had known for countless years. She wrapped her arms tight around her waist, but she leaned subtly forward as if to call him back to her side.

I want you so.

He felt her need; It pulsed inside him. His body grew taut and aroused. He fought to remind himself of the result of their last encounter. He had pursued her without hesitation, he had held her hand and kissed her cheek, and told her he wanted her even on the first night they met. He'd made no secret of his attraction for her. Ariana had seemed surprised and hesitant, as if she doubted his sincerity. He remembered her questioning whether he said this sort of thing to all women, and how surprised he had been, because he had never felt anything like the closeness he felt with her.

He had been too aggressive. She didn't want him, not really. It was unfair to pursue her now when she was weak and tired. He allowed himself one last look at her, one last flash of sweet imagination as he pictured himself bending to kiss her, and her reaching for him. She seemed to be trembling—he had stayed too long, he was overstepping his bounds.

Taran turned his head away. "Good night, Ariana. Sleep well."

He didn't wait for her answer. He had to fight every impulse in his body, every demand of his soul, to walk out into the hall. He closed the door behind him, shutting her away. He heard her footfalls coming toward her door and he froze. If she opened it, if she asked him back in . . . His heart throbbed with excruciating hope.

He waited, not breathing, but the door didn't open. Instead, he heard the harsh sound of a lock being set. His hope crashed with such force that he felt actual physical anguish. He stood for a moment, longing to go to her, and knowing he never would. When he turned to catch up with Emilia, he knew he was as closed in by his own fear as Ariana was locked in by her door.

Chapter Four

Taran was on the far side of a large manor, and she couldn't see him. Ariana lay in her bed staring at the candlelight as it flickered on the ceiling. At Nicholas's abode, their workshop cottages were side by side. She could throw a rock from her bedroom window to his. She hadn't realized how much comfort his nearness had given her, but she felt his physical absence more keenly than she had in years.

Emilia's guest room was warm and comfortable, the bed soft and the pillows fluffy. Ariana punched one, but couldn't settle herself into a better position for sleeping. Taran had looked at her, that certain way, and her blood still tingled. Sometimes, she wondered if she misread desire in his dark eyes, but whatever it was seemed fleeting, ephemeral.

She had thought he might stay, because the look in his eyes told her he wanted to. But then he had left her. He had lured her with desire, then turned her away when she answered. She scowled. Maybe it was just his pride, after all, that had to get a reaction. Maybe he was just proving to himself that he still had the upper hand between them.

Ariana rolled to her left side, then onto her back. If only he were in a closer room, she might find the courage to visit him, perhaps under the pretense of discussing their strategy. Ariana sat up, then stood and went to the window.

She could see the west wing through the glass, but not clearly enough. She hesitated, then opened the French doors and went out onto her ice-covered balcony. The snow had ceased, leaving a dark, starless sky. The cold night air cut through her thin nightgown and into her flesh, but then Taran appeared in the last window across the way. She couldn't move.

He stood there a moment, silhouetted against the warm glow of a hearth, then moved out onto his balcony. Ariana's hair was ruffled about her face, moved by the icy night breeze. Her nightgown molded to her body. With the light of her room behind her, she knew he could almost see through it. She knew it, and she wanted it that way.

She felt the exact moment when he saw her. She felt his desire, primal and overwhelming. Ariana closed her eyes. *Please, come to me. Show me I mean more to you than a conquest.*

They watched each other for a timeless while, and desire flooded Ariana like waves on an endless sea. He must know she wanted him, but did he understand that she needed him to come to her first?

The image of Taran standing far from her, out of reach but intensely focused on her alone, burned itself into her mind. She held it there, cherished, then went back into her room alone.

He had to come to her. Her fingers tingled from cold and nervousness. When he came, she would be waiting.

And if he had any doubts as to her desire for him—and how could he—then he would know the truth the moment he saw her.

Ariana returned to her bed and lay on her back. Her heart refused to slow its wild beating. She adjusted her hair to fall evenly, yet casually, around her head and shoulders, then selected a thick wave to draw along her breast. She tried to close her eyes, so he wouldn't know she had been waiting when he arrived, but she couldn't keep from watching the door.

Every sound struck her; every squeak might be the floorboards heralding his approach. Someone walked to her door, and Ariana jerked up in bed, her hand over her heart. But the person passed by, and another door closed across the hall. Ariana flopped back onto the mattress. It was too soon, obviously. Taran would wait until everyone in the household slept, then come to her.

He had to come. She wanted him so.

The rafters outside her window creaked in the cold wind, but she heard no other sound. It was possible that Taran wasn't coming to her, after all. She had misread his interest so many times, and been hurt because of his indifference. Whenever she had thought he wanted her most, he ignored her, proving how wrong she could be.

Ariana's eyelids drifted shut and her breathing deepened, but her chest still felt tight from sorrow. Why did she allow herself to hope this way, when everything that passed between them destroyed that hope further?

She had an answer: It had been a long day. She had been removed from a position she loved, cast out into the snow, almost frozen, then tossed into a group of people who needed nothing. With her former lover at her side, it was natural she might feel some vestige of their brief passion.

If only hope didn't return, even in its smallest measure, her attraction for him might fade over time. Everything did. But every time he turned his dark gaze her way, the fire between them started again.

Sleep approached, but Ariana couldn't stave off her disappointment. She blew out her candle, then lay on her side, curled up and facing the door. The light from the hall seeped beneath her door. A shadow darkened it, and Ariana blinked. Her heart skipped a beat and she sat up, staring at the shadow. Someone stood outside her door.

She felt him there and her breathing quickened. She closed her eyes and whispered, "Yes," but the door stayed closed. She remembered that she had locked it, because she had been angry that he left.

Ariana slipped out of her bed and crept to the door. She placed her hand on the lock, then stopped. If she looked out, it would seem she had been waiting for him. She hesitated. It would be better if he had to knock.

She felt his presence as if she could see and touch him, and her body burned with need. He had to knock, to ask her. And she would hold him and kiss him, and make love to him with a fire he had never dreamed possible. But first, he had to knock.

She waited for the sound, but none came. After an eternity of waiting, the shadow moved soundlessly away, then disappeared. She waited, but no further noise came, and beneath the door no shadow blocked the hall's light.

Ariana went back to her bed. She had made a fool of herself. The desire in her body cooled to shame. Ariana curled up on her side, facing the window, and by the strength of her will, forced herself to sleep.

She woke with the same ache in her heart that had accompanied her to sleep. Ariana sat up in bed and felt as if her limbs were made of lead. He hadn't come. She had been a fool to think he would. Ariana bowed her head. Tonight was Christmas Eve. They had so little time to find the person Nicholas spoke of, and then even less to find a cure for that person's sorrow.

If she could focus her attention better, she might see what was wrong. But all Ariana could think of was Taran. One more night, and she would lose him. He would return to his homeland, so far away, and she would go back to the dark woods of Wales.

I will never see you again.

They had destroyed their chance at happiness, so perhaps it was for the best. Still, while Ariana didn't expect his love anymore, she wanted to see him every day, to know what he was doing, to feel the sweet comfort of his presence.

Someone knocked on her door, and Ariana jumped. She pulled her cape over her nightgown, adjusted her hair in the looking glass, then ran to the door. She stopped, drew in a quick breath, then opened the door.

"Good morning, my dear." Lady Emilia stood holding a breakfast tray, but Ariana's heart sank. "I've brought you some sweets and cakes and tea for breakfast. I hope it's not too early."

The cold winter sun slanted through the French doors, low on the hilly horizon: Ariana sighed. "Thank you. It was very kind of you to think of me."

Emilia entered the room and set her tray on a table. "The snow has cleared, and my guests will be going for sleigh rides today. I have a winter picnic planned on the frozen loch. I hope you and your cousin will join us."

"I'm sure we would both enjoy such a venture." It might prove a good chance to view Emilia's guests, and a chance to spot grief among them. "Please tell my cousin to make ready."

Ariana seated herself at the table and realized she was extremely hungry. Emilia smiled and held open the door. A thin maid brought in a second tray and placed it beside

Ariana's. "You can tell him yourself, my dear. His room is cold, so I thought he might enjoy breakfasting with you."

Ariana tried not to smile, but she trembled with anticipation as she waited for Taran's arrival. Emilia left, and Ariana heard him greet their cheerful hostess. Her nervousness soared, so she pretended to sample a scone. What if he mentioned her behavior last night, that she had stood out on the balcony dressed in only her nightgown? What if he knew she had been trying to entice him?

He came into the room and said nothing. She didn't dare look up. Her hands shook as she lifted the teapot. "Would you like some, Taran?"

He seated himself opposite her. "You do it on purpose, don't you?"

She looked up at him, still holding the teapot aloft. "Do what?"

"Play with me."

Ariana splashed tea over his cup, then smacked it back down on its stand. Her face felt hot, both with anger and shame. "I have no idea what you're talking about."

He cocked his head to one side, lips curled in annoyance. "You went out on that balcony and stood there dressed like a goddess, with the light behind you, which you know perfectly well shows every curve of your delectable little body . . ."

A small squeak burst from her before she could stop it. "I was hot!"

His brow angled. "Indeed? As was I after watching you." He gave her an intense glare.

Wild tingles coursed through her veins. At least, he didn't claim indifference. "I did nothing provocative."

"Is that so? You stood, with your arms to the side so that I might see every portion of you, looking at me. You're a fiend, Ariana. The worst kind of fiend."

Tears burned her eyes. "Your conceit astounds me. Yes, I went onto my balcony. It was hot in my room, and I wanted cool air to clear my thoughts. I saw you come out on your balcony, so naturally I looked at you, but I meant nothing by it. I was surprised to see you, so I forgot to cover myself." She paused, her lips tight in annoyance. "And at that distance, I don't know what you could see, anyway."

He leaned toward her, bracing his elbows on the lace-covered table. "I could see your hair fluttering in the wind. I could see the curve of your bottom, which is enough to entice any man. I could see the tips of your breasts—"

She squealed again and hopped up from her chair. "You could not!"

His glittering brown eyes defied her as he stood, too. "You may as well have been standing naked before me."

Ariana felt weak. "It is not I that am the fiend, but yourself."

He drew nearer, but didn't touch her. He reached his hand out to her cheek and just held it there—close but not touching her—as if he could feel the raging energy of her body nonetheless. "I am a man possessed by desire. A desire that I would thank you not to enflame at every opportunity."

"You started it!" She rose up subtly on tiptoes to better face him.

"In what way?"

She pointed her finger at him. "You know perfectly well." Ariana leaned closer to him, then snapped back to stop herself from seizing his long, black hair and pulling him to her. . . . She paced in small circles before him, then spun back. "When you said good night to me, you worked quite hard giving me a look—standing there so tall and strong, as if you could do anything to me, and I would thank you for it in the morning." Ariana

361

clamped her hand over her forehead and groaned, then shook her head miserably. "Why do you make me say such things?"

She felt his hand on her shoulder. It seemed comforting, so she let him draw her into his arms. He stroked her hair, gently, then kissed her forehead. "We torment each other. Maybe, when we're separated by both time and distance . . ."

She fought a sob and closed her eyes tight. She rested her cheek against his chest and listened to the strong beat of his heart. "I'm sure that will be for the best." The words hurt to speak. She didn't mean them. Her life would be empty without him, but if he thought he would be better off without her, then what more could she do?

Taran smoothed her hair from her forehead. "Neither of us seem capable of protecting our hearts. For mine, and for yours, it is probably best to never see each other again. Even if we must give up our work for the children."

She couldn't stop her tears. "If that is what you want, then we should abandon our quest and accept our fate."

He hesitated, and she knew he wanted more. He looked at her, and he seemed shy. "Is that what you want, Ariana?"

She couldn't meet his eyes, so she bowed her head. "What I want . . . hurts so much." Ariana turned away to look out the French doors, and he stood behind her, his hands on her shoulders. "I want to go back to the way we were, living in the Vale, working on our toys." She peeked back at him. "I promise to be kinder to you, and not to trouble you as I did. I am sorry I caused you such grief."

He ran his hands down her arms and she shivered with brief pleasure. "Not grief, Ariana. Distraction. But I will tell you a secret. Not a day went by when I didn't look for you to pester me in some way, nor a night when I didn't dream up some way to provoke you."

Ariana smiled and felt warm. "I must confess also to enjoying our encounters. I like to see you angry. It's almost like . . ."

He turned her in his arms, and she saw his desire. "Like passion?"

Ariana bit her lip, but she nodded. "Yes."

"I thought so. I could swear I'd noticed . . . When your eyes are glittering with mischief, it's not so different from the way you looked when . . ." He swallowed and she held her breath. She felt sure he was going to kiss her, if she held very still and didn't stop him in any way.

Ariana reached up and fingered his hair, then finished for him, "When I want you to kiss me."

He looked vulnerable, as if he didn't quite dare to speak. "You are looking at me that way now, you know."

She gave him a tentative smile. "Am I?"

He closed his eyes. "Ariana, when you look at me this way . . ."

"Maybe I should do more than look." She entwined her fingers tight in his hair, pulling him down to her, and kissed him. The feel of his firm mouth drove all doubt from her mind. She parted her lips against his to taste him, then slipped her tongue along his. His arms closed around her, his heart thudded and her whole body seemed to mold to his.

His hands shook as they traveled down her back, holding her closer to him. So much passion raged between them, and so much tenderness. How could she lose him now, when she felt hope flaring inside her so brightly?

Ariana kissed the side of his face, then wrapped her arms tight around his neck. She had to stand on her toes to hold him. "There is so little time. What are we going to do?"

He rested his forehead against hers, and their noses touched. "We still have a day left. Emilia has some sort of sleigh party arranged. Maybe we can find the person we must save there."

She nodded, but her fear refused to abate. "But what if we can't?"

"Nicholas wouldn't have sent us on a hopeless quest. We must trust that he knew what he was doing, and that there was some chance of us succeeding."

From downstairs, she heard the sound of Emilia's guests readying themselves for the outing. "We must join them. Finding the right person is our only chance."

Taran gestured at their untouched breakfast trays. "You haven't eaten."

Ariana seized a scone, pinned her gaze on Taran, then stuffed it in her mouth. She was frustrated, sexually and emotionally, so she ate with particular vigor. Taran watched her for a moment, then took a flat cake and ate it. He ate sensually, probably with the same thoughts that filled her.

They sat opposite each other, never looking away. She poured a fresh cup of tea and he drank, his beautiful dark eyes glittering as he watched her over his cup's rim. Ariana drank, too, then licked her lips. Taran reacted to her every action as if their bodies were touching in passion.

She ate everything on her plate, and finished every drop of tea. Taran's plate was left empty, too. They stood up at the same time. She cleared her throat, and tried to sound formal. "That was quite good. Truly, I have not enjoyed a breakfast so much in a long while. Ever."

A slow, teasing smile grew on Taran's face. "If breakfast affects us this way, my dear nemesis, what then will dinner do?"

"Lady Emilia has promised us a 'winter picnic,' whatever that is. We will see there, shall we not?"

He touched her hair and played with a thick spiral. "If you practice your arts on me today, you're likely to distract me from our purpose." He was teasing, but Ariana's eyes widened and she bit her lip.

"You are right!"

Before he could speak, Ariana snatched a blue velvet dress from a wardrobe closet. "Tell Emilia I'll be right down. We can't afford any distractions now."

He went to the door. "We must keep our eyes on our task, lest we lose . . . everything."

Taran left, but Ariana stood awhile, motionless. She placed her hand over her heart and closed her eyes. "The only thing I fear losing is you."

Emilia's winter picnic proved less useful than Taran had hoped. Many of her guests had already returned to their homes since the storm had cleared, and those that remained seemed blissfully happy. The old man sat in a sleigh, informing them of prime "toading" areas near the loch, as well as where pollywogs might be found in spring. Jane and David walked together holding hands, and the pear-shaped woman chatted amiably with Emilia, though she too often found occasion to grope Taran's arm for his taste.

The low winter sun rose to its highest point, then began its journey back to night, and still, Taran had no idea of who might be suffering even the slightest discomfort.

It was hard enough to concentrate on others when his own discomfort seemed so obvious. Over and over, he relived Ariana's kiss, and the look on her face when she pulled his face to hers. He recalled the utter delight she took teasing him, and her natural sensuality as she ate.

She had denied, weakly, any attempt to entice him the night before, but she had countered with the satisfying claim that he had done so himself. Apparently, she found him nearly as desirable as he found her.

Maybe they had to be kicked out of their comfortable existence in Nicholas's domain, in order to rekindle the passion that once enflamed them. Taran had never lost that desire, but he had learned to hid it. Here, in Scotland, hiding was impossible—especially with the pressure of time upon them.

Ariana sat beside him in the third sleigh, to which was harnessed two heavy-boned gray horses. Emilia had placed a strange bonnet on Ariana's head, which covered her ears and squeezed her cheeks into unusual roundness. Taran couldn't stop looking at her, wondering with a laugh how a woman who so closely resembled a chipmunk could hold him so utterly enthralled.

She stuffed her small hands into a white muff and looked out at the snowbound loch as if at the end of the world. Purple and gray hills etched an endless line on the horizon, casting shadows that darkened the frozen water. The end of the world.

Ariana fixed a dark glare upon two wolfhounds who frisked ahead of the party. "Everyone here is happy. Even the dogs." She spoke as if an army had utterly defeated her own, leaving no hope for survival. "And it's Christmas Eve."

Taran eyed the dogs as they rolled and jumped through the snow. "Perhaps we'll find they've been troubling the housekeeper's cat."

Ariana sniffed. "How can you joke now? When we're about to lose . . . everything." She hung her head, which had the effect of further rounding her cheeks, grown pink in the winter air. Snow that had melted under the morning sun had turned to ice and hung in crystal droplets from tree branches. It was a beautiful day, and it felt tinged with eternity.

This could be his last day with Ariana.

Taran placed his gloved hand over her muff and squeezed. "We have to be missing something. Someone."

Ariana looked around at Emilia's guests. "The trouble is, we don't know these people well enough to judge their temperaments." She paused, thoughtful. "Emilia knows them best. Perhaps we should consult her."

The party made ready to leave, and Emilia said her farewells to the other guests. She climbed into the sleigh beside Ariana and patted her pink cheek fondly. "You look chilled, my dear. We will get you back to the manor at once and pour you a nice cup of tea."

The two other sleighs turned in the opposite direction, and Ariana clutched Emilia's arm. "Where are they going?"

Emilia looked at her in surprise. "Why, they are going back to their homes—to spend Christmas Eve with their families. Tomorrow night, they will return to dine with me."

Ariana glanced at Taran, then at Emilia. "So you're by yourself on Christmas Eve?"

Emilia smiled. "Not this year." She placed her hand on Ariana's shoulder, then reached to pat Taran's arm. "I have you two, and it is a joy to me."

Ariana's face betrayed sudden eagerness and hope. "Are you usually sad on this night?"

Taran held his breath for the woman's answer, but Emilia laughed. "I am not sad to be alone, no. Christmas Eve is a time of peace to me, when I reflect upon the many blessings of my life."

"Oh." Ariana's face twisted and her brow puckered. This was not a woman to conceal her feelings. She thought for a while, then turned back to Emilia. "Why have you never married, Lady Emilia?"

The question didn't seem to trouble the noblewoman. "I suppose I never met a man I wanted to marry." She paused and gazed over the frozen loch. She didn't look unhappy, but Taran recognized her expression as familiar. Who did she remind him of? "I had many suitors in my day, but when their proposals of marriage came—and they inevitably did—I couldn't accept. I wanted more, you see."

Ariana sighed. "I understand, perfectly." Taran watched Ariana's small face as she, too, gazed out over the frozen loch. What had she hoped for during her life in Wales? Her words indicated that like Emilia, Ariana had a vision of the man she would love. His heart felt low and heavy in his chest. Maybe that explained her withdrawal from him. She had desire, but not whatever image of love she cherished.

Ariana shook her head as if to rid her mind of unpleasant thoughts, then pinned her attention back on Emilia. "Has the lack of a husband made you unhappy, Emilia?"

Their hostess arched her brows. "It has not. I have seen my cousins and girlhood friends marry, and to be honest, many chose unwisely. Oh, they picked men of good standing, men of wealth or breeding. But I see their faces now, and they look so tired, as if all the success of their match was lost in that lonely space that forms between two unhappily wed people over time."

Ariana slumped miserably between Taran and the older woman. Emilia noticed her downcast expression, right away, for Ariana had no skill at deception. "What troubles you, dear child?" She glanced at Taran. "Do you fear your family's reaction to . . ." She paused as if broaching a sensitive subject. "To the choice you have made?"

Ariana peeked up at her, confused, but Taran took Emilia's meaning. She thought they were secretly betrothed, and fearful of her Welsh family's reaction. Taran patted Ariana's shoulder. "In my cousin's family, it is customary on the Christmas holiday to find one person whose life they might better, and help that person. Because we have seen no shadow of pain at your household, Ariana fears she has failed in that effort."

Ariana straightened and looked at him in amazement. "Brilliant!" Taran rolled his eyes and she coughed, sputtering, then turned with a broad smile to Emilia, who looked confused. "My cousin is quite right. Don't you know of anyone nearby who is suffering and might benefit from our help?"

Emilia shook her head. "I am sorry, but no. I, too, have found joy in my life by bringing such help to my neighbors." She looked proud. "I have done so well that I fear your family's custom isn't likely to be needed here." She smiled and patted Ariana's cheek again. "But don't worry, dear. After what you've been through, I'm sure your family will understand."

Ariana sighed, and it sounded like a moan of despair. "I suppose so." She sat back in the sleigh as they rode home and watched the darkening sky. Taran sat close beside her, as one by one, bright stars appeared. It would be a perfect night, clear enough to see forever.

Emilia looked tired, but she invited them to dine with her. Ariana fished more for possible hidden unhappiness in their cheerful hostess, but found none. Taran spoke little. Defeat seemed inevitable. Tomorrow, he would be gone, returned to a world he barely remembered. Ariana would be left again in her Welsh village.

She was brave and determined, but he doubted she had learned anything in the Vale of Snow that would protect her from the raging onslaughts of battle that had troubled the land she had come from. The assaults of the English in her time were relentless. She would be vulnerable, and this time, there was nothing he could do to save her. Nicholas would recruit neither of them again.

After dinner, Emilia wished them good night and retired to bed, leaving Ariana and Taran alone in the great hall. They stood silently together before the fireplace, staring into the flames as if they viewed the vision of hell.

Ariana seized a deep, shuddering breath, then turned to Taran. "We have failed."

He couldn't argue, but neither could he speak the words. "I can think of no other effort we might make at this late hour."

Tears welled in her eyes, but she didn't cry. "If I thought it would help, I would hunt the whole night through." She bowed her head. "But I see no hope now. There is no one left but us."

"If we must accept this fate, then you must be careful once you're returned to Wales, Ariana."

She didn't seem to care. Her lips formed a move and her chin thrust out. Every time he looked at her face, her sad expressions tore at his heart. He could watch her face forever, and read every emotion there, and never tire of the sight. "You were in grave danger before Nicholas rescued you. If you must go back, then you must take care."

"I would have escaped. I had already loosed my binds and was well on my way to breaking free."

Taran frowned. Her self-confidence would see her killed. "A warrior was coming for you, my dear. He bore an ax."

Ariana eyed him suspiciously. "How do you know?"

He hesitated, then turned his attention to the fire. "I was with Nicholas the day he chose you."

He felt her staring at him, and he knew when she

moved closer to his side. "Truly?" She paused, seemingly amazed that he hadn't objected.

He had kept this secret for many long years. Many times, he had resisted the temptation to tell her the truth. Partly for her pride's sake, and partly to hide his own interest. But tomorrow they would be separated, forever.

Taran faced her, and he felt raw inside. "Can it be, after all this time, that you don't know?"

She was trembling, but she shook her head. He wanted to hold her, but he couldn't move.

"It wasn't really Nicholas who chose you, Ariana."

He looked into her eyes and saw the cool thrill of recognition form inside her. Her lips parted and her breath came in a shuddering gasp. Very slowly, she reached to touch his face. He felt her palm against his skin and the infinite tenderness she possessed.

"Taran . . ." Her voice came with the sweetest wonder he'd ever heard, and he knew that no distance, not time or space, could ever keep him from loving her. "It was you."

Chapter Five

"Why didn't you tell me?" She couldn't stop trembling. Taran looked both extremely vulnerable and strong. He had chosen her. "Why?"

He gazed up at the ceiling, and she realized he was shy. "Nicholas had let me watch those people who were being considered. I was studying warriors in your land to learn what armor and weapons they used. As I was watching the English army invade a Welsh village, I saw a girl. All the townsfolk were fleeing, running from their homes in terror. But this girl was running *into* it. I cannot tell you how frustrated I was, to watch that girl and not be able to help her. I watched her go into a burning hut, and I wondered what inside could be so precious."

Tears dripped down Ariana's cheeks. "A doll."

He smiled and nodded. "A doll. But not her own. I watched in wonder as she brought the doll to a weeping child, and I knew I'd found a truly great soul."

Ariana sniffed and dried her cheeks on her sleeve. "But I don't understand. That happened when I was a young girl. Nicholas didn't rescue me until I was twenty-three."

"That is true." He seemed hesitant to continue, but their time together was so short, and she had to know. "It takes a lifetime to earn such an honor, and not all candidates are selected."

"You watched over me."

He didn't meet her eyes. "I feared for you. A child so brave would turn into a woman utterly without caution, and a penchant for risking her life for others."

Ariana frowned. "You found me foolish."

Taran grinned. "I found you familiar. I had been the same, after all." He looked into her eyes and she saw his heart shining there. "I thought you were the bravest, most beautiful woman who ever lived. I could do nothing to help you, nothing but watch. I wanted you to live fully and to be happy, but every time I spotted a man courting you, I endured such an agony of jealousy . . ."

He stopped, but warm happiness flooded through Ariana. "I do not recall giving you much cause."

"It didn't take much. I watched you pining for men I considered far beneath you. I watched you through heartaches, and I watched you try to love men for whom I knew you felt nothing."

"I wanted love so badly," she admitted. Her brow furrowed as she remembered the young woman she had been, ages ago. "But after even my most ardent of my infatuations passed, I felt nothing. No flicker of real passion remained. What I felt had never truly been love. Those who pursued me I cared for, but I could never muster the feeling I believed I should have."

"Your life in Wales ended too early. You would have found it, otherwise." He didn't sound entirely happy about the prospect of her discovering love. "You may find it still, when you return."

"Taran." She waited until he looked at her, and she smiled. "You know better."

"It is possible." He seemed nervous. "You are a beautiful woman. There's bound to be someone, eventually, worthy of your heart."

She shook her head. "You know better."

He moved away from her and braced his arms on the mantelpiece. "Once . . . once I thought differently."

Ariana went to him. All her fears gave way to a woman's tenderness. He had watched her, and he had cared enough to be jealous when another man sought to claim her, enough to watch her for many years. "If I go back to Wales and live a hundred years there, I will never find the love I hoped for."

He glanced at her, his dark brow furrowed. "You can't know that."

"I know it, better than I know anything." She laid her hand on his shoulder and touched his long hair. "I cannot find it in Wales, because I already have it here."

He didn't speak, but his chest rose and fell with sharp breaths. "Ariana."

She rested her head against his shoulder and felt the power and tension flow inside him. "I have been such a fool."

He turned and drew her into his arms, holding her close, surrounded by the fear of what they would lose. "It was I that was a fool, Ariana. I should have told you."

"Why *didn't* you?" She looked up into his beautiful face, a face that had become so dear, not because he was handsome, but because he was part of her, a part she would never forget, no matter what kept them apart.

He pressed his cheek against her forehead, then kissed her. "Pride, I suppose. I didn't want you to feel beholden to me. I hoped you would want me for myself, and that you'd come to recognize that we were the same, more right for each other than anyone else could ever be."

Wonder filled her. It seemed too good to be believed, too much beyond even her fondest dreams to be trusted. "I was afraid you were toying with me. I wanted to believe so much, and I did not trust myself. And because other men have spoken sweet words to me, made promises that had no weight, and left me feeling foolish for ever having trusted in the first place."

Taran ran his hands through her hair as if he coveted each strand. "I cannot say I haven't spoken such words to women before. But until I met you, I had no idea what they meant. Ariana, I didn't know how much I could lose, that without you, my life would be empty."

His words felt like a dream. At last, he said everything she had longed to hear. At last, her heart filled with the love she had kept at bay for so long. But it had come too late, and now nothing could keep them together.

"I am so afraid." She bit her lip and stopped, but he ran his finger along her cheek.

"Of what, Ariana?"

She closed her eyes, but tears slipped out and dripped to her cheeks. "I'm afraid I'll never see you again. I wanted to go on as we were, fighting and being near each other all the time. But we haven't found anyone suffering, and tomorrow is Christmas Day. They will come for us and send us back to where we came from. And I will never see you again."

He looked as if he wanted to believe her, but still held some wariness, some terrible inner fear. "Does it truly affect you, the thought of being separated from me?"

"It is the worst pain I have ever known." She was crying, but she had to tell him, now, before she lost him forever. She wrapped her arms around his waist and hugged him close. "All I wanted, I found the moment I first saw you. It was fear, the most awful fear I've ever known in my life, that kept me from saying so. I was waiting for you to prove that you really wanted me, but now I know nothing you could have done would have been enough. I thought I was safer at a distance; fighting with you was easier than laying my heart bare before you."

"I found that, too."

She peeked up at him, doubtful. "I always thought you hated me."

He smiled. "So much that I lifted you off your feet and carried you to my bedroom and made love to you all night?"

A spasm of embarrassment and delight twisted through her. "I didn't think you hated me that night." She paused, suddenly shy. "I didn't think at all that night."

"It was the happiest, most wonderful night of my life. But somehow, it went wrong." He looked down at her and she saw anguish in his eyes. "I have never known why."

"I didn't dare to trust you, so I pretended not to care."

"I gave you no reason to trust." Tears welled in the warm depths of his brown eyes. "You were the gift to my life, and I destroyed it, all because my fear dominated my love. Have we really been so young that protecting ourselves means more than the magic we might have found together?"

She nodded, sniffing. "Now we will lose each other, and the chance we had will be lost."

He sighed. "One night left . . . after all the nights we might have had."

One night. Ariana backed away from him and stood beside the giant Christmas tree. "If one night is all we have . . ." She closed her eyes and tipped her head back. This night would have to be timeless; it would have to last her forever. She looked at him, and saw that he felt the same. "Taran, fear has ruled me. It has ruled us both.

I need to know that you want me more than you fear me."

He stood there by the fire, tall and strong, so beautiful, her heart ached to look at him. "And I need to know that you trust me more than you doubt."

A shiver ran through her, because she knew this was their last chance. They had one night, and that was all. She felt small and alone in the center of the room, reaching for a man who would be gone before daybreak. "Then I tell you now, I want you, more than I have ever wanted anything." Her voice quavered with emotion, but she didn't cry or allow herself to beg. "I will go to my room and I will wait for you. If you come to me, I will take you in and I will love you with all my heart, and give you all myself. But you will have to come to me on your own, because it is your desire—not because I've thrown myself at your feet."

His dark eyes burned with conflicting emotion. "Ariana, are we not making this more painful? If I come to you, if now—at last—we share all that we have feared to share, won't losing each other be that much worse? Wouldn't a taste of what we might have known be worse than simply dreams?"

"I can't say that it won't." She swallowed hard. He still wanted to protect himself, and her, from the pain they would feel. And she couldn't blame him.

She met his gaze and held it. For a timeless while, they looked at each other, and in his eyes, she saw all that might have been. She saw herself and Taran together, happy, in love. She saw herself with his black-haired baby in her arms. She saw herself, a woman beyond doubt, finally able to trust, and in love for all time to come.

She looked at her feet and imagined herself alone, tormented by might-have-beens and the knowledge she had thrown away her one true chance at love because she had been afraid.

Ariana closed her eyes and turned away. She didn't look back as she left the room and climbed the long staircase to her bedroom. She undressed as if held in a trance, then lay on her bed staring at the ceiling.

She felt the same agony of waiting she had endured the night before.

But this time, her door was unlocked.

For the first hour, every sound brought her upright, her heart pounding with expectation. When the next hour passed, expectation turned to merely hope. When midnight approached, hope had turned to despair.

She tried to sleep, to forget, but she knew how close they had come to sharing something wonderful, and with each second that ticked by, that she was losing him. Ariana sat up in bed and stared out the window into the night. There was no moon, but the stars seemed bright enough to cast shadows over all the surrounding landscapes. Frost stuck to her window, closing it in slowly, and she saw her own heart, desperate to live and to feel, slowly frozen because she was alone.

Her long hair fell loose around her face and shoulders. The frost spread like diamonds over sand, and one by one, each star disappeared from her view. Ariana bowed her face into her hands and wept. She cried until her throat was raw, until her face stung from her tears.

At last, Ariana rose and wiped the frost from her window, straining to see through the pane. Taran's window was dark, and her grief nearly crumpled her to the floor. He was not going to come. Still, nothing she did could stem her wanting. After so long searching, denying, and hiding, she had finally found her true love. No other man would ever do now. Separated by a lifetime, by time and distance and hearts too frozen to feel, Ariana would still love him.

378

With that grim certainty, Ariana sank back on her bed. Night encircled her, bright and clear with a thousand stars looking down through the window. She closed her eyes and allowed herself to relax.

Just as sleep was about to overtake her, the door creaked, then opened. Ariana lurched upright in bed, her hair falling around her face like a veil. She shoved it back, breathing so fast that she felt dizzy. The light from the hallway illuminated Taran's tall, powerful body before he closed the door behind him.

He carried a thick candle, which he set on her bedstead. He didn't speak. Her heart beat so fast that she barely breathed. His dark eyes seemed to glow, and the fires of her own body kindled in response.

She drew her knees up to her chest and wrapped her arms around them, fearful despite her desire. He had really come. She hadn't expected him, not in her deepest heart. But now he was here, and she had no idea what to do next.

He noticed her posture and his brow angled. "You invited me, my angel. I have come. Is this how you greet me?"

She dampened her lips with a quick dart of her tongue, nervous, then swallowed. "I don't know what to do."

He smiled, not simply an expression for reassurance, but one that said he had made his decision, and that they were about to share something amazing. His gaze fixed on hers as he pulled off his clothing and tossed it aside. He stood naked before her, and Ariana gaped. He had been beautiful before. She knew that he was well-built, strong, and firm, but each time she saw him, the effect grew more overwhelming.

She chewed her lip. "What are you going to do?"

His smile deepened. "I'm going to give you something so that in a lifetime apart, you won't forget me.

379

Whatever happens, Ariana, you will remember this night, and what I do to you now."

She gulped, but he pulled back her sheets. She shuffled herself to the side to give him room, but he didn't lie down as she expected. Instead, he traced a line with his finger over her bent knee, to her ankle, then back along the same path.

Rather than lie down, he knelt by her feet. Ariana choked back a startled squeal when he edged her knees apart, then maneuvered himself between. She wore only a thin chemise, with nothing underneath, so she tried to adjust it to cover herself, but Taran caught her hand.

She felt giddy and terrified. The first time they had made love, they had been caught up in a whirlwind of passion. She barely remembered how they reached the climactic moment, just holding him and feeling his body inside her, driving her to the sweetest delight of her life.

This was different. Taran was different. He held her hand and kissed it, but she found her nervousness double. Ariana caught her breath. "Aren't . . . aren't you going to kiss me?" She sounded as breathless as she felt.

He leaned toward her, dangerous and strong and so beautiful she couldn't look away. "Oh yes. I'm going to kiss you, my sweet, beautiful angel. I'm going to kiss your mouth and your face and your neck. I'm going to kiss every part of you until there is nothing in your memory or in your dreams expect me."

She wanted to tell him he held that honor already, but no words came. He bent to her. His lips molded to hers, and he tangled his fingers in her hair, pressing her back to deepen the kiss. Ariana moaned deep in her throat. Taran's touch, his kiss, they were so powerful. Everything he did was sensual. "Every part of you . . ."

Her legs curled around him and her chemise bunched at her waist, but she didn't care. He was caressing her with his mouth, and she wrapped her arms around his wide shoulders, gripping his muscles to steady herself. She kissed him, then tipped her face to look at him. "This is what I've wanted for so long."

He didn't answer. He pulled off her chemise and kissed her again. She ran her hands greedily over his firm skin, delighting in the hard contours of his chest and back. She pressed her mouth against his chest and licked, tasting his skin, loving him. Her hands traveled down his stomach, meeting his arousal.

He groaned when she touched him, and her assurance increased at his reaction. She wrapped her fingers tight around his swollen staff, squeezing as she massaged him. She felt his body quiver as she pressed her lips fiercely to his throat. "Taran, I want you so, and I've waited so long."

Taran caught his breath, then grabbed her hand. His breath came in harsh gasps, and she felt intoxicated by seeing the effect she had on him. "Not yet, my dear love. Not yet."

She puffed an impatient breath. "You want me. I want you, too."

He smiled. "Do you? I think you can want me more."

She shook her head vigorously, certain he was wrong. "I can't. I'm sure of it."

"Lie back."

Ariana hesitated, then obeyed him. She expected him to enter her, but when she lay back, he began kissing her neck. She felt his firm, purposeful lips grazing her flesh, and his tongue tasting her skin, lower as he cupped her breast in his hand.

He teased its small peak with this thumb, then took it between his lips, laving it until she moaned with pleasure. He lavished attention on one breast, then the other. Her whole body demanded him. Liquid heat filled her woman's center. Her hips squirmed with need, but he made no move to take her as she desired.

His kiss left her breast and moved across her stomach. He woke every nerve with a light touch of his tongue, and his hands slid with sensual ease over every curve of her body. Wherever he touched came alive, yielding to him before he asked it.

He slid himself lower so that he knelt between her legs. Ariana watched in astonishment as he bent to kiss her there. She clamped her knees together, but he laughed and held them apart. "Ariana, all of you. It was a promise I intend to keep."

He met her eyes, then slipped his finger along her woman's cleft, dabbling in the moisture he had inspired. His lips curled into the most seductive smile she'd ever seen, and then he followed his touch with a kiss.

Ariana bit her lip to keep from crying out, but his kiss turned sensual, too. She felt the tip of his tongue as it swirled out to taste her. It flicked over her small woman's peak, and she gasped his name in surprise.

He looked up at her, his eyes heavy and dark with passion. "You will never forget me, Ariana. No matter where you go, or what comes between us. You are mine."

He didn't wait for an answer. He returned to his sweet, excruciating attention, teasing her until she flopped back on her pillows and gave herself over to his skill. He licked her and sucked and teased until every breath she took was a gasp and a plea for release, but each time the moment came upon her, he slowed, then resumed again. She wrapped her legs over his shoulders, and he kissed her and teased her until she had no secret left inside her, no restraint to the depths of her soul.

As the first sparkling waves of ecstasy swept through her, she seized his hair. With all her fury and passion, she pulled him up, arched her back, and curled her legs over his hips. He held back for a moment, watching her, then drove himself into her.

She cried out his name and writhed around him, shaken all through herself with the pinnacle of bliss. It faded, then started again as he thrust inside her. He filled her, and withdrew, and filled her again, moving in unison with her until she lost all sense of time and place.

Nothing stopped them. His release came, shaking him, pouring into her, but he didn't stop. They moved together, unable to part, until the fires took hold of them both, and started again. They made love until Ariana went weak, her legs dangling over his, but still she held him, demanding and murmuring as he filled her. His release came again with shuddering intensity, and her own spiraled around his.

At last, when every star burned through the frost and shone upon them, they stilled and lay quiet in each other's arms. Ariana refused to release him, holding him so that his body stayed inside hers. "I will not let you go. We will fight, when they come to separate us. I will not lose you."

She felt Taran nod.

They looked at each other. Ariana steeled herself to an unimagined blasphemy. "We're going to oppose Nicholas?"

Taran hesitated, but his expression firmed. "If we must, if it's the only way to stay together." He paused. "Although, you realize what that will mean."

She laid her palm gently against his cheek and her eyes filled with tears. "I would rather be in hell with you, Taran, than in heaven without you."

Chapter Six

"What in God's name are you two doing?"

Emilia appeared carrying a tray of tea and breakfast cookies, aghast as Taran and Ariana pulled down every one of Gurthington Manor's ancient swords and shields.

Ariana turned to her, wearing the smallest mail shirt she could find. "I'm sorry, Emilia. We know this is odd, but it is necessary." Taran helped Ariana with the belt, but the shirt still hung past her knees. She looked small and adorable, and his heart filled with love as he looked at her.

Emilia stared at them, astonished by their sudden turn to crime. "Is it?"

Taran tried an old war ax, found the blade dull, then set it aside for a shorter Saxon scramasax. "I'm sorry this had to happen in your home, Lady Emilia. We bear you no ill will, and are grateful for your kindness."

"Well, this is a fine way to show it!"

Ariana seized a sgian-dhu, then tried a wobbly rapier. "I wish she had a wooden bow! I was proficient with the bow."

Emilia gestured toward the hunting lodge across the gardens. "I believe the gameskeeper has a bow for deer hunting. . . ." She clamped her hand to her forehead. "What am I saying? This is hardly the way to celebrate Christmas morning! What are you two doing?"

Ariana's chin firmed. "I'm afraid for us today, this is the only way."

Emilia placed her hands on her rounded hips. "And who is it you two plan to fight?"

They looked at each other. Taran saw no reason to lie now; he laughed at the absurdity of the situation. "You would know him as Saint Nicholas."

Emilia exhaled a long breath. "Saint Nicholas. The patron saint of children? I see. And you're going to fight him."

Ariana tried a stab into thin air. Her fighting posture was remarkably good. Taran tapped her elbow. "Keep your arm up, aim straight, slice up."

She nodded, but Emilia grimaced. "You cannot be talking about stabbing and slicing the patron saint of children."

Ariana winced, revealing a spasm of guilt. "Only if he attempts to send us back." Emilia popped her lips. "Back where?"

Ariana stuffed the sgian-dhu into her belt and abandoned the rapier. "It's a long story. We assist Nicholas in his task serving children."

Emilia's brow rose. "You're *elves*?"

Ariana looked confused, then glanced at Taran. "Elves?"

Taran frowned. "I don't like that term."

Ariana shook her head, too. "Nicholas employs people who have aided children to assist him in the Vale of Snow. We make toys."

Emilia liked that. She nodded as if she understood and accepted what they said, much to Taran's surprise. She studied them a long while. For a reason Taran didn't understand, a small smile formed on her lips. "You are both very dramatic young persons, I see. It is your instinct to fight when all else fails?"

Taran hesitated, but since he was armed with a broadsword, couldn't deny the obvious. "We fight only as a last resort, but we will fight."

Emilia's smile widened. "I do not approve of violence, but something tells me this battle isn't going to be violent."

"I hope not." Taran touched Ariana's shoulder. "It is my hope that Nicholas will let us live in peace."

Ariana looked small and vulnerable as she peered up at him. "Will we stay here, then?"

"Is that what you want, love?"

"I have never loved a home as I do the Vale of Snow, but where you are . . . *that* is my home."

Emilia looked back and forth between them, perhaps assessing the depth of their feeling for each other. "The Vale of Snow. It sounds lovely. What kind of toys do you make?"

"I make dollhouses. Taran makes toy soldiers with perfect little weapons." Ariana checked the window and Taran came up beside her. "Nothing yet."

Emilia glanced out the window, too. "What are we waiting for?"

"He'll come for us in his sleigh."

"And then you'll *ambush* him?"

Ariana peeked up at Taran.

He hesitated. "As desperate as I am, I cannot imagine attacking him without warning. He is a good man, even if he has forced us to desperate straits. We will give him a chance to let us stay here, together."

Ariana's brow puckered. "Nicholas is a kind man, but he can be stubborn. If he refuses . . ."

"We fight."

"Where does he want to send you?" Emilia broke in.

"He's sending me to Wales, where I came from—but long ago. Taran would have to go back to his mountains, back to his home, too."

Emilia seated herself in a comfortable chair. "I'm sure such a man as Saint Nicholas has much to do. I'll offer him tea when he arrives, in case he is chilled." She paused. "Tell me of him. Is he handsome?"

Ariana eyed her doubtfully. "He is somewhat stout. But his presence can be imposing."

Emilia nodded. "Sturdy of build. With a fine beard?"

Taran fingered the blade of his sword. "He takes pride in its fullness, yes."

Emilia poured herself a cup of tea and ran her fingers along the rim. "And his wife . . . is she of a similar temperament?"

She sounded overly casual, so Taran stopped to study her expression. "Nicholas has no wife. His life has been his work, bringing joy to children."

Ariana sighed. "He is a good man, although stubborn at times."

Emilia looked confused, and not without reason. "You care for him . . . and yet you still plan to . . ."

Ariana moved close to Taran. "We have *no* choice. We failed in the quest he gave us, so he will feel it necessary to send us away as he vowed."

"Why has he punished you this way?"

Ariana looked embarrassed. "Our fighting became tiresome to him, so he sent us on this mission."

"What were you supposed to do here?"

Taran held Ariana's hand in his. Every second now was precious. "He told us to find someone who was suffering, where no pain showed, then solve their problem. Unfortunately, we found you, and you have already alleviated any lack in all those nearby."

Emilia looked thoughtful. "I can think of no one in

this area who needs your help. I am sorry. It appears you will have to fight him after all. But I can't believe he would be so stubborn as to keep you apart—it's so obvious that you love each other."

Ariana's lips curled at one corner. "I'm afraid it wasn't obvious to us, until last night."

Emilia rose from her chair. "Then this has become my quest as well as yours. I have great admiration for a man who devotes his life to children—whoever he may be— but it is plain he has gone too far."

Taran looked at Ariana, but she looked equally baffled by Emilia's meaning. "You're going to help us?"

"I am."

Taran hesitated. "How?"

Emilia seized a medieval helm and placed it on her round head, then picked up the war ax. "I'm going to fight, too. What else?"

The winter sun reached its highest point. Emilia stood beside Ariana, holding her ax with surprising strength. Taran positioned himself in front of them. From the sun's pale golden center, a shape appeared and took form. It was the sleigh of Saint Nicholas. It lowered, then came to the ground before them. The Laplander elves sat perched behind him, and bounced down to tend its team, whose coats steamed from exertion.

Nicholas took one look at the trio, dropped the reins to his lap, then burst into the deepest, heartiest laughter Taran had ever heard. He hopped down from the sleigh with agility much belying his shape, then laughed again. He drew a breath to clear his amusement, but his blue eyes glittered. "I take it you have failed."

Taran gripped his sword, but pain filled his chest at his own intention. He loved this man, this kindest of men. Could he draw a sword against him? He glanced to where Ariana stood with Emilia. She held her sgian-dhu, but her hands were shaking and tears glittered in her eyes.

For Ariana, he would risk all, but what good would their love do if they won it at the expense of another? He met Ariana's gaze, and they looked at each other, filling themselves with the love they shared, and would always share.

Together, they dropped their weapons. Ariana fell to her knees before Nicholas. "Please, sir. Send us away if you must, but please send us together. I'm sorry we failed. I'm sorry we fought as we did, but we were so afraid, and it was easier to fight than to love. But here we have learned that love is stronger than fear. Please, can't that count for something, even though we found no one suffering?"

Nicholas looked down at her and touched her head gently. "Dear girl, do you ever draw a breath when speaking? Your capacity for chatter amazes me."

Taran dropped to one knee beside Ariana. "Sir, I beg of you, too, don't part us. We have done much ill, and many times made mistakes and taken wrong turns. But I can't let you send her back. It's too dangerous, and she's too brave. I can't let her go where I can't protect her."

Nicholas arched his heavy brow. "She's affecting your speech, too."

The sound of ringing steel came from behind. Emilia swung her ax in a dramatic arch, then stomped forward. "You let these dear young people stay together, or I'll . . ."

A broad smile formed on Nicholas's face as he looked at the headstrong woman. "Or you'll fell me like a Scotch pine, my lady?"

"If I have to."

Taran and Ariana looked at Emilia, surprised by the ferocity of her tone. Nicholas, however, seemed intrigued. "Is true love worth so much to you, madame?"

"I imagine it's worth everything. And I won't let you stand in its way—no matter how handsome you may be!"

Nicholas stepped over Ariana and Taran and went to her. Taran helped Ariana up and they stood watching, astounded by the change in the old man's demeanor. He suddenly seemed . . . suave. Masculine. Taran exchanged a quick glance with Ariana, and she gripped his arm.

"Taran! I know who she reminds me of, now. It's *him!* Nicholas. She had the same expression on her face yesterday when she was gazing across the loch as he did looking out his window in the Vale. I know what it is now."

Taran took her hand in his. "Loneliness."

She nodded, tears in her bright eyes. She whispered, "I never imagined that he might be sad . . . in the same way I was. In the same way we were."

"We should have recognized it sooner."

She rested her head on his shoulder. "How could we see it when we were drowning in it ourselves?"

Nicholas turned to them. He lifted the helm off Emilia's head and smiled at her pinkened face. "I should have realized that when I sent you here. How could you see into Emilia's heart when you didn't understand your own?"

Ariana peeked around Nicholas to Emilia. "You are lonely, aren't you, Emilia? You seemed so happy."

"Aye, and happy I am, my dear. But lonely . . ." Emilia looked up at Nicholas and her face glowed. "I thought love was for the young and the truly fortunate, like yourselves. I hoped for a man, a great man, when I was young, but the years passed and hope faded. I made the best of my life, and I have lived it well. But I've been lonely . . . for someone to share my thoughts and my heart. Is there anyone on earth who hasn't felt this longing?"

Taran looked between them. "This isn't the first time you've seen Lady Emilia, sir."

Nicholas grinned and he patted his new beloved's plump hand. "You're not the only one to see a woman of amazing virtue from the Vale of Snow, my friend."

Ariana's eyes misted with tears and she hugged the old man. "I'm so sorry we considered fighting you, sir. We were desperate. I hope you will forgive us."

Nicholas laughed. "You are forgiven, my dear. You and Taran share a warlike ancestry, so your lapses are to be expected. And rarely have I enjoyed a scene so much as that of you mail-clad and ready to skewer me. And rather than saving this gentlewoman's heart, you have turned her into a Valkyrie. I haven't laughed so well and so hard in a long while."

Emilia tapped his arm. "Before you journey onward, would you care for some tea?"

"That would be welcome indeed." Nicholas tucked her hand on his arm and covered it with his own. "Perhaps you have tired of living alone in this manor, so far from everything? It may be I can offer you a more interesting home."

Ariana fidgeted. "What about us?"

"You have given me the two gifts most worth having, Ariana. Laughter, and love. All the pride, doubt, and fear in the world can't hold a candle to the power of these two."

"Does that mean you'll let us come home to the Vale with you?"

Nicholas smiled. "As peaceful as your absence was for all of us, I find I missed you both. Of course I will let you return. The children have need of you."

Ariana beamed and Taran breathed a deep sigh of relief. "We will not let you down this time."

391

"See that you set your shops in order. While you were gone, your helpers commenced baiting each other, and have been scuffling far too much. Also, Hakon has taken up with Kiya, and I fear another such quest as your own will soon be in order. A Viking and an Egyptian . . . Who would have thought?"

They went inside the manor, and the Laplander elves seated themselves with cookies before Emilia's beautiful tree. Ariana looked happier than Taran had ever seen her, content and peaceful, a woman rather than a fearful child. Emilia skittered around the room, serving tea, and lavishing attention on Nicholas.

Ariana watched them, smiling. "What will you tell your friends and relations, Emilia? You can't very well tell them you're going to live with Saint Nicholas, after all."

Emilia tapped her lip. "We will stop at their homes on our way. I'll introduce Nicholas as a German nobleman, whom I have decided to marry after a whirlwind courtship. I'll explain that I plan to go abroad at his side. That is true enough, as far as it goes. I'll bequeath my home to Jane and David. I do not think they would deny me joy in my declining years, do you?"

Emilia bade her friends farewell, and was met with the warmest delight from all. She had given others such compassion and happiness that no one thought of denying her own. Her friends stood at their doorway while Nicholas drove his strange harnessed animals across the snow. The creatures resented the strain of picking their way on foot, but he kept them earthbound until the sleigh had moved out of sight.

Taran held Ariana's hand in his, treasuring each second at her side. She had changed. They both had changed, because the energy they had spent in fear and in doubt had finally turned to love. It had been love that

392

inspired him to take her from her violent country, ages ago. And love that kept him beside her through every battle since. As the sleigh lifted from the ground, he knew it was love's wings that carried them now.

The stars kindled like fire around them and the frosty air sparkled with hope. Tiny sleigh bells rang as Taran bent to kiss Ariana. Around them, all else was forgotten, and as they kissed they heard Nicholas's booming voice.

"Merry Christmas to all, and to all a good night."

Three Heartwarming Tales of Romance and Holiday Cheer

Bah Humbug! by Leigh Greenwood. Nate wants to go somewhere hot, but when his neighbor offers holiday cheer, their passion makes the tropics look like the arctic.

Christmas Present by Elaine Fox. When Susannah returns home, a late-night savior teaches her the secret to happiness. But is this fate, or something more wonderful?

Blue Christmas by Linda Winstead. Jess doesn't date musicians, especially handsome, up-and-coming ones. But she has a ghost of a chance to realize that Jimmy Blue is a heavenly gift.

___4320-3 $5.50 US/$6.50 CAN

Dorchester Publishing Co., Inc.
P.O. Box 6640
Wayne, PA 19087-8640

Please add $1.75 for shipping and handling for the first book and $.50 for each book thereafter. NY, NYC, and PA residents, please add appropriate sales tax. No cash, stamps, or C.O.D.s. All orders shipped within 6 weeks via postal service book rate. Canadian orders require $2.00 extra postage and must be paid in U.S. dollars through a U.S. banking facility.

Name_____

Address_____

City_____State_____Zip_____

I have enclosed $_____ in payment for the checked book(s).

Payment <u>must</u> accompany all orders. ❏ Please send a free catalog.

Christmas means more than just puppy love.

"SHAKESPEARE AND THE THREE KINGS"
Victoria Alexander

Requiring a trainer for his three inherited dogs, Oliver Stanhope meets D. K. Lawrence, and is in for the Christmas surprise—and love—of his life.

"ATHENA'S CHRISTMAS TAIL" Nina Coombs

Mercy wants her marriage to be a match of the heart—and with the help of her very determined dog, Athena, she finds just the right magic of the holiday season.

"AWAY IN A SHELTER" Annie Kimberlin

A dedicated volunteer, Camille Campbell still doesn't want to be stuck in an animal shelter on Christmas Eve—especially with a handsome helper whose touch leaves her starry-eyed.

"MR. WRIGHT'S CHRISTMAS ANGEL"
Miriam Raftery

When Joy's daughter asks Santa for a father, she knows she's in trouble—until a trip to Alaska takes them on a journey into the arms of Nicholas Wright and his amazing dog.

___52235-7 $5.99 US/$6.99 CAN

BLUE CHRISTMAS

Sandra Hill, Linda Jones, Sharon Pisacreta, Amy Elizabeth Saunders

The ghost of Elvis returns in all of his rhinestone splendor to make sure that this Christmas is anything but blue for four Memphis couples. Put on your blue suede shoes for these holiday stories by four of romance's hottest writers.

___4447-1 $5.50 US/$6.50 CAN

Dorchester Publishing Co., Inc.
P.O. Box 6640
Wayne, PA 19087-8640

Please add $1.75 for shipping and handling for the first book and $.50 for each book thereafter. NY, NYC, and PA residents, please add appropriate sales tax. No cash, stamps, or C.O.D.s. All orders shipped within 6 weeks via postal service book rate. Canadian orders require $2.00 extra postage and must be paid in U.S. dollars through a U.S. banking facility.

Name_____
Address_____
City_____State_____Zip_____
I have enclosed $_____ in payment for the checked book(s).
Payment <u>must</u> accompany all orders. ❏ Please send a free catalog.

THE MAGIC OF
Christmas

Emma Craig, Annie Kimberlin, Kathleen Nance, Stobie Piel

"Jack of Hearts" by Emma Craig. With the help of saintly Gentleman Jack Oakes, love warms the hearts of a miner and a laundress.

"The Shepherds and Mr. Weisman" by Annie Kimberlin. A two-thousand-year-old angel must bring together two modern-day soulmates before she can unlock the pearly gates.

"The Yuletide Spirit" by Kathleen Nance. A tall, blonde man fulfills the wish of a beautiful and lonely woman and learns that the spirit of the season is as alive as ever.

"Twelfth Knight" by Stobie Piel. In medieval England, a beautiful thief and a dashing knight have only the twelve days of Christmas to find a secret treasure . . . which just might be buried in each other's arms.

___52283-7 $5.99 US/$6.99 CAN

Winter Wonderland

Emma Craig,
Leigh Greenwood,
Amanda Harte,
Linda O. Johnston

Christmas is coming, and the streets are alive with the sounds of the season: "Silver Bells" and sleigh rides, jingle bells and carolers. Choruses of "Here Comes Santa Claus" float over the snow-covered landscape, bringing the joy of the holiday to revelers as they deck the halls and string the lights "Up on the Rooftop." And when the songs of the season touch four charmed couples, melody turns to romance and harmony turns to passion. For these "Merry Gentlemen" and their lovely ladies will learn that with the love they have found, not even a spring thaw will cool their desire or destroy their winter wonderland.

___52339-6 $5.99 US/$6.99 CAN

Dorchester Publishing Co., Inc.
P.O. Box 6640
Wayne, PA 19087-8640

Please add $1.75 for shipping and handling for the first book and $.50 for each book thereafter. NY, NYC, and PA residents, please add appropriate sales tax. No cash, stamps, or C.O.D.s. All orders shipped within 6 weeks via postal service book rate. Canadian orders require $2.00 extra postage and must be paid in U.S. dollars through a U.S. banking facility.

Name_____
Address_____
City_____State_____Zip_____
I have enclosed $_____ in payment for the checked book(s).
Payment <u>must</u> accompany all orders. ❑ Please send a free catalog.
    CHECK OUT OUR WEBSITE! www.dorchesterpub.com

RAVE REVIEWS
FOR THE AUTHORS OF
MISTLETOE & MAGIC!

Lynsay Sands

"Readers are swept up in a delicious, merry and often breath-catching roller coaster ride . . . a true delight! 4½ stars!"

—Romantic Times on *The Deed*

"Filled with bravery, passion, complex characterizations, humor and clever story lines, this romance will heat up the cold winter nights with a warm, fuzzy feeling."

—Romantic Times on *Sweet Revenge*

Lisa Cach

"Lisa Cach spins a charming and witty tale that is sure to capture your imagination."

—Romantic Times on *The Changeling Bride*

"Ms. Cach weaves a story rich in humanity and emotional intensity. 4½ stars!"

—Romantic Times on *Bewitching the Baron*

Amy Elizabeth Saunders

"Ms. Saunders's charmingly arrogant hero and the interweaving of two timeless love stories makes the reading of this lovely tale a truly enchanted time."

—Romantic Times on *Enchanted Time*

"A marvelous story!"

—Romantic Times on "A Time for Joy"
in *Christmas Angels*

Stobie Piel

"Ms. Piel's touches of humor and sparkling dialogue make this one a classic! Excellent! First-rate storytelling!"

—The Literary Times on *Midnight Moon*

"A rousing adventure with blistering sensual fire!"

—Romantic Times on *The White Sun*

MISTLETOE & MAGIC

Lynsay Sands
"The Fairy Godmother"

When the fourteenth-century maiden loses her father, young Odel learns from her aunt that she must marry—and that a handful of fairy dust can separate the men from the mice.

Lisa Cach
"A Midnight Clear"

Returning home in time for Christmas, a New England beauty finds she needs a little help in seeing that true love comes from within and not from a handsome spectacle.

Amy Elizabeth Saunders
"Angels We Have Heard"

During the holidays, even mistakes can be rewarded. And for Rose Shanahan's family, one little error—when caught and remedied—brings about a loving Christmas, indeed.

Stobie Piel
"Here Comes Santa Claus"

Thrown together to vanquish suffering in an old Victorian home, two of Saint Nick's helpers have to sort out their feelings and find true love before their master returns.

Other Christmas anthologies from *Leisure*
and *Love Spell:*
UNWRAPPED
FIVE GOLD RINGS
THE MAGIC OF CHRISTMAS
BLUE CHRISTMAS
SANTA PAWS
CHRISTMAS SPIRIT
A TIME-TRAVEL CHRISTMAS
HOLIDAY INN
A WILDERNESS CHRISTMAS
THE NIGHT BEFORE CHRISTMAS
THEIR FIRST NOEL
A FRONTIER CHRISTMAS
AN OLD-FASHIONED SOUTHERN
   CHRISTMAS